FLIGHT

After flying passengers, Bob Winrush then worked as a 'freight dog', flying consignments of goods, sometimes people, all over the world — including bush-strips in war zones. But he walked away from a deal that didn't smell right — something a freight dog should never do. Now a pilot for an Emirate prince in Dubai, that refusal is catching up with him. A marked man, he flees to a remote Scottish island. Pursued by armed assassins, he struggles to re-fashion himself in this barren, beautiful place, taking on another identity. But the stakes are rising, despite the presence of Judith, the alluring environmentalist; memories of his uglier flights haunt him. Even in the furthest Hebrides his past is with him . . . and the predators are closing in.

Books by Adam Thorpe
Published by The House of Ulverscroft:

THE STANDING POOL

ADAM THORPE

FLIGHT

Complete and Unabridged

CHARNWOOD
Leicester

First published in Great Britain in 2012 by
Jonathan Cape
London

First Charnwood Edition
published 2013
by arrangement with
Jonathan Cape
The Random House Group Limited
London

British Library CIP Data

Thorpe, Adam, *1956* –
   Flight.
   1. Suspense fiction.
   2. Large type books.
   I. Title
   823.9′2–dc23

   ISBN 978–1–4448–1484–2

Published by
F. A. Thorpe (Publishing)
Anstey, Leicestershire

Set by Words & Graphics Ltd.
Anstey, Leicestershire
Printed and bound in Great Britain by
T. J. International Ltd., Padstow, Cornwall

This book is printed on acid-free paper

The impression left after watching the motions of birds is that of extreme mobility — a life of perpetual impulse checked only by fear.

Richard Jefferies

Part One

1

If you're having an affair with a freight dog's wife, you should check the world's weather.

A final flight to Zambia was cancelled because of flash floods: the airport runway and all alternatives round about were rendered unusable. It was Bob's last haul for that trip, which had been the usual mixture of things, although the last few days had been toing and froing for Glencore with machinery for the copper belt. He came home two days early, not warning his wife so he could surprise her — even finish tiling the bathroom, fix the outdoor light, mow the lawn. He was looking forward to it.

Then he remembered that Olivia wouldn't be at home until early evening. The twins, of course, were away at school. He hated them boarding — nothing to do with the considerable cost — but it was her decision. Worcester, she claimed, was mostly obesity in cheap jeans and there was some sort of serious drugs ring: at fifteen, the kids had begun to have dodgy friends.

So he had a couple of hours in which to shower, nap, find his land legs. He was glad. He smelt of sulphur from the strip mine at Mufulira, the wind blowing southerly over the town and its scratch airport. The acid gas from the smelter was still in his mouth. He was glad the rains had come.

It was the mid-afternoon of a cloudless and cold October day, mulch and woodsmoke nipping the air, as unmistakeably English as an old churchyard. The ancient mill-house, modified for the twenty-first century, seemed braced for another thousand years under its fresh thatch (and so it ought to have been, if expense was anything to go by).

He closed the car boot and took a slow breath, filling his lungs. It took longer, these days, for the ground to settle. The country air felt deliciously damp and green after the dryness of the cockpit, from which he'd barely emerged except to sleep. Home is sweet and silky, he thought. Home is good. Celandine House. Olivia's idea, the name. Celandine all the way up the grassy approach track, before the council turned it into a runway for the posh new estate.

He crunched across the gravel drive, unlocked the door, planted his bag on the hall carpet.

An unfamiliar smell. No pets (the twins were allergic), so it was usually a mixture of fireplace, cinnamon from the carpet cleaner and Olivia's fruity hairspray, with an underlying hint of hay-bale from the thatch. Now there was lavender. A lot of it, oily but pleasant. Olivia's latest fad, no doubt. You could never smell much in a cockpit, but hours of being cooped up with his co-pilot's armpits and Hugh 'Al' McAllister's low-tide breath (not improving over the many years Al had been his loyal flight engineer) made him appreciative. And that last copper town had been something else: sewage, sulphur and slag dust.

'Asthmaville,' Al had shouted over the unloading, eyes as red as a ghoul's, wheezing horribly. 'I'll sue Glencore for millions!'

You never know what you'll find at the other end.

He heard sobs from upstairs, was only surprised for a moment: the telly was left on for security purposes when there was no one in. Some emoting afternoon soap. Or perhaps tennis, without the *knock-knock* of the ball. Just the grunts.

A nature documentary, he realised, as he poured himself a glass of mineral water out of the fridge: peculiarly like the moans and screeches of the equatorial forest he'd spent the first part of the trip flying into — the landing strip like a dropped pin on a rug, somehow rotating to a scar wide enough for your considerable wingspan. *Bump squeak bump*. A testing time for the landing gear. Then he remembered it was early-closing day, which Olivia's boutique was unusual in honouring. It was part of her class act.

He climbed the stairs and opened the bedroom door. When it comes to emergencies, a pilot's reaction time is faster than other people's: the seconds break their own rules, slow down, become brown and viscous. Otherwise pilots are dreamier than most. This is why it took Bob Winrush a long moment — really, a split second — to recognise that his wife, crouched stark naked on their double bed, was not examining her own feet. She was gripping the feet like a pair of throttles, while a pair of shiny-knuckled hands

5

covered her breasts from behind. They were not her hands, she didn't have four arms: the broad nails were clipped to the pink, the wrists were thick. And her own legs were not stretched out in front of her, but tucked up either side; the legs in front of her were someone else's, swirled with dark hair, a tuft on the bridge of each big toe.

She was frozen in shock, staring back at Bob. Or would have been frozen, if her moaning partner hadn't continued to rock her up and down. The room was heady with lavender oil: Olivia's neck, shoulders and clavicles were glossed, as was her open lower lip and the tongue resting on it. There was a ball of tissue, grey with moisture, by the man's shin. Her buttocks were on the man's belly. It was all any old how.

At first she said, 'Job. It's his job.' Then she reached for the duvet rucked at the bottom of the bed, pulling it up over her long body as if her husband had never seen her naked. She squeezed her eyes tight shut.

'Oh shit,' she said.

The rocking stopped and a shiny face appeared behind her shoulder, someone familiar to Bob. A neighbour. Luke, the therapeutic bilingual masseur. *He lets you keep your bottoms on*, Olivia had laughed, once, in the kitchen with her friends. Luke from Montreal.

'You've not got your bottoms on,' Bob heard himself say from high overhead.

Olivia's dorsals were being pushed at by Luke as he wiggled his hips, prising himself out of her; Bob spoke through the slow viscosity of a split second and told him not to move, not a muscle.

6

'Hey,' Luke said. 'Hey. Let me explain.'

'Not right now,' said Bob.

That was his own pillow those elbows were digging into: pale-blue John Lewis pillowslip, wedding present from his late aunt. He'd always been fussy about pillows, given his own scrunched internal clock. He pulled up a chair, the chair he'd drape clothes over when changing, and sat on it. If he hadn't done so, he would have fallen down — the deck pitching and rolling, his heart enormous in his chest.

Olivia said, peeping out from the duvet, 'Well? What now? Christ.' She sounded annoyed, as if a teapot lid had been broken by his own careless hand. Really, though, Bob knew she was scared. The ex-stewardess, trained in first aid and all types of emergency.

'Sustain velocity. Go right through it.' He was trying to think. The impossible happening. Something you'd never been trained for.

'It's tantrism,' she said. 'A religion. A way of being part of the universe. Luke?'

Nothing came from Luke but a squeak, the beginnings of words. He coughed.

'Energies,' she went on. 'This is the first time, ever. *Ever*.'

'Said Josephine,' Bob whispered. He didn't mean it to be a whisper: just staying upright and functional was taking most of his strength, and he was a muscular, broad-shouldered man who kept in trim. He needed another glass of water: the acid fumes were filling his mouth. He was back on the runway at Mufulira, eyes watering, feeling sick, kids in torn shorts running about beyond the fence. 'Said Johnson,' he added, with a chuckle that was strange to him.

'Truly, it is precisely that,' Luke drawled. 'Meaning a very ancient tradition, no barrier between physical and spiritual. About releasing energies? And one time is enough, truly.' His voice trembled.

Bob looked at him properly at last. 'That's what we pilots say about birdstrikes: *once is enough.*'

'This truly is not a birdstrike,' said Luke. Then gave a little involuntary snigger.

'Sucked in. The fan blades twisted. And that's it.'

'This is truly just really about healing.'

'Those big bald-headed vultures are the worst,' Bob added. His stare, augmented by a faint trembling of the head, was more effective than a fist. Luke looked up at the ceiling, his lips drawn back in a snarl.

'Let's get dressed, Bob, meet you downstairs for a chat,' said Olivia, attempting her no-nonsense tone. Her eyes and nose were moist.

He was staggering about in the considerable debris field of his marriage, and all she wanted was a chat.

Luke twisted round, putting his weight on his one elbow, digging deeper into Bob's pillow.

'Don't move. I won't say it again. Once is enough.'

The man sank back, hand over his eyes.

'Well,' Bob continued, adopting the sing-song voice he'd use over the intercom back in his passenger days; 'this is it. This is what I think. Listen. I think you should stay up here while I fix myself a stiff whisky, and we'll go on from there, like grown-ups.' Somewhere deep in his mind's tangle, at the initial sight of Olivia's buttocks pressed on another man's belly, a tiny glowing valve of arousal had been switched on. He wanted to smash it.

'Oh, Bob, good idea . . . ' Olivia sounded faintly relieved, which annoyed him.

He left them and went steadily, step by step, down the creaking and scarred oak stairs, using the banister. He could wrestle a pig of a plane through almost any storm without missing a heartbeat, but *the worst usually happens when you least expect it*.

He unzipped his bag by the front door and drew out the pistol, a battered Makarov with a notched wooden grip.

There was the sound of the bathroom latch dropping (each door having its own familiar acoustic), and he loped back up. Olivia stood alone in her underthings in the bedroom, shivering and saying something. He kicked the bathroom door open.

Luke's glossy fingers were on the windowsill, next to the raw area of wall that Bob had been planning to tile. Then they vanished. Bob leapt to the window, forgetting to duck under the bathroom's low beam, and saw the tantric healer slide off the outhouse roof below, to end up sprawled stark naked on his back in the hydrangea bed.

By the time Bob and his throbbing head had

joined him by the conventional route, the man had managed to crawl some distance over the lawn. He had done something to his ankle, and his knees and hands were stained red with Worcestershire clay.

Catching sight of Bob, he curled up in a foetal position and sobbed into his knees. 'Please, please, oh please, yow, oh Christ.' He looked up, hopeful. 'I've broken my ankle? Really bust it?'

The lawn's grass was definitely on the long side. It needed cutting. Bob pointed the gun downwards and took aim.

It was a hinge moment, but he was already several hundred nautical miles ahead, thinking out the consequences.

He saw himself driving, driving north until he got to the very edge, then just carrying on.

He said, 'If I ever see you near my wife again, your brain'll be couscous.'

He went straight back to the house, rescued his bag, tried not to notice the twins' photos here and there, thought about shooting up the kitchen, and drove away spitting gravel, after standing by the car and sending one bullet up into the clear blue sky. The shot was surprisingly loud. There was no sign of Olivia: he learnt later that she had stayed in the bedroom with the double bed pushed up against the door, and called the police.

2

His naked body glistened, sweat pooling in the hollow of each collarbone. He was down at the tail end of a converted DC-10, stuck on the tarmac in Roskilde while mechanics in hi-vis smocks replaced a valve on the starboard engine. The plane, en route between Paris and Dubai, belonged to an Emirati prince. As the crew were leaving the cockpit for a smoking-zone tour and to deal with the landing fees, His Excellency had invited the captain for a spell in the sauna. This was situated in the rear of the fuselage, working off ground power by special request.

It was a sleety winter dusk in Denmark. Bob left François, the co-pilot, to the tea and medals and followed Sheikh Ahmed down to the sauna at the aft end.

The two men were quite naked but for small white cotton towels around their midriffs. Bob had only ever seen the prince in his desert robes and tinted glasses, and was surprised by the enormity of his belly, the furriness of his chest, and the dark patches around his eyes, like bruises. For a man in his mid-thirties, he was in poor shape. Bob, on the other hand, prided himself on keeping in trim: he worked out, pulled weights, jogged.

They were uncomfortably close: the sauna was tiny, with the back wall stepped into a couple of benches, and so new there was resin oozing in

11

gobs from the pinewood cladding. The air was an accurate rendition of Dubai's in July and August. I must be mad, Bob thought.

No girls, which he'd been half-expecting. Just the plump prince and his sing-song drone, broken now and again by a lazy chuckle. Because of the misbehaving valve, they'd had no choice but to land at Roskilde, where the biggest runway is barely 1800 yards. Not exactly an emergency, but the prince was impressed. Or maybe scared.

'Piece of cake,' Bob reassured him, adding that the complete conversion had added less than a ton to the aircraft and there were only twelve bodies on board, so it didn't really matter if they were 3,000 feet short of tarmac. His Excellency had flown himself, taking lessons on a brand-new Grumman Tiger he'd received on his eighteenth birthday back in the early 1990s, between educational stints at Wellington and Cambridge. But he ran off the runway somewhere after a gust caught him from behind, the aircraft flipping over when the nose landing gear collapsed. This had clipped his wings, he joked.

He leaned forward, indicating the scars on his face; Bob had always thought they were acne trails. The prince wanted to know what the DC-10's reputation was among pilots.

Death Cruiser 10.

'Fairly viceless. FedEx bought a lot of the old fleet off American and United Airlines, which says it all.'

They also talked football while their faces

glistened. Apart from his home team in the Emirates, the prince supported Chelsea. In fact, he wanted to buy it. Bob was more a cricket man, but kept up his end well enough, if only to please. At fifty-one, he didn't fancy being thrown upon the shrinking aviation job market, or not in his previous capacity as a freight dog: apart from anything else, he'd end up in the usual hot water. Saunas may be hot, but they don't scald. His Excellency threw a splash from the jug onto the false coals and Bob had to close his eyes against the rush of steam. When he opened them again, his employer was smiling strangely.

'Captain Windrush. Captain Windrush. Is this really your name? It sounds like a Frederick Forsyth novel.'

'I once met an interior designer by the name of A. M. Gay.'

This made Sheikh Ahmed laugh out loud, teeth very white against the black beard.

'Actually,' Bob went on, 'it's Winrush. Without the *d*. For future reference.'

'I know, I know. I employ thousands. Our good old teachers remembered all our names at Wellington, except for mine, which they pronounced completely wrong! You know why we are meeting in the sauna?'

'Because it's November in Denmark,' Bob said, 'and you're missing base.'

'I am usually too chilly at base, with all that overdone air con.' He leaned forward and put a plump hand on his captain's knee. 'By the way, are you married?'

13

Bob glanced at the door, almost indistinguishable from the walls in the poor light. Nothing until now had ever suggested that he was anything more to the prince than a minor member of his vast entourage.

'Right now I'm in the middle of a divorce, Your Excellency. It's fine. I mean, it's not sticky. Painful, but straightforward.'

The hand left the knee.

'Painful?'

'I still love my wife.'

'I suppose she has a job?'

Bob explained: she had been a BA senior flight purser, left her job to bring up their twins, studied with the Open University for a business-studies degree, put it into practice by selling smart once-worn cast-offs — Chanel, Jaeger, Saint Laurent — from their front living room, and then opened her own shop in downtown Worcester, called Holier Than Thou.

The prince, who had three wives, gave a non-committal nod. 'I will tell you why we're meeting in here. Because here no one will be listening to us.'

'That suggests we've got something worth listening to.'

'Exactly.' The prince twitched his nose, reflected. 'Captain Windrush, Winrush, whatever, have you got enemies?'

'Why, have you?'

'I asked you first, Captain.'

Bob's throat was dry. He hadn't drunk enough during the flight from Paris, fretting about the dodgy valve. And now it was hard to distinguish

14

his heart from the distant knocking of the repair job, making its way through the aluminium tube of the fuselage to this tiny sweltering pod.

'I think you've been watching too many TV dramas, Your Excellency.'

Watching TV dramas (on various huge widescreens, two of them on board) was exactly what the prince did spend most of his time doing, while being paid a fortune for not working as a corporate executive in several Dubai companies. Bob had made a gaffe.

'In TV dramas,' said the prince, eventually, wiping his face with his towel and so revealing a groin demurely shielded by his belly, 'the journalist seeking information is usually a beautiful young blonde with perfect dimples, so one does not mind being badgered. In this case, it's a male Jew with glasses.'

'An Israeli?'

'I prefer the term Jew. He came to see me in Dubai two weeks ago. Just before we left for Paris. He claimed to be a restorer, interested in one of my broken Florentine putti. Once we are alone, this fellow says very smartly that he is in fact a journalist, a journalist for a left-wing paper in Tel Aviv, that he believes a certain Robert Windrush is working for me, and that he needs to know your whereabouts. Now I know our agreement, when you joined me, was that your contact details should never be given to the press, nor to anyone else for that matter. As much for my benefit as yours. And the idiot did not even know about our address system.'

Bob smiled, despite himself. Dubai had no

postcodes and few street numbers; it was all PO boxes or a map drawn on the envelope. Underneath, the city was still nomadic — built on shifting sands. Nevertheless, he'd been there two years and felt almost settled. He liked the plane, the undemanding regularity of being a winged chauffeur, even the managing of the crew.

'Not much of a journalist,' he said.

'I can't even check that out,' the prince frowned. 'When I asked him for his name in turn, he refused. All he said was that his investigation would destroy — crush, was the term he used — the present ultra-right government in Israel. No doubt an exaggeration, but still.'

'Investigation?'

'Of a certain arms deal.'

'Old, old news,' Bob said, watching the sweat well up from nowhere on his thighs.

The prince blinked slowly. 'I think he felt it would encourage me,' he went on. 'It did quite the opposite. I asked him if he feared Mossad. Here in Dubai, I told him, we know all about Mossad. He said Mossad do not target Israelis. Sheena put her chin on his knees and I think he was more frightened of her than of any secret service.'

Sheena was a cheetah. The prince kept a number of juvenile big cats in cages, and would let one loose in his office to impress visitors. It had always impressed Bob. 'I told him he was foolish even to think about it,' the prince sighed, wiping his glistening face. 'Does any of this make sense? I see you are sweating.'

Bob chuckled dutifully and wiped his face in turn, heedless of nakedness now.

When all this tricky business had first brewed up two years ago, he had cleaned and oiled his pistol — the old Bulgarian Makarov picked up in Liberia — and fired it into water: the expanding bullet's splay was like orange blossom made out of metal. He saw it now entering his flushed thigh and flowering out and doing an awful lot of damage. And it wouldn't just be one, and certainly not in the thigh. They might not even bother to waste a bullet; smothering was more their style. The journalist would probably be hit first, but that was meagre comfort.

'Your Excellency,' he said eventually, 'I am very grateful to you for telling me this. And, I presume, telling the journalist nothing.'

The prince settled back, looking cross. 'I don't have the slightest idea of what deal the Jew was referring to.' He reached up and turned the dial clockwise a few notches. 'Have *you* ever overshot the runway, Captain?'

Bob thought at first he was speaking metaphorically, but the prince generally stuck to traditional metaphors to do with tents, moons, oases, camels and desert blooms. Bob took a deep breath, parboiling his sinuses.

'When I was knocking about in Africa,' he admitted, 'my wheels did carve my name in the airstrip's grass a few times. And back in my commercial airline days, flying a BAC I-II, I rattled some chimney stacks when the water

17

injection system failed, as it had a tendency to do.'

He looked up. Sheikh Ahmed was sitting back with his eyes shut, sweat trickling down his sideburns, dripping off his chin, seaming the folds of his belly. 'Don't leave the job before you've flown me home, will you, Captain Winrush? Your co-pilot cannot do it on his own.'

Bob frowned, his guts turning a flip. He allowed a little hot silence to fall. 'I had no intention of leaving the job, Your Excellency.'

There was another pause. 'Well, you realise my difficulty.'

'What?'

The prince opened his eyes, angled his head with a sad smile, spread his hands wide, then went shut-eye again.

'I think in plain English,' said Bob, 'we call this firing somebody?'

There was a slight frown above the dark lids. 'Let's call it reluctantly letting you go, for your own welfare.'

'Ah, right. Compassionate leave.'

The joke was lost somewhere in the sweaty blur, or maybe in the cultural chasm that lay between them in spite of their similar schooling. The sheikh nodded. 'Yes, it makes my heart awfully sore, but there we are. The nail-bed of life. Just take me home first, Captain. My secretary will do the rest. Concerning you, I mean.'

Since the prince had some twelve homes in twelve far-flung locations, Bob very much hoped he still meant Dubai, where the ejected pilot's principal belongings awaited him on the twenty-fifth floor of a block with a view of the usual construction site, rumbling and ablaze at night. As for his own home, in the proper sense of the word, he had no idea where that lay, not these days.

'I see your point, Your Excellency. What a shame. There goes my long service award. Just give me a letter of reference. My impeccable landings.'

'Of course.' Sheikh Ahmed opened his eyes and stood up, the towel thankfully in place. He stared at Bob. It wasn't an Emirati-style joke, after all. 'Jacuzzi? You must tell me what exactly you got up to, knocking about in Africa.'

His gaze was fixed, his face unsmiling: nothing on the clock except the maker's name in Arabic, as the expression goes.

He smoked in the jacuzzi: a Dunhill Infinite whose ash swirled into the bubbles. Bob refused the offer, as if out of principle.

'I think I know what pile of ordure this journalist is sniffing around, Your Excellency. When I was doing freight, I made a mistake. I walked away from a deal.'

'When?'

'Year before last. Just before I joined you.'

'Cigarette?'

'No, thanks.'

What he wanted was water. The prince was drinking a chilled bottle of sparkling, but had failed to offer one to his pilot. Perhaps it hadn't occurred to him. 'Why did you walk away?'

'It wasn't my deal: a freight dog is just a flying

truck driver.' He felt grumpy, but decided to overcome it. The prince was not someone you could make an enemy of. 'The deal bothered me. I can't tell you what the deal was, but let's say that money throws bridges over geopolitical gulfs, makes arch-enemies into clients, and this particular deal went right up to the highest levels.'

'Of the Israeli government?'

'Don't go there. It's not worth it. Pursue your enquiries elsewhere. We're off the blocks in an hour. My job is to fly you safely back to base without spilling a drop of this fine jacuzzi, and then walk off into the sunset. Right?'

His Excellency smiled and drew deeply on his cigarette: it smelt very costly. Bob still hoped the walking barrel would change his mind, so kept polite. He let the water jets pummel his broad shoulders, tried not to think of the future, of being thrown back yet again into freight, its dodgier tributaries. The surging waters turned the prince's chest-hair to straggles, like the beard found on mussels.

As they were towelling themselves dry in the changing room with its cream-leather pouffes, the prince pointed to Bob's right leg.

'I see you have a history, too, Captain. I had noticed you were ever-so-slightly lame.'

Despite the cooling bubbles, the sauna's heat had retained itself as a flush everywhere but on the old wounds, so they snaked their way happily over Bob's calf and shin like white nylon cords, with a shiny granny knot over the knee. At times the scars would turn dark red, like strips of salami.

'Never make a landing in the Congo forest in the rainy season unless you have floats in place of wheels,' he explained. 'Not with a DC-10, anyway. A Cessna or a Cherokee, maybe. They told me the airstrip was hardened and it wasn't. Builders' mud, basically.'

'Then you did more than carve the grass,' the prince said with a slight air of rebuke.

'It wasn't a question of overshooting. We just lost it. Skidded. There was a tree in the way. It sheared off the aft end of the fuselage. To be honest, she was no great loss: she'd had the arse flown out of her. Purchased with two years of life left, and we'd done eighteen months. Much more and she'd have joined the notorious fleet.'

'And what is that, Captain?'

'Ageing freighters whose entire makeover consists of repainting the registration letters on the tail. I know the feeling.'

When the prince asked him what the cargo was, with the air of a man who knows the world, Bob gave him the usual spiel about building materials for a sawmill, how in crashing it they'd saved a lot of trees. By now the man had donned his snow-white dishdasha, slipped his *ghutra* over his head — and looked like any other sheikh: one of those fat white queen ants fussed over by everyone else.

As they walked down the aisle past the bedroom suite and the two lounges, past the galley gleaming with stainless steel and the dining area with its medieval crossbow collection, past the TV room with its Blu-ray and four giant speakers and library of crap DVDs, the prince never once turned his head. By the time the two men reached the flight-deck door, he was the flight's self-loading cargo and Bob was just the thirsty cameleer. Servants and their masters never, in the end, mix.

★ ★ ★

About ten hours later they made their approach into Dubai against a strong wind made more interesting by sand. Bob thumped it in somewhat after a gust dropped them suddenly.

'The goodbye bump,' said François.

Bob hadn't mentioned being shown the door, of course, only that an opportunity had cropped up.

'And now the goodbye drink, skipper?'

They went as usual to Caspar's, a club the prince started a few years back and to which of course they had free membership. The floors were slate, the tables teak, the walls purple-lit, with a glass wall fronting the outdoor pool and its free viewing of the local talent in what were, apparently, very expensive bikinis — which, given their minimal surface area, they must have been. They settled in one of the sofas closest to the glass, metaphorically pressing their noses against the sweet-shop window. François was about forty and not yet at the age where girls seem to get more and more attractive, but his preppy air concealed an aficionado. It also concealed a somewhat disreputable past, as far as Bob could gather, including a narcotics run in a twin-engined Cessna that came down over Kentucky. Bob never wanted to probe: drug-trafficking was way outside his envelope.

'Resigning so soon is not good,' François commented. 'You will put a bullet in your feet.'

'Maybe. Anyway, I didn't have a choice.'

'That is not resigning, then.'

'Whatever. Keep it to yourself.'

The Belgian looked at Bob in his usual nonplussed way. 'So, I will keep mute.'

Bob made sure he eked out the Scotch, as his tongue had a tendency to wag under the influence, and he felt this might not be a good idea. François had heard most of his stories, including the one about tantric Luke, and had suffered his glooms in the cockpit during the worst moments of the divorce: perhaps the man didn't mind the prospect of a new skipper. At any rate, instead of weeping over the departure, he spent the rest of the hour ogling the costly bikinis while Bob pretended to know some of their contents: 'Oh, look, that's Olga, from Bucharest or somewhere. And there's Leonora, she of the perfect shoulders. And if that isn't Jessica, the pearl still in her navel, I see.' As François began to inveigle himself with a Latvian dish working the tables, his skipper slipped away, barely saying goodbye.

There had been equally little regret from the prince, emerging from his suite as they were taxiing to the GA apron. He was planning to enjoy the next fortnight in his miniature antiquities-bloated Versailles the other side of the city, so the impromptu loss of a pilot hardly ruffled him. There were hundreds queuing up for the job, younger and perfectly qualified, and his fleet's young ops manager, Greg Tennyson, had all the usual contacts.

Perhaps that's why the boss left the plane without a glance, although the captain stood by the cockpit door like a waiter expecting a tip. Or an apology. Bob wished His Excellency an afterlife of a permanent holy month where the sun never set: no food, chewing gum, drink or girls. Or water.

* * *

He was nervous, standing outside the glass tower of his apartment block. It was late, and the nights were beginning to cool, but the breeze felt very warm after Paris, the smell of the desert always strongest in those first hours of arrival. He craned his neck to count the floors up to his own: the apartment was dark behind the dazzle of reflected crane-lights. Couples passed on foot, laughing, along with the usual two-bit Ferraris with their sonic booms of inboard music. He'd parked the Audi (not really his — it came with the job) in the block's underground car park, but had avoided the lift. Instead, he'd taken the fire stairs and emerged in the service area at the side, which always smelt of sick.

I'm small fry, he thought. I'm below their radar. I'm as small as a grain of sugar in a crate, even as small as the cannabis crumb the Dubai customs men found one day on the sole of a shoe — whose owner thereby copped four years

24

in an Emirates prison. How do you know when you matter to someone? When he was on the flight deck he mattered a great deal, especially in the days when his cargo was hundreds of men, women and children. Even when it was freight, he mattered. Mattered more than presidents, but probably not more than surgeons. This mattering business was what made him addicted to the job — along with the actual flying.

The lobby was empty apart from the porter, Vakim, who doubled as the security man. He asked Vakim if anyone had asked for him while he was away. 'No, sir,' Vakim said, flustered because he'd been watching the TV behind his desk, had not noticed Bob coming in, the sigh of the sliding doors inaudible under the murmur of an Arabic soap. The little fountain trickled, its pool brimming flush with the lobby's tiles: it was the only feature he liked about the lobby, which otherwise reflected the prince's taste for mirrors, pointy shapes and much gold on much black. 'Are you sure, Vakim?'

'Certain, sir. Apart of your friend.'

'What friend?' As if he didn't have any. He was already chilly in his short sleeves, whose epaulettes Vakim's eyes would always stray over, his own being merely decorative. 'Which of my many friends, Vakim?'

'Mr Sharansky, sir.'

'I don't know a Mr Sharansky.'

Vakim smiled, a bad sign. 'He said he knows you very well, he was one in your family.'

'I have no family apart from my grown-up children. When was this?'

25

It was the day before yesterday, the caller sounding American — although Vakim was unreliable on this; he had once thought Bob Winrush was American.

'Did he leave a card, Vakim?'

'No, sir. Just this message and this telephone number. I told him the day on when you were . . . returning. Which is this day, in fact,' he added with a sharp laugh.

Bob took the slip of paper and wondered why Vakim hadn't given this to him straightaway. Maybe he'd learnt suspense from all those soaps. The note was headed *URGENT* in Vakim's awkward hand, and asked Bob to phone the number below on his return. It was signed (in block capitals) *MATT SHARANSKY*. The name had a faintly Israeli ring.

The lift doors slid open and Bob swivelled round and a woman he recognised as being a resident clicked out on high heels, her small but exquisite fluff of a dog in tow. Tomorrow he was due to brave the cheetahs, sorting out his forced departure with the prince's busty green-eyed secretary.

He ascended in the lift alone. Its merciless mirror showed a grim, pale face that he temporarily adjusted with a smile. In some ways, he had been waiting for this episode from the moment he'd walked out of the deal in Istanbul, a couple of years back. Instead of going straight to departures, he'd visited the Topkapi palace, something he'd always wanted to do. Jewels and gold leaf and harems and scimitars: what else powers the world? There was a crush of tourists around the bigger jewels; none of them knew what this tall well-built man among them had done — or rather, what he had not done. He had not taken a brown envelope containing $90,000 in cash, to be divided among a three-man crew, in return for a simple ops. He took off his shoes and walked into the Blue Mosque: you could fly a Cessna up in its dome, if you banked tight enough. Glittering, resplendent walls. Something, some divine hand, then patted him on the head and said, 'Good work, Bob.'

You bet. He'd hopped out of a window at Istanbul Airport, hailed a taxi and escaped some grumpy men with visible shoulder holsters. A few days later he'd emerged spluttering in a pool in Dubai, city of tomorrow's today, where memory's an unwanted guest and the past is sand.

* * *

He stepped out of the lift and was quietly relieved not to find someone waiting for him. The corridor to his apartment was as quiet as ever, its tiles gleaming from the attentions of the scrupulous Filipina maids. Maria, who always dealt with his mess, brought a dazzling shine even to the waste drain in his bathroom basin, let alone its taps. The doorknob had received a particularly eager polish. His key slid in and he opened the door with a caution that struck him on the one hand as sensible, on the other as silly. The apartment itself was as still as a grave, only animated by the frenzy of Dubai's lights coming in through the glass. It really did not feel crouched and waiting. It even felt a little bit like home.

Nevertheless, he touched no switches. The flat's glassed-in walls were visible from myriad vantage points in the vista of bunched skyscrapers — from right out beyond the marina, if the observer was using binoculars powerful enough to pick out his particular strip. So he moved straight onto the terrace with a splash of whisky, tipped out three weeks'-worth of sand from the lounger, sat back and reflected. Sharansky might well turn out to be a minor dealer in rosé wines, or a recruiting sergeant for the local amateur dramatics. The cranes were swinging through the air, lights ablaze, all distant booms and crashes. Since he'd been away — less than a month — the forest of towers had been stretched by at least five storeys. In fact, he could have sworn an entire new ziggurat-like structure had gone up in what he remembered as a wide gap. And when Bob had first arrived, just two years ago, there was desert. Black air at night, and stars. An unadulterated wind. He'd loved looking out at the desert, marred only by the slow wink of climbing and descending planes.

He thought about calling Greg 'Drip' Tennyson, his immediate boss, to double-check his dismissal, but decided to wait. He didn't much like Greg: too full of himself, with a tendency to go on about aims and objectives, ticking boxes, flexing one's approach, all that. His nickname was nothing to do with his macho

persona but because he'd always be telling you
to 'light up and smell the coffee'. Bob would
never forget the first time Drip showed them
round His Excellency's DC-10.

'In terms of conversions,' he said, 'this is the
dog's bollocks.'

François raised his eyebrows, asked what that
was.

Greg pulled a face: 'Don't you know that
expression?'

'Well,' said François, 'I can *visualise* it . . .'

Right now Bob's skin smelt faintly of jacuzzi
— not chlorine but some musky scent the prince
had sprinkled in. He would miss the dog's
bollocks, but not the prince. Middle Eastern
bad-ass. Wrong. He'd met bad in his time, on the
job: they can really hurt you. This one was just a
fat-ass. With spare cash. Bob would always try to
see the best in people, a dangerous trait. And it
wasn't always easy: he had a very good nose,
both literally and figuratively. Luke, for instance.
He'd always found Luke the masseur a living
proof that manure has intelligence.

He toasted the view and considered Leila. She
was a petite big-busted twenty-five, he was
fifty-one. He could almost make his thumbs and
forefingers meet around her waist when she
breathed in hard. The relationship was come and
go, as she put it. They'd go their separate ways
for a while — easy in Dubai if you don't mind
glimpsing one another in clubs, bars, gyms; now
it was come-together time. He phoned her
number and left her a message.

He enjoyed the first splash too furiously and

poured another, the ice sticking to his fingers. He had never flown with a drop of alcohol in his body, but off duty was different, even in the Emirates. The whisky soothed him: he no longer imagined every rustle as a chap in a frogman's outfit swinging in over the balcony with a knife between his teeth. Yo-ho-ho and a bottle of rum.

The ring of the fixed phone startled him. He hesitated before picking it up, then reckoned it might be Leila. It was Greg Tennyson, confirming the dismissal.

'Past catching up with you, Bob? That's the trouble with freight dogs. You never know where they've been.'

'I didn't. I chose not to go. I walked out of a deal. That's why I'm in trouble. Maybe Our Excellence didn't bother with the detail.'

Greg Tennyson never listened. It was too much trouble to listen; he just got on with his own thing. 'Anyway, Bob, I'm sorry to hear it. I've enjoyed working with you.'

'The dog's bollocks, was I?'

'A change strategy, that's what you need now.'

'I think it's called coping with involuntary redundancy. Not nearly as pleasant as involuntary emission.'

Greg sportily chortled, then snapped into his suit-and-tie voice. 'You'll have to pass by with all the relevant paperwork, of course. Your files, keys, badges and so on. You know the drill.'

'Yup.'

'Terrific.'

'The cat's pyjamas. Into the valley of death rode the five hundred.'

30

'Come again, Bob?'

'Learnt it by heart at school. A poem. By your namesake. A famous poet. Always wondered whether you were any relation.'

There was a momentary pause. Puzzlement. Bob felt triumph brimming over inside him.

'Actually,' said Greg Tennyson, 'he was a cousin of my great-grandfather, was our Alfred. Our Alfred Lord T.'

'Oh. You never said.'

'Didn't reckon you'd have heard of him, to be frank, Bob.'

'Wrong there, Greg. Well, that explains it.'

'Explains what?'

'Your way with words. Inherited. Y' know — flexing your approach, smell the coffee, move the change forwards to another peg.'

Another pause, a touch heavier.

'Bob, want to know what your prospects in the executive-jet line are?'

'Not really.'

'Mush.'

'Well, better than the rock at the bottom.'

It didn't pay to upset Greg, but he'd done it. So he left it at that.

He thought about Leila as he went back in to shower and change, defiantly flicking the lights on. He felt a dark shaft of apprehension as he did so, but he was tired and slightly drunk. He planned to have a bite at the nearby Indian, fit in his thirty lengths in the apartment block's ten-metre pool, nick a lemon from one of the waterside trees in their great earthenware pots, fix up an ice-crammed vodka and tonic, then pack, then sleep — assuming Leila didn't get back, offering the comfort of her warm velvet skin, her sheltering inlet. He shaved, just in case. He looked raddled. Mirrors are spiral staircases, he thought, once you reach a certain age: *clang clang clang*, down we go.

There wasn't much kit to cram: most of it was still in storage after he'd been refused re-entry by Olivia (the gun had been a bad mistake), plus a few bits in the Crowthorne flat. Up to now he had always avoided any professional bother; or rather, up to the moment he'd walked away from the deal — which wasn't his deal in the first place. It never was. The agents, the brokers, the governments, the rebels — one great mish-mash in which the pilot stayed a pinhead, doing his job. But since that rashly sensible moment in Istanbul, followed by an unpleasant phone call, he'd half been expecting a spot of bother, as you do when you play truant. Now it was here, potentially, all he could feel was the Glenmorangie sliding down his throat, easing him up.

Then, padding towards the bathroom, he noticed how the tiles didn't shine.

The apartment had been cleaned by Maria; he could tell because she had placed his cutting boards in descending order of size, polished the knife holder as well as the knives, washed his long-dead mother's tea cosy so that its greyish purple was now bright red, and left a spiral of green cleaner in the toilet bowl. Nevertheless, there was a fine flouring of sand on everything: the tiles, rugs, covers, the tops of picture frames, the giant fridge, the TV, the hi-fi, the leather sofa, and the family photos — mostly of Sophie and David from babyhood to teens — that were ranged on his desk. Except that a couple had fallen flat, as if the maid had tried to open one of the sticky drawers. The picture of Olivia laughing in his arms on their wedding day was still defiantly standing, if a touch faded. He stood the two upright again.

It reminded him of Glencore's copper mine at Mufulira: white powder from the slurry blowing all over town, dusting his face, a gauze over the rising sun. That taste of sulphur. Here, it was 100-per-cent natural. When the doors and windows were closed, there was no sand: the desert flowed around the glass tower like one of those films he used to watch in school physics. On the balcony, yes, it would pile up in folds against the corners, shift over the tiles, lightly coat the loungers, the metal chairs and table. But not inside, unless you left something open.

The millimetrical thickness of the sand meant that the doors had been open at some point for a few hours. That was something the maids would never do: it let the cool out, and the heat and sand in. It was like shouting in church. The prince, who owned the building, made sure his manager made that clear in print, along with numerous other stipulations (no barbecues, no alcoholic shenanigans on the balconies).

Yet the sliding glass doors were locked when he'd arrived: only a cat burglar with a head for heights might make it over from the neighbouring balcony. A James Bond extra, a stuntman. He'd wanted to be a stuntman, long ago.

The bedroom door was open. He hadn't yet looked in the bedroom. It had a French window and its own little perch of a balcony no bigger than an aircraft's galley. He went to the safe in the hallway wall and took out his Makarov with the notched wooden grip, eased off the safety catch, switched the bedroom light on. The French window was closed. The drawers of the bedside table were shut, its five unread books piled in descending order of size, the double bed neatly turned back in the American manner, and absolutely nothing looked amiss.

Yet, unless there was a secret fissure, an unseen crack, someone had been in here since the maid had cleaned, and for more than a few minutes. An hour or two, say, with the balcony doors slid back — maybe only a little. He looked for spoors or fingerprints, but the sand-dust was so fine that a mere breath would shift it: even the air conditioning's unfelt eddies. All he could see was his own trace here and there, especially around the fridge.

He opened various drawers and felt that someone had rifled them, although there was no tangible proof. The whisky was making him feel reckless, and recklessness is very bad news for pilots, unless — like his dear-departed father — you were strapped into a Spitfire at a time when recklessness was indistinguishable from bravery. But he wasn't his father: nothing like. He sat on his white leather sofa — a sofa he disliked, along with most of the furnishings — and checked the pistol was fully loaded. This

34

was sensible, he thought, not reckless.

And then it occurred to him, and he felt relieved: if anyone had somehow found their way in, it would be the left-wing journalist. Left-wing journalists were not dangerous, or not directly. They stirred stuff up that might lead to a spot of bother, but they wouldn't hurt you or shoot you or throw you in jail. However, left-wing journalists weren't necessarily adept at breaking into a twenty-fifth-floor luxury apartment and leaving no trace. Anyway, there was not much here to find. Most of his papers were in Crowthorne, apart from his logbooks and various post-freight documents. A brief spasm of worry about Olivia and her foxy solicitor vanished with the last of his second top-up. No one had been in here. The wind had been particularly strong when he'd landed the beast, the air cloudy with sand. He wondered whether November, the start of the cooler season (cooler meaning slightly less oven-like), was a particularly bad month for sand. He felt very tired suddenly.

Nevertheless, just to make sure, he levered himself off the sofa and went to his desk beyond the rubber-tree plant. He kept the logbooks — three of them, he'd been flying that long — and all relevant papers in the bottom right-hand drawer, unlocked since he'd mislaid the tiny key.

There were two logbooks, the corners bumped and the covers scuffed. Two instead of three. He checked every other drawer. Then he checked them again: he knew that whatever you're looking for — sunglasses, keys, Sellotape, wallet

— has magical powers, can turn invisible. He sat in his swivel chair and put his head in his hands. This was what Olivia would have called an 'oh shit moment' with her lovely, nervous laugh.

One of the logbooks was missing: the last logbook, recording all his flights up to the Dubai job. He'd started a new one for Dubai, since he was no longer in freight. It seemed right. His logbooks went back to 1985, when he started with Sabena. The reason he wasn't screaming and shouting, apart from having an experienced pilot's resistance to screaming and shouting in emergencies, was that he'd photocopied every page in all three logbooks some nine months ago. This followed an incident when he had taken them down to the pool for perusal and returned without them, distracted by an exceptionally lovely pair of coffee-brown shoulders. Fortunately, they were found by a cleaner, but not after the hard covers had been pummelled by the fists of a very strong sun. Copies were essential, and he'd left these with other copied documents in his flat in Crowthorne on his next trip to England. He'd assumed that Mossad, or whoever it was, had not sufficient nous to raid, let alone trace, his second address.

He checked every single drawer in the suite, having a vague recollection of showing the books to skinny, desirable Leila; he virtually ransacked the place, looking for it. But it was gone. It had been taken. He had walked away from a deal, but the record of that deal (or the Deal) was in the missing logbook. Not the cargo, not the kit, but

36

the time, the places, the company, the crew, the lot. And after it he'd put: *SECOND LEG REFUSED*.

★ ★ ★

He'd often wondered how he would react, coming out of low night cloud in a full 707 and seeing the surface of the ocean no longer tens of thousands of metres below but close enough to spot the dark swell roll, the foam glisten and fleck and disperse.

Right now he felt as though he was in a similar flat dive, but not yet realising it. The night and the clouds were still thick.

Of course, it didn't have to be a cat burglar. He thought: anyone who's important enough can walk their way into anywhere in this country. Vakim would not say, 'No, sorry,' to certain important people, especially if they proffered a brown envelope. He had even seen one important person — not the prince — walk airside right through the police control and customs without waving a thing.

They had come up here, or just possibly risked their necks, and searched his rooms with a window open or the balcony door slid aside. That was presumably in case they were surprised by his premature return. But if they'd entered via Vakim's trembling keys, such an escape was unlikely to be necessary. In fact, the whole business struck him as unlikely, except that it wasn't. He'd been bothered enough times in his career to know that it wasn't. People could get very anxious, and very angry, when you got in their way or refused to obey an order.

He very much hoped it was the left-wing journalist who'd pinched the logbook, and not those he was set to make an enemy of. After all, Sharansky had talked to Vakim. Maybe Vakim had covered himself by telling him a white lie. But the more he considered this, pacing up and down the living room and muttering aloud, the less likely it seemed. Surely a journalist's job was to talk and persuade, not steal. Then a dreadful thought came to him: the only evidence of his knowledge of just what this deal entailed was not in the logbook but in his private thoughts — and these were on display in his half-a-page-a-day diary of that year: nothing elaborate, just curt scribbles, keeping track of his hopes and fears, likes and dislikes, between lists and appointments.

He kept these (uncopied) diaries under the bed, along with a batch of *Clipper* magazines in a tatty Pan Am shoulder bag with a difficult zip, the legacy of a long-ago fling with one of the World's Most Experienced Airline's sky-blue crew — not Olivia, who started with Pan Am but who came into his life a bit later, but a girl called (if his memory was serving him correctly) Nikhil.

He sprang to the bedroom and yanked the bed to one side, slipping on the rug. The strap of the shoulder bag was showing. Relieved, he hauled it out and it came too easily, precisely as light as the blue canvas it was made of. It was empty, apart from a biro, a paper clip and a courtesy sweet from a Bangkok hotel.

The zip had evidently annoyed them, because the opening was a long and jagged tear, made by what he supposed was a serrated combat knife.

Maybe they were just Pan Am souvenir nuts, he thought, before pouring himself a third whisky with a hand that was trained to be shake-free, but was having a day off.

3

'Never pretend you are anything more than a flying truck driver, the pilot of a whispering warehouse. What's in the cargo bay is not your business, and, until it's being loaded, you've no idea anyway.'

Ed Trimble repeated these words to every new boy. Then he'd always say, 'Listen, why does Africa exist? To let white guys make bucks round the clock. Same with Asia, only there it's more the Asians making money round the clock. You get in the way of that process, you get in trouble. Oh, now where's so-and-so gone? Nobody knows. Nobody ever will know. We're not talking Staffordshire; we're talking wildness. Pure wildness.' He had white cropped hair and a thin gold chain round his neck, had started his working life as a quarry man in Mozambique. He was their loadmaster, knew exactly where to shift crates in the bay to the nearest centimetre, or so it seemed. Their life was in his hands, as they generally flew very near to maximums. Being nose-heavy in a fog over the Congo, looking for a badly maintained strip, would have been a one-way headache.

Just over two years back, Bob had ignored Ed Trimble's advice. There was a direct link between that moment of inattention and the current emergency getting the ice ringing in his Scotch. It was The Deal, the one that had hit him like a stepped-on rake: partly his fault, partly the fault of whoever had placed it there, and partly because Olivia wouldn't have him back. That was why he'd been inattentive.

He'd called on her in the shop. Apart from anything else, he wanted his old aeronautical charts, lit by laser-like spots on the stripped-back eighteenth-century brick between the gesturing dummies and racks of unbought clothes. The shop had been on a downward curve since the crisis, Olivia claiming she wasn't so much sick of it as the other way round.

'You used a gun.'

'I shot at the clouds. A farewell signal.'

'So you say. I thought you'd killed him. It was dreadful. He said you threatened to blow his brains out. He'd twisted his ankle.'

'There's a whole universe between using and not using a gun on someone, Olivia.'

A woman entered, a customer. Olivia signalled to him to leave as if he was a pocket of dust and turned her back. She had cheated on him, and he was the one being booted out — or rather, not being allowed back. It meant that his concentration on the job in hand, a few weeks later, was muddied by a fierce undertow of rage.

He had carried all sorts before, including atomic equipment, to many strange places, mostly out of Ostend or Bratislava in the old days, but he had always kept as wise as the three monkeys. Mostly it was stuff like tinned pineapple or bandages or baby milk or spare parts for the oil industry. This time round it was

41

meant to be medical supplies: there'd been a serious earthquake in southern Turkey, and they would be flying into Istanbul out of Plovdiv, Bulgaria.

He never suspected anything else, and anyway it was, following Ed's rules, none of his business. The only reason he was alone in the 727's cargo bay, checking out the crates, was because he'd taken a weekend break in Norfolk after twenty days' flying for an ad hoc charter in lieu of another stand-off on the gravelled drive with Olivia. He had jogged along the beach barefoot, and got a cut toe: not even dead-flat Norfolk was without its dangers.

He was looking for antibiotics, as the small cut was now infected. The top of his foot was flushed and a touch swollen. He knew this little infection could turn into cellulitis, and he'd been in Africa enough to know how swiftly it could all deteriorate: infected cut to cellulitis to septicae-mia to coffin. He also knew exactly which antibiotic to take, and that it was as likely to be in a consignment for earthquake victims as it was unlikely to be available on a wintry Sunday night in Plovdiv International.

So there he was in the dimly lit hold, prising open the lid of a crate with MEDICAL and SAVE THE CHILDREN FUND stencilled on it, when he was suddenly looking not at bandages and bottles but at naughty green boxes. Lots of them. Less to his surprise, these contained brand-new AK-47 assault rifles and their ammo in plastic bags. The crates stretched away in the dim bay, as useless to him as a piss hole in the snow.

42

He disguised his intrusion with a tarp and went off to find the boss, or rather the anonymous boss's agent, a fattish young chap called Lennie with straggly flaxen hair and a cut-glass English drawl, although he claimed he was Swedish — full name Lennart. He was due to come on-board with Team Bob, and perhaps out of nerves he was drinking beer after beer in the airport bar. Maybe he was an uneasy flyer. He asked Bob why he was limping. 'I've limped since I crashed some years ago, but now I'm limping on both legs. It's just more obvious. Talking of which, can I be reassured that our final destination is Istanbul?'

'Of course. Why?'

'I've a feeling the equipment we're carrying might not be very medical.'

'Sorry?'

'It makes no difference to me, I'm just the pilot. I'm not involved in anything other than getting us from A to B, but I do need to know for fuel reasons. I don't want you telling me to take a sharp left or right when I'm thinking to go straight on and finding my maximums are maxed out somewhere over fucking Libya.'

Posh Boy reassured Bob that they would certainly be landing in Istanbul, and reached into his briefcase to flourish the relevant documents, including a flight plan, an export licence, an end-user certificate and a letter from Save the Children which, if Bob had studied it properly, would no doubt have revealed itself as a fiction full of spelling mistakes.

He was as good as his word. The plane left

Plovdiv at midnight with a touch of snow on the runway, and the usual 727 shake-it-about on take-off had Posh Boy gripping his shoulder harness.

'A piece of cake,' Bob told him. 'The wings were bolted on in Seattle, not Shanghai.'

The flight engineer gave a throaty chuckle. This was, as usual, Hugh 'Al' McAllister. Bob had known Al for years and looked on him as a friend, even a good one. 'But the tail was made in fucking Aberdeen,' he growled.

They touched down in Istanbul after an uneventful few hours peppered by reminiscences of Eton; the lad had been sent there by his millionaire dad, who ran a company near Stockholm making industrial refrigerators. Bob had no doubt that the Swede was an old-fashioned adventurer — money certainly wasn't the object. If Bob had known something about Eton he might have quizzed a bit more; instead he admitted going to several very minor public schools, none of which had wanted him for long, ending up in a sixth-form college where he was moderately well received.

'Which university?' asked Posh Boy, leaning forward in the jump seat, his beery breath filling the cockpit.

'The university of life,' Bob replied.

'The best, the best,' said Al. 'The dog has always eaten your homework.'

'And what about yourself, Lennie?'

'Christ Church Oxford,' he announced. The co-pilot — ex-Swissair — looked impressed. The man's a liar, Bob thought. A consummate liar.

He had to tell him to shut up as they began the landing check at 1,500 feet over the Bosphorus.

He expected the cargo to be unloaded, no doubt intended for use by or against the Turkish Kurds; instead, once the cargo high loader was operating, the space in the plane's hold was filled by a jeep and a couple more containers. Then a refuelling truck rolled up. They were on one of Atatürk's remoter aprons next to a curved Nissen-like hut, one of those corrugated relics of a bygone age you find in the unglamorous parts of most airports. Dawn was rising in inverse proportion to his heart, which was most definitely sinking.

He stood shivering on the tarmac (it was winter even in Turkey) looking distinctly grumpy. He repaired with Lennart to the hut and Bob said he needed to sleep. 'A few more hours and you'll all be $90,000 happier,' said the Swede.

Bob tried not to show his delight. Reluctance would put the price up even more.

'Where are we going? Angola's peaceful these days.'

'Turkmenistan.'

'Bigger earthquake, was it?'

Posh Boy smiled wanly. 'There's a lot of bucks in it.'

'Eton old boys don't say *bucks*. They say *small change*. Which airport? Krasnovodsk?'

'Is that the same as Turkmenbashi?'

'Everything's Turkmen-something, I believe. You inspire great confidence in me, but then you did go to Oxford.' Bob sat down at the plywood table on an unstable metal chair with a splintery plywood back, folded his hands and rested his chin on them. Posh Boy avoided his eyes as Bob spoke. 'Look, I've landed there a couple of times. A very smelly place. All rocks and rusting pipelines and little black pools and not a blade of grass. Crude oil. Much smellier than kerosene. It takes ages to get the smell out of the cockpit, in fact. And this operation smells. It would smell less if you'd given me an honest flight plan. The type of cargo's neither here nor there, it just annoys me when the flight plan's hidden from the pilot. That's unusual. I'm not happy with it.'

Posh Boy looked around as if the response lay somewhere in the hut. Its interior was a time warp: there was a telex machine covered in dust on the table and a yellowed Vickers Viscount flight manual on the shelf. A BOAC calendar girl with bright red lips and a woollen bikini grinned from the wall, next to a Brylcreem'd and ageless Atatürk. Bob guessed the place had been padlocked for years and they'd lost the key. The only modern item was the other man's mobile, sitting between them and faintly illuminating his hairless chin.

'I can arrange for a bit more,' he said.

'I'll need to talk to the crew. I don't like the look of this. It's got all the appearance of an illicit arms transfer. If the hardware had been for His Esteemed Turkmen-Highness, no need to hide it.'

'Hardware?'

'All those medical supplies, complete with ammo. And now a jeep and maybe Christ knows what else. It's dangerous goods. They don't appear on the Loadsheet and you didn't notify the captain. That's me. I need to know their loading positions, I need to sign the NOTOC, in case of emergencies. Or the so-called aspirin could give us all a fatal headache.'

The Swede smiled, in the way a kid does when caught fibbing, but his eyes were anxious. 'Please, Captain. Just take it there, pocket the money, and fly back empty. Like you've always done, notification or no notification.'

'Not always. Sometimes I've not liked the look of it. There are wars in Africa, and people need guns like they need medical kit, but there's no war in Turkmenistan.' As no answer came back, Bob gave it to him: 'There is, however, a big war next door. So why not fly straight to Kabul or Bagram? I've done that quite a few times. Field hospitals, tents, even military stuff. There's no embargo. As long as it's not, of course, the Taliban.'

The reaction Bob had deliberately wished to trigger was unexpected, but it imparted the same message: the young man laughed. Not a laugh of derision, but a high yelp-like thing of embarrassment. He looked up at the ceiling, its askew panels defying the forces of gravity. 'Well, it's an awful mess,' he sighed. 'No one knows where anything ends up, really.'

'Mess is the operative word,' Bob said. 'I have two golden rules in this job: no flights to Libya, not since Lockerbie, and don't touch the Taliban. For a start, they burn down schools, which despite my scholarly record is not something I approve of.'

'There's worse in Africa,' said Posh Boy. 'Joseph H. Kenley, for example?'

Bob glanced at him: the young man's stare was meaningful. The eye pouches seemed to have grown suddenly, adding ten years to the pallid area under the straggly flax.

'I was a charter pilot,' Bob said, 'doing my job. Standard operations, in and out of the bush. Short hauls, an hour each way. But you had to know what you were about. Real aviation.' He reiterated that he'd said no once or twice, when it was not to his liking.

And that was true: Bob Winrush had said no to some very unpleasant so-called rebel colonels, who'd end up shouting a lot too close to his face so he could smell the drink. But he would stick to his guns, despite losing money. 'And as for Kenley,' he said, and paused. 'There was a war on. You don't know who the stuff's intended for. It's on the tarmac. You load it, you fly, you unload it. Equipment or men. This business is different.' He brushed the table's dust from his uniform sleeves, folded his arms and sat back. 'This has critical alert flashing all over it. I know what I'm talking about. And my foot's infected. I need to get to a doctor immediately.'

Lennart reached into his briefcase once more and produced the flight plan and a plastic folder with the relevant flight charts, approach plates and so on. He removed the charts and flattened them out. Most of the route was over water: the Black Sea, the Caspian. As for the flight plan, it was a new one: it started at Plovdiv, but its destination was marked as Turkmenbashi. All signed and above board, Bob noticed. Not that anyone in Turkmenistan could have cared a hoot.

'I said we'd fly into Istanbul, Captain, and we did. Our return to Bulgaria is rerouted due to bad weather,' he added jokily.

'Yes, we did fly into Istanbul. And I'll bet you went to Eton, too — on a day trip with your very minor public school. Or comprehensive, even. Forget it. Find another skipper. I'm off to the doctor's.'

Bob stood up, swigged the last dregs of the coffee he'd somehow brought out with him to the shed, and limped slightly dramatically to the door. Posh Boy started to talk in Swedish, which Bob thought was silly until he realised the man was, without picking it up, addressing his mobile. No doubt it had been relaying the entire conversation. As if in sympathy with its owner's feelings, Bob's foot drew attention to its condition with a needle-sharp stab of pain. But the man hadn't wanted to hear about the foot. Clearly, when millions of Tali-dollars are at stake, sourced probably from the limitless wells of Saudi Arabia, a pilot's minor medical ailment does not count for much. This piqued the pilot more than anything.

Naturally, when Bob tried to open the door, he found it locked. He looked out of the grimy pane of glass that constituted the shed's window and saw at least three burly men, the kind you know have halitosis, standing outside with shoulder holsters in evidence. He turned round.

'Look,' Posh Boy said, 'you and I are in this together. I went to Eton, but I got expelled. You know, drugs, being too individual and all that.'

'Who's your boss?'

'He's not paying you. He's just the client. You'll be paid on landing.'

'What, the mad mullahs are just going to come on board waving a brown envelope?'

'Yes. Their representatives. In Western suits.'

'Well, I hardly expected them to board in Taliban T-shirts,' Bob said. 'So who *is* your boss? Viktor Bout's in prison, these days. Barrett-Jolley, too.'

Posh Boy switched his mobile off and looked thoughtful. Then he said a name, quietly. Bob got him to repeat it. The Swede didn't want to, as if he'd had second thoughts on hearing himself say it. Bob actually refused to believe him. Ed's advice was swept away.

'Evron Bensoussan? It's not possible. He's an Israeli. Even Mr Bensoussan wouldn't sell arms to the Taliban. Are the guns booby-trapped or something?'

'It's crazy, I know,' Lennart said, turning pale. 'But I'm just the agent. I'm not even Jewish. And, by the way, I didn't lie: I never said delivery was in Istanbul.' His pale blue eyes stared, but oddly unfocused, as if through the bottom of a glass.

Bob could either fly and risk a lot of trouble, or not fly and risk a lot of trouble. The payment was not just for doing it but to keep your mouth shut, after.

'I see I'm free to make one choice,' he said.

Posh Boy stood up and shook Bob's hand. 'I'll get you more money. Another $20,000, just for you.'

'No. Divided three ways. I can't fly the beast on my own. But what about my foot? I may get delirious on the plane. In fact, I'm feeling pretty rough already.' Lennart said they couldn't hang about. 'They've given us a slot?' He nodded. 'So what's our CTOT?' The agent said take-off was in four hours fifteen minutes, which seemed plenty to find a doctor, but he didn't want Bob to find one. It would draw attention, lead to stamped documentation.

Bob expressed surprise that they were flying in daylight. 'We're freight,' he enunciated, as if talking to an idiot, 'and I believe it's hot out there. It's mostly desert.'

'Actually,' said Lennart, 'deserts get pretty cold in the Caspian. Right now it's under ten degrees. There's a doctor in the airport here, emergencies. I'll get it sorted. Go sit in the plane. What do you need?' Bob scribbled out the name of the antibiotic on a slip of paper. It was almost illegible, like a real prescription. He did feel rough, but not just from his foot or lack of sleep; no man feels good when his marriage is disintegrating in mid-air, frame by frame.

He told the Swede that the identity of the boss was just between themselves, that he wouldn't tell the crew that it was Bensoussan. Posh Boy didn't seem to take it in, so Bob told him again. He dismissed the assurance with a wave of his hand and tapped on the door, which opened. He said something more in Swedish — or maybe it wasn't Swedish, maybe it was Martian — and Bob was escorted back to the flight deck, his limp even more pronounced.

All Bob said to his crew was that there was twenty more grand, because their destination was a certain benighted country that stank of crude, felt a bit stony, and had not a tree nor a blade of grass, except maybe around the presidential palace. Five guesses.

'Not fucking Iraq,' said Al.

'No way.'

'Afghanistan?' suggested ex-Swissair.

'Close. Think the latter end of the alphabet. We fly from A to Z, as you know. It has a famously lousy airline.'

'Ireland,' joked Al. 'And I don't mean Aer Lingus.'

Ex-Swissair pointed out that Ireland had a lot of grass. This was getting silly so Bob told them. Al groaned. He'd once flown Turkmenistan Airlines to Birmingham out of Ashgabat as a passenger after his own plane was grounded. The toilets were flooded, the food was foul and the cabin crew had not a word of English between them. 'But they're pretty-looking planes,' he added. Bob wondered whether to tell them who their clients were, remembered Al had done a few flights for Viktor Bout (no stranger to the Taliban, it was rumoured), and did so. They weren't aware, of course, that the cargo and the cargo manifest did not join up.

'Christ,' said Al. 'The Taliboys. So who's brokered this deal? I'll bet it wasn't Save the Children.'

'That, my friend, is out-of-bounds knowledge.'

'The Saudis, I'll bet. My situation awareness is improving to a point I don't want it to.'

'Ignorance is joy,' said ex-Swissair.

'Bliss,' said Bob. 'Ignorance is bliss. As I can confirm from personal experience.'

'Bliss?'

'Rhymes with kiss.'

'And piss,' growled Al. 'As in fucking grand piss-up.'

They were standing by the cockpit door, backs to the cargo bay, where the second container was being rumbled in. Napalm, probably. The heavies stood on the steps. The trio passed into the cockpit and consulted the charts. Bob spotted another man down below on the tarmac, near the nose, passing what looked like a curry comb over his black knee-length coat.

'I wonder who he is.'

'The devil, grooming himself,' Al said. 'Well, it's pretty obviously never just medical supplies, is it? I'll bet you it isn't. Istanbul's not called the crossroads of Europe and Asia for nothing.'

'I suggest you speak in dulcet tones,' Bob said, lowering his voice. 'I'm not happy with this operation, but we're stuck in it. Never walk away from a deal. You're probably right,' he added, just to cover himself. 'It's bound to be green boxes and stuff, but we'd better not check.'

He didn't fancy letting on that he already knew.

Ex-Swissair said, 'I've need of the money.'

'And what are those guys all about?' asked Al, squinting through the port window at the three guards, now happily smoking where they shouldn't.

Bob popped his head out of the exit door with a pretend look of dismay and asked them to extinguish their cigarettes. They laughed and blew smoke towards his face.

'Over to you, Al,' he said.

'Where's your authority, skipper?'

'Authority requires some kind of system. The only system here is naked greed.'

Nothing much in this hopeless, hapless world could surprise him these days, but Bob was genuinely shaken up by what Posh Boy had told him. Evron Bensoussan! The biggest Israeli arms dealer! For all his experience of naughty cargoes and dirty brokers, this one had still managed to take the bolts out of his jaw. 'Let's go kick some tyres,' he suggested, 'while we're waiting.'

They passed the guards on the steps and the guards followed them down while they half-heartedly went through the motions of a general look-over. Bob wondered about finding a hairline crack in the fuselage, a loose bolt in the wing stub, but didn't trust his acting abilities. The three heavies stood about under the belly smoking away until the guys in the refuelling truck yelled at them in Turkish and English, and they obeyed. The cockpit crew kicked the tyres and then gathered in a thoughtful knot.

'I don't believe I'm that desperate for money,' said Al, as if he was two people. 'They can find another crew.'

'We know a certain amount, though,' said ex-Swissair.

Al said, not very convincingly, 'We'll collectively reassure them of our silence. We'll say nothing about it. Strictly hush-hush. I've been in this position before.'

'Listen, I haven't told you everything,' Bob said, 'so you're safe. If I told you who the client was, the boss man himself, you wouldn't be safe. You may not believe it, either.'

'Tony Blair,' suggested Al. 'No, the Pope!'

They laughed. In fact, either might have been more credible than what Bob had just been told.

'If it's just medical,' said ex-Swissair, 'then maybe it is in fact the Red Cross. They have no political bias.'

'That's a point,' said Al.

'No way,' Bob insisted. 'That's aiding and abetting terrorism.'

'Aye,' said Al. 'I can see the Jesus sandals coiling around your feet.' The refuelling truck had wrapped up its hose, and they were enveloped in kero fumes. Bob kept an eye on the heavies. The man in the knee-length coat had vanished. 'You know,' Al went on, 'I was flying into Damascus some years back in a seventy six, with a Reuters man on the jump seat, the last one out of Iran after the Shah fell, and he told me the Ayatollah was a US stooge. As we were landing he told it me. I said no one talks when landing except to count down the feet, but it stayed with me. I think the experiment backfired.'

'Let's take a vote,' said Bob, cutting in. 'Who's happy to go?'

Only ex-Swissair put his clean, almost glossy

hand up, although tentatively. 'I wouldn't say happy,' he admitted, 'but I need the money.'

'I'll tell you what,' murmured Al. 'There isnae going to be a cargo check here, and there isnae going to be one in Turkmenbashi. They're in it up to their necks.'

'What're you saying?'

'That if you say yes, skipper, we'll follow your lead. Otherwise it's no.'

'I don't want to say yes, given I know too much. But that's not fair on you. Your state of blissful ignorance makes you party to nothing. Even that crew caught flying on the Barrett-Jolley jaunt got away with it, because they genuinely did not know what they were carrying, or who the customer was.'

'Where did you pick up that piece of shite?' scoffed Al, quite put out. 'B-J's crew went down for a lot o' years. You'd better tick the box that says, 'I don't know — anything.''

When Posh Boy came back, he had a small white box of antibiotics. Clearly a man of influence. He was beaming from ear to ear as he handed it over.

'What's this?' asked Al. 'Have you a migraine, skipper?'

'Terminal illness, as it were,' joked Bob. 'Nothing to worry about.' He turned to Lennart, taking him away from the others to the foot of the steps. 'We've been parleying,' Bob said. 'And the conclusion is not good.'

The beaming rotated to a scowl. The better light now revealed the man to be in his late thirties, possibly more. Or maybe ten years had passed in his absence. He said, 'There's no more money.'

'Listen, we're not fooling about. This is not a safe operation. If we're caught . . . I mean, we're hanging about here with the doors open. I haven't told my crew about the real nature of the cargo, nor about your boss. Only about the source of the brown envelopes. And they're still unhappy.'

Posh Boy shrugged. He was so much more in control of his nerve that Bob wondered if he'd taken a snort in the airport toilets. He fluttered his hamster eyelashes. 'The extra cash,' he said. 'We expected more crew. You're only three. I won't reduce it.'

'727s always have a three-man crew,' Bob said. 'You don't know your equipment, do you?'

'You'll only get the cash on arrival,' the Swede pointed out. 'For this leg, nothing.'

'Fancy thinking a 727 uses a five-man crew,' Bob muttered, shaking his head. 'Young people today, I dunno.'

In truth, Bob Winrush was flummoxed. The money was very good, the flight was no challenge, and he was used to brown envelopes from all sorts of curious personages. The runway at Turkmenbashi was no bumpier than Frankfurt, and always dry. But everything inside him was wanting out. Pilots feel this sometimes: premonitory warnings. They know the aircraft better than themselves: they can give you the thread diameter and metallurgy of the four bolts that secure the engines to the fuselage on a 727, but not how the human head swivels on its neck, or what nerves connect the fingers to the brain, or why the heart should suddenly contract for no concrete reason.

The man had lied to him. That was it. He hated being lied to. He hated being cheated. It was humiliating. It was an invisible undertow of rage that was pulling him out of this deal, taking him out into open water. But rage hardly ever paid.

'I thought your kind were tough,' Posh Boy sneered, getting his own back.

'Tough and crazy. A blindness to danger and an eagerness to die: I should join the Taliban. I'll ask them if they need recruits. Can't wait to wear my explosive vest and walk into a school for girls.'

'They're actually very polite,' the Swede said, seeing a glimmer of hope. 'It's all just politics,' he added vaguely.

The airport's ops agent, a frighteningly young man in an impeccable white shirt under his fluo jacket, came up with the papers to sign, handing Bob a biro with Snoopy decals down the side. He could see there was no way out. The only solution was to do a bunk. He watched the high loader go off and the cargo door close, then turned to the simpering Swede.

'OK. I guess I've signed my death warrant. Hello, death. When have we got clearance exactly, Lennie?'

Posh Boy went over and talked to the ops agent, who consulted his sheets. They had just over four hours. 'Fine,' said Bob. 'Time to visit a Turkish toilet, take a shower, brush my teeth, swallow a couple of these pills, a brief shut-eye, then be fresh for ops. It's called crew rest.'

Al and ex-Swissair seemed quite happy when their skipper told them that they were on. The three heavies accompanied them to the airport hotel, which at that hour was all massively empty conference spaces humming with the odd Hoover. The crew booked into a business class room equipped for four adults, with a long frosted mirror and a trio of spotty prints. It was hard in such a place to imagine they'd be bumping onto a dusty desert in central Asia before the day was out. The heavies watched satellite TV from one of the twin beds, but the crew complained and when that didn't work phoned Posh Boy Lennie. 'Our room's overweight on the live load,' was how they put it. 'By three armed oicks.'

The heavies grumblingly exited, standing about in the corridor studying their mobiles as once they'd have studied their nails.

Bob closed the door on them politely and checked out the window height: the room was on the second floor, luckily, and below it was the kitchen quarters' flat roof. He asked Al to come out from the bathroom; his long-time flight engineer emerged dripping from the shower, skirted by a fluffy towel.

'Listen, chaps,' Bob said. 'You don't know something I do.'

'The wing's got woodworm,' Al joked.

'Worms don't go for balsa.'

Ex-Swissair, in his underpants, applying eau de cologne, asked what the hell was going on.

'Don't mind him,' Bob said in a Fawlty voice; 'he's from Lausanne.'

Al laughed his very loud and raucous laugh, which was Bob's intention. Unless they were very stupid, the heavies would be listening to the way the room's voices were intoning, or for silence. So Bob kept up a slightly manic tone: 'You know what? I am not doing this one. I'm scarpering. Out of that window. Maybe it's my foot. Maybe the operation's too hot. But I am not doing it.'

Al grimaced. 'It's not airworthy, or what?'

'No, it's to do with the boss. The client. As I said, that stupid public-school boy told me who's setting up this deal when he should have kept mum. It's done my head in. That's the only reason. Oh, and a bad kind of premonitory feeling.'

'I never care who the fuck the client is,' said Al. 'And the client doesn't care about me. As for feelings, I get a bad one every time we roll out.'

'Really?'

His flight engineer all but glared at him. 'You're committing a runner, skipper.'

'Keep your voice down. This wasn't in the contract. We were bamboozled.' He had to explain 'bamboozled' to ex-Swissair.

'Fuck a duck,' said Al. 'They'll shoot us.'

Neither of them wanted to come with their captain, though. 'This is always happening to me,' Al moaned. 'It happened to me in Kigali. The captain scarpered in the night. They really took it out on me. Fists, boots, the lot.'

'They were military, that's why,' Bob said. 'Far

from civilisation. This lot'll find an equally disreputable replacement with proper stripes in minutes. This is Turkey. One foot in Europe.'

'I tell you what: you could raid our drinks bar,' Al suggested brightly. 'One J and B miniature would push your levels way over the FAA limit.'

'I don't suppose that would bother them.'

'Ginger ale'd do it, probably.'

Al had been in rehab before shifting out of passenger into freight. He was still bitter about it, as he'd always been careful to stop being an alcoholic the stipulated twelve hours before each flight. Ex-Swissair shrugged. Bob was to find out later — when it was necessary to do the research — that the man wasn't actually Swiss, but formerly of the East German air force, and had a profitable sideline selling Stasi files to interested parties.

Bob told them to lock themselves in the bathroom. 'Wait inside about ten minutes, with some tap activity, then come out and alert the bouncers with shock and awe in your voices. Alternatively I can hit you, suggesting you struggled to hold me back.'

'I suppose in the bathroom is better,' said ex-Swissair. It was hard to picture him faking shock and awe.

Al looked worried. 'In the bathroom together?'

'I'm sure they're broad-minded, underneath,' said Bob.

★ ★ ★

The modest jump was painful only because of his foot. There were windows looking down on him, but presumably everyone was still asleep, or simply assumed a randy pilot had been caught out by the unexpected return of the husband, boyfriend, girlfriend, whatever. He hadn't changed into his civvies for fear of meeting Lennart, in which unfortunate instance he could plead his need for some duty-free. He avoided the hotel itself and limped to departures and its taxi rank, where a sleepy-looking driver deposited his small case in the boot, but in slow motion. Bob kept low in the back seat, feeling very unprofessional, and picturing the three heavies emptying their handguns into his co-pilot and flight engineer: he could even see the bullets shattering the TV screen, Al's brainpan disintegrating like JFK's.

The captain had abandoned ship, walked (or rather jumped) out of a deal. But he told himself that he'd fulfilled the original contract: he'd done nothing wrong except refuse tens of thousands of dollars. Other men would have gone ahead — Bob Winrush might have gone ahead a few years earlier despite a happy family and comfortable home. But he was older now and lacking a certain zip, and his concentration was not crystal-clear at present. Things on his mind. Domestic interference. He remembered how out in Angola or the Congo or Sierra Leone, you'd meet old hands, yellowish by now rather than white, whose total analysis of the human character had boiled down to this: there were those who fucked everything in sight and all the time, and those who were choosier and fucked every now and again. He knew which category he slotted into: a third, unmentioned one. Those who were fucked.

But he still managed a cultural tour of Istanbul, waiting for the night coach to take him to Izmir. He certainly didn't fancy returning to the airport. And he hadn't even had a shower, so he booked an hour in a historic hammam he remembered from years back when he was doing the Heathrow — Istanbul run.

He splayed himself naked on the slippery expanse of marble along with a bulky party from Rickmansworth, some assorted Chinese and a few young Turks discussing what sounded like football. He stared up at the ancient star-punctured dome and deeply regretted his late action. Not because of what it might lead to — he was never in the business of alarmism — but because he had denied himself a challenge. Right now he'd have been at altitude, in control, in his element, off the airwaves and not talking to anyone on the ground, beyond the ordinary limits yet still secure, just resting on his own wits and skill and the machinery.

Proper flying.

Raising his head, all he could see were corpses with towels on their groins, laid out on a massive slab. It reminded him of a fish stall in the souk. He could have been in the front office with his hand resting on the throttle and some tens of thousands of dollars waiting to greet him. He told the masseur to avoid his foot, but the man made up for it on everything else: not a joint missed. Slappable fish-meat. The bones sounded like distant firecrackers. Or guns popping off from behind rocks in some waterless Afghan gorge. Afterwards Bob poured freezing water from the faucet over his head, drank several glasses of applemint tea in the hammam's café and felt fantastic.

It was time he called it a day. Freight. All that lark. He should retire early and open a little pub. The pleasant divorcee with the sympathetic ear, pulling the real ale and spinning his yarns. And as if his personal angel had suddenly remembered his existence, a portly man flashing a gold tooth caught his eye at the next table and asked him where he was from.

'England,' he said. 'And you?'

'I am from the Emirates,' the man said, with pride. 'I am a royal cook. My name is Muhib. Actually, I am Moroccan in birth. I work for a prince. He has a house here, in Istanbul. A big house. He has one in Paris, too. Very big. But the biggest is in Dubai,' he added, as Bob's attendant angel screwed up the original flight plan and unfolded a brand-new chart. 'Many fountains, trees, so beautiful. Gold taps. Many old things. Very very old.'

When Bob said he was a pilot, the royal cook raised his hands in admiration and said that his prince had just bought his own big jet, a DC-10, because when he flies on a passenger plane, even first class, the time comes to pray to Allah, and he must stand because you must always stand before Allah with obedience, and that is not allowed when there is turbulence, and often no one can tell him the direction of the *qiblah*. And this jet was being refitted in a way you would not believe, with a sauna, jacuzzi, all that stuff.

Bob asked him if the prince had appointed a flight crew.

'Not yet,' he said, and spread his hands. 'Allah has brought you to this spot, I can see. Praise be to him.'

Bob chuckled, then saw the man was being deadly serious.

'Allah does seem to know best,' he said, raising his glass of applemint.

Then came the coarse ringing of an old-fashioned phone, the kind you'd still find on airport desks in places like Bangui or Ndjamena a few years back. Bob looked about him before he noticed his new-found friend pointing at the mobile winking away on his serviette. How reliable is a pilot who can't recognise his own ringtone? Bob picked it up with an embarrassed snort, but without a qualm: Olivia, for instance, only sent emails. Or rather, her solicitor sent emails; it was a kind of autism, as Al had put it, this refusal to communicate like an adult. 'That's not very fair on autistics,' Bob had replied.

As for walking out on the deal, he seriously considered that, as generally happened in this sort of situation, he was in the clear. The organisations involved are far too preoccupied to start worming out some bit player, especially a bamboozled pilot, and bothering him. But here was a voice he didn't know, with only a slight if unidentifiable accent, being fairly unpleasant (and loud with it) into his ear. The line was bad, like a vast and echoey room, but the content and the tone were clear: menacing. He kept up a mildly joky expression for the benefit of his friend, but in fact it was wholly natural: it was hard to take this voice seriously. His heart thought otherwise, apparently slamming its oleaginous bulk into his upper chest-wall as the voice droned on.

Basically, it was most unfortunate that a professional pilot of the rank of a captain should walk out of an operation of such delicacy with all the facts of it still in his head, as if intent on informing others for his gain. Did he wish to be famous like Brad Pitt, or something? Bob turned his head slightly away from Muhib, and told the Voice that he had been strong-armed into a deal and that was not the way he operated, but the Voice talked over him halfway through in a most irritating way, and Bob's own voice was acting up, it sounded strangulated instead of firm and confident. The Voice repeated that what he, Bob Winrush, had done was unfortunate, not only for them but for himself. What was he going to do about it? Bob reassured him that he was going to forget all about it, that he wouldn't even think about it, that he had already forgotten the details.

'If you say one word, you will be dead by Monday,' the Voice said matter-of-factly.

Bob replied that this was understandable, and he had no intention of dying, and that luckily he'd said nothing about what he knew to his crew, who he assumed were unharmed. A hoarse sort of rasp sounded, which Bob read as a sardonic snort, and the Voice said to his great relief that the crew were already doing their professional job, unlike a certain scumbag. Bob asked if that was all, and the phone went dead. He turned back to Muhib, who was distracted by some teenage girls hovering in front of a shop opposite, their long gold earrings waving at the two men to look and admire.

'Plenty of beautiful girls in Dubai,' said the royal cook, nodding sagely. 'Eyes like jewels, lips like roses, dimples like wells.'

'Hey,' Bob said, feeling a little nauseous suddenly, a little faint, 'maybe Allah wants me to meet them, Muhib.'

4

You will be dead by Monday.

That two-year-old phrase returned, dusted off and beautifully polished, as he sat in his apartment, pondering the loss of his logbook and diary. Why not by Sunday? Maybe they only worked on Mondays, these hit men. Maybe they went home on Friday evening, watched telly, took their kids to a football match, grumbled about work to the wife, woke up Monday morning thinking, Christ, I've got that pilot job this afternoon, over in Dubai. Never any break. There's always someone in my cross hairs. The point, of course, was that arms smuggling is all smoke and mirrors: it probably wasn't Mossad so much as some mafiosi types, of which there is no shortage, hired to deal with the small fry like himself.

He thought of Mike Perceval, a pilot with a dodgy hand-sewn outfit called Worldwide Wings Inc. He had disappeared without trace in Belarus some years back after, apparently, refusing to fly a creaky 707 freighter to Yemen. The seven-oh had a kid's collage of faded logos on its tail and no maintenance records, and was packed to the gills with Albanian military hardware. Bob had heard this from Mike's Latvian co-pilot, unlicensed and about as trustworthy as a BAC 1–11 was quiet. Mike got cross and was then driven off in a BMW at Minsk airport by men in dark glasses, and that was that. 'Putin,' was all the co-pilot would say, 'Putin pay a lot of that attention to detail.' But then he hated Russians. Mike was a character, with the sort of moustache you expect to be ripped off with a triumphant snarl, but one couldn't say he was sorely missed.

Bob decided not to phone Matt Sharansky, although he half-suspected him of breaking in: after all, a Mossad operative might well pose as an investigative journalist, on the same principle as anti-arms campaigners pose as arms dealers, or butt-grabbing wife-stealers as bilingual thera-peutic masseurs. He did consider, for all of ten seconds, telling the police about the break-in and theft. Dubai, the glittery city of intrigue, of deals in wraparound shades. Money falling over itself to make even more. Trust? That's the real luxury in this city built on sand, where the streets can blow sudden whiffs of sour milk or the stench of sick into your face, as though to remind you.

What the prince had said in the jacuzzi suddenly came back to him over his internal tannoy, like his old recurrent nightmare in which he heard his own flight — the flight he should be captaining — announced in the former Wool-worth's in Sudbury, fitted by the dream engineers in their hi-vis smocks as a departure lounge in Chicago: 'I see you have a history, too, Captain.' Maybe Sheikh Ahmed had done a bit of research. Easy as falling over, these days. You don't have to shift your plump carcass an inch.

Bob made no change to his plan to eat, swim, pack, sleep and depart the following day — until he saw that all flights were full out of Dubai except for one that cost over $800. He wasn't going to risk going subject-to-load on a British Airways flight (which as an ex-BA pilot he got a lot cheaper), only to find himself stranded when the load turned out to be at max. It was the same story in Abu Dhabi; Doha was way too far.

So he booked a flight to Heathrow for the day after, first thing in the morning, giving himself more time to sort out business with the green-eyed secretary among the cheetahs. He did a quick Google-search for the main actors in the game, and fell upon a Matt Sharansky who seemed likely: worked for an Israeli paper he hadn't heard of, author of articles about the arms trade and general politics from a leftist angle, no photos. He began to hope it was this guy who had stolen the logbook and diary for his own benefit, and not some nameless shadow in shades, hired by big-time Bensoussan. Matt Sharansky had attracted a lot of bile from fellow countrymen to his right, some of it strikingly venomous.

Bob had a bite in the luxurious local tandoori among expat executives in the construction business (every one of them with self-shaved heads, as if pretending to be workers), and then, still in the pre-digestive period, got the pool slapping its sides with a vigorous crawl under the night's glow. He had the water and lemon trees to himself.

Better than the sheikh's chic sauna's heat. Tongue-twisters would keep them from nodding off in the cockpit. *My landside folder's glider flight guide's filed.* The tower would presume they were speaking Japanese, or something.

As he towelled down, he felt his life had divided itself into two versions which were running in parallel: the normal version whose emotional centre was a hole once occupied by his ex-wife, dangerously plugged by a pretty-looking DC-10 and (at present) lovely Leila; the other a patently absurd one in which a deadly secret service or one of its acolytes thought him important enough to break into his apartment and possibly do him harm.

The one time he had crashed a plane was memorable for the way everything slowed right down in the preceding seconds: the touchdown, the brakes not responding, putting it into full reverse, mud and stones rattling through the engines as they ingested the runway, a nice view of the forest's trees straight ahead instead of to port and starboard, their foliage expanding as the yards in between reduced. He understood why birds and winged insects are said to have a slowed-down viscous sense of time: all those acrobatics. As he dried himself by the pool, this was the time he was moving in. Not because he felt in someone's cross hairs, because he didn't. No, he just felt he was about to crash. The man without his logbook. The man without his diary. The man without his job. The man without his house. The man without his wife.

The pilot without his plane.

I must phone Leila, he thought. As Al had advised him when he'd turned up in Maidenhead from the trip up north after the

71

catastrophe, 'You're at rock bottom, pal. Start to dig.'

He liked the glow of the city's night sky on the pool water, all those wobbly lozenges on the bottom, the scent of lemon blossom over the chlorine, the little blue-and-white tiles at his feet, the cool desert air on his skin. He didn't really want to leave this for his Crowthorne flat, or worse. For nothingness. But the crash felt imminent.

As he went up in the lift, it occurred to him that his son, David, might know this Sharansky character, if only by repute. David had recently gone student-political and joined various activist groups, including AAW, or Action Against Weapons; so he was annoyed that his father had stopped being a freight pilot, he could have serviced their campaigning needs, provided info. David would quizz Bob on what he had seen exactly on the tarmac in Entebbe or Accra or Ostend or Minsk. The Ilyushins, the Antonovs, the refitted 707s. Dad was not a lot of help, mainly because he hadn't seen much except crates on pallets, containers, goods hidden under shrink wrap.

One day David had phoned Bob after some weekend conference or other and said straight out, 'How could you do it, Dad?' With the zeal of the convert.

'Do what, David?' When his son explained, Bob said, 'I just fly. It's always a mixture of things. Polio vaccines, tractors, livestock, art works, sweets.'

'But you flew for Viktor Bout.'

'I didn't know I was flying for Bout.' Bob had told him yet again how a plane could be leased and chartered three or four times over by various holding companies. He compared it to banks putting your savings into arms, plastics, nuclear stuff, pesticides while their adverts showed a happy family in a flowering meadow. 'We're all flying along totally compromised, David. Angels are only found in heaven. You need to introduce some nuance.'

'And Africa?' David persisted. 'The Congo? Uganda? Rwanda?'

'Africa's Africa. Lots of different stuff came up. You just went along and did it. General cargo or military or medical, you just did it. Freight dogs aren't vicars, you know. We don't exactly pull the triggers, either. And I'll bet even vicars have some malicious, malevolent members in their congregation. But they still carry on with the service.' Since Olivia had started going to church in the village, this was an obvious reference, and unnecessary: Olivia was neither malicious nor malevolent.

At the end of these conversations his son would get grumpy, and Bob would try to change the subject to rock bands, which names had been playing gigs in Dubai, but he could never remember them correctly unless they were called something like Pink.

The more he thought about it, the more plausible it seemed that David had put Sharansky onto him. These guys talked to each other at conferences, on Facebook, via campaign websites. No one else, or hardly anyone, knew precisely where he lived: he'd drawn a map for David so he could copy it onto the envelope if he was sending his father a card or a letter. Since David had forgotten his birthday last year, and only ever texted (usually for money), the map remained unused. Until now, possibly.

What's more, David knew about the logbooks. He would see them as a kid, on the desk in Bob's box-room study. Recently, David had asked his father if he could cross-check a logbook against some cargo histories they were looking at: his overlords in the campaign group had paid a considerable sum for satellite photos of tanks being disembarked at Addis Ababa, but Bob could truthfully tell him that he'd never landed there. Then he compromised. 'OK, if you want to take a look, you'll have to come to Dubai. I'd love you to come and see me here, as you know. Great clubs, nice beaches, incredible girls.' Too late, he realised that these would not be a draw for David in his new guise as world saviour.

'You can scan it, email it to me.'

'No way. Absolutely *nyet*.'

The more evasive Bob was, the more interested his son became. Sensitive material, all that. Bob ended up asking him if he really wanted to get his old dad into trouble. The reply reminded him of what a smoothie rebel colonel riposted when he wondered about human rights in some airstrip shack near Kisangani: the man had swatted mosquitoes from his nose and said, smiling, 'Human rights is a bourgeois concept.'

What David said was: 'Your trouble, Dad, isn't quite as serious as the victims' trouble.' His father said he'd think about it.

Anyway, he now felt disappointed, and all sorts of angry rubbish flowed in to do with Olivia and that glossy-fingered Canadian prick. Before long he was out on the terrace with another large chaser and a beer to be chased. He stared out upon the usual glitz and could have sworn another few storeys had been added by the cranes and diggers grinding and banging away.

He was itching to phone David, but it felt a bit late. He liked phoning his children from Dubai. David or Sophie. Sophie or David. Both at seats of learning so that, whenever they answered, it was with a real pub's racket behind and he could say, 'Glad to hear you're in the library. I'll whisper.'

Instead, he tried Leila's number again but it was still on message. She'd be at work, busy behind the bar. Behind him — or rather at his shoulder, where he could keep half an eye on it — the apartment felt slightly alien. On coming back from his swim, he had smelt a strange aftershave as he stepped inside. It was doubtless the trace of another resident passing in the corridor, swirling in with him, but it did make him especially alert as he picked up a few things and snapped open a couple of suitcases, before succumbing to the drink — which he eventually noticed had a film of dust on its oily-looking surface (the beer was straight from the bottle). Construction-site dust, that's what it was. Not desert sand. Or maybe both. He'd never thought about it, really. But you could see clouds of it, like smoke, in the cranes' floodlights as they winched and whirred.

It was fine to be leaving.

★　★　★

He couldn't sleep, of course. It was a tangle of things: losing his job, the drink, the feeling that someone else was in the apartment. He was nose-heavy and over his maximums, as they always would be in Africa — ten or twelve tonnes over max landing weight at times. Just enough to make it delicate, to reduce the get-out clause to zero. He was wiggling away at the analog switches, knobs, pressing what have you, pushing the throttle and so on, and there was no response.

He tossed and turned, got up at 3 a.m. to watch some international pap on cable, swallowed down a basinful of bottled water, then tried to lure unconsciousness with earplugs (which simply drowned out the grumbling air con with the dim baboon-shrieks of his tinnitus). He considered phoning Al. He hadn't talked to him properly for ages. He stood shivering on the balcony, disco beats faintly pounding as the place partied, but Dubai's glitz was completely overruled by a full moon.

This reminded him of an old, recurring nightmare: he was flying a 747, filled with pax to the last seat, between the skyscrapers of some unnamed city, his rate of climb so weak as to be pretty well invisible; but he'd always do a great job of squeezing the fuselage between two towering glass edifices, and somehow the wings followed. 'Piece of cake!' he'd shout over the shuddering yoke. At last a gap would prove too narrow, and he'd wake up practically on the floor unconstrained by sheets. But what he most remembered about the dream (it stopped when he only carried freight and the odd self-loading batch in the form of hundreds of soldiers) was that, just before the fatal moment, a cabin attendant with a huge beehive perm like his first stepmother's would whisper in his ear, 'At least it's a full moon, Captain.'

He did drop off, about half an hour before the alarm (set for eight o'clock), but he didn't fly between skyscrapers. He was bringing a heap of loose flowers in his arms for his master, Doug Rydale, an ex-Pan Am pilot near retirement who had done the Berlin airlift run and flown the Beatles twice. Doug was definitely the nicest, kindest man Bob had ever known. It was under Doug's captaincy (he'd moved to BA after Lockerbie) that Bob had begun his own real-time flying career, so fresh out of the simulator that he was, as Doug joked, 'still out of focus, in two dimensions, and distorted'.

Bob learnt many things from Doug Rydale. Most of all, how to treat everyone as your equal — including the service crew, the ground staff, the cleaners. How to look the steward or stewardess in the eyes when you say 'Thank you' for bringing you coffee, and not just when you want to date them. Doug was what used to be called a gentleman, with a moustache made for twirling. He only read the *International Herald*

Tribune, and hailed from Minneapolis. 'That's the outside world,' he'd say, when some unpleasant event was reported. 'That's the outside world big time. When all we want is beauty, justice, and at least two engines working.'

In Bob's dream, Doug (who had died suddenly on the eighteenth tee in Florida about ten years ago) was still alive and in a retirement home. A pretty nurse came up and said, 'It's all through-carpeted,' and then Bob entered Doug's room. It was empty. He came back out into the corridor and the floor was awash with muck and blood: the corridor was as slippery as the worst runway in the Congo or Uganda or the Central African Republic. Bob couldn't get out; he couldn't get to a clean place, no matter how he tiptoed and lurched. It was foul.

He woke up, nauseous. He didn't need to be Sigmund Freud to realise what the dream was all about. Doug Rydale was his hero, his master, his ideal. And Doug had gone. Instead, there was blood and ordure and old age.

★   ★   ★

The phone went at eight, while he was packing. He thought it might be Leila.

'Hi there.'

'Hello.'

'Am I talking to Robert Windrush?'

Young voice. Thin, nervous, clever. Accent: North American, plus slight foreign inflection.

'Is this Matt Sharansky?'

'It is. Hello, Captain Windrush. Great name.'

'It's Winrush. Win-rush. I've lost my job because of you.'

'Oh, that's too bad. How come?'

'My boss got scared. Are you scary?'

'Not at all,' laughed Sharansky. '*He* was pretty scary, though.'

Bob couldn't help smiling back. 'He's very rich. That's the scary bit.'

'I guess so. Can we meet? I have a few questions.'

'I'm not going to answer them. I'm never going to answer them. I know nothing about whatever you might be interested in.'

'That's too bad. I'll be in Virgil. You know Virgil? If you fancy a free breakfast.'

'Of course I know it. But I'm not answering any questions.'

'Because it has to do with a deal that defies all geopolitical realities?'

'I wasn't part of that deal.'

'I know you were. Strictly in confidence. If you don't help me, I'm obliged to mention you by name. And where you live. When I write my article.'

'That sounds like a threat, Mr Sharansky.'

'It's good journalism. Virgil. In about an hour?'

'If you bring my logbook.'

'Logbook? What logbook?'

There was a brief silence in which strange clicks could be heard. Perfectly ordinary clicks, of course.

'I'll be wearing a cream jacket,' said Sharansky before Bob cut him off.

Virgil was a wholefood joint about a mile from his building, at the peaceful end of a mall containing the biggest aquarium in the world, where sharks lived mysteriously at peace with thousands of succulent titbits that rippled prettily over your head as you shopped. The café overlooked a concrete pond pretending to be a lake, and had good roasted coffee.

He stood in his bathroom and wrapped his pistol in a handkerchief and hid it in the inside pocket of his jacket. The gun's bulk looked obvious in the mirror, so he put it back in the safe and set a new combination: the twins' birthday date, backwards.

He felt a touch rough, but decided to walk it. The streets of Dubai worked better when you lacked sleep; it was that sci-fi, surreal look, slightly crazed. He could never quite work out why desert air could feel humid, but that morning was damp, the fumes circulating along his sinuses. It was too early, thank God, for the cruisers in their sports models, although he counted five Lamborghini Gallardo Superleggeras pretending to be on their way to work, booming out Shababi. His shirt was clinging to the tighter areas within minutes, and he took off his jacket, thumb-hooked it over his shoulder: it always took a few days to adjust to the sauna effect, even in the cooler season.

It was, as usual, chilly inside. Apart from an obese couple working their way through the Big Breakfast, there was a young man with dark curly hair, his brow beetling over intense eyes; his wide nose shadowed either unshavenness or a scanty beard. His rumpled cream jacket was too broad for his shoulders; he would have looked more comfortable in the olive T-shirt underneath.

He glanced up and saw Bob, immediately raising his hand. Bob settled into the colonial-style wicker chair opposite, the table uncomfortably small.

'I don't like being threatened, Mr Sharansky,' Bob said, refusing to shake hands.

'Call me Matt. Hey, I'm just giving you an opportunity to remain anonymous.'

Bob smiled, despite himself. 'Most grateful for the opportunity, Matt. Have you seen the sharks?' he added, waving airily in the direction of the mall.

'Of course. But I could only picture the glass breaking.'

'Yeah, you're not the only one.'

The waitress came up and they ordered: the left-wing journalist, to Bob's surprise, requested a hot chocolate with whipped cream. He had a notepad in front of him, and a tiny Sony Dat recorder.

Bob said, 'I don't like to be recorded.'

Sharansky shrugged, putting away the recorder in an Eastpak shoulder bag that had seen better days. 'Pencil notes OK?'

Bob nodded. 'Can I ask you a question first?'

'Sure.'

'How did you know where I lived? Via Sheikh Ahmed or his secretary?'

'I have to protect my sources.'

'Was it my son David?'

The striking hazel eyes, burning through surrounding lines of weariness, moved down to the paper. 'Sorry, I can't say.' He cleared his throat. 'So, does the name Bensoussan mean anything to you? Evron Bensoussan?'

Bob kept expressionless. It was the reason he'd walked away from the deal. 'Of course. Major arms trafficker. Would sell his old granny for a fiver.'

Matt Sharansky nodded. 'His nickname's Dutch. I mean that's what it is. Dutch. Evron 'Dutch' Bensoussan. Either in honour of Dutch Schultz, the infamous New York mob boss, or because he once flattened a rival under a freight truck's tyres, over and over, until most of the guy was stuck in the treads. Holland's flat. Geddit? Anyway, take your pick.'

'Maybe both,' said Bob.

'He's certainly not from Amsterdam or Utrecht. In fact, he's from Bethlehem. And not the one in New York State. He has knees that look like a pair of gonads. Horrible. They were smashed up when he was in special operations on the Golan Heights some forty years back. But he generally wears shorts. He walks a little stiffly.'

Bob nodded, trying not to smile. Once, walking out to the plane in a hot dry place, he had seen Evron Bensoussan outside a shed, ten yards away: a paunchy sixty-year-old in shorts and flowery shirt-sleeves, face shiny with sweat, knees strawberry-red, smoking furiously and yelling into his mobile at the same time. The floweriness was a mistake: huge carnation-type blooms taking him over. Bensoussan was too busy to do more than nod in Bob's direction: he was not carrying the man's cargo, but still. The wader-in-blood was still yelling into his mobile when Bob took off, the plump little form jellified by the heat shimmers off the asphalt before Chad's shrivelled lake took over with a tinfoil flash under the starboard wing.

Breakfast arrived — muesli and yoghurt, the hot chocolate with its piled-up wig of whipped cream, Bob's frugal coffee — and there was a brief hiatus. This time Sharansky noticed the waitress, and she clocked him with a smile.

'Check out that bomb,' Sharansky nodded, his eyes following her across the café.

'Yup, she'd melt the frost off a cold-soaked wing,' said Bob.

'Hey, don't look at me like that. It's my chocolate. You know why I'm not drinking coffee? Because that's all people do in my country. You know the joke? Why did we take forty years wandering in the desert? We kept stopping for cappuccino.'

Bob smiled. 'I always found Israel very appealing,' he said. 'Although I'd only stay a couple of nights, mostly in my passenger days. His Excellency prefers to avoid it.'

'That's because he hates Jews.'

'Beats me why.'

They began to eat. Matt Sharansky's spoon hunted for the hot chocolate through the whipped cream, which he seemed to begrudge.

'It's presumably down there somewhere,' said

Bob. He felt benign towards the young man, surprising himself.

'I guess so. Everything in this city is extreme superfluity. It's pure surplus. For the rich, the whole world's a whorehouse, but this is the big couch. I can smell it's going to be degraded cocoa powder. Paris is good for hot chocolate — I know the places. And the cafeteria of my old university in Jerusalem. I don't know why it was so good in there, but it was.' There was a pause. The journalist picked up his pencil. His voice went lower.

'These are the facts, Captain. Just over two years ago, a converted Boeing 727 left Plovdiv, Bulgaria, with a cargo of so-called medical supplies. In reality, these were mainly AK-47s and a helluva lot of ammo. It stopped in Istanbul for a fuel-up and some more military hardware, including a jeep, then flew on to Turkmenbashi airport, Turkmenistan. Everything's called Turkmen-something in Turkmenistan. Did you know Plovdiv is the oldest city in Europe?'

He glanced at Bob, who nodded as if on his own train of thought.

'OK,' Sharansky went on, tapping his pencil on the pad. 'From reliable sources, we know the guys who paid off the cockpit crew were the Taliban. So far, so not very interesting. What makes this pure dynamite is that the broker of this deal was Evron Bensoussan, the man with the testicular knees. I don't whether you knew that, seeing as each layer of the flexible export market in weaponry or narcotics remains hermetically sealed from the one above and the

84

one below. Finding their air tubes is truly a challenge.'

'I didn't know that,' Bob fibbed.

'This key player in the global war economy is my fellow countryman. He is also a close friend of several of our ministers, including the current prime minister of Israel.'

'Whose name I can never spell,' Bob said.

'Exactly.'

'This seems incredibly unlikely.'

'Doesn't it just.'

'And where do I fit in?'

'You were the pilot.' He took a sip, eyes on Bob over the rim. 'Yay, as I foresaw, it's low-grade powder, sub-Starbucks even.' He grimaced, leaving behind a frothy tidemark on his scanty beard, but none on his nose.

'There you're wrong,' said Bob.

'Hey, Bob, I've been in Israel since the age of six. I love my country. It's not like other countries; it's quality. It's deeper and it's special. You know a quarter of our population is Arab? Nobody questions that. So don't get me wrong: I am actually a Zionist, or maybe a post-Zionist. I'm no transnational freak, anyway, I leave that to the neo-fascist capitalists who run the world. They're mostly idiots with receipts, like Evron Bensoussan. But I feel an outsider because I am not a caffeine addict and I hate military hardware and I have some tedious notions of civil rights and pluralism and Palestinian nationalism and so forth. But, because of my views, I am hounded. When I was called up, I told them I heard voices to avoid the army. It worked, can you imagine? But the whole country hears voices! They belong to Adonai, apparently. That's God, to you. Good old God. We reckon we have him by the balls.'

Bob said, 'Or by the knees?'

Sharansky gave a loud laugh, like a yelp. Others looked.

'I've not got all morning, by the way,' Bob added.

'Sure. What I am saying is that I don't rely on some abstraction; I rely on concrete evidence. Especially written. Not that you can trust words, either. Not all words. But some are irrefutable. So that's why I'm figuring that my assumption is ontologically correct.'

'What assumption?'

'That you were the pilot.'

Bob ate his muesli and pretended to cast his mind back through thick mists of forgetfulness, clacking mentally through countless flights like an old-fashioned departure board. This young man was exhausting him with his prattle.

'Well, Matt, yes and no. I did fly from snowy Plovdiv to Istanbul just over — well, crikey, two years ago it is. I think it was in a 727. But I've never had the privilege of touching down at Turkmenbashi. And I didn't get a dirham for my efforts, by the way.'

Matt Sharansky's eyes narrowed. 'But the plane did arrive, for sure. We've acquired the amended flight plan and the shipper's declaration. You are definitely marked down as the captain. Words. Irrefutable, in this case.'

'That shows naivety.'

'Sure, flight plans can be cooked, but we use the originals. And this one was not falsified, except of course for the nature and quantity of the goods, which were most certainly not medical supplies. The flight hours are consistent with a 727 cruise speed and the cargo's declared tonnage. Why would they change the crew list?'

Bob sat back in the wicker chair and wiped his mouth on his napkin. The female half of the obese couple was pointing her camera at something on the artificial lake: a wind-up swan, maybe. A few other customers had come in, including a pair of squash players. None looked dangerous, but looks can mislead. A pumpkin seed had caught in his teeth.

'Take dictation, Mr Sharansky. Pencil sharpened? Right. I flew that first leg to Turkey, walked out of the deal, got threatened via my mobile in Istanbul, kept my head down for two years here in sunny Dubai flying a poverty-challenged sheikh around — and now just when I need clear water in the glass, given some serious personal issues to do with my marriage, you've made it go cloudy.'

Sharansky began to speak. Bob leaned forward again, raising his hand. The squash-playing pair looked like a comic routine: one tall, one short. 'At some point over the last few days, my apartment's been broken into. My logbook and personal diaries have been borrowed, I guess permanently. I would like you to return them, please, or I'll mark them as overdue.'

'OK.' The young man nodded, looking impressed rather than shocked. 'We didn't take

87

them, by the way. That's a promise. I wish we had. A pilot's logbook is the kind of thing that makes us unable to retain our waters.'

Bob nodded. He believed the man. 'OK, then I suggest you drop the matter. For your own safety. And mine. No blab. My lips are sealed tighter than a camel's ass in a sandstorm, as they say round here. And that's it. That's really why I agreed to see you. To tell you to back right off.'

Sharansky looked pained. 'Did you record that particular flight in the logbook?'

'I recorded all my flights. It's part of the job. We landed on runway 24. Atatürk. The following leg I marked as *REFUSED*.'

'So someone wants to kick ass. Our world gets smaller and smaller. This is cool, Bob.'

'No,' Bob said. 'Evron Bensoussan is not cool. Business before pleasure, each and every time. Iranians selling arms to the Taliban, that's business as usual. A highly connected Israeli selling guns to the Taliban? Surprising, but again, that's business. I'm afraid you anti-arms campaigners are throwing sponges at a giant concrete bunker called naked greed.'

The other snorted. 'Not greed. Politics. One of a series of mechanisms designed to keep most of humanity superfluous and dirt-poor, using the tools of mas-cu-lin-i-sation.'

'In plain English?'

'An AK-47 is a jumbo prick extension.'

Bob was beginning to find Sharansky's youthful enthusiasm irritating. 'Sorry, that doesn't explain this particular deal. Money does.'

'OK. Put it like this, Bob. The best enemies to have, as the saying goes, are those who are busy killing each other. Say, in this case, Muslims killing Muslims, taking the West's eye off the ball, off Gaza, off the world banking conspiracy, you name it. Elementary tactics. You've just got to keep stoking it with weapons, and don't let them run out of bullets.'

'On that happy note.'

The journalist leaned forward with a slightly manic look in his hazel eyes. 'The enemy of my enemy is my friend.'

Bob pulled a face. He was the one who now felt naïve. He should have spotted that equation earlier; it sounded convincing. But pilots are famous for being naïve. Head still in the clouds when they're down on the ground. Always thinking a few hundred nautical miles ahead, even when trundling a trolley down the supermarket aisle — or eating breakfast down-town.

'You're not convinced, Bob.'

'Quite. But not entirely.'

'OK, how about this hot shit?' Sharansky glanced around, eyes taking in the café's sanitised colonial look, its benign-seeming customers, with the flickery movements of a bodyguard's. He half-whispered, so that Bob had to lean forward, head cocked: 'We've a hunch, based on visual evidence from an informant, that the plane came back with a few kilos in its belt of Afghanistan's main cash crop, helpfully refined by the Taliban.'

'Heroin?'

'Possibly. Perhaps even probably. Or for damn certain.'

'The return flight could've been for another client.'

Sharansky spoke from under his hand, as if afraid of lip-readers. 'The big B was obliged to return the aircraft home, back to Plovdiv. Officially empty. Just the crew and a lot of space behind their heads.'

Bob shook his head. 'Your informant needs new lenses. With the notable exception of Monzer Al-Kassar, I've never personally known arms and drugs to mix, not in the freight world, and especially not with Bensoussan.'

'Don't underestimate that type. He has mafia links. There are eighteen mafia families in Israel. They breed like rock rabbits. They keep blowing one another up in their cars.'

'So you don't know about Bensoussan's daughter?'

Sharansky's eyes narrowed. He looked piqued. Bob told him what was public knowledge: Bensoussan's daughter, an ex-model, was in a wheelchair. She'd lost both her long and beautiful legs in a car crash in Tel Aviv. The driver tested for coke and heroin. He'd hit the accelerator pedal instead of the brake and demolished a wall.

'So Bensoussan is very, very against narcotics. And where I'm concerned, drugs are also a non-starter. If I know we're carrying an illicit substance, I'll refuse to fly.'

'So that's why you refused the second leg.'

'No, I didn't know about the return snow in

the hold, how could I? I refused for the reasons I've given.'

'Ignorance is easy, Captain Windrush.'

'It's Winrush, but never mind. Without the *d*. Sorry to interrupt.'

Sharansky scratched his broad forehead. 'It's called looking the other way. When my grandparents were dragged out of their Warsaw flat in 1943, by their hair, every fucking neighbour looked the other way. And now Gaza's so close you can throw a frisbee into it.'

Bob stared at him rather crossly. 'It's a personal issue. I won't carry drugs. Drugs are evil. That's one thing Evron Bensoussan and myself would agree on, if I ever had to meet the guy.'

'And weapons are not evil?

'Guns are neutral, like an animal's claws. My father flew Spitfires. He was tall, like me, and had to crouch a bit in the cockpit. Once he pulled out of a steep 600-mph dive and fainted for a few seconds. You know what his motto was? Take your time, but punch hard. He got five confirmed kills, lost all his friends, lost a leg, didn't look the other way, helped save the world from Hitler. I really don't want a philosophical discussion.'

'It's not philosophical. It's a bunch of concrete. Armaments kill and maim, whoever fires them. They cause pain, terrible pain. Did you make a copy of the logbook?'

One of the squash players was glancing across at them from his table, talking into his mobile. Bob looked away, eyes following the waitress. A

91

sudden diamond twinkle from the obesities, and their photograph had been taken — or at least a snapshot in which the two of them were central. He leaned forward towards Sharansky.

'Keep looking the other way. We've been caught on camera. Basically, I think we're being shadowed.'

'What?'

'You'll have to forgo your summer-fruit yoghurt bomba and think of a way out of this mess. What day is it?'

'Friday,' said the journalist, looking puzzled. 'Why?'

'The same as last time. I've got until Monday.'

'What?'

'That's what they said to me on my mobile in Istanbul, two years back. *You will be dead by Monday.* If I blabbed. They don't work weekends, apparently.'

'Who?'

'Mossad. Evron's boys. The Syrians. The Iranians. MI6. Whoever. Lighten up. Guys in squash kit, obese couple. Don't do more than glance.'

Matt Sharansky glanced, then chuckled. 'My heart's down in my pants. They look really like Mossad.'

'Mossad don't always wear black zip-down combat gear and do stunts. Not in public. Anyway, it might not be your countrymen. It might be mafia, the Russians, aliens, the super-rich who have the universe by its balls, who knows?'

'This is almost like the time in the Sudan

92

when I was kidnapped.'

'Kidnapped? You're joking.'

'Well,' Sharansky admitted, 'I was kind of politely told I couldn't leave this shack. Twenty-four hours. It was OK.'

'So, Matt, I'm not blabbing to you and never will. What do you suggest? Just in case.'

'Play a game for the tab?' said the young man, drawing out a pack of cards. 'I'll teach you *yaniv*. I have a simplified version.'

He explained how to play and the game began. The obese couple paid up and waddled out. Surprisingly, a few minutes later, the squash players, Tallie and Shortie, followed them. The only people remaining were a French-speaking family — parents, grandma and two weenies. He waved the waitress over and asked her about the squash pair. She flashed a becoming smile at his breakfast partner, who flashed one back.

'They are lawyers,' she said, raising one butter-smooth shoulder. 'They are coming every week for at least two years. Why?'

'I may want a game,' Bob said.

'Let me know,' said Sharansky, giving her a wink.

She cleared the plates and left. Sharansky pursed his lips. 'What a bomb. Too bad you're leaving Dubai,' he said. '*Yaniv!* Show me your hand. I think I've won.'

He had. Bob checked the multi-dirham tab and shrugged. 'You know me,' he said. 'I never walk away from a deal.'

★　★　★

93

When he got back to his apartment, not in the greatest shape, there was a surprise waiting for him. It was in the form of a couple of strangers in his sitting room, lounging back either side of the coffee table in expensive long-sleeved shirts with fancy cufflinks, their jackets neatly folded beside them, their crossed ankles ending in white socks and mirror-finish dark leather shoes. They were thirtyish, clean-shaven, smiling. Bob froze with shock. His pistol was in the safe, behind a fiddly combination lock. But at least he was thinking ahead, clarity kindly supplied by Adrenalin Inc., seconds treated like minutes. He regretted slipping his own shoes off, as he would always do inside the flat: it was hard to feel like James Bond in socks.

The chap sitting on the white leather sofa, his arms stretched amiably along the back, asked him to sit down. No apology for breaking in. There was a sort of creak behind and a third man stepped out from the bathroom, rather bulkier than the other two and with a shoulder holster sprouting a pistol grip, and stood between Bob and the front door. There's always one of them, he thought: a muscular oaf. It was precisely the same in Africa, except that there everyone was in uniform and shouted a lot, the worst that had ever happened being a brief spell in a Nigerian jail until the release cash arrived, most of it destined for the colonel's son's fees at Harrow. Or so they explained. This was different. This was a little more serious.

'Mr Windrush, do sit down. We must have a chat.'

'As long as it's just a chat.'

'Just a friendly chat, Mr Windrush. I like this name, for a pilot. The rushing wind.'

The man smiled more broadly, revealing dental work that involved much gold. Bob ignored both the obliteration of his rank and the usual inaccurate version of his name, and sat down on a chieftain's stool he'd bought years before in Douala; he'd always fancied it had some sort of mystical force, encircled as it was by carved heads, authentically cracked and wood-wormed. Gold Teeth's partner looked as if he'd had a flare pistol fired at his face, but it was probably acne. The heavy stood in the little hall, leaning on the door jamb. For the first time, Bob regretted living on the twenty-fifth floor: falling off Dubai balconies was something of a local speciality.

'So?'

'We have come to ask you some questions.'

'ID? This is my private home.'

'Irrelevant.' The expression hardened. They were doubtless of Middle Eastern origin, as the papers say, but God knows where. Emirates, Israel, Syria — anywhere. Central Asian, even. Their English was heavily accented but good. They reminded Bob of the sharks in the aquarium. 'You've been meeting up with a journalist.'

'Quite untrue.'

'We saw you.'

'Obese or squash-playing?'

95

'Sorry?'

'He's not a journalist. He's a friend of my son's.' What a very silly thing to say. Dragging in David.

'He writes articles concerning the trade in arms.'

'I told him nothing. Ask him. I'm very good at forgetting all about it. I told him, as we say, to get lost.' He felt dream-like, a little floaty. His rear end was tingling, just as it had at school before a caning. 'You don't fly freight around the world and then blab, if you want to stay out of trouble. My aim is to stay out of trouble.'

The other man, Flare Pistol Victim, leaned forward and said, in an accent thick enough to make interpretation challenging, 'You should not have met with him at all. Why do you do such things?'

'For personal reasons.'

Gold Teeth raised his eyebrows — rather patronisingly. Bob felt like pulling rank.

'All I try to do is my job, as captain. It's a highly skilled job, too.'

'You don't do your job well enough.'

'You're a pilot, are you?' Bob felt pretty nettled.

'A pilot flies a plane. You refused. We don't know why.'

'I didn't like the look of it.'

Flare Pistol laughed, which means that he laid his tongue between his teeth, shook his body and wheezed, gazing at his expensive shoes.

'What's so amusing?'

His partner explained: 'On one side, a

96

hundred thousand bucks. On the other, not liking the look. This is funny.'

'Your money or your life, I think it's called.'

'So you knew what the cargo was, who was the broker, who was the client.'

'Are you the Dubai police?'

'Yes,' he said, after a telltale pause for reflection: an amended thought plan, clearly.

'I'd like to see your ID.'

'In our own time.'

'OK,' Bob said, trying to keep ahead. 'I can tell you exactly what I knew: that the cargo was military, that it was being sold to the Taliban, that me and my crew would be paid, as you so rightly pointed out, a lot of bucks. I didn't like the look of it, so I quit halfway.'

There was a pause. 'You're quite a bad liar,' said Gold Teeth. 'You see, your eyebrows go in,' he explained jovially, indicating his own rather thin pair and helpfully frowning. 'Next time, you control your eyebrows and we might believe you.'

'Next time,' chortled Flare Pistol, shaking his head at the sheer, outrageous drollery of it.

This little speech and its response got Bob shivering. He shifted on the stool and took a grip on himself by folding his arms. 'Maybe my eyebrows went inward because I'm stressed. It's not pleasant coming home and finding strangers. Even the police. I love your country, by the way.'

Gold Teeth narrowed his eyes a little, perhaps feeling he was being mocked. Bob suspected his country was Israel, but he could hardly start heaping plaudits on Israel. He was stuck. Gold

Teeth glanced at his partner, a glance Bob didn't like. He remembered that Israelis are banned from the Emirates — at least, they can't get visas — so these two must have entered on false passports. Given the country's welter of queue-manufacturing bureaucracy, of documents required and form-filling and God knows what else, this was a disappointing lapse.

Flare Pistol sighed, reached into a briefcase next to him, and dropped Bob's logbook and last year's diary on the coffee table.

'Thank you,' Bob said. 'I was wondering where they'd got to.'

'It's clear you knew all the positions. So don't lie.'

'I told you, my job is to forget — '

'You quit freight. Instead you fly a rich Arab all about. Why?'

Definitely Israeli: a sour relishing of 'Arab'. But Bob had no idea whether they were Mossad or rogue elements or simply Evron B's henchmen. Matt Sharansky's item about heroin on the return trip introduced all sorts of ugly possibilities.

'Maybe I'm getting too old. Or tired of being mucked about. Could I just remind you that the agent on that ops, the guy from Sweden, really did muck me about? He sprang the second leg on me at Istanbul. Ask him.'

As soon as he saw Gold Teeth's smile, oddly like a smug vicar's, he knew what it meant. 'Lennart? How can I be asking questions to him?'

There was a pause. Bob had no intention of

giving them the satisfaction of reporting how he died. Gold Teeth was showing him a creased passport photo of a dark-haired man in his late twenties or thirties, with large eyes equipped with fatigue bags above a pointed nose and tapering chin. Oddly, he'd be the Mediterranean type that Olivia would go for, but to Bob he looked faintly psychopathic.

'Who's he?'

'You don't know him?'

'No.'

'A pity. His name is Pedro Diez.'

'May I go to the loo?' It was a genuine request. His insides appeared to be melting.

Gold Teeth smiled, his eyes moving beyond Bob's head, its owner reacting too slowly. The heavy seemed to leap like a mastiff let off its chain — it was more instinctual than obedient — and before Bob could so much as flail, had him in a headlock that made him bite his tongue. The stool rolled over and knocked against the wall. Bob's arms were brought up his back to their sockets' maximums and then seemingly beyond, judging by the pain.

He was pretty certain he was about to die, if only from cardiac arrest, and just hoped it was quick and clean, that they didn't mess about responding to various dark and hidden urges. For instance, he'd rather die than have his testicles turned to dried apricots by a firm heel. At the same time, he imagined the episode as having a kind of timetable, that they'd finish him off and then he'd brush the dust off and start again, somewhere a long way away. In these situations, one never quite grasps the finality of it — or rather, the opposite. That there is no end. No arrival. Nothing. Certainly no timetable.

Heavy had him like many a school bully he once knew, and he merely gripped the man's slippery forearm, feet struggling to find a grip on the floor to relieve the weight of his own body on his neck. This bully had unpleasantly sweet aftershave and peppery armpits. The other two then each grabbed one of Bob's scrabbling feet and he was carried out to the balcony like a sack full of live eels. Of course he struggled, but his efforts were put paid to by Heavy's iron-like bicep on his throat, which virtually stopped him breathing. He noticed silly things — the fact that the lounger had dust on it again, that the unwashed whisky glass had been left out. The clumsy caterpillar somehow avoided the latter, and he was taken to the rail, which was at the standard safety height so that in normal times you could rest your elbows on it and watch other skyscrapers inching up to join you. He was raised, trying to catch his last breaths — his struggles exceptionally feeble for a tallish, fit and broad-shouldered man — to just above the rail. An ant scampered along it, which was quite a sight; animal life was rare on the twenty-fifth floor. It was quite unaware of the drama. In a few seconds he would know nothing about ants or drama or anything else. Of course, they ought to have been visible from neighbouring towers, but he guessed they were too small to make out without binoculars, and by the time the Dubai police came he'd be a boneless *plop* far down.

Up to then, the men had said nothing beyond their grunts of effort, but neither had Bob: he didn't even swear. He just concentrated on trying to kick, with a faint air of disbelief that this should be happening to him at all.

Long ago, when he was still small for his age and a bunch of older kids were taunting him at school and about to throw him into a heap of Lincolnshire manure, he had shouted, 'Stop! It's Mother's Day tomorrow! I need to send a card!' He said it with such conviction (it was a lie; his mother was dead) that they looked worried and released him and he ran off. This time, he failed to shout anything at all. He was about to be launched from the twenty-fifth floor, free as a bird. Except birds are never free, of course; they spend every moment of their waking hours on the job, surviving — flicking all sorts of mental switches inside their translucent skulls.

5

What he should have yelled was something sporting and witty, to prove they were no match for his English gentleman's nerve. Something like 'I prefer to take the lift, even though it's slower!' Or 'I say, you've forgotten the drink before take-off!' Something scripted, anyway, for a James Bond movie, the kind British Airways used to show on the Atlantic haul, that he and the crew would discuss at some point on the flight deck with the stewardesses in their pyjama-striped kit, along with recipes for the best cocktail or where to find the perfect bagel in New York or how to sleep in full daylight when your circadian rhythms say it's two in the morning. Bob's secret regret was that Pan Am pilots had to be American: their sky-blue girls wore white gloves and served hot towels with silver tongs. The grass is always greener, and so on.

No pilot scares easily: they're schooled in keeping cool. Black boxes prove it. Nerves don't snap as long as there's someone to engage with over the radio, except maybe in the last fraction of a second, when a scream is permitted or a 'That's it, I'm dead.' But generally it's 'Pull up, pull up, pull up!' to the last full second. What pilots never do is mess themselves, at least not before the scream. You've got a full tube of passengers behind you and the flaps have gone or the rudder's misbehaving and the plane is converting into sheer tonnage thousands of feet up in the air, and it's all physics, aerodynamics, mercilessly so — but you don't mess yourself. Bob Winrush didn't when he crashed and lost consciousness. But when those three bullies began to lift him so that he could see cars below like slow-motion pellets and feel the drag of vertigo in his gut, he did mess himself. He also squeezed his eyes shut and prayed.

They dropped him. The ground hit so quickly, almost simultaneously, that he felt he must have passed out for a second or two with shock. When he came to, he found Gold Teeth kneeling down next to him on his balcony.

'Stick to carrying diapers, Mr Rushing Wind. More useful to you than guns.'

Except that he pronounced it 'driapers'. And the appreciation of his wit from the other two made Bob curl up into a foetus position, feeling damp.

The drop had bruised his coccyx and winded him and made the back of his skull tender — but it was the good side of the balcony rail. The life-preserving side. His ribs were being rapidly clouted by his heart, but he was alive. Shamed, shivering, but alive. Gold Teeth added some advice about Bob going away, a long way away, because next time they wouldn't miss, it would be on the correct side. 'A real long way away, OK? Far over the seas and away.'

Bob nodded, wanting to snivel, and croaked, 'Nothing I'd like better.'

'You like living?'

'I enjoy it, yeah.'

'Some bugs, they are living only one day, but are more beautiful.'

He snapped his fingers, and the beaming threesome left.

They'd been very nice to him. They could have killed him, and they hadn't. Yes, he felt like a tenth-rater who'd done six rounds in the boxing ring, his hopes ending with a liver punch, but he was alive. They'd even left his logbook and diary — minus the offending pages, neatly sliced out. That was really quite sensitive.

They were very effective bullies: they'd made him grateful to them. He would have kissed their smart shoes in gratitude. This was how he'd felt when he'd been bashed about a bit in Somaliland, his hotel room turned over, a few years back. Things could have been a lot worse.

★　★　★

It struck Bob during his ensuing power shower that they'd sounded Russian with an American gloss, which could mean anything. They'd sounded like the pilots coming in and out of places like Kisangani back in the 90s; he'd have a drink with them now and again, only those guys were a lot friendlier. Brilliant flyers, too. This lot could have been from Turkmenistan or one of the other ex-Soviet Asian states — they hadn't been fair enough to be ethnic Russians.

And then he remembered an Israeli friend once saying that Israelis speaking English sound like Russians after a couple of years in New York, and Israelis aren't exactly identifiable by sight. Whoever they were, they were sent by someone serious. He wondered whether Matt Sharansky had been paid a visit. As Posh Boy had been. Swedish Lennie. The man who'd saved his foot. Expelled from Eton, then from life. A bullet in the temple or run over by a freight truck, body vanished. Tough being an adventurer in the twenty-first century.

After the shower and a sorting of his shame with the washing machine's hottest cycle, he smoothed out the rucked rug, locked the front door and slipped the chain across, vacuumed the sofa and wherever else they'd been, put an old Earth Wind and Fire vinyl on the stereo, poured a triple Scotch raised up to the rim by crushed ice, tucked the pistol under a cushion within immediate reach, and worked on getting his heart back to boring old cruising speed. The sun poured in out of a cloudless sky, keeping the air con on its toes. The Scotch reminded Bob of his bitten tongue.

His coccyx felt fractured, but it probably wasn't. The soft leather sofa kept engaging it.

He wondered whether to warn Sharansky. All potential leaks had to be plugged. They'd started with Lennart, and then — With a lurch, Bob thought of Al and ex-Swissair. To eliminate a paid-off crew really was outside the envelope, but he'd made a gaffe: he hadn't informed his visitors that, whatever he'd put in the diary about Evron 'Dutch' Bensoussan, he'd told neither his co-pilot nor his flight engineer who the big-time broker was. Unlike himself, they had actually been part of the ops, shaken hands with the Taliboys (or hugged, or whatever the latter permitted) and touched the cash. Israel's enemies would be most interested in their testimony. The happy soul beat moved his foot in time but didn't make it to his muddied thoughts. He never usually drank before sundown. He wanted to dance, to work out, to run. But his balance system was made of jelly.

He must phone Al.

He realised that he'd hardly talked to Al since the fateful ops. Time pauses for no man; and men, Olivia would say, are bad at communicating. His new life in Dubai, his and Al's tendency to be thousands of feet up, or sleeping it off, meant that they'd mostly texted, and usually for some precise or pragmatic reason. Apart from a couple of Christmas duty-cards with nothing written on them except *From Al and Jane*, that had been it. Texts, plus one long phone chat when Olivia had set the solicitor on him last year, during which Al's advice was, 'Man up and throw some plates around.' On such flimsy piles is the house of friendship built. And a massive beam called Flying Together. But he did feel that his doing a runner might have damaged things: it was a kind of betrayal. He'd felt a cooling-off.

He would have to warn Al, however, as he didn't think the Maidenhead area fell into the 'long way away' category. He turned down the soul pulse and dialled the Berkshire number. It was, as usual, on message. Al was a keen gardener. He tried Al's mobile. Surprisingly, it was answered straightaway.

106

'Al?'

'Bob, blow me. Blow me to Bermuda. How's it going with the belly dancers in DXB?'

He's in a good mood, Bob thought.

'I left messages.'

'Christ, skipper, I know. I've been so damn busy. We've bought a place on the Virgin Islands.'

'Nice one. I'll house-sit any time.' How the hell did Al do it? The house in Maidenhead was decent. Jane didn't work. They had no kids, of course. No boarding schools hoovering up the greenbacks.

'And I've been under a cloud, Bob.'

'For the last two years?'

'It's Jane. She's not well.'

'Oh dear. What's she got?'

Bob was expecting the big C, but Al gave him some medical mouthful of a name that wasn't 'life-threatening, but it's got every bloody symptom going, including extreme irritability with your nearest and dearest'.

'I think it's common name is menopause.'

'Bob, if you said that in front of Jane, you would be raw mince garnished with your intact balls.'

'Talking of which, Olivia's symptoms were, as you know, a hugely increased sexual appetite.'

'Aye, and she couldnae wait for the captain to come home and furl his sail.'

'Well put,' said Bob, gamely, but flinching within. 'Now listen, pardner.' He explained briefly why he was phoning. The logbook and diary. His visitors.

'Christ.'

107

'Spot on.'

'Did they, um, manhandle you?'

'Yeah, but not really. It was psychological. I'm on the twenty-fifth floor and they pretended to send me the quickest way down.'

'I always wondered what that might be like. You know, to fall from a great height. Like that stewardess sucked out from the Pacific Airlines jet, where was it, over the Pacific anyway — you know, whether she lost consciousness immediately.'

'The cold would have killed her. Thirty-five thousand feet. The shock. Anyway, Al, just watch out. Keep a low profile, even in Berkshire. The main thing is, you don't know what I know, do you? About the broker. Of that deal.'

'Our man Evron B, you mean?'

'Oh.'

'Yeah, Lennie told us. That poofy Swedish feller. He was a little worse for wear. Drink, maybe drugs. The fumes from the pools of crude, maybe. Terrible.'

'A great pity, you knowing.' In fact, he felt curiously relieved: a problem shared and all that. He was also beginning to feel nauseous, presumably an effect of shock. The back of his skull was hurting and his hands were shaking. 'Al, Lennart's no longer with us. This lot told me, in so many words. I mean, I definitely know he's dead, and they implied it wasn't an accident.'

Now Al sounded concerned. 'That's no fun at all,' he said.

'Who was your skipper, in the end?'

'Well, he acted like he was one of their own people.'

'Was his name Pedro Diez?'

'Doesn't ring a bell, Bob. Took hours to get him. We lost our slot. He hardly said a word. Though the guys at the other end were very polite, with the fat brown envelope and all. The ones beginning with T. I expected turbans and machine guns, but they had Western suits and terrible spotty ties of *Twin Peaks* vintage, all very smiley. Lousy coffee at Turkmenbashi, though.'

'Did your new skipper have serious eyebags and a kind of dark, brooding look?'

'Aye, I suppose he did.'

'That's Pedro. They're looking for him, too. A rising tide lifts all ships.'

'Oh.'

Bob could hear a television on in the background, maybe Jane's voice.

'They didn't show me your handsome mug, though. Where are you, Al?'

'Chemnitz. We're loading in an hour. Like the early days, eh?'

Al was referring to a series of mysterious flights he and Bob made in their first year on freight, back in 1999, shipping out classic artworks and antiques from eastern Germany to the States — near Washington, going into an old USAF base. The old commie cadres, they presumed, and their illicit plunder. But they weren't paid to presume; they were paid to carry, complete with an amended flight plan from Madrid.

'So,' Bob concluded, 'if an Israeli journalist called Matt Sharansky or anyone else contacts you, you're to refuse point-blank to cooperate.'

'Ach, you know me, skipper, I love to swap yarns. But I always obey my captain.'

They talked shop for a few minutes. Al had passed his medical but hadn't done much flying recently, just enough to keep his hours. They'd up-sized in Maidenhead, massive garden, he kept bees and made honey, had entered the fascinating world of koi fish. Then someone called him away with a faint shout. Bob had forgotten to mention the return flight's bonus of heroin, but that seemed irrelevant anyway: the possible icing on the cake. The cake was the thing.

Bob felt better, however — not least because he'd assumed Al had been cross with his skipper since the bunk; he didn't appear to be. Bob wondered whether to warn ex-Swissair, but reckoned he was safe, somehow. Too boring to bother with.

He found the folded bit of paper with Matt Sharansky's number in his back pocket and called. He was instructed to leave a message, but he didn't: it was a moot point whether the phone was still in the boy's hands. Even journalists were fair game, these days.

He was fishing out his trousers from the washing machine when the flat's phone went. Hardly anyone phoned him on the landline, these days. He picked it up carefully, as if it harboured toxins. It was Ellen, married to Dinesh, both in their early thirties and Fijian.

Why would anyone from Fiji want to come and live in Dubai? Bob had met them at some do put on by Drip Tennyson, and liked them — they were part of the same expat group, although he kept on the fringes. She was glad he was in: Dinesh was bad. 'He's totally depressed, Bob. I'm going to join him with a breakdown. Please come and talk to him. He respects you. You're his hero.'

The last thing he could face was seeing Dinesh and Ellen. They had been a bright, jolly, high-spending couple until Dinesh's three-year visa had run out and mysterious Emirati forces had refused a renewal: so his employers, an enormous construction company, fired him. Or maybe the other way round. Anyway, for some weeks now he'd spent his days in bed. Bob had tried to help by asking the prince's secretary to tap princely contacts, but to no avail.

'Ellen, this is an awkward moment for me. I've had a spot of bother and I'm having to leave Dubai tomorrow. I've also been given the boot. By His Highness.'

Ellen began to cry, very softly. Bob's sympathies were restricted by their connection with Fiji, which he'd flown 747s into for refuelling on the New Zealand route, and would have problems leaving every time. But apparently there were no buildings in Fiji higher than seventeen storeys, and Dinesh's particular skills were not required. Now, of course, she was insisting he must come and say goodbye. He wondered if Dinesh's self-defeating depression might have been solved by having the kind of near-death experience that he had just had. There was elation in the post-trauma air. He was not Dinesh, for a start. He was not depressed.

'OK,' he said, 'after I've packed.'

So it was well into the afternoon by the time he was ready for the off. He bought a big box of chocolates for cleaning-whizz Maria (and another for Dinesh and Ellen) in a vast and gilded mall shaped like a ziggurat between their place and his. He'd fixed a slot to see the prince's secretary around teatime, which gave him about half an hour with the depressed Fijians. He was somewhat nervous, driving. In fact, he'd checked and rechecked the bottom of the car before starting it: watching too many action films had left him with an inner simulation of cars transforming into fireballs. A loop tape of the balcony incident was running through his head, in which the ant played a starring role. His driving was so bad that it no longer stood out.

Dinesh and Ellen lived in a needle-like block with a lawn and fountains fronting it and a sweep of marble steps in case you were still in any doubt. Bob was held up at the bottom of these by a photo shoot, with a model sultrily descending and a dozen or so cameras heavy with lenses snapping away; their operators were mostly young women or men just past retirement age, and his expectations concerning the model were dashed: she was a gauche teenager, clearly an amateur, there for the benefit of what looked like an expat photography club, directed by a grey-haired American dame. They were being snapped in turn by a Middle Eastern guy with the stoop and hurriedness of a pro.

Bob's mobile rang; otherwise he would have fled.

'I want you,' came a throaty, familiar voice.

'You're reading off your Love Hearts. The next one'll say *Blue eyes*.'

'No, it says *Ever yours*.'

'Uh-oh.'

'What's that noise in the background, Bob?'

'It's an expat photo club, laughing coyly.'

'You're such a weirdo. Are all pilots weirdos?'

'If they aren't already, they become it. By the way, I'm off tomorrow morning. For good.'

'Blimey. Where to?'

'Far far away, but I don't know where. I can't really let you know, either.'

There was a silence. He ought to throw a farewell party. Leila (probably not her real name) was from deepest Birmingham and worked in a bar in one of the smarter clubs. She was a drifting, good-time girl, heading for thirty without a care in the world. She had nice butterscotch shoulders, so she was on his list. He'd tell her romantic stuff about his passenger-flying days, except that he'd swap BA for Pan Am, setting it back twenty years in the Golden Age instead of the late decline, after the split with National. She was so bad at maths she never noticed. 'You really worked for Pan Am?' 'I cannot tell a lie. I did.' She was excited by his conspiracy theories about Lockerbie, and aghast about his days in freight, ducking in and out of

African hot spots. Never did she wonder what he might have been carrying; she'd just stroke his chest and snuggle up to her pilot hero, pretending to be his concubine.

There was a crackle on the mobile. 'Bob, I'm really going to miss you. Honest.'

'D'you know, that was too long for a Love Heart. I think you're being sincere.'

'I bloody am, Bob. Where are you, precisely?'

'In Abu Dhabi,' he lied. 'If I ever come back, I'll tell you.'

'Gerroff. You won't. You'll forget me. Your floozy. Are you going somewhere where it rains?'

'No idea.'

It was then that he had a startling image of soft bare hills and horizontal rain, while the sun-struck photo shoot seemed to evaporate.

'Hope so,' she said. 'Ta-ra, then.'

This was silly. He cleared his thoat of desert dust. 'How about a farewell bite tonight, Leila?

'Love bite? Or nosh?'

'Both.'

'I'm working. You're away.'

'I'll drive back just to say goodbye, maybe.'

'Buy the barmaid a drink.'

'Done. And after?'

'We'll see.'

After that interchange, he was even less inclined to see the Fijians.

Dinesh looked terrible. He was lying on the bedcovers, one sock off, in his suit trousers and shirt, but with a dressing gown on top. Ellen wrung her hands in the corner. While she was what used to be called mulatto, Dinesh, despite

114

his name, claimed to be descended from Captain Bligh; Bob reckoned he did look like a handsomer version of Charles Laughton, and had once told him so at a well-fuelled party in Jumeirah. Now he suggested anything was better than staying at home all day, and maybe people should be less fussy about the kind of job they wanted. He wasn't really concentrating on the matter in hand. It was a duty call. His hands had only just stopped shaking.

'You mean, become a builder,' Dinesh scoffed. 'Earn peanuts. Wear filthy overalls. Go get pissed and then knifed in Jebel Ali. Those Asian guys are slaves, more or less.'

'They worked under you, didn't they?'

'No, not under me. I just drew plans and calculated stresses. I'm finished, man. This place swallowed me and now it's spat me out. The bank phones every day. So do the credit card companies. I feel like killing myself.'

'So Ellen told me. I'll have another chat with the sheikh's well-endowed secretary. Otherwise, I suggest going back to Fiji. Nice beaches. Let's face it, Dubai is fairly unpalatable unless bucks are your sole object.'

'There's nothing in Fiji. What's more, we can't. We owe too much, even if we sold everything. Our mortgage is crazy. We had medical bills, for Shonika.'

Shonika was their small daughter, allergic to both Dubai's dust and its seasonal steaminess.

'OK, open a little South Sea stall here. In Karama, say. Work your way up. You know how I started in the airline business? As a handyman's assistant. For instance, mending burn holes in the Clipper Club's carpet in Heathrow. I was crawling around all these expensive shoes with a Stanley knife, plugging holes with cuttings taken from behind those plush curtains. I overheard the smoky conversations. I was eighteen. I said to myself: one day I'll walk in here and everyone'll look up to me instead of down to me. So what did I do? I got a job in Pan Am wash-up, where we'd drain the liqueur glasses on the trays fresh off the Atlantic haul. We were permanently blasted.'

'I thought you were British Airways?'

'Later, after the RAF. Pan Am were nationalistic when it came to pilots, but dishwashing was international.'

That extracted a smile from both of them. Dinesh told Ellen to leave the room. She said she'd say goodbye now as she had to go to her gym class (presumably on credit). She gave Bob a squeeze and that was it. He thought: people come in and out of your life.

Dinesh sat up and beckoned him to crouch down. He spoke softly in his bad aviation ear. 'Bob, listen to me. I don't know what to do. After I heard about the job, I got trashed on Singapore Slings at Barasti. I was a crazy idiot. I went with a downtown whore. I think she was Chinese. And I had this tiny fresh cut on my finger. I went right up her with it, you know? But I didn't go the whole hog.'

And he'd heard how some of Dubai's numerous sex workers were not necessarily free of HIV, but he didn't dare to have a test. He looked at Bob in expectation.

'Dinesh, you're a hypochondriac, a coward and a lecher. Shame on you. Get the test. You're clear, for certain. Remember, I was in Africa. I know all about it. I got worried once, too.' A disarming look of relief came over Dinesh's sallow face. 'Oh, and here are some chocolates. For Ellen. You're already spoilt.'

Bob dropped them on the bed, gave his friend's hand a squeeze, and left.

The upshot of all this was that he was late for his appointment at the princely palace, partly because they'd swapped the roads about in his absence: the old one seemed to be stranded on pillars in the middle of a wasteland, or maybe that was the new one. Anyway, by the time he'd drawn up in front of the Chelsea-style wrought-iron gates, there was just a hint of indigo in the sky overhead and a flush of green on the desert horizon (the latter only being visible because the prince owned the land right up to it and probably beyond). Although the secretary worked till six most evenings, and it was now six thirty, she had waited for him. He had phoned her from the car. The secretary's name was, for some reason known only to her Colorado parents, Filberta.

The cheetah was in her office, as ever, and apparently hungry. It eyed Bob expectantly, just as Dinesh had done, but probably for more primal reasons. Filberta showed him what a sweetie it was by putting her face to its face and allowing herself to be licked on the nose, mouth, eyes. It really did have the most impressive fangs,

117

just as the fit golden-tanned Filberta, when she crouched to her green-eyed double, revealed an impressive depth of cleavage.

The Drip was away in Switzerland — 'client sourcing', apparently: His Excellency's private fleet included a Gulfstream V and a Dassault Falcon 7X which were available for charter — a sign, perhaps, more of his greed than any actual need. Bob had taken a spin in both when required (not often), which had made the overall job good fun. He emptied his bag of files, papers and sundry items like keys, sat down gingerly in a seat that sighed, and started on the business of departing from the princely empire. He was owed a month's wages, as technically he should have received thirty days' notice, as well as a refund for his flights home, and his unused holiday pay. Filberta found all this faintly amusing, clicking her tongue and shuffling papers and making American-style noises patented by TWA stewardesses on being asked to come up to a hotel bedroom during a stopover.

To get to her lair he'd had to pass down a long and gilded corridor crammed with so many priceless antiquities — lamps, brooches, jewel-studded swords, hammered-gold necklaces, Greek vases, Chinese horses, Florentine putti and so on, all set higgledy-piggledy behind glass or just scattered on tables, with life-size marble sculptures greeting him every so often (a missing hand or nose proving their credentials) — that he found this hesitation a touch distasteful. 'I think that's not only about 0.001 per cent of a billionth of his fortune,' he said, 'but those are my rights. He may be an affable chap, but he'd be acting wrongfully if you denied me my rights.'

Filberta suddenly looked like Filberta. She may have crammed a pair of honeydew melons down her silk front, yet there was an ice-forming austerity in her gaze. She cocked her head on one side and said, 'It's not up to me. But what I do know is that it was kinda urgent. An emergency.'

'What was?'

'Firing you.'

'You mean, he was dangled over the side of his biggest yacht or something?'

She snorted disdainfully and folded her arms. Perhaps she had detected that Bob's field of vision, although apparently aimed at her face, included her bust if he concentrated enough. It was a kind of trick: you peered through the perspex at the sky, but you saw the control panel and its winking lights.

'OK, Bob. So long, and thanks for flying us around.'

'I've just been dangled from my balcony,' he said, spreading his arms, 'but would you know?'

She chuckled a little uncertainly. 'It's been great,' she added. Nothing more.

He patted the cheetah goodbye, and it instantly lifted itself and placed a paw on each of his shoulders, wreathing him in its low-tide breath.

'Well, Princess Tiffany seems to like you, anyway. Sheena died, you know. Ate something bad.'

'I'll bet the prince was heartbroken, being

such a sensitive soul.'

'You bet.'

When he got home, there was a message on the landline. It was Ellen. She didn't know what he had said, but Dinesh was a new man. It was a miracle. 'You're like . . . *Jesus*,' she cried. Never in Bob's life had he been likened to the Son of God. Then it occurred to him that maybe they had in fact thrown him over, and he had risen again. Up to a point.

★ ★ ★

Jesus went to the bar to see Leila. Say goodbye, no hard feelings. Leila, from Birmingham, was petite, half-Indian, with very thin wrists and long fingers. She was also busty, but that was only in relation to the rest of her, which was slender. She had large and perfectly dark-chocolate eyes, a straight, sharpish nose and lips that were always set in the smiling position. She existed to have a good time, but looked the opposite of blowsy. She had the prettiest feet he'd ever seen. A serious dancer once, she'd done something to her knee and, anyway, as she put it, 'My boobs were getting in the way of my splits, yeah?'

Her face lit up across the bar when he appeared: the place in question, called Wushu, was very twilight, very trance and vaguely Japanese, with the occasional live band in the corner who always seemed to be about to start, their glittering instruments looking lonely under the spots. Tonight was no exception, but it meant he could talk across the bar's alabaster sheen.

Leila had never looked lovelier, Bob reckoned, probably because she was unreachable, hard at work, like a stewardess in flight. She was certainly busy: on the stools there was a row of fat bottoms belonging to assorted consultant-types, loud and chatty, almost permanently on their mobiles. He insisted on buying her a flash cocktail, and they managed a few sentences before she had to serve up at the other end. The youthful but plump customer next to him, in a white linen suit with the store's folds still visible, used her absence to start chatting: he was from Bristol, over as a solar-panelling advisor, the next big idea being to turn the desert into a massive generator. As if Bob didn't know.

'Pity about the desert,' he said.

The man laughed, pushing up black retro specs. 'And you? You seem to know the local talent well.'

'I'm a pilot.'

His manner changed instantly, but Bob was used to that, 'Big planes? Proper ones?'

'Mine have wings, yeah.'

The man laughed again. 'Wow. That's a real job. And you're keeping us in business.'

'How?'

'Greenhouse gases?'

'Oh, yeah,' Bob smiled, chewing his vodka-sodden cherry.

Then the usual line, so common Bob could almost mouth it: 'I fancied being a pilot myself, as a kid. Hitting above my weight, I think they call it. So you live here, then? Great place to do business in.'

'For the moment.'

'Which airline?'

'Oh, a private outfit.'

'Of course. Here, this is my card. Call me Craig. Actually, I can't believe the amounts still swilling around here. It's almost kind of wrong. But it does keep our particular ball rolling. In the UK it's like they've got three responses: *no, no* and *sorry, great concept but*. Even before the bottom fell out. Chicken soup in a basket, these days.' Craig laughed again. His hair was shaved to the roots, but the premature balding had a giveaway mirror-finish.

Bob told him that in the Burj Al Arab hotel, a glass of Macallan single malt would set him back around 27,000 dirhams.

'What's that in sterling?'

'Around 4,500 quid?'

'That's about 500 quid a bloody sip!' he cried.

'*Little* sips, yup.'

Craig was now pursuing the financial crisis, how he'd noticed the empty towers, the stalled building sites.

'Plenty going up,' Bob pointed out. He was feeling cross with the prince suddenly. Murderous, even.

'And still great for doing business in,' Craig agreed, pulling his tie down, undoing his top button. 'To be honest, this whole banker business is what I call a — ' He made a noise rather than a word, like a kid's imitation of a bullet zipping past.

'What's that?'

'The sound of something going way over my head,' he chuckled.

'Oh, right.'

He's on the edge, Bob thought. Things are not going well. He asked Craig what he did before, just for something to say.

'Oh,' he laughed, 'jobbing electrician.'

'Good for you,' Bob nodded, not really concentrating. The drink was soothing him, the music was soporific, and Leila was wearing a dress cut so low at the back it all but touched her coccyx. She was busy, busy with orders, her shoulder muscles darting about under the soft skin.

'Yeah, well, I saw the opportunity,' the man said, hitching up his white trousers. 'Growth area. Climate change and that. And you've got a bit of the old sunshine here.'

'On the side of the angels, eh?'

'Well, not on the side of the devils, anyway,' he chortled, looking at Bob as if unsure whether to take it further, to rib him for leaving his dirty contrails behind. He decided not to, it seemed, and asked Bob what he was having. 'Yeah, we actually specialise in the copper solar panel: doesn't stress or pinhole, doesn't UV-degrade. Natural product. Long track history, you might say. Beautiful stuff.'

Bob nodded slowly. 'Ever been to the Zambian copper belt? Say, to the town of Mufulira?'

'Can't say I have.'

'Thought not, Craig.'

★　★　★

Maria came the next morning to clean. Fortunately, Leila had left by then. She'd agreed to eat something after her shift, which ended at midnight, by which time Bob was full up on odd-coloured Japanese nibbles and somewhat bored by the ins and outs of solar panelling, Asperger's (the man's brother), the best pubs in Avon and Craig's final tearful admission to his sexual confusion: married to Christine, but gay. The trouble with bars abroad is expats and their tendency to drunken release. By the time Leila was free, Bob felt he had known Craig all his life, and even before.

They ate in an expensive Italian bistro in the Venetian quarter; she was bubbly after her work, he'd had four White Russians and was now lowering the level of a fruity Grignolino rosé. They sat outside but it was still hot, or felt it, and there was a whiff of ripe drains from the waterworks. His head felt tender from his recent adventure: Leila leaned over the little table and stroked it at one point and he winced.

'S'up?'

'I knocked it on something.'

She touched it tenderly and then kissed him.

'I like your shirt.'

'It's what's in it that counts.'

'No, just the shirt,' she giggled.

'Leila, I'm going to miss you.'

'It's the soppy music.'

'Are you going to miss me?'

'I reckon I'm gunna.' She kissed him again, tongue slipping over his, the sound of her breath making it past decades of jet-turbine abuse.

Couples were glancing over. Maybe they reckon she's my escort, Bob thought. Old enough to be her dad. One morning he'd woken up and was no longer young.

'Let's skip pudding,' he said, holding her small and perfect chin.

'But there's zabaglione. Or lychee pannacotta with mango jelly. Luscious. I love lychees.'

Bob told her that she was his pudding.

'I preferred it when you said *bird*, Captain Robert. *You're my little bird*. How much does a little bird weigh?'

'What did I tell you?'

She put her hands together and thought. A glisten of sweat on her upper lip caught the light that was busy turning the nearby twenty-foot fountain mauve, orange, mauve. They virtually had to shout over it. 'A few ounces, you said. It wouldn't be pounds, would it?'

'Ounces. An ounce, probably.'

'Don't you know?'

'Depends on the bird, I guess. I like your dress. It's so low I can see your birthmark thingy.'

'Gerraway,' she said, glancing down. 'That's just under me nipple.'

'Is it? Oh. It's many years since I've seen it.'

'Ten days.'

'That's years, in my book.'

An hour later and he was checking it out. She insisted on undressing in the living room, with the sliding doors open to let in the warmer night air because she said the flat was 'parky'. She walked around on the cool tiled floor in nothing but a sheen of Dubai's lights, spread beyond the balcony so like a cockpit's night-time avionics that he kept wanting to check the readings. He sat on the sofa equally naked and watched with his legs wide, as strictly ordered. George Benson was crooning on the hi-fi (which came with the flat), and she swayed to it softly, rampant with her own future that seemed right now so much richer and further than his. It was a game that she and her fun-loving friends in Dubai played, and he went along with it because he was feeling careless and sad: her favourite pilot had to keep his 'jumbo on the runway' for ten minutes — if it took off there would be no sex. He wasn't allowed to close his eyes or look away.

How could he look away? The lack of correlation between Leila's breasts and the rest of her, slim and slippery, was always a marvel to Bob.

Cause angel we can fly you and I

She eyed him from under her loosened black hair, so long it touched the dimple in each hip. But then she was small, about five foot two, so the hair didn't have far to fall. Her arms swinging loosely with the ease of a trained dancer, the narrow supple waist, the twinkles of moisture on her straight back as she swivelled, paced, faced him and then giggled and moved off again . . . Oh, Leila. Dubai's midnight seethe was oblivious. He didn't want to leave here. He could marry Leila, once the divorce was through. The big fridge coughed and began to purr through the open kitchen door. Faint tootings, the whine of crane machinery. He could nestle into her every night, she into him. She said something and he didn't catch it. She stood there against the window, hands demure behind her back, so she was rimmed by the blue glow and white points of dazzle, an hourglass silhouette, each curve lightly downed — he'd never noticed that.

'I think you've won, Mr Pan American,' she said. 'That's either amazing self-control or you're going off of me.'

'It's sadness,' he said. 'I might never see you again. My altimeter's gone.'

She placed one hand on a smudge of breast, the other over her groin, which was reduced to a neat; dark strip; he could just about see her fingers moving there, up and down, as if striking a safety match against it.

'Vroom,' she said, swinging her hips a little. 'Vroom. Look!'

'Yup, it's making an important life decision.' No taxiing: take-off had been a Hawker Harrier's — vertical, instantaneous. All angle and thrust. The tubular weight defying gravity in the unlikeliness of flight. 'Will you marry me, Leila?'

She laughed, said he was barmy, knelt down in front of him, her eyes slightly cross-eyed as she inspected her triumph. 'Oh, you've got sand on it.'

He stroked her hair, wanting to cry; its silkiness smelt faintly of almonds.

'The sand gets everywhere,' he said. 'We'll all be desert soon.'

'Between my toes, on your dick. Do you know, lychees with the skin on really do feel quite like a bloke's knackers.'

She licked the grains off, little cat-licks sparkling on the tip.

He took a deep breath. 'I mean it, by the way. Will you marry me, Leila?'

Her fingers held his; she leaned her cheek on his thigh, looking up into his eyes. Her cheek was burning hot.

'W for wow, but not right now, Bob. I'm too happy.'

'Are you always happy?'

She pulled a face, still smiling, white teeth undaunted. 'Gerroff, it's only a mask.'

'But you make other people happy, just by smiling.'

'Do I?'

Bob drew her up over him and against him so she was kneeling either side of his legs. She straightened up and rested her belly on his face, her hands spread on the sofa back. He planted a kiss on her navel, in which luckier grains of sand nestled. 'I'll bet a lot of people are glad you were born,' he said. He was tired.

'And you? Do you make people happy?'

'I could make you happy,' he said. 'Why don't you come back with me, Leila?'

She laughed, her smooth belly skin vibrating against his ear. She lowered herself a little, poised and just making contact, teasing him with the open secret behind. 'Back to England? You gotta be joking.'

'OK.'

They lay down on the white leather sofa that up to now he hadn't liked, her softness under him. His own buttocks were slightly cold, his coccyx ached, he was worn out, he felt vulnerable to an attack from the room's darkness. He kissed her on the crease beneath each breast, on their rounded underparts that were moist and harboured a saltiness when lifted, wondering why this might not have been enough, bothered by her instant refusal. 'It was worth a try,' he added.

She stroked his shoulders — she liked their hardness, the idea of him keeping them taut in his fifties — and he kissed her on the mouth. He was all but asleep; her lips enveloped him in pulpy comfort and then there was a sudden clawing or scraping sound, close. His mobile, which he'd deprived earlier of its ringtone, was in the process of nudging itself across the glass top of the coffee table, a tiny underwater glow moving through the darkness. He groaned and reluctantly stretched across and picked it up as Leila wriggled under him. 'You don't have to answer,' she said, 'not this late.'

'I won't.' He was knackered. It was a text, in caps. He checked the number, one he didn't recognise: not an Emirati code, anyway. A distant siren floated up from twenty-five floors down.

'Bob . . . '

'Just a sec, honey.'

'ONE SWALLOW IT DOES NOT MAKE A SUMMER, CAPTAIN'

Now what the hell did that mean?

'Bob?'

He was on one elbow and looking up at the ceiling, at the fixtures, the grilles where the cold air would swirl in silently, the dark fisheye in the smoke detector. That he'd always assumed was a smoke detector. Gold Teeth was fond of such expressions. He must have a little dictionary of them. Suitable for any occasion.

'I don't care,' he said, dropping the mobile on the table and summoning himself back to Leila. He felt alert again, at least — prodded into alertness. 'I don't care.'

'Was it from your wife?'

'Trust is everything,' he whispered into her softly beating neck. 'Trust me, we're going to be fine.'

⋆   ⋆   ⋆

Maria was shocked to see no pictures on the walls, except for the large one of pink clotted palm trees he'd long hidden in the wardrobe and which had come with the flat. There were no hidden cams, after all — or not that he could see. The smoke detector had worked, emitting a shrill pulse when he held a smouldering roll of paper up to it the next morning. He gave Maria the chocolates and her diminutive frame gave him a big hug in return. She was in her forties and rather keen on Bob, pressing him to her multi-pocketed apron so firmly that its various contents — brushes, bottles of cleaning fluid, a scourer, the Hoover's head for awkward corners — impressed themselves a little painfully on tender parts.

'Goodbye, Captain Bob sir.'

She was unhappy with Dubai's glittering lifestyle, mainly because she was part of the backstage support team and entirely excluded from the show itself. She had particular difficulty with a fun-loving distant relative of the prince, who at nineteen or so had the entire top floor of their block to himself, and was not renowned for his homemaking skills; she would spend much of each week picking her way through his detritus, while he called her names from his bed. But she was kind and Christian, feeling sorry for him because he was so fat he could barely walk, let alone get out of bed. Bob felt less sorry for him, seeing the fatness as self-afflicted, but she taught him to try to see the good in people. Bob thought: I will never forget Maria. I think she may be one of the few people never to forget me.

He said goodbye to trusty Vakim, handing over the keys. He was pretty certain that the man had been strong-armed or bribed into letting in the visitors; nevertheless, he shook Bob's hand with alacrity and many smiles. Bob wondered if it was a test to see if he was real, and not a zombie back from the dead. The car was to stay put, as it had come with the job, but he'd ordered a taxi — on his tab, of course.

Needless to say, the taxi was late, and by the time the Pakistani driver had negotiated Dubai's usual dogfight of traffic and taken a brand-new, uncharacteristically well-signed peel-off to the airport which ended in sand and lots of fluttering paper litter, Bob only just made it before the check-in closed. There were cars blocking the drop-off point, with the taxi driver determined to play dodgems, and the final sprint was behind a dicky trolley under the hall's giant palms. In the summer Bob would have run three feet and dropped dead from heat exhaustion, or equally dead from the sudden glacial shock of interior air. A brief hiatus when he couldn't find his boarding pass ('It was a late night') resolved into apologies when it appeared by his left foot.

Off-block time was bang on and then they sat on the apron for an hour. Bob looked through the porthole and smiled, thinking of what Leila might have said. He'd insisted that she shouldn't see him off: the less she was seen with him, the better. But he didn't tell her that. 'Ta-ra,' she'd said, after a long final hug. 'Ta-ra, Captain.'

One swallow doesn't make a summer. Great quip. Thank you. Meaningless, in the context. But it had taken the edge off his final performance, despite Leila's slavering attentions. Now he'd give anything to be with Leila again: she made him laugh, and she was sweetly tender, at least on the outside. Inside she was (he suspected) as hard and smooth as a lychee stone.

Finally they were aloft. Bob was a poor passenger at the best of times, checking unseen instruments every time an aircraft yawed or lifted or turned, but that day he was worse than usual. He was in the window seat over the wing, and the flaps were bouncing. That's it, he thought to himself. Jesus gave up carpentry; I'll give up flying. I'll stop telling bad jokes. I'll open that quiet little pub, tell aviation yarns over real ale in some quiet corner of somewhere nice like

Devon, if that sort of thing still exists. Maybe it doesn't; everything seems to be Tesco these days. Above all, he'd get it right with the kids. With David and Sophie. Hardly kids. Let nothing rankle. Let nothing submerged rise to the surface and spoil everything.

He was flying Emirates Airlines, so the in-flight magazine was mostly duty-free diamond key chains and so on. He admired the usual crop of sea-beaded bimbos, then dropped off. Naturally, the submerged thing rose in his dreams. The dodgy aircraft in trouble, one engine gone, bad weather, fifteen tonnes over the maximums . . . and every time he failed to make it, in his dream. When Bob emerged through unbelievable noise into a real-life murmur of turbines, he found his neighbour looking at him, surprised. He must have cried out, or twitched violently as the thick forest canopy leapt up. It wasn't a good dream to have: in the dream, the crash would always bring relief; on waking up, the relief dissolved because he'd instantaneously remember that he did not really crash. He'd landed his cargo safely. And what followed had been much worse.

'I think this is yours,' said his overweight neighbour, handing him his boarding-card stub.

Bob blinked at him. He felt they'd met somewhere before.

'Solar panelling? In that bar? Brother with Asperger's? You're married to Christine but gay? Didn't we . . . ?'

'Sorry, no.' The man grinned. His calorific plumpness was compressed into the space dictated by the armrests, but a bared arm, swirling with hair, protruded, as did his smell. 'Sales. Machine tools. And you?'

'Not sure. I'm working on it. Sorry, I'm not a good flyer.'

And Bob closed his eyes as if to sleep. The thought came to him again in the form of his own, clear voice: that's it. I've done with flying. If I fly, it'll be in my own home-made Sopwith Camel that'll take years to build. A work of love. Fuck the agencies. Fuck being a haulier with wings. Fuck being a chauffeur. That's it.

'A drink, sir?'

Eyes as dark, polished and smooth as lychee stones.

'That's it,' he murmured, gazing into them. 'That's it.'

6

Whenever he'd mention having a place in Crowthorne, the clever clogs always said something like, 'What, a room in Broadmoor? They agreed to have you, did they?' Others would mention Wellington, the stiff-backed public school that the prince had attended, although it didn't stiffen *him* up very much.

The reason Bob Winrush had a one-room studio flat there was purely practical: it was well under an hour from Heathrow, unless there were a few too many bollards on the Frimley Interchange or wherever, and yet it lay properly outside the airport's aura. Praise be to motorways, he'd think, despite the nuisance of other cars (he'd remember with nostalgia the empty asphalt sweeps around Bratislava back in the 1990s). It was also a quick train ride to Gatwick. There were nice walks in bluebell woods, and Crowthorne was unassuming and not small enough for his comings and goings to be a subject of interest. His pad was at the other end of town from the BA pilots' traditional burrow, the pricy and posh Edgcumbe Park: he didn't want to talk shop all night.

They'd bought the flat when they moved from London to Worcestershire, in the days when he was doing a lot of shuttle stuff and Olivia had got tired of walking hundreds of miles just beneath the stratosphere (she wore a pedometer on all her flights). He would have preferred the family home to have been in the pilot's outer commuting zone — somewhere up on the downs near Newbury, say — but Olivia wanted to be near her parents, one of whom had dementia, although Bob could never remember which. She'd had her eye for years on a ramshackle thatched place which they grabbed the moment it came on the market, despite an alarming surveyor's report. 'It's been standing for 800 years,' the agent assured them. 'That's the best insurance.' This particular myth was nailed by the hard science of deterioration: a main joist was being held up by a kitchen cupboard, itself ancient. Recent doors had perforated the load-bearing walls. They had to call in a building pathologist, who defined every opening as a 'point of discontinuity', discovered fungal decay in 'moist' beams, and pinpointed unfortunate composites of the old and the new that interfered with elasticity, tension and stress.

'Sounds like me,' was Olivia's remark.

'Anyone'd think it was going to fly,' was Bob's. He was lightly fingering a masonry join that suddenly fell out in a clump.

The house, although listed, had to have a virtual rebuild, using original materials. It hoovered up so many brown envelopes that he lost count.

And now it was going to be hers, not his. After all that.

England felt wheedling, somehow, after the matter-of-fact heat of Dubai. It was raining and surprisingly cold; apart from a brief and spectacular gash in the clouds above the M25, the day's light stayed begrudgingly dimmed all the way to Crowthorne, when it almost went completely, and then promptly did, replaced by gaseous orange street lamps.

The flat smelt musty and unloved. He ran a bath and noticed bruises; the back of his head was even tenderer when he leaned back, perhaps because Leila had knuckled it in the throes of passion. He wondered if his coccyx was fractured as it rustled over the residue of bath salts — Sophie's present for his forty-ninth. 'They're retro, Dad. They're making a come-back.'

So it got dark at four o'clock, and you never saw it happen. He'd forgotten that. He'd last been here in June, when the communal garden's trees were out and its lupin beds were abuzz. The flat was in a wing of a purpose-built 1980s block, the brick type that had probably looked friendly when new, and now resembled a barracks. Fire and security precautions meant that he had three heavy code-operated doors to grapple with before he reached his pod, and their self-closing systems left about half a second to pass through. He noticed the sills on the triple-glazed windows were rotting.

At last, with some reluctance, he checked in the metal filing cabinet where he kept his papers and photocopies of his papers. Nothing had been touched. The Taliban flight was still there, in copyshop A4, each page from the logbook framed in black shadow. So was the cash, rolled up in Sellotaped Jiffy bags. About £30,000, most of it from the flights he'd done after Olivia had refused him back, adjusting her halo, the massage huckster still limping about town with the post-traumatic shakes. As if he'd never been waved at by a gun before!

'Why should he have been?' Olivia had remarked. 'Most normal people have nothing to do with guns, if they're not American or Somalian or whatever. It's totally illegal to carry one, since Dunblane.'

'Because he's a serial adulterer,' Bob had replied. 'Like a pop-up target in a shooting range.'

'The police have said that if you come back, and I don't want you here, they'll have you in for questioning. Illegal possession of a weapon, if nothing else.'

'Right. I noticed the mammoth manhunt when the armed would-be killer went missing.'

'They were extremely annoying,' Olivia snorted. 'Said it was a private matter and they couldn't chase up everyone with a gun or they'd be doing nothing else. Oh yeah? In Worcestershire?'

'Fancy you even phoning them.'

'I was bloody frantic.'

'So was I, honey.'

He yanked the curtains shut on Olivia's face looming out of the November night. He felt more glum than cross.

He stood holding the copied logbook, snapping the elastic on its yellow file, wondering if he should physically eat the relevant page. Instead, he looked for somewhere secretive, but the flat had no nooks or crannies. He eventually put the file in the oven. It was the one place (he'd read somewhere) that burglars never look. He unfolded his laptop and spent far too long circling around Matt Sharansky, Evron Bensoussan, Pedro Diez and even the sheikh. Sharansky's articles were annoyingly sober and reasonably accurate: he was on Bensoussan's tail, that was clear. No mention of the Turkmenbashi flight, not yet. And nothing else of real interest, no wires touching with a flash. Fingerprints are visible everywhere on the net, but it's the latent ones that are crucial. And you can't scatter powder over the Web.

The next morning was all leaflessness and very low houses, the grey spitting on the glass. He smoked an old cigarillo from a packet in a drawer, relic of an old habit he'd kicked (at Olivia's insistence) a few years back. It was worryingly pleasant, but he felt he deserved it. Dubai had made him horizontally challenged and light-insensitive: here the buildings really were crouched, like crabs, with a few exceptions that needed to be reported for obstruction. He went out to the corner shop up the road for fresh milk and provisions — custard creams, Marmite and other such native stock, horribly overpriced in Dubai — and he smelt the street before he saw it: a queue of cars, chokes metaphorically out, windows fogged so they looked driverless. The daily commuter rush. Work.

He was out of work, unless he phoned up the agency in Brighton. They gave you anything: he'd flown a Hercules around the Congo for them at one point. Not that he'd ever liked flying

Hercs, but the Winrushes were overstretched some five years back: the shop not doing so well, plus the school fees, the house repairs, the mortgage, Sophie's cello, his medical insurance. 'Dodgy agencies here I come,' he'd said. 'I'll phone those Brighton boys. They've got this nice big Herc. Lovely to fly.'

Fat brown envelopes, he was thinking.

So was Olivia, but you wouldn't have known it from her tearful look, gazing out on the orchard, the trees just emerging into blossom: old apple varieties, damsons, an ancient pear that long-haired growers would come to graft from. He remembered that look now. She was imagining the twins back in the dodgy local gang, or the cottage up for sale. Seven days of brown envelopes could pay for an awful lot: a year's education for two, for starters. If he were to do the Goma general cargo run — which was 'dangerous-*ish*', as Al would say with classic understatement — he could clear seventy thou in a week. Who was he to deny their kids a decent education?

So he'd done it.

Now, post-Dubai and bruised, it was late, he was in bed and he couldn't sleep. The flat made strange, alien noises. Footsteps. Dripping sounds. Sighs in his ear. He was hanging on by his shirt tab to a spike on the edge of a cliff. The headmaster would beat him if the tab broke, because it was the third time he'd allowed his games kit to drop onto the bench. 'I don't have a mother to sew it on properly, sir.' 'You're lying, Winrush. I talked to her at the

140

beginning of term.' 'That's my stepmother. My real mother's dead.' 'One swallow maketh not a summer, stupid boy.' He was falling, but at least he wouldn't be beaten. Then the whole school were after him, yelping and baying; as he plunged on through mud the siren began. That was it. Now the whole world knew.

He woke up to the Broadmoor siren's Monday test, a dreamy version of a police chase. Ten a.m. on the dot would be the ideal time for a psychopath to escape, because no one would take any notice. The all clear sounded. He felt relieved. He was still alive.

He hit the coffee, did a clothes wash, phoned his son David and left a message about wanting to see him. He wondered about phoning Sharansky, not to talk about his writing skills but to warn him, tell him about the Gold Teeth trio, about Lennart's involuntary exit. But a little bird told him not to meddle. Another day was over before it lasted long enough to be properly counted.

The next morning, feeling brighter, he searched around for the journalist's number. He looked through the tumble-dried wash and found a stiffened piece of folded paper in a back pocket, the number just visible. He was instructed to leave a message by the same breathy English rose that fielded his own phone. Imagining Matt Sharansky's mobile in the hands of those unwanted guests of four days ago, he aborted before saying a word.

He made another call: Al's landline. Jane answered and told him that Al was up to his waist in ice-cold water near Berwick, fishing for salmon.

'Do come and see us when he gets back, Bob.'

Jane: the Olivia that might have been. Jane: Miss Gatwick 1979, against stiff competition (though having been shown the group photo, Bob reckoned it had been a walkover). Now on the inflated side, having given up smoking. He didn't mention her health. He left Al to his angling.

He tried Sophie, who answered his text around lunch. Bob told his daughter that he was back for good, that there was no more flying. She was studying music in Newcastle.

'Dad, you've said that before.'

'Never, sweetie. I've never said it because I've never thought it.'

'So what's up? You're retiring?'

'No. Resurrecting. Life change. I've got a bit put by, can sell this place — '

'Not your little-pub-in-Devon project?'

'What's wrong with that?'

'Dad, you'll get *so* bored. Boring old men whinging on about their carrots and cucumbers. It's *such* a bad idea.'

'Oh. That's pretty encouraging.' Private education had given his daughter not just a posh accent, but a sort of world-weary gloss. It was hard to tackle.

'I mean,' she went on, 'you have to admit. You're the type that needs excitement, adventure. Your little-boy side will just go *completely* crazy.'

'I haven't got a little-boy side. That's Mum's

invention. I fly because I love flying. I'm gonna
fly for myself, from now on. A Sopwith Camel.
Which I'll build myself, over years. In the field
behind the pub.'

'Yeah, Dad. And it'll crash. You'll be really
quadraplegic or something.'

'Or just dead.'

★ ★ ★

Bob had already given up flying — once, just for
a few months. This was about a year before Luke
struck lucky. Olivia's argument had been honed
over afternoon wine with her friends: the shop
was tiring, she came home to no one at all in
term-time, it was depressing. 'But it was your
idea that the kids should board,' Bob reminded
her. That was no argument. She burst into tears.
He agreed, under pain of a separation, to give up
flying for a local desk job; they'd sell Crowthorne
and manage.

Not only had his reputation gone before him
(some obscure piece on arms smuggling,
blown up and copied and preserved for
eternity on the Web), but there were not a lot
of openings in Worcestershire for a man in his
late forties. He got hired as an account
manager for a firm making disabled-access
equipment on an industrial estate in Worcester,
and survived a couple of months: sitting in a
swivel chair all day in the same room as a
triple-chinned secretary shouting about her life
down the phone proved too arduous. As for
Crowthorne, there was one of those property

dips and the buyer pulled out on the last swerve.

Meanwhile, Olivia had started therapeutic massage sessions with some Canadian guy or other on the new estate that had replaced the paddock beyond their garden. She seemed less bothered about her husband being on and off, here and away.

He called the agency in Brighton. 'I'm back in,' he said. They laughed, almost dirtily. The great unwashed.

'I'll end up in Davis Monthan Air Force Base,' he told Olivia the day he handed in his resignation. They were in bed, reading. It was late.

'Where's that?'

'Arizona. They call it the boneyard. It's where obsolete aircaft end up, rusting under the hot desert sun. Rows and rows and rows of them.'

He touched her smooth upper arm with the back of his knuckles.

'Bob, this isn't working.'

He lifted the sheet. 'It's working all right. I just need to smell you and it works. Because you are you.'

'That's just physical,' she said.

'It's not. It's because I'm nuts about you. I am. Day after day.'

'Don't stroke me like that. Please.'

'It was only your arm.' He lay back, hearing the secretary's unfortunate voice, smelling her bacon crisps. 'You're not nuts about me, on the other hand. That's a problem, I grant.'

She allowed in an air pocket of silence. She

144

used, he recalled, to call him her 'hunk'.

'It's not you, per se,' she said. 'It's the whole thing.'

He failed to find an answer. At the time he thought it was because she'd had a grand total of three customers in the shop the day before, and had laid off her teenage assistant. Or that she was pining for Miami, those far-off days with the World's Most Experienced Airline. Being a naive pilot, it never occurred to him that a pleasant Canadian guy could be a wife-sucking ghoul, his massage parlour merely a portal to various caves of wonders. But that wasn't the whole story in itself. He recognised that, now. A plane only stays up in the air if it's going not-too-slow, not-too-fast. Their marriage had slowed, he felt, but not yet run out of juice. He simply misread or ignored the data: it was, in fact, in a stable, stalled, horizontal descent, an unnoticed death spiral. It happened: pilots trying to fix a mild problem in slightly bumpy night conditions while the surface of the ocean is hurtling up, their vessel as airworthy as a lump of rock. Full realisation had to wait for a crisp, clear October afternoon, a nip of woodsmoke in the air, a smell of lavender oil in the hall. The water about to cleave into a phosphorus bomb.

* * *

David got back to Bob in the afternoon. He'd just returned from what had been a decent little Crowthorne pub, the Star and Garter, but was now an offshoot of something like Cut-Price

Records, judging from the ambient music and the quality of the food. They discussed this and other things. Remembering Sophie's response, all Bob said was that he'd left the job in Dubai, that he wasn't going back. This was no news to David, as his father had been flitting all his life, a kind of blur that coalesced at regular intervals into a dad he'd once been proud of and was now embarrassed by.

'How's uni?'

'Fine.'

Bob asked him if he knew a journalist called Matt Sharansky.

'Oh yeah.'

'Personally?'

'No, just his articles.'

'David, did you put him on to me? Give him my details?'

'Why?'

'Because he knew where to find me.'

'Dad, anybody going on the Web can find out you live in Dubai.'

'My address is just a PO box. Otherwise you have to draw a map.'

'I did not draw a map. I didn't give him your address. Don't get on my nerves, Dad.'

Bob nodded, remembered you could hear a smile, so he smiled. 'Isn't that exactly what dads are for? Hey, I quite liked the guy, in fact. We had a useful chat. Trouble is, it turned out I wasn't on the dodgy flight in question. So it was all a waste of time.'

'Is Sharansky why you're leaving Dubai in such a hurry?'

Bob looked down on the bedraggled communal gardens. His bruised coccyx was saying, *You bet it is*. 'No. Other reasons.'

'Mum.'

'Well, partly. Tricky time. But getting back to this Sharansky character, he's in very murky waters. Best to avoid him.'

'He usually is. He's a fearless campaign journalist. We can't avoid him. Did Mum tell you I'm in trouble with my tutor?'

'She tells me nothing,' he said, unable to stop himself.

'Well, he's thirty-five and he's got seriously bad hair, literally like early Pink Floyd? I said so on Facebook and someone else showed him it. He was extremely cross,' he added, laughing. 'But it's seriously, seriously bad hair. And strawberry blond.'

'*I* once had hair like early Pink Floyd,' Bob said. 'Before the RAF.'

'Yeah, Dad, I know. But that was then.'

That was then. And now is now.

'I might take a trip up, David. Come and bother you in sunny Manchester.'

'Seriously?'

'Seriously.'

'About this journalist? Don't bother, Dad.'

'Just to see you, mate. Truly. Dads like to see their sons from time to time.'

'Hey, you don't want to give a talk, do you? Might be a bit rough, though. A few pointed questions. Wear your body armour and all that. Could be pretty cool. What d'you reckon?'

Bob promised he'd think about it and they

said their goodbyes, chummily. He stayed staring out through the rain-spotted glass onto a brown-and-grey muddle that was toying with the idea of being England. His own hair was dark chestnut and flight-deck short, but there'd be no more flight decks. Could that be true? Another empty vow.

He opened the window. A man was leaning against a tree on the far side of the road beyond the garden. A bird was hopping about on the grass below. A squirrel rippled up a trunk. The traffic hummed away unseen, overmastered by the beefier drone of a jet on its approach to Heathrow. And then another, and another. So large and loud a sound. He thought: I've completely forgotten what it was like before jets were hush-kitted. The BAC I — II was the loudest. *Let the noise be with you, skipper.* Birds manage it with no more than a faint sort of whispery thumping at most, if their wingspan's big enough. But then the body of the biggest eagle is no bigger than a rat's, or that squirrel's on the lawn. An Antonov 124 is seven storeys high and can carry fifty cars.

The air in his face did feel a touch too fresh after Dubai. Everything saturated, as if the country needed wringing out. And the spaces between all the brick and tarmac — green, matted, soggy! It was too cold to keep the window open. When he closed it he got condensation: rain-in-the-plane. As a kid he'd enjoy following the drips, seeing them join up, each individual journey. For want of anything else to do in deepest Suffolk. David had put

148

Sharansky on to him, obviously. The key was to peel David away from this whole business, as the man down there had peeled away from the tree. Looking up at him. Walking off.

Never mind the weather; he needed a drive.

7

Bob opened up his garage in the row adjoining the flats. Inside, in a pleasant smell of oil, leather and petrol, was a two-seater Austin Healey Sebring, a souped-up replica of the 60s racing model, built in 1988, with a Ford V8 engine and convertible top in tan, nicely setting off the dark red body. It was a present to himself after the Congo accident, cheap therapy at around £9,000. The kids had loved it, and got to ride in it in turn. Now safely under lock and key, he never bothered to check it beyond kicking the tyres. He reconnected the battery and it started straightaway.

He gave it a spin around the lanes, had lunch in Tadley, blew the dust off. He wished it was the summer, the wind in his face, blurred hedgerows. Instead, the windscreen kept fogging, the wipers wiping. When he got back, he went straight to the gym and renewed his membership. It was no good going slack: he felt like an animal in predator territory. And he was missing Leila.

He called the McAl at home again, but he was still battling with the salmon.

'Can't I try his mobile?'

'It doesn't pick up where he is. Deepest Highlands.'

'Is he semi-retired, or what?'

'Why do you say that, Bob?' Jane sounded

indignant. 'Just because he keeps some bloody bees?'

'He seems to have spare time.'

'Don't you?'

'I guess everyone's entitled to it,' Bob said. He wasn't quite sure why he'd started this: envy, perhaps. She asked how things were.

'You mean the divorce. We're almost dissolved. Sealed, signed and delivered. A few more stressed-out months of Olivia high on pulsatilla, and then it's done.'

She laughed, always the same high laugh. 'That's for colds. You make it sound like a death certificate.'

'You bet. And you?'

'What do you mean?'

'I mean how are you? Al said you were not A-plus, healthwise.'

'Did he now?' Far from going cold, she went on for another half an hour. By the end, there was nothing that Bob did not know about fibromyalgia in all its manifestations, most particularly, the one that increased your sense of smell a hundredfold. So how did Jane put up with Hugh 'Dog's Breath' McAllister?

Marriage is a human mystery, Bob thought. Divorce is an exposed rock, by contrast.

*   *   *

Saturday was sunny, between high white banks of cloud. He drove off again, but slightly further afield, up on the downs towards Hungerford. Olivia and he had taken the occasional break in a

151

picturesque village up there in their early years. An old rectory of a hotel, as she'd put it. He just needed to be looked after for a weekend — he might have gone to friends, but had to play the lone wolf for a while. Crowthorne was a safe house. Even the prince didn't know about Crowthorne.

He hit metal with the pedal and overtook most of the cars on the M4, enjoying the noise. He didn't like driving: other people in the way, bossy road signs, no views to infinity. He found a compilation Procol Harum that took him back.

Did you hear what happened to Jenny Drew?
I couldn't believe it, but it was true.

Too sad, too sweet: he whipped past Chieveley Services with Creedence Clearwater Revival blasting out so loud it made the gearstick vibrate. Old memories. He'd have to keep on Olivia's good side, for the sharing of family yarns, within limitations.

The Old Rectory Hotel, Ulverton was now a mere link in a chain, and a weak one. The receptionist was smoking mournfully in the porch, but smiled broadly on seeing him, her blonde hair scraped back. A client! She was from Estonia, so they chatted about Tallinn, in and out of which he'd flown freight. What he hadn't banked on was off-season, post-crash sadness: the hotel supper was a juiceless flap of steak with oven chips and a something sundae, the dining room so empty it smelt of tablecloths. Thanks to a wedding the previous weekend, the bar was out of almost everything except Stella Artois.

'But last weekend's six days ago.'

'Yeah,' said the Serb barman, grinning. 'Much problems with delivery. Reminds of back at home. There we go. That's life, sir, eh?'

Bob had a long bath, dried himself on a spotless fluffy-white towel that, once wetted, smelt of cigarettes. The huge telly was on a dodgy bracket; he switched on gingerly and lay back on the bed, zapping through frantic tosh. This is no good, he thought. Fuck Sharansky. Fuck Bensoussan. I was enjoying Dubai. I miss the converted crate. Handled well, had class. He couldn't face the village pub and had a bad night, dreaming of Olivia and Leila in cahoots behind him while he was flying over Worcestershire with the illuminated instruments about as useful as the dial on a food mixer.

During breakfast in the chilly dining room downstairs, sepia ploughmen on the walls and a salesman-type picking at his fried egg while studying a folded *Daily Mail*, Bob placed his English mobile on the table and switched it on, and it immediately rang. It was a message from Matt Sharansky, received the previous night. He wanted to talk, urgent. Bob sipped his fruit juice. The Old Rectory was dull. Nothing needed him, here.

'Matt Sharansky?'

'Sure. Bob, hi. Where are you these days?'

'Ever heard of hacked phones?'

'Oh, come on. I'm in our office in Tel Aviv. I feel bad.'

'What about?'

'You losing your job. But, you know, make hummus not war.'

153

'I wasn't making war and I'm not a great hummus fan. More serious is that I got back to my apartment after our meeting and three hired guns almost sent me over the balcony. Twenty-fifth floor.'

'You're kidding.'

'For once, I'm not. That's why I got out of Windy City without stopping at Go. They told me to. Remember I said we were being shadowed? I think you should take extra precautions, Mr Sharansky.'

'Scare tactics. This is how the goofballs keep control. They won't bother you now. Do you know Radom?'

Bob blinked. 'I presume you mean Radom in Poland, famous for its air show.'

'And for other things. Thirty thousand Jews lived in the ghetto. All killed. Did you fly out of there, ever?'

'Listen, the guys that mistook my balcony for the lift said I wouldn't have a second chance.'

'They don't need to know. I've been beat up a few times. It didn't work: I still carry on. They try it, it's scary, but as long as you're not Hamas you're OK. And you're somewhere nice in England, not the city of a thousand slaves. Did you ever fly out of Radom, Bob?'

'Maybe.'

'Carrying arms? AK-47S?'

'Radom has a very large arms factory. I was never on that leg to fly nappies. But I stress it was always just part of a many-legged tour which did involve a lot of stuff like nappies.'

The salesman-type was pretending not to

listen, but he'd been reading the same page of the *Daily Mail* for too long. It was so quiet in the hotel words were tannoyed. 'I believe the arms you saw in the hold in Istanbul, those AK-47S, were made and packed up in Radom.'

'Quite possible. So?'

'I'm accumulating evidence. Tracing it all back to the source. I've been faxed the packing list of an Ukrainian subsidiary company called Fine-track Ltd. It's actually controlled by one of Bensoussan's outfits, but the connection's a zigzag in a sewer. The packing list was for the first leg of a flight, to Bulgaria. Radom to Plovdiv International, where you then took over the flight with a substitute packing list.'

'Medical supplies.'

'Actually, as we all know, assault rifles, pistols, sub-machine guns. Great for the health.'

The Estonian girl, waitress for this shift, approached with more weak coffee, and Bob held out his cup. She had electric-blue eyes you could dive into. 'You would like something more, sir?' You bet. He reluctantly told her it was all fine and returned to Sharansky's voice, which was going into more detail about the sticky web of companies on which Bensoussan the spider sat. 'Mr Sharansky,' he interrupted, 'you're young; you think you'll live for ever. I know I won't. Behind every scar lies a story.' The salesman-type was glancing over now. The rain spat and dribbled on the glass, distorting the view of the village church. 'Nothing more to report. Sorry, chum. Can't even point you in the wrong direction. Make this our last contact.'

'Podgorica.'

Bob's thumb had been flexed over the red button. It froze. This left a rather telling pause.

'Sorry?'

'The flights, back in 2000. Podgorica to Somaliland. Hundreds of boxes of miniature manhole covers. Landmines, courtesy of one Pierre Dufort, now in jail. I have the freight documentation. You signed all the papers, being the captain.'

'If you say so. What's the description on the loadsheet?'

'Mechanical parts. Nice and vague, huh? As ever. But I have solid proof they were landmines. Worse, they were not anti-tank mines, they were anti-personnel mines. The type that blow kids' legs off, years after the war is over and forgotten. I went to Montenegro and did my homework. The manufacturer was Fiat.'

'I'll bet you were always good at your homework.'

'When it mattered. At school it didn't; you just had to be nice to the rabbi's wife and bring your own toilet paper.'

'Daimler made landmines, too. Toshiba Tesco KK, Nissan. They were all the rage. British Aerospace PLC.'

'Anti-tank mines. Yours were AP. Trucked south to Somalia, naturally. I found that out from a frightened guy in Mogadishu, where they behead you for saying *schmuck*. Somalia was not a legitimate destination, as you know.'

'I flew into the autonomous region of Somaliland. It was seriously in need of arms for

156

its defence. Berbera, to be exact.'

'Bob, I do not wish to have to post what I know about your Podgorica jaunts on the Internet. You know what my mum used to say to me? 'Never forget you're Jewish, because no one else will.' Now why does that remind me of the Web?'

Bob reacted smoothly. Underneath he was more than a little cross. 'I'm not sure exactly what you want to coerce from me, Sharansky. I've told you as much as I know.'

There was a sigh at the other end, over the sound of car horns and voices. The window must be open on Tel Aviv, or maybe the journalist was sitting in a square. The hot sun on his face. Was Israel hot in November? Nice and dry, anyway.

'OK, I believe you. But your flying buddies know more. First Officer Hans Schmitt. Flight Engineer Hugh McAllister. Apparently you're not acquainted with the fascinating Captain Pedro Diez.'

'What my crew do when I'm not commanding them is none of my business. I was not their captain on that leg. Do your own spadework, chum.'

There was a brief pause. When Sharansky spoke again, it was in a higher, strained tone. 'Look, I'm gonna be putting the final touches to my landmine article this week. Feel free to change your mind, Bob. Let's say your deadline's Friday after next? Today's Tuesday. That gives you ten days. Here's an extract. I corrected your name, thank you for that. 'The aircraft, flown by mercenary pilot Captain Robert Winrush and his — ''

'That's crap, for a start. I'm not a mercenary.'

'Then I'm not Jewish.'

Bob felt a surge of annoyance. The man had the stubborn tenacity of a ferret, a yapping terrier, a leech. 'Oh, look. While you've been wasting my time, my champagne's lost its bubbles. I was enjoying this little break. Just what the doctor ordered. Put whatever you don't know much about, anywhere you want, Sharansky. No one's interested. Least of all me.'

He cut off the reply, caught the salesman-type looking at him and flashed a pilot's reassuring smile. The man got up and left, blushing. The rain had stopped, as if the scene in the film was over. David would be interested, of course. Unfortunate. There wasn't a lot of nuance when it came to landmines in the popular imagination.

The blue-eyed waitress cleared the salesman's table. Olivia always told Bob that his eyes were grey, not blue. Grey-blue, at the very least.

I'm not partial to men with blue eyes.

She had said this the very first time they met. It was at a friend's wedding. Bob was barely weaned off simulators, but had clocked up a long haul or two. Her own eyes were green, her dark hair imbued with a citrus smell. She was exactly his height that day, in high heels. They were all hanging about for the happy couple in the ancient country churchyard. She explained to him that her name used to be shortened to Liv, but when she made friends with a Liv (the bride) at the age of nine, she became Olivia.

158

'Not Ol?'

'Too male,' she said in her throaty voice. 'And Olivia was also Olivia Newton-John, I'm afraid. We were fans.'

'I'm Bob. The groom's Rob. We're known as Bob 'n' Rob.' She found this funny. Her hand touched his elbow.

'What do you do, Bob 'n' Rob?'

'Fly planes.'

'You've got to be joking. Who for?'

'BA at present. I've just got my stripes. I think I know where the brakes are, now. You don't look impressed.'

'I'm Pan Am. Serving drinks and sick bags in white gloves. Based in Miami.'

Of course, hers wasn't a top-model look; it was the post-Pan-Am-training look. The straight back, the elegance, the looking-into-your-eyes. The bergamot oil against jet lag.

He asked where her Florida tan was.

'I'm an English rose. And the fuselage doesn't get the sun.'

'So are those the same gloves?'

'What a cheek.'

'Pan Am doesn't believe in British pilots, alas.'

'And nobody believes in women pilots. Not yet.'

'The day will come,' Bob said, secretly thinking it never would.

They began to read the tombstones, like the other guests. Her high heels got stuck in the lumpy turf and he had to hold her silk-covered arm. They got engaged a year later.

The rain was still switched off, so he went for

a run up on the downs, Ulverton extending into them in the form of a new estate crammed with posh houses in tiny gardens, window staring into window to check out who was sleeping with whom. He imagined it at night, full of snores and giggles. The only other walkers were people with dogs, looking wind-bitten and healthy under bobble hats. His Dubai tan must have struck them as inauthentic. The downs felt bleak and the tracks were as slippery as cream, but he appreciated the space and pushed himself a little, stretching his lungs and burning them on the cold air, so that by the time he was back they were flaming. He doused them in steam from the shower on the homeopathic principle, thinking about the DC-10's sauna and how the prince had been so quick to get rid of him. Fat white rabbit, scared by the foxes. The wolves, maybe. Bob wasn't sure. Sharansky was the hunter with a kid's catapult.

The phone grumbled as he sat there in his ash-smelling towel, feeling steamy and picturing Leila in a waitress's bib apron and nothing else. A text message from his soon-to-be-ex, finishing 'LOL OLIVIA'. She still shouted at the end. No crosses. She didn't now mean the lots of love; it was automatic. Otherwise she'd still be calling him grey-eyes, as in the old days.

She wondered when oh when would he take away his 'bits n pieces'. Twenty-five years of marriage ending in *bits n pieces*. He ignored it for the moment. He must go up and see David. He wasn't sure whether Olivia had told the twins about the bloody Makarov, that single sky-shot she still heard as entering her lover's head, whatever the evidence to the contrary. They did know about the Canadian prick, though. For the moment they hadn't taken sides; they were helpless spectators. For how long? Olivia was growing vindictive, maybe out of shame.

It had taken him three weeks of brooding in the Grampians, and a lot of staring into a lodge hotel's roaring fire, to forgive her. Before the bullet had had a chance to come down to earth again, he'd spat the drive's gravel, sped along Worcestershire's golden lanes, blended into the motorway, whipped past Birmingham, Stoke-on-Trent, Warrington and Wigan, shot past Lancaster, Kendal and Carlisle, and hit Scotland's hills after hours behind the wheel, using up all the CDs trailing about in the car, music at full volume, sliding past Glasgow at dusk, the lights coming on around Stirling, stopping at last in a pub in Killiecrankie and downing a foamy pint of Red McGregor over a Stilton risotto, talking to no one, easing his back, then on over the Drumochter summit and into the night, aware of the great mountains all about, the very cold air, the freshness, keeping the window down in case he went to sleep — which he did anyway at about two in the frosty dark, but not before he'd pulled off the A9 onto a lay-by north of Carrbridge, to be woken after dawn by the throb and squeal of a lorry touching down in front of him.

All for nothing: Olivia didn't want him back. She'd not told the kids that he'd vanished, not in their A-level year, and so had absorbed all the worry into herself. With the help of her book-club friends, between chapters.

You need your own life, they'd advised. You no longer love him, do you? Always off on his jaunts. Coming back grumpy, like ours are all the time. He's probably having the life of Riley. Go for it. Attagirl. Njoy. *Clink clink*.

So easy to slip up in real life. The split-second decision. What was she telling the twins now? After all, David hadn't come to see him in Dubai: ideological reasons. Sophie had had a ball, though — in the clubs, on the beach, in the pools, on the slopes.

No, David was the worry.

He checked at the desk about the salesman: he was an IT manager heading for Swindon. He'd paid and left. His car was not in the hotel's car park: the deep gravel exhibited impressive ruts of wheelspin, as if he'd left at a lick. Bob wished the waitress, smoking in the porch again, a happy life.

'No problems. Bye bye, sir. Thank you for your visit. I really love your car!'

Bob offered her a spin. To his great surprise, she agreed. There were no guests; she had an hour before preparing the lunch tables. His heart was hammering with expectation, like a pimply youth. But she was the age of Sophie, by the look of it. He glanced across as she climbed in and was touched by her child-like delight, the innocence of it.

He would behave. He would be honourable. She trusted him.

His wheels left as deep a mark as the IT

manager, but that was just showing off. They threaded the downland in lanes banked either side by grass and slashes of brilliant chalk. The sun had emerged; he lowered the top but the cold air allowed them only a few minutes of exhilaration. She was laughing, her lips glistening, clutching her coat to her neck. He took her up to Uffington; they walked to the White Horse, stood in its grassy eye, sunlight scudded over the tussocks, over her angel hair which she loosened so that the wind rippled it out behind her. It's so easy, thought Bob, to fly to somewhere else. Split-second decision. Because it was a chill weekday in November, they were alone. She had worked at the hotel for six months, but had never come up here, not ever. Her electric-blue eyes were enormous, looking at the view of the downs spreading southwards. 'I must do my table setting,' she cried, checking her watch. On the way back he played her Manuel Poveda, the flamenco voice turning the bare sweeps of chalk slopes all around them into something passionate and heat-rending. 'I love Spain, Estonia, England!' she shouted out of her window as the Healey swallowed the banked lane. I'm mad, thought Bob. I've fallen in love again.

'That was the best hour of my life,' she said, before running back into the Old Rectory Hotel, ten minutes late and risking her job. They were very strict, she said, these Serbs. He didn't even know her name.

'And mine,' he shouted after her, his voice vanishing into the laurel bushes.

He phoned Sharansky and left a message. The

deal was on. He was perfectly polite: he'd made the decision in the eye of the horse. Or rather, it had been made for him, threads of angel hair tickling his cheek.

★ ★ ★

He had called Jane to check if the angler was back. He was. Bob stopped off on the return leg back to Crowthorne: the sensible man still lived near Maidenhead, but had relocated to a fancy Edwardian mansion with an immaculate garden, complete with heated pool, statuary and his other hobby: roses. Bob was taken aback; it might almost have been one of Sheikh Ahmed's spare homes. Lots of brown envelopes, careful investment, a childless and rock-solid marriage, but it still surprised. The next fishing trip was to Norway, once the rivers had unfrozen. McAllister hadn't even been a chief pilot, thanks mainly to his reputation as a brawler. (There had been a single incident in the bar of the Hotel Ter Streep near Ostend airport, where the low-lifer crews tended to gravitate; it had got around.) Perhaps that rankled: if so, Al never showed it. Bob was always the skipper-that-must-be-obeyed, without irony.

Jane was out getting her perm reconfigured, which meant the men could yack. Al's extra two years were cancelled out by a healthy tan, and his sandy hair showed no signs of greying. Somehow he looked more strapping, or perhaps it was due to being semi-retired and fattening up. Bob's own Dubai bake was beginning to fade. They inspected what Al called 'the grounds': he had six hives, made sweet Maidenhead honey. The gliding koi had names: Pretty Lady, the Count, Popeye. So did the roses, presently pruned right back to thorny sticks but apparently Jane's chief love — closely followed by her husband, Al joked.

'Bee, koi and rose breeders,' Bob remarked. 'Impressive.'

'At least we've bred something,' Al murmured. 'A human being would've been nice.'

Then they did the 'guided tour' of the en-suite bathrooms, the breakfast room, the lot.

'Jane's done everything in shades of green and grey,' Al pointed out. 'That's her domain. She has an eye. This one's called Elephant's Piss, or witever,' he growled, gesturing at the dining-room walls. His mobile kept ringing and he'd talk into it in single-word sentences, puffs of marshy breath.

'The world loves you,' said Bob.

'When it suits it to,' Al muttered, switching the phone off. 'You know I've a new hobby, to go with my passion for koi?'

A tall walnut cabinet of thin drawers in the study held Al's collection of butterflies: African, Indonesian, Himalayan and so on, with one drawer full of more modest home specimens, some of which Bob recognised.

'I've always been tentative about this kind of thing,' he said.

'Don't be a wet,' said Al. 'Billions of 'em live and die and we don't even notice. Remember the clouds that'd rise up in front of you in the bush?'

'Sure do. That's my point.'

The pin through the thorax, the shimmering colours pushed out of sight. When Al pulled out a drawer entirely and lifted its glassed lid, there was a smell of camphor. He pointed to a specimen with iridescent blue patches as bright as police lights, marked *Prepona werneri* in Al's attempt at a neat hand.

'Remember seeing this in Ecuador?' said Al. 'On that great big leaf? Rare. We were damn lucky, you and me.'

★ ★ ★

They skipped tea and hit the gin straightaway: Al could never drink it in front of Jane, it was one of the smells that made her ill. He favoured gin over whisky, oddly for a Scot, as long as it rang with ice and was lidded with a thick slice of lemon. Oh, and the tonic had to be splashed, not poured. Otherwise he wouldn't touch it. This is what made Al something else to fly with, Bob thought: he was fussy, but he savoured life.

They touched glasses.

'Tea and sympathy,' Al said. 'Sounded nasty. But no worse than anything in Africa.'

'It was worse.'

'But you look good on it, skipper. Sparkly eyed.'

'Clearing the dust off in the Austin Healey. What is the actual speed of light, by the way?

'Now that's straining my brain cells way beyond their capacity. Why? Is that what you reached?'

'The speed you can fall in love. Visual information, eye to eye.'

'Who this time?'

'Someone.' Bob shrugged. 'A hotel waitress. Remember Ulverton? That nice pub? I think I took you up there one time.'

'Vulva.'

Bob chuckled, after a puzzled pause: someone had sprayed a V on the village sign when they'd visited, back in the 1990s. Al remembered everything.

'Ach, that's just post-separation trauma,' he said.

They drank to that, Bob disappointed that Al was not more interested.

'So now what, skipper? Start a gliding school for blondes?'

'Yup, with an engine to cover their blonde moments. I know that one.'

The two men sipped their gins thoughtfully.

'Well, Bob. You've had a prowler.'

'If you mean the journalist, he's dealt with.'

'Dealt with?' Al looked genuinely alarmed suddenly.

Bob laughed. 'No way. I mean I've verbally shown him the door.'

'Good news. What a little wanker. So who's your new dish?'

'I haven't got one.'

'Oh. I thought you said.'

There was a silence between them. *Little wanker* was not quite right for Sharansky. *Pain in the arse* was better. Doing his job. The real wankers were the men who'd misled them into a

167

deal none of them liked. And one of those wankers was dead.

'He's not a bad sort,' Bob continued. 'He'd better be careful, though.'

'He'll be fine. We're not in a film.'

'Maybe that's what Lennart thought.'

'The poof? He had short life expectancy written all over him.'

'Did you come back empty, Al? From Turkmenbashi?'

Al frowned. 'Full of air. A terrible waste, I thought. We could have hoovered up some of them puddles of crude, at least. Why?'

Bob leaned forward, keeping his voice down. 'No extra kilos of a certain poppy derivative?'

Al paused, as if in shock, then snorted. 'Was that a question? A lean-forward question, from the look of it?'

'As I told him, you'd have known nothing about it.'

'Heroin? Christ. You've got to be pulling my leg, Bob. We flew back with wall-to-wall air in the hold. Where's he picked up that scrag o' shite from? Eh?'

Bob held up a calming hand. He'd not seen Al so worked up since a loadmaster claimed his men weren't responsible for damage to the cargo door in N'Djamena, the tarmac melting in the heat. Maybe it was the strain of Jane. The strain of not flying enough. Of not having his gin whenever he wanted. 'I've no idea. I told him, arms and drugs never mix. Chalk and cheese. Oil and water.'

'Bloody hell,' said Al. 'Now that's a thing.

Heroin! Taliboy brown sugar! Terrorist skag! Christ alive!'

He looked out of the French windows, and so did Bob. The glorious garden looked mopish, it being November and grey in the Maidenhead area, but it was still impressive. The statuary around the covered pool, the weeping willow by the pond, the comforting spiral of smoke from a huge heap of leaves.

'I see you've put in a copper beech,' Bob remarked, noting the pool of red beneath a tree on the lawn.

'For the future generations,' said Al. The outside light fell on his face: he had developed some more capillaries over his cheeks since the last time Bob had seen him — which was standing in a hotel room in Istanbul, watching the skipper jump ship. Al sucked on his lemon noisily, then munched it.

Bob said, clearing his throat, 'Well, I never quite trusted ex-Swissair.'

Al turned to him sharply. 'Apart from being Swiss, nothing wrong with the guy.'

'And Pedro Diez?'

'Who?'

'Pedro Diez. The skipper for Turkmenbashi. My fascinating stand-in. Surprised you've forgotten.'

'Oh, him.' Al shook his head. 'Nah. Ex-Iberia. Could barely speak English. When he did, you couldnae understand him. They scraped the barrel, I can tell you. Don't believe everything you read in the papers, Bob. We all know Bensoussan is never into narcotics — he has a thing about it. His crippled daughter?' 'Disabled daughter. You'll get into trouble. Yup, that was my conclusion. So if the info's reliable, and apparently it is, then the stuff was planted behind Evron Bensoussan's small but compact back. Lennart knew?'

'What is this?' growled Al, spreading his arms. 'Twenty questions? Sherlock fucking Holmes?'

Al could look ferocious: those genial creased eyelids turning hawkish around the pale blue stare. Rare, but in Africa it was useful. He'd never wear sunglasses out there, and his long eyelashes were bleached hamster-white.

Bob made light of it. This wasn't working. Sharansky would publish and David would never speak to him again. Or not for years. 'I'm worrying for our health, Al. That's all. If one green bottle should accidentally fall, that's fine: it's an accident. Any more, it's deliberate.'

'You didnae fall.'

'Next time, I will.'

'Who told this scribbling fella there was heroin?'

'I said, I've no idea. He called it protecting his sources.'

'Bensoussan's a big-time arms trader. Even without his junkie daughter in the wheelchair, he wouldnae readily deal in narcotics, not in the real world beyond men's feverish imaginations. And I'll tell you what I think,' Al went on, leaning forward himself, his freckled forehead glistening: 'I think someone's out to nail Evron Bensoussan with false information, and your writer-wanker's swallowed it. Cogs within cogs,

170

Bob. That's the Jewish mind for you. Political scheming.'

'The arms alone are a scoop, though. An Israeli selling guns to the Taliban? Wow.' But it struck Bob that Al was possibly right. For someone who wanted to bring down a right-wing government, Sharansky the young left-winger was the perfect conduit. Why hadn't he seen that straightaway? 'Anyway, all I know is that Evron Bensoussan has connections up to the highest level. And his daughter was never a junkie, by the way; she was sitting in a car driven by one. Be careful.'

'Ach, she was in that lousy crowd. And the highest level's God. I don't think God's in the same neighbourhood. Neither are we.'

'Nope.'

'You don't look convinced,' Al said.

'Anyway, now you know.'

Al fixed him with the sharp engineer's gaze that had saved their lives on at least two occasions. 'Don't get involved, skipper. Someone else's dirty games.' As Bob nodded, Al went on: 'The thing is, between you and me, war wouldn't be a bad solution.'

'To what?'

'Yob culture. Mop the louts up, siphon off their testosterone levels. That, or send them down the mines, re-opened especially for the occasion. Girls are no better. Underage, on the job, off their heads on poof juice. Another?'

Bob drained his glass, but still had a few miles to drive, so wavered for a few seconds. 'Weaker, Al, weaker. I've a feeling Sharansky'll try you on, now that I've said no. Even if it's just the naughty green boxes. Your official line is: one, you were just doing your job; two, you are a peacenik.'

'The fella can fuck off. No, seriously, Bob,' he went on, handing his late commanding officer a glass writhing with oily swirls, 'go take a pecker at the centre of Maidenhead of a Friday or a Saturday night, if you don't mind the risk of getting twatted. Smashed glass and vomit. You can feel it sliding down into a second Bracknell, God help us. Next time you see me I'll be in a fucking shell suit. This country's only held together by Big Macs and smack.'

'There you go, smack.'

Al looked goggle-eyed for a moment, then laughed. 'You have to eat properly with it, though.'

It was a gas, flying with Al. Bob leaned back in the white furry sofa and sighed. The gin was jolly. 'Weren't you a lout once, Al? Up in Fife?'

'Very, very briefly. No, I'll just tell your namby-pamby scribbler to write about the town of Maidenhead instead.'

'He's more interested in the town of Radom.'

'Radom as in Polish massive arms factory?'

'Yup. Pursuit of the ongoing investigation.'

Al pulled a face. 'What a little wanker, eh? Writing whatever he likes. It only takes one rotten apple to ruin the entire box.'

There was a silence, apart from the tick of a fancy grandfather clock. Al, despite his politics, had saved them from a graveyard spiral in a full seven-oh freighter by closing the throttle

— before Bob had even detected the dive — during a night flight into Kigali. Bob could tell they'd accelerated but not that they were banked, and he was about to push the nose up. Al took over and put them into recovery mode within five seconds, which was about all they had. It wasn't Bob's fault, but it did make him think that Al was the more sensitive pilot. As in sixth sense. Which is why he'd ended up with what he'd got: posh house, a pad in the British Virgin Islands and serious time for his hobbies. He hadn't yet asked about Olivia, the divorce, the house, the twins. He seemed distracted. For his own part, Bob had the impression, as he studied the misty garden, that he was losing everything — wife, kids, home, job, friends — in a kind of receding or miniaturising step-by-step fashion, and that nothing could stop it. He'd have to get a cat.

'Jesus, Al,' he sighed suddenly. 'The stranglehold of life.'

'Transitional. Sling a few girls over your shoulder and enjoy yourself. You're still a fucking draw.'

'Thanks for the in-depth advice, friend.'

There was a kerfuffle in the hall and Jane came back in from the hairdresser's under a snappy little bob, all streaked and glazed, that jarred with her weight. She looked drawn and pale, held her hand over her nose.

'Gin,' she said. 'That awful smell. One of the ones that makes me literally sick. I'll get used to it. Hello, Bob darling.'

The two men had to get rid of their

half-glasses down their throats instantaneously, flambéing their tonsils. Bob was over the limit and was made to stay the night. Jane magicked up a fine supper, partly by plunging into their vast freezer in the garage. She went to bed early, overcome by nausea from the fumes of ordinary life. No wonder Al was under strain. A very expensive private clinic in California was booked for the new year: Jane talked of little else during the meal.

The two men stayed up late relishing Al's best malt in sensible amounts. Bob already had a headache. It was, he admitted to himself, a little like the old days. Their hands re-enacted various approaches onto unmarked jungle strips of compacted earth fitfully lit by kerosene markers about as big as birthday candles; in between, Al kept poking and prodding about Olivia, at last — as if there was the remotest chance of a reconciliation.

'What did she cite in the petition, apart from the fact that you're a complete fucking prat?'

'Oh, I don't know. Not hanging out the washing enough, or something. Using too many clothes pegs. Whatever.'

'Amateur psychology, skipper, but what I reckon is that she feels guilty when you're around, and is projecting that guilt onto you. You know, about her fling.'

'As in Highland,' Bob joked. Al had always been partial to Olivia. What normal male wasn't? He realised he'd taken up a peculiar recumbent position in the massive sofa and levered himself up somewhat painfully.

'Easy does it, old boy,' Al said, in a gruff, colonel-out-in-Inja voice. One thing about Al: he could always do a mean imitation, would once upon a time entertain the kids as a rollicking Santa Claus for the BA staff Christmas do in Hanger Lane.

'I know,' Bob said. 'It's annoying. I don't want to be stiff. I keep pretty fit, jogging, workouts in the gym. Press-ups.'

'Ach, I can just see you, in poofters' black leggings.'

'There's a general lack of oil.'

'Still clocking up the miles down there?' Al smiled, patting his crotch.

'C'mon, Al,' Bob said, wide-eyed. 'Loud and proud. It wasn't *that*.'

'Girls get lovelier and lovelier,' Al sighed. 'Especially the foreign ones.'

'That's because you're getting uglier and uglier. And more Scottish. Now, remember that last copper mine in Zambia? We were freighting machinery into the copper belt, the Glencore ops. What was it called? Slagsville. All that sulphurous shit in the air.'

'Mufulira. Christ, yes.'

'The flash floods that made me come back two days early? Nature is to blame.'

'It always is,' said Al. 'Who else is responsible for the human race?'

'So, listen. I walked into the house with the taste of that sulphur in my mouth. African copper-mining sulphur. And I walked straight in on them, coupling. *Coupling*.'

'What position?'

'Oh, she was on top, facing his feet. Tantrical or whatever.'

Al's face was one of intense concentration. 'But imagine if he'd been in a gorilla suit.'

'Two years later, and I've still got that actual sulphur taste in my mouth. Slightly, but all the time.'

'That's psychosomatic,' said Al, gravely. 'You need tae suck on a girl's boobs smeared with lavender honey, every day after meals and last thing at night.'

'Thank you, Doctor. Not lavender. Clover, maybe.'

'You're a fussy one, Captain. As if I could care less what damn flavour the honey was, in those precise circumstances as previously just described.'

They drifted along thus, on a slipstream of Glenlivet.

'God, I wish you'd been in my crew for the sauna with attached DC-10,' Bob said, the room circling him slowly. 'I was stuck at first with a Syrian co-pilot who thought a flame-out was a fire.'

'You can't half-know how to fly,' Al growled, 'but any little cunt can write.'

At about three o'clock, when they were more asleep than awake, they made a decisive move to stir and go to their respective beds. Bob tottered upstairs and lay mysteriously revived between the crisp, expensive sheets, thinking about the waitress. He hadn't even asked her what her name was. It made it purer, somehow. All he knew was that she had sprinkled happiness over his day, and therefore over his life. Clover honey would be just fine.

He eventually slept, but uneasily. We carry far too much about with us, was his final waking thought.

★ ★ ★

'Half and half,' he said. 'Crowthorne in my name, Worcestershire in hers, and she gets part of my savings to notch it all up to fifty-fifty. I pay maintenance until the kids earn, which'll probably be in about ten years' time, at this rate. All very amicable, except it straps us both to some extent. Well, quite a bit. Improverishment no, budget cornflakes yes. The court's verdict is imminent.'

Over breakfast, Al had asked how the finance side of the divorce was playing out. It was eleven o'clock and they had a headache apiece. Al was definitely running to fat, competing with Jane: maybe he lost it during the day.

'That's good and bad news,' he said. 'She gets the house and the kids, you keep your penis and your soul. As they say.'

Bob chuckled gamely. 'Given that Olivia reportedly agreed with her charming friends to do me for whatever she could, I think it's all fairly good.'

'You've got more grounds than her to clean her out,' Al said, checking Jane wasn't in earshot. She was in the garden, feeding the koi or whatever you do with koi, avoiding the stench of their toast.

177

'Al, I have no intention of cleaning her out. Anyway, the financial shenanigans have nothing to do with the conditions of the divorce. It's ancillary, as the slimy solicitors call it. She could have had 500 Canadian masseurs all at the same time and refused me her favours with an evil cackle over the entire marriage and still walked out with fifty-fifty, if that's what the court decided were her needs.'

'Brown envelopes required,' Al said.

'No way. I think I may've retired without knowing it.'

'So you said. You've said it before. There are some offal flights going begging out of Niarobi, if you want them. Various destinations. With a few spare parts for the oil industry thrown in, no doubt.'

Organ transplant flights were usually at night and paid well. Bob could feel himself hesitating. He could feel the pull. But he shook his head. 'I'll sell the flat. I've got a bit put by. I need to stop, reassess. Give myself a break. Run that little pub, build the Sopwith Camel.'

'You'll turn smelly and unshaven, skipper.'

'Like a true freight dog.'

Al wondered what the flat was worth.

'I'll be lucky to clear £200,000. Needs a bit of a refit. Rotten sills. What can you buy for two hundred thou that's halfway decent?'

'Depends what you're looking for,' said Al. 'And where.'

'A bolt-hole,' Bob said, after chewing and swallowing thoughtfully. 'Correction: a home. I'm looking for a proper home. In this country.

The twins. I think Olivia might take over the controls if I'm abroad. Ease them away from me.'

'Interesting. Take a pecker at this.'

He was stroking his BlackBerry next to the toast, poking, opening a file. A mostly slate-roofed house swam into view, long and low, in a windswept tussocky plot lit by brilliant sunshine.

'Looks more like the Falkland Islands than the British Virgin Islands,' said Bob.

Al laughed. 'Was that a joke? This is fucking Scotland. The home country. 'A real rarity', see? Yours for a hundred thou. The Outer fucking Hebrides.'

The property belonged to Al's bachelor cousin in Glasgow, now suffering from advanced Parkinson's. The island was called Scourlay. 'Pronounced as in moor,' said Al, 'not fucking dish-pad. *Scoor*lay, right? This is the view, Crusoe.'

Low mountains, bright blue water, a great deal of sky. Bob felt something rush like sherbet through his chest. Al was saying he didn't know what to do with it: no one wanted to buy it, and as executor he wasn't allowed to drop the price below the market value. The price was less than half the value of the flat. Three beds, five acres.

'Lovely and quiet,' said Jane, who had joined them by now.

'Although let me warn you,' said Al, 'being an honest feller, they took that photo on the one day in the year that the sun shines.'

'He does exaggerate,' said Jane, stroking Al's broad back in its blue cardie. She had earrings

179

that looked like real diamonds, flashing in the grey day. 'Though it might get blowy.'

Al chuckled some more. 'I can tell you, up there you forget what the colour blue looks like in its natural state.'

'I've been a year in Dubai,' Bob said. 'You know I love it wet and gusty.'

'Well, on the off chance. Give it a try, I thought. It's my inherited headache. If the bugger was in the Grampians, now . . . '

Jane left off stroking Al's back and went to lie down.

'She's a doll,' said Al fondly, rolling his large shoulders. 'Did you see how she rubbed my back?'

'Rent?'

'Aye, he was always happy for folk to rent full time. Anything to keep out the damp. It's been on the market for over two years. Never, ever be an executor. The damp's terrible. Character-building. And the midgies. You'd be back screaming after a couple of weeks, pursued by midgies.'

'I think my character's built,' said Bob. 'From about seven years old.' He turned and indicated his earlobes. 'Those rocks of Jane's, were they real?'

'Aye,' Al grunted, 'and so are her diamonds. Why?'

'You're doing very well.'

'So?'

'Al, don't look at me like that. It makes my headache worse.'

Later, as Bob climbed into the Austin Healey,

Al held the door open, leaned in and said, 'You jumped ship, skipper. Stay on shore.'

'Meaning?'

'Drop it. Leave the crew alone. Hans, Diez. Me. No more queries. That's my advice.'

Bob held his gaze, which wasn't easy. Sometimes Al could look like Major Hench, the worst of young Bob's five headmasters. 'You know the score, don't you?'

'There isnae a score. There's just carrying. May we open cargo holds and approach the staircase. Confirmed. That's it. Pallets. It's very simple. There's no score. We'll keep in touch, skipper.'

He slammed the Healey's door. Bob braved a smile, and had problems sticking the key in the ignition: hand-tremble. He waved as he drove off, but Al was already on the phone under the pillared porch, shaking his head in some unseen veto.

*   *   *

Back in Crowthorne, Bob called various local estate agents, asking them to re-evaluate the flat for a possible quick sale. They shot round the same day; he told the pimply youths that he was awaiting the divorce court's verdict any week now. 'No problem, sir. We'll be right on hand when you're ready.'

There were various steely edges to the settlement that were in Olivia's favour, but friends had warned him that contesting merely expands the solicitor's bill. A hearty wave is free

181

and a lot better than a scowl.

He had an 'oh shit' moment that evening: he'd forgotten to phone Olivia about his *bits n pieces*. Sophie answered, to his surprise: she was down from Newcastle — her degree's reading week. Mum was in the bath. He had a good chat with Sophie, battling against his own crosswind of grumpiness, a feeling of family exclusion. Her course was going well, Newcastle was fab, she was clubbing a lot. He wondered if Olivia really was in the bath. Sophie was going no further south than Worcester, with just a brief detour to a rock gig in Birmingham. Dad wasn't included in her itinerary; the message that he was back from Dubai had got to her too late — she'd already bought her train tickets. He offered to pay for the additional leg south. To no avail.

'OK, sweetie,' he said. 'I'll come up to Newcastle soon. Can I speak to your mum?'

To his surprise, she went upstairs with the phone and called out. He could see the landing, the bathroom door, the exposed beams and crooked floors; he could even see the shaggy patch of plaster between a V of rafter and joist that no amount of insulating and specialised paint had ever cured. His wife came on the phone — dripping in her wrap-around towel, no doubt. Her firm and lengthy forty-eight-year-old body with its dense breasts; her quick, high voice, her long fingers.

'Oh, it's you.'

'Who did you think it was?'

'Sofe didn't say,' she sighed. 'Yes?'

'I didn't say anything.'

'I'm getting drips on the new floor.'

'What new floor?'

'The joists underneath were rotten. That's why the boards felt sort of spongy. Mike did it, with planks from an old church or something.'

Mike was the local thirty-odd carpenter: a charmer who played the guitar.

'I thought he wasn't supposed to be much good.'

'What difference does it make to you?'

'Well, we haven't actually signed anything yet,' Bob pointed out. 'Until then it's still mine as much as yours. Technically.'

'Did you get my message about all your junk?'

Bob stiffened, took a deep breath, studied the flat's wheat-meal carpet. 'I've carried junk, when I was flogging round Asia. Plastic junk, made in Chinese slave factories. Half of the stuff I *ever* carried was junk. I've flown over the junk floating in the oceans: circles of plastic the size of France, visible from the cockpit. Half of the stuff we carry in our heads is junk. But my bits and pieces are not junk.'

'And?' she said impatiently. She would always claim men went on and on.

'I'll sort out storage, hire a big white van and clear it next week. As long as you can put me up for the night. It'll take more than a day.'

'A whole day?'

There was a pause. He mustn't comment.

'You can have David's room,' she said in a posher voice than usual.

'Thank you.'

'So?'

'Are you still dripping?'

'I've stopped,' she said. 'But there's a mark.'

'Sorry. All my fault.'

Instead of saying something like, 'Exactly, it always is,' in a tone he used to love because it was funny and sardonic, she ignored his remark. She was just being efficient. Her shop voice. Holier Than Thou.

The voice said, 'I'm moving, by the way.'

'Moving?'

'I've had enough of the Worcestershire malaise.'

'Where to?'

'West. To Shropshire. I don't want to be actually *in* Wales. We need to discuss what we're deciding.'

'Nice idea,' Bob said. He knew the area from the odd holiday they'd spent in their early London days: Clun, the Long Mynd, hiking across the heathery Stiperstones. 'But you told the solicitor you were deeply attached to the house.'

'So? It's in my name and I can do what I like with it. It's got too many painful memories. It's a weight.'

'Nice painful, I hope.'

Bob decided not to point out that, technically, the house was still his. She was doing no more than he was: planning the future on the rubble of the past. As for the shop, he would be sharing its debts, but they were minor. The agent was in negotiation with a kebab chain.

'When you come,' she went on, 'remind me to

give you some pots of wimberry jam. And you can mend the tap in the kitchen. It drips. I don't trust plumbers.'

'No, I wouldn't trust them an inch,' he said. She was softer, almost back to normal. 'When would suit — '

'Oh, look,' she interrupted. 'Can you hold a minute? There's someone at the door.'

'I'm holding,' he said to the clatter of the receiver. 'Burning holes in the sky. Piece of cake.'

This was not like divorce in the films: he'd even imagined them having another crack, later. It had happened to friends of his. But the idea of Celandine House soon being up for sale, having absorbed so much of his life, let alone his earnings, was somehow disturbing. He could get rid of the Crowthorne flat without a qualm, but the house was where they'd brought up the kids, made a go of everything.

When she got back a few minutes later, she was brisk but jolly. They agreed he would come round this Saturday, when she would be in (the flag flying, as he almost joked). Their goodbyes were amicable.

He felt fairly annoyed with Olivia. She knew that calling his stuff 'junk' would annoy him. Why did she want to annoy him? So that he would lose his cool and she could go to her solicitor and say, 'He's aggressing me.'

It was a close-run thing. Although pilots keep their cool in emergencies, delays on the tarmac can get their blood pressure up to stroke level. And that's when they make mistakes, smudge procedures, move with the bridge still attached. Not recommended. His own solicitor had warned him that provocation was habitual in divorce cases, although it generally made no difference to the court's decision concerning the ancillary settlement. This was the kind of lingo being used about his marriage, his private life, his Olivia.

And he thought he'd heard a male voice in the background; she wouldn't have answered the door in her towel. He hadn't wanted to probe: probing had just gone badly with Al, for a start. Mike the carpenter. Thatchers were a danger too. The bilingual masseur had long found other bodies to master.

I'm not the probing type, he decided. But at least he could tell Sharansky in all sincerity that he had tried. That none of the crew were aware of the in-flight smack. Would that be enough to remove his name from the Podgorica piece?

Somehow, he doubted it. It felt too easy. He should get in touch with Hans 'ex-Swissair' Schmitt, at least. A touch risky, in the circs, but why should anyone else know? They couldn't know everything. And the man himself was no squealer. He scrolled up Schmitt and called him.

Nothing, just a non-operational buzz.

He wasn't dead; he'd just changed his number. Al would have his fresh coordinates. But Al had said, in so many words, *disengage*. On the other hand, Al wasn't his skipper. He didn't have to obey. That was just Al stepping out of rank.

The next day he got himself a Hotmail account under the name Mad Hound and found a couple of freight-dog Web forums that seemed well attended. Within twenty-four hours, his question had been answered. Pedro Diez ('El Cid') was flying cars for IQS out of Hanover and had spotted the authentic 007 Aston Martin palleted in a warehouse somewhere; Hans Schmitt was currently in and out of Saudi Arabia for a cargo outfit wet-leasing mainly to Syngenta, carrying pharmaceuticals, pesticides, what have you.

The outfit, called Speedstrap Ltd, gave him ex-Swissair's new mobile number. Hans Schmitt answered straightaway. Typically, he didn't seem surprised to hear from Bob. There was something else, though: a coolness that bordered on the frosty. Of course, the skipper had walked out on his crew. Bob filled him in on the last two years. Hans replied monosyllabically. Soft music in the background, Arab voices.

'Yeah,' Bob continued regardless, 'I'm sorry about walking out on you, but it didn't smell right. I hope it paid handsomely. What did you think of the coffee at Turkmenbashi?'

'Why are you calling?'

Good question. He was calling because a two-bit left-wing journalist had blackmailed him. But he could hardly ask the guy whether he'd noticed some brown sugar in the empty hold.

'Listen, Hans. Someone's putting the heat on me about this trip. Because I was skipper on the first leg. Did you come back from Turkmenland empty?'

'Who's putting you the heat?'

'The usual pain-in-the-arse campaigner.'

'You want me to tell you all what I know about this two-days trip?'

'If possible.'

'Fuck nothing.'

'As opposed to fuck all.'

'Yeah, exactly.'

'Hans, you flew the plane.'

'I repeat, I know fuck nothing. I flew the plane, that's all. These smiling guys in ties and suits came in the aircraft, gave out the brown envelopes, very friendly. We go back to Istanbul empty. That's it. I was doing my job and I know how to do that.'

'Are you sure she was completely empty?'

There was a pause. The music was funky; there was laughter among the male voices. 'Yeah,' said Hans. 'As far as I was observing. Why?'

'This journo pain-in-the-arse thinks there was narcotics involved.'

'In sport?'

'Eh?'

'He's joking?'

'No. Deadly serious.'

'Drugs is not ever, ever our business. Eh?'

Bob made an approving noise. Hans Schmitt worked cocaine and counterfeit tools, among other things, for mafia types. Or so the rumour went.

Schmitt was piling on the blah. 'He thinks

we're crazy? Drugs? That's for idiots. I have to go. OK?'

'I'll tell him you know fuck nothing. And listen, Hans, take care. I was paid a visit in Dubai, knocked about a bit. Maybe Bensoussan's heavies. Whoever.'

'Really? Is that why you're getting into touch with me now?'

'Yeah. That's why. Any more info? Mysterious packages? This guy Pedro Diez, your replacement skipper? It would really help.'

'El Cid? So bad English I couldn't understand a word of the procedures. Not even 'tripfuel'.'

Bob laughed. 'OK, he's Spanish.'

'Mexican.'

'Mexican? Wow. Pedro Diez is Mexicano, huh? Anything else?'

'I'll think about it. I'm with my friends here. We try to have fun during our boring job, yeah?'

'We try to. Thanks, Hans. Call me some time this week. I've got until Friday.'

'So long, skipper.'

That was nice: *skipper*. Bob had been getting a bit worried there. He felt pleased with himself, scribbled down the points he'd garnered. Probing had its moments. He'd always loved detective movies. He remembered those long hauls to New Zealand in his early days, when pretty well all they talked about over the night-time oceans was *Twin Peaks*, the illuminated avionics turning the crew's dim faces an eerie blue. 'Oo-er, it's evil Bob,' someone would always say.

He texted Sharansky to keep him quiet: 'Probe ongoing. McAllister and Schmitt deny all knowledge of extra return cargo. Schmitt getting back with more info? Mystery man Diez a Mexican — interesting . . . No reply necessary or even desired. BW'

On the side of the angels, as ever.

8

He'd started working out in the local gym, with its overcrowded cardio equipment and its tattooed shaven-headed heavies. He was adding a plate on the free weights bar when he was struck by an unattractive thought.

He skipped the sauna, went straight home on grumbling legs and googled 'Celandine House' and 'For Sale'.

There it was. He wiped his face with the towel and felt almost clever.

'Breathtaking', 'distinguished', 'resplendent', 'rural'. He thought 'resplendent' was a touch exaggerated, while 'breathtaking' was simply untrue. 'Rural' was technically correct, but the photo failed to show the overlit access road to the estate, let alone the hum of the A4103. The orchard, exposed beams and mature garden were 'features'. The price was disappointingly low.

She had jumped the gun. Although the court was fully expected to approve their amicable settlement as a result of AIDS — aviation-induced divorce syndrome — this broke the rules. No wonder she'd wanted his 'junk' out of the place.

However reasonably he broached the subject of the premature sale, she would scream at him. Then he remembered that he was seeing her anyway in two days' time. He would turn up without a hired van and do some broaching. The house must be withdrawn until the settlement was approved, or they would find themselves in a legal quagmire. If she refused, he would call his solicitor.

★ ★ ★

He rolled up in the Healey at the appointed time late on Saturday morning. There was no FOR SALE notice in sight. He was nervous, had chosen his clothes with care — smart jeans, new leather jacket — and brushed his teeth. He was going to be up close and personal and he realised this might be the last time ever. She'd stolen his heart and wouldn't give it back.

She had never treated him as captain, like everyone else. Not even when she was cabin crew (he wasn't a skipper then, but it would have been the same). And Olivia liked to wear the stripes — all four of them. It was relaxing for Bob. He could come home and be ribbed, no longer in charge, no longer responsible; this was probably why, in the long list of her grievances, she cited his 'absent-mindedness'. Or was he just exhausted, his night become day, and vice-versa? He liked her joshing him, knocking off his captain's cap; it was touching, the way she sighed at his inability to hang out his washing correctly. It made him feel close to her, because she wasn't bothering to pretend in front of him. In front of others, she was completely joined up: the perfect hostess from hors d'oeuvre to crumble; the svelte boutique owner; the elegant mother at the school play. Immaculate even in gardening gloves. Pan

Am training, for God's sake.

The day was greyish, but not gloomy. Someone on the newish estate — more visible now the curtain of leaves had fallen, and the fruit trees were bare — was strimming his no doubt impeccable verges, hedge, leylandii, whatever. Either Olivia had got a new car or hers was in the garage and there was a visitor: a bright-red hatchback disturbed the overall effect of breathtaking, rural, and resplendent.

He looked briefly at the orchard: the late apples were bright red or golden spots in a kind of chaparral of branches, while the purple-blue damsons had all been picked. There was the same fur of moss on the old stone bollard surviving at one end of the brick-laid antique terrace at the back of the house. The other bollard had been nicked just before bilingual Luke came along. Maybe it was now in Montreal.

He stroked the moss, lost in his thoughts. All of a sudden Olivia appeared, looking slightly younger if anything: perhaps because she'd let her hair grow out, styled to curl on her umbilical neck. He felt like a trespasser.

'Where's the white van?'

'Being treated for white van syndrome.'

'Unfunny.'

'I'll explain inside. Over a cup of coffee?'

'Uh-oh,' she said, turning on her heel and leading him through the French windows at the back, her desirability enhanced by a long black clinging cotton sweater, her slim legs going on for ever in tight black trousers. Maybe she was

193

planning his funeral.

He was careful to remove his shoes, as she had a thing about that. The rear sitting room was bereft of the African art he'd brought back from his trips: bronze statues with exaggerated breasts or lifelike penises; masks with nasty teeth; naughty ivory. All gone — he assumed waiting for the white van. He found himself hovering instead of plonking down, as though he needed permission. He was a guest in his own house. It was still his own house. But the smell had changed: different wood in the fireplace? The low ceiling was whiter between the beams. Of course: the house was on show.

He followed her into the kitchen, about to ask whether she'd changed her car.

A man was at the sink, filling the electric kettle: the man said *hello-o* over his shoulder, in a way that was a mixture of friendly, terrified and contemptuous, then plugged the kettle in, wiggling the dicky connection Bob had never quite solved. For a moment he felt physically nauseous: the intruder wiggled it in the same way. At first Bob thought the man was in his early thirties, as the jet-black hair — clearly dyed — had a youthful, even boyish cut, and he wore jeans with zips in peculiar places and a T-shirt that said *Sorry, not in service*. But his face had the crumpled, used look of someone a lot older. Around Olivia's age, Bob guessed: late forties.

'This is Ben,' she said. 'He teaches in Tewkesbury.'

'And I'm Bob, obviously. What do you teach?'

'Art, mainly.'

'Oh, right. A bit rough, Tewkesbury?'

'Kids are manageable. It's the parents're the problem.'

He sounded as though he'd spent years chipping away at a posh accent: the result was unconvincing. He opened the dishwasher and began loading it — wrongly, of course. Bowls where the plates should go, sharp knives pointing upwards, thirsting for wrists. They'd clearly had a late breakfast. The two of them. Bob inwardly winced as Ben slotted in a side plate crookedly.

'You paint as well as teach?'

'Nah, more video art.'

Bob nodded, not being up with the times when it came to art, and changed the subject to apples.

'Bumper crop,' said Olivia.

'Really fantastic,' said Ben, dropping a teaspoon into the dishwasher's belly and not retrieving it. He was clumsy.

'Like last year,' added Olivia.

Bob felt the bumper crops were tied up with his two-year absence, so he didn't comment. Instead, he thrust his hands into his leather jacket's pockets and talked about the weather, as one does when inwardly bothered. His right hand found the Makarov, which he'd completely forgotten about, and he let it lie. He tended not to go out, now, without his old companion.

Long ago, Bob had made the mistake of taking the kids, aged six, into Pratley's, Worcester's well-known china shop: the plates were stacked up in leaning towers down narrow passage-ways, cups and jugs had elbow-ready handles sticking out. The present conversation reminded him of those twenty minutes in the treasure trove of Pratley's: nothing broken, in the end, but only by sheer luck.

All the time he knew that it was utterly finished between Olivia and himself, for here was the new boyfriend. No last-minute pulling up, after all. The boyfriend taught art and would not have much money. He was connecting with Olivia's creative side and no doubt her bank account, too — enjoying the cash that Bob had earned most of through day after night of often tricky flying. While he was facing down colonels of profoundly violent tendencies in some unfortunate part of the world, or struggling to find an unmarked strip in dense jungle with, say, a couple of armed Pilatus Porter bush planes out to shoot him down, this other man was running an art lesson in Tewkesbury, his biggest headache how to stop Darren flicking paint at Cindy.

They would suit Shropshire, Bob kept thinking: a small-holding, long walks, hens.

He thought he was being pretty agreeable. Olivia drew him into the back room on their own, to talk stuff over. She asked him why he was being so 'hostile'. Bob wobbled his head, bewildered. 'Going on about how you never did any art,' she added.

'I didn't do any. You know why? I was distracted by the newspapers they covered the tables with, especially *Titbits*. It seemed more interesting than in the kiosk.'

'He's just a friend,' she went on. 'He's not my lover.'

'Oh, that's a relief.'

'Bob, I don't think you've got the point. We're separated. I've my own life and can do what I like with it. Stop judging me. Ben's wife died of cancer two years ago and he's struggling. His videos are really landscapes — they're beautiful, light changing on fields and woods, that kind of thing. They're not what you think.'

'I didn't think anything.'

'No, I don't suppose you did. Now, where's the white van?'

He squared his shoulders. 'I'm not about to move my stuff anywhere until the court has approved the settlement. Meanwhile, I think it'd be a lot more sensible if you took our house off the market.' Supposing Olivia died of cancer? He would be more than 'struggling'.

She looked startled for a moment. He explained that he had looked on Google and was a touch surprised. She scoffed, saying it took ages to sell anything, the market was crap, the settlement was all but signed and sealed. She was just getting a bit of headway. They'd had very few people round to look. Bob could hear Ben doing useful things in the kitchen. Maybe he was getting his paints out. No, tripod and camera. Bob stood and looked out on the garden and the orchard: pure autumnal gold. The lawn felt bereft without the kids running about squealing. But that was years ago. From about fourteen to when they'd left for uni, they'd sat indoors mostly, in front of screens.

'You haven't sold my African art, have you?'

'Of course not. It's in boxes upstairs. Ben's

been really helpful.'

'Ben? I hope he's not been handling my stuff.'

'Bob, if you think I can hump it all about on my own, given my back problems . . . And your study was a complete tip, papers covered in dust.'

'If he's been in my study, that's probably illegal.'

She put on a pained expression. It was then that he reminded himself, heart hammering as it was, that she'd become very skilled at provoking. He decided to split as soon as he could.

'I'd better check the study, then go,' he said.

'We've not thrown anything away,' she reassured him, which made him even crosser. She folded her arms and he was surprised at the sharpness of the elbows against the loose-sleeved sweater; on the other hand, he'd always thought her weak point was their boniness.

'No, but there are private papers, bank dossiers, letters. And fragile things.'

'He's not the type to snoop, for God's sake. He's just helping out. I'm on my own.'

'That was your choice.'

'Can't you sit down?'

'We had a good life, Olivia.'

'With you away most of the time, me holding the fort?'

'Someone had to earn the serious money.'

'You certainly did that,' she said, nodding slowly and knowingly, making her long coppery earrings shiver. They were new: these days she never wore the big chunky malachite ones he'd brought back from the Congo.

He frowned. 'Pardon me?' And could feel the pull of the current, everything heading for Niagara Falls.

'You certainly did earn the money,' she said. 'In every which way.'

'What the hell do you mean by that?'

She shook her head slowly and looked to the side — a movement which usually went with a faraway air of infinite sadness. Decoded, it meant, *Game over*. She could go off-signal for an hour afterwards: all day, sometimes.

'Olivia, I hope you're not implying something about my job.'

She raised her eyebrows slightly. That's exactly what she was doing. Never in their whole life together had she implied such a thing. Ben next door was now breaking plates, it sounded like, as if to remind them of his presence. The family plates, purchased from Pratley's.

'Since most of the money's a result of that job,' he said, only his eyes keeping above the flames, 'then you'd better return it, if you're having qualms.'

Of course that was a silly thing to say. She told him to get out of the house. He said what about the pots of wimberry jam, or was that another broken promise? She said he didn't even deserve the damson (of which she always made too much, with annoying little rock-hard stones that had once broken one of Bob's fillings).

He insisted on seeing the study — a small room under the eaves with a step down to it.

He went upstairs with both of them yelling, she from the hall, he over his shoulder as he climbed. He expected the door to be locked, somehow, but it wasn't. Instead, the curtains were drawn.

'Jesus Christ,' he shouted.

Everything was boxed up in the gloom, except for the African pieces, which were dotted about looking very resentful and bad-tempered, his favourite mask from Cameroon scowling at him from the top of a Costcutter carton.

What did he expect? That this room in which he'd spent so many years happily working on his accounts, writing letters, calculating nautical miles flown, dreaming of building a biplane (life-size, not a model), would stay intact, like a museum? He didn't even like museums. They gave him the willies. Then, drawing the curtains for daylight, he noticed a small black bin-liner, stuffed to the gills but still open at the top. Junk from the look of it — the kind of glossy dross that slips out of the newspaper, offering lawnmowers or laser eye ops or whatever — but at some point he must have thought it would be useful. He shouted again and would have sat down but there was nowhere to sit.

This room contained his life. Melodramatic, but it was how he felt. Its total volume was a tiny corner in the average cargo bay; you would hardly have noticed it. This was it. What it all came down to. Over twenty years of marriage. His peak years.

The mask went on scowling at him. He used to plant a cheroot between its serrated teeth — the twins would scream with laughter. He used to light the cheroot, imitate the voice of the mask in a broad cockney. Well, they did like that. They certainly did. He smoked a lot of cheroots back in those days — even in the cockpit, waiting for the ramp agent, his feet up on the instrument panel like a cowboy. He was notorious for that: the ramp agents would tell each other, *The guy smokes cheroots in the cockpit — it's so cool, it's like a film!* Good ol' McAl bought him a Stetson in Dallas to complete the show, which really wowed them. He was a character: he cheered them up.

He stumbled downstairs to Olivia somewhere behind her crossed arms and Ben furtively having a fag at the open back door. Bob didn't like furtiveness, so he shouted a bit more and then Ben interrupted him: 'I told you; I told you it was the wrong thing to do, Liv.'

Bob frowned. 'Liv? That's your old name.'

'Yup,' she said.

'Jesus.'

She insisted that the stuff Ben had chucked was 'literally junk'; Ben started to confirm this gently from the back door; Bob said that his — Ben's — videos were probably junk but he wouldn't dream of touching them; Ben objected and stabbed the air in Bob's direction with his cigarette, then the doorbell went before they could come to physical blows.

They all froze, then Bob said, in a moment of inspiration, 'That's OK. I'll get it. It's still my house.'

Olivia started to move but Bob moved faster. She was not far behind him in the hall when he opened the door on an attractive young woman in a natty grey suit, holding an attaché case. She beamed at him, sparkly eyed, and said in a sing-song voice, 'Hello, Mr and Mrs Winrush? It's Wendy from Perfect Locations. Sorry I'm a bit late.'

'Bad timing,' Bob pointed out. 'We're having a flaming row. Really sorry to have wasted your time. And it's *Captain* Winrush. And this is Liv.'

Wendy was startled, lost her smile. Bob shut the door on her. Olivia said he had no right to do that and made for the door. Bob blocked her like a bouncer, with crossed arms. Olivia asked Ben to intervene, but Ben waved the dishcloth about like a surrender flag, saying he'd rather not. As the gravel signalled that Wendy was heading off, Olivia said, 'Ben, you're a wimp.'

'Yeah? End up getting shot?

Bob frowned. 'Who says I'm armed?'

'Your reputation goes before you,' said Olivia. 'He's absolutely right. What you're doing is totally illegal.'

'What am I doing?'

'Carrying a gun around. This isn't Florida.'

'Unbelievable,' said Bob. He would have said more, but his mobile went off. It was David's number. A text. Despite the circumstances, the first few visible words made Bob scroll down the rest.

'What's really unbelievable is that you're more interested in your mobile than anything else,' Olivia scoffed.

'That's mobiles for you,' said Ben. 'My students are just the same.'

Bob held up his hand, as if for quiet.

Olivia gave a snort. 'Is that an order, Captain Winrush?'

'He's gone chalk-white,' Ben pointed out.

Bob blinked at them, still holding up a hand. The two of them had folded arms, like bouncers. 'Got to go. Sorry. You'll be hearing from Jenkins, I suppose, the solicitor.'

He spat gravel and on the sharp bend nearly went into a knot of primary kids coming back to the estate from judo or whatever: Kirsty, Aidan and Lisa — he did recognise them, just. Sophie had babysat two of them when she was about fourteen. He stopped in a services and read the text again, then replied to it thus: 'A helluva shock. Don't do ANYTHING till we talk this evening. I'll phone u. LOL Dad xx' He saw his hands were trembling on the Formica. He could do nothing about it. But it could all have been so much worse: he might have skidded into the kids.

★ ★ ★

He had made a decision, at least. Back in the flat, fuelled with a Scotch, he phoned Al on his busy mobile; he didn't think the landline would be a good idea. It was on message. He told Al to call him back, urgent.

There was nothing about Sharansky on the net. Not yet. Bob could hardly believe it: the man was the kind of sparking live wire you couldn't grab, let alone cut. The news should have come as a kind of relief, but Bob had human feelings and behind it loomed a lot of night fog: questions, questions. It might just have been an accident: Polish driving. Lack of motorways. Long, straight, narrow roads where lorries swerved to avoid potholes, especially fun when someone was overtaking the other way. Bob'd had a white-knuckle ride or two in Poland.

He double-checked the chamber of the Makarov and went out to the nearest less-loud pub; wearing through the carpet in the flat was safer, maybe, but did similar damage to his nerves. His son phoned while Bob was absently watching football spread-eagled across a massive flat-screen.

Outside, shivering in the November gusts and choking in the smokers' downwind pall, Bob listened as David told him that no one knew the details, but it was hit-and-run. Matt Sharansky wasn't in a car, it seemed, but walking along the road. No info yet on the car that did it, but the area had been quiet.

'Near the arms factory?'

'According to Google Earth, about half a mile away.'

'Near enough. Which way was he walking, away or towards?'

'We don't know, Dad. We're pretty shaken up.'

'People do get run over, especially in Poland. Was it at night?'

'Very early in the morning. No one saw it; he was just found on the verge with the right kind of injuries. He was facing the vehicle, they reckon. The police aren't necessarily treating it as suspicious, though, as it happens quite a lot:

drunks and stuff. Our campaign colleagues in Israel are dealing with his computer before Mossad or whoever get to it. They'll send us the files by email. They've got some problem with his computer's password. Not even his boyfriend knows it.'

'*Boyfriend?* Are you sure?'

'Yeah. A problem, Dad?'

'Nope. Nope.'

'And his mobile's missing.'

'Oh.'

'Yeah, that's a drag. He did a lot of texting, maybe the kind of thing you wouldn't want enemies to see.'

'David, can I ask you to voluntarily retire from this operation?'

'No, you can't.'

'I could try really hard over some nosh tomorrow. The Healey could make it by midday. Will you be up? I know you're on Australian time. Name your restaurant.'

David agreed, almost with alacrity. Anything for a free lunch. 'By the way, Dad — '

An explosion of laughter from the smokers drowned out the rest of the sentence. Bob asked his son to repeat it.

'I said, by the way, Dad, whatever did you say to Mum this morning, exactly?'

'Crikey, that was quick.'

* * *

From their teenage years, the twins had been switched off from his professional life. Whenever

Bob came back from what Al would call a scrotum-tightening ops and try to tell them about it (emphasising the part of the cargo that had pacifist credentials), their eyes would glaze over or flicker back to the screen. After the SBO, or seriously bad ops, in the Central African Republic, from which he returned physically intact but with his nerves neatly diced, he would wake up from nightmares making a bit of a noise, and that had to be explained away, as did his temporary hand-tremble. But the twins were somewhere else in their heads, dealing with the tricky approach to the big-time airport of adulthood, for which there was no flight plan, evening class, nothing. He concealed it pretty well, took the pills, and Olivia actually did a grand job. She was a natural nurse and confidante, although he'd given her a Cert U version of it all, no worse than the TV news.

It was soon after the SBO, in recovery mode, that he'd tried his hand at being a normal person with the disabled-equipment firm. During the holidays, fifteen-year-old Sophie took to staying out late, driven about by lads who hadn't yet spotted the difference between Worcestershire lanes and the M1 (probably because they were stoned at the time), while David justified the school fees by being able to grunt in several languages and taking up the drums. They weathered all this together, as parents do; he had gone back to flying, but given up on the jungle strips, or at least avoided places like the Congo or CAR unless it was tarmac plus tower. If he occasionally carried cargo with a brown envelope attached, it was mainly because the plane had been commandeered by the local psychopath in khaki.

Once, getting back from one of these hotter legs into a March downpour that soaked him as he removed his luggage from the boot and ran into the house, he found David slumped in front of his PlayStation on the main telly in the back sitting room, legs stretched out longer than ever.

'Hi, David. Where's Mum?'

'Out shopping wi' Sophe.'

His son had barely looked up, twiddling his way out of what looked like an SS ambush in a winter pine forest, snow sliding off the branches like lumps of plaster.

Instead of acting all sad and grumpy, Bob slumped down with him, hair dripping, collar wet, and they had a whale of a time on two controls. But the decent father did come down with a heck of a cold.

He thought of that moment now, getting ready for bed: they were in this one together, but it wasn't a video game. Al hadn't got back. The journalist's mobile was missing. Bob reread the text he had sent to that phone. It mentioned the crew by name. When he thought about who might have eliminated Sharansky, he saw a crowd of shadowy figures. Bensoussan was in there, with his knees instead of balls or balls instead of knees, but there were a lot of others, too. The whole lot vaguely looking in his direction.

★　★　★

'Bob? Got y' message. Whassup?'

'Israeli journalist, Al. No longer with us. Hit-and-run in Radom.'

'Christ. The long arm of Mossad, no doubt. That's got us out of a pickle.'

'Ten green bottles, Al.'

'Och, c'mon. The guy was a meddler. You tried to warn him off, no?'

'Correct. But the others are carrying on.'

'What? Carrying on what? Who else have they got?' Al sounded alarmed.

'I mean his campaigning mates. The anti-arms lot over here. David's involved with one of the groups.'

'Warn him off, skipper.'

'Al, you sound worried.'

'Not half as bloody worried as you do!'

Bob took a deep breath. He had made the decision, he should stick to it. It was all for the best. 'That's because our Podgorica jaunt is bound to be on Sharansky's computer. David will read all about it. I don't want to lose David, like I'm losing Olivia.'

'Our Podgorica jaunt? Which one?'

'Anti-personnel mines to Somaliland. Among other nicer stuff.'

'Your sloppiest landing ever? At Berbera? And just about the longest bloody runway in Africa? That the one?'

'If you say so, Al. It was very hot and shimmery.'

'How do you know it's on this fucker's computer? Sorry, Jane. I'm moving into my study. We were in the middle of *Mad Men*, but it's a DVD. I'm in the study. Now tell me all, Bob.'

Bob did not tell all: he said that he knew Sharansky was writing a piece about the landmine flight; he did not say Sharansky had been blackmailing him with it, forcing him to probe.

'Wear flares, grow your hair long, swing your beads,' Al chuckled.

'You're about thirty-five years out of date, Al.'

'What I mean is: everything comes round again, skipper. What else is on that computer?' he asked airily.

'Well, the Turkmenbashi flight, obviously. Outbound and inbound. Of great interest to the late man, as you know.'

There was an audible sigh. 'So he was using the Berbera flight to force you to probe your old loyal crewmate from Fife about the Turkmenbashi caper.'

'Don't be crazy, Al.'

There was a short pause in which the flat's walls seemed to close in on hydraulic pistons. A blackbird was hopping on the wet lawn, pulling worms. Al was always quick in emergencies; it was easy to underestimate his mental agility.

Al said, 'We were empty on the return. I've told you till I'm blue in the face.'

'Are you blue in the face now?' said Bob with a smile to it.

'No, I'm red. Red with fucking resentment. That maybe someone planted a packet of snow on my flight, without my knowledge.'

'You know what, Al? I talked to Hans Schmitt.

Interesting. And Pedro Diez is Mexican.'

'You mean it might have been them? Bastards.'

'You don't always choose your crew. Like siblings. But then, I'm an only child. I think we should meet up. Talk strategy.'

'What did Schmitt say?'

'Nothing,' said Bob. 'It was the tone. The hesitation. Or maybe it was just a bad line.'

'Look, I've got to go trim the syringa. Jane's hands are bad today. It comes and goes. She's being tested for Lyme disease. It's in fashion.'

'I thought she had fybromalgia or whatever it's called,' said Bob, discreetly tapping 'MATT SHARANSKY' into Google.

'Well now, don't go busting yourself with sympathy, will you, skipper?'

Reuters, repeated in various newspapers: 'Israeli journalist dies in hit and run'. So it was true; he now believed it. It was the same when his father died: the brief obituary in the *Daily Telegraph* made him believe it. The report said nothing he didn't know, but he knew more than the report. There was no mention of Sharansky's mission, just that he was in Radom, home of a major weapons factory, 'investigating illicit arms deals', and that the police had not ruled out murder.

'Bob? Are you still there? Can you hear me?'

'Loud and clear, as ever, Al.'

The guy knew the places to get the best hot chocolate in Paris, and he'd taken this with him to the grave.

9

Since his gap year, mostly idled away in South America, David was bearded; at least, an irregular growth of dark hair fringed his jaw and chin. He also wore a shapeless hat. Now an earring had been added, and a silver piercing in the side of his nose.

'Bet you a fiver you've got a tattoo.'

'Can't afford it. Next birthday present, if Mum lets me.'

'Or Dad lets you.'

'Yeah, well.'

Bob had nipped up in the Healey, or would have nipped if the traffic hadn't congealed around Risinghurst. Manchester, he thought, looked more and more like a Lego version of Dubai. In the cheerful Thai restaurant, they were struggling. The move to Shropshire came up.

'Even deader than Worcestershire,' said David. 'Average age about seventy.'

'Have you met the art teacher yet?'

'Her new bloke?'

'Oh, she denied it,' Bob said, crestfallen. 'Just a friend.'

'Dad, you're so naive.'

'She seemed very sincere.'

'Anyway,' David said, 'it's nothing to do with me.'

Bob grimaced, staring at his giant glass in which a quarter of a bottle of red was nestling at the bottom. 'Nor me, really. Except when he touches my things.'

'Hands off my toys,' said David, with a nervous smile.

'You bet.'

Bob stopped himself mentioning the study, the bin bag, the African art. He'd flown with pilots who couldn't resist telling you, and if you were flying Europe and doing all four legs with them, the same stuff would come round and round and in exactly the same order. Like being trapped in a bad marriage. He felt so cross about the fact that Olivia had lied to him concerning her lover but had said something else to their son — and Sophie too, no doubt — that he couldn't actually speak. He was crosser about the lie than about the bloody boyfriend himself. It broke the rules. It was hidden stuff. He hated hidden stuff.

There was a silence. Bob looked up from his crab. David was frowning over his pak choi. Bob felt a pulse of love that cleared his chest, relaxed his vocal cords.

'Any more news on Sharansky, David?'

David looked relieved at the change of subject. 'Yeah, they've done the autopsy, according to his brother. Basically, judging from the tyre marks on his legs, they're looking for a four-wheel drive. With a dent in the bonnet, where his forehead hit. He was facing the vehicle, they reckon, which is why his pancreas split open and he kind of jackknifed down face first. Maybe he thought it was someone he was supposed to meet.'

Bob pulled a face. It wasn't quite real. David

212

could only talk like that, paradoxically, because he *hadn't* seen folk split open, bits cut off, all the rest. 'The thing is, David, I had a brief and friendly chat with him, poor guy, and found he'd got it all wrong. He was investigating a flight that I had actually *walked out on*. I walked out on it precisely because the job was dodgy.'

'Not evil?'

'Dodgy and evil, I guess. Didn't like the smell of it. Can't say more. Anyway, I didn't fly the plane on that leg. Snag is, it's usually more dangerous to walk out than to stay in. You're no longer in their debt.'

'Were you ever bribed, Dad?'

'What?'

'He reckons you were bribed. To do certain flights.'

Bob smiled. 'Wrong term, bad journalism. A pilot's price goes up if the chance of his dying goes up. Fair enough. But I don't want to speak ill of the dead. Seriously, I liked the guy. He'd have made a good future prime minister for Israel, in a nicer world.'

David nodded. He seemed uncomfortable.

'The thing is, my campaign colleagues reckon you know who might have done him in.'

Bob frowned and shook his head. His son was looking at him furtively. Olivia's clear green eyes. 'David, I was a cargo pilot. I carried everything.'

'*A complete mixture*,' said David, miming quote marks with his forefingers.

Bob felt a rush of dismay. 'Well, it was. Let me finish. If you're a passenger pilot, it's the same: you carry a complete cross-section of human

213

society, good, bad and indifferent. Cargo's what? Aardvarks to zips with mostly junk in between.'

'Junk?'

'Been shopping recently? OK, exaggeration, but a cargo pilot just carries cargo, full stop.'

'Wow, Dad. That's such breaking news.'

Why had he chosen crab? You had to concentrate, or you couldn't extract the flesh from the fiddly bits. And it wasn't even good crab, it was thawed out and tasteless. In his mind's eye, he saw a huge bright-red crab being lifted from the belly of a pirogue in the Wouri estuary, the grinning fisherman in his loincloth, and remembered the spitting fire they cooked it on, that lovely burning stench of Africa that sits on the tongue.

'You didn't *have* to do all that stuff in African war zones,' David said, who'd always had a tendency to read his father's thoughts. 'You and Al the McAl. Mum reckons he was a bad influence. I was too young to realise. Now I realise.'

'Al was my flight engineer. Mum found him a bit large and rough, that's all. He saved my life at least twice. Look, I loved Africa. Loved it, most of the time. Not all the time. But you can't love anything all the time. It was grown-up flying. Remember what we called a long-haul passenger plane?'

'A boredom tube,' said David, as if bored.

'Exactly. Actually, I never found it that boring. Other people like an office to sit in, I like a cockpit with nothing but sky outside. However, give me a bush airstrip of compacted earth that's about 300 yards too short and a couple of mountains to chew on, and I'm really happy. I miss it. There were these cholera vaccinations that had to be got in kind of urgent and I put my hand up. That was well paid, but bloody difficult, fog and too many trees. Saved a few lives. Maybe thousands. The locals crowding round you. It's whatever comes up. Sometimes of course it's military.'

'So you've always told us, Dad.'

'But it happens to be true!'

The trouble with families is that they say the same things to each other over and over.

David looked up properly. 'You know what you did say once, when I asked you what the weirdest cargo you ever carried was?'

'Live dolphins swaying in that clapped-out DC-8 to Brazil? Those two little baby gorillas in a Seneca, really cute, and two years later I had to fly them back to Stuttgart, now full-size and grumpy, in a 747?'

'It was only one gorilla going back.'

'Of course.'

'No. You said, *I could tell you but then I'd have to shoot you.*'

Bob chuckled unconvincingly. 'Did I?'

'Yup.'

'That was just to impress your mates.'

'I was on my own.'

'I'm sure I said it with a smile. Aviation humour.'

'Yeah, it was really joky.'

Bob abandoned his crab. The debris was about three times the volume of the original. He scanned the room: mostly the next table, very long, full of loud teenage girls apparently dressed for a Honolulu beach. He felt the weight of his Makarov under his shirt: he'd now got it holstered at the waist, but didn't like the feel. At least he'd got it pointing away from his penis. You could never quite trust a pistol.

'I've got another one, David. Bloke says to his wife, 'Hey, do you know what the milkman just told me? He said he's had it away with every woman in our street — bar one, of course.' 'Oh,' says the wife, 'that'll be the old bag up at number seventeen.''

David couldn't help smiling. 'Changing the subject, yeah.'

Bob sighed, leaned back, wiped his mouth. 'Look, the irony is, I was trying to help him, our over-keen Sharansky. The proof is on his mobile, which you said was missing. I was an idiot. I sent him a text, with names.'

'Uh-oh.'

'Yup. That may mean I'm a target. For whoever wants this thing to go quiet.'

'Seriously? You really helped him?'

'In a minor way. I liked the guy. But what I would truly like, David, is for you to totally disengage yourself from this particular job. If you don't disengage, I'll be in far more danger. Never mind your good self. Like father, like son. Ten green bottles. Two down already.'

'Two?'

'One, the crooked agent overseeing that crap flight. Two, poor Matt Sharansky. Unusual, where arms deals are concerned, but this flight

216

was not the usual arms deal.'

David's eyes were shining. The wrong tack. He had no idea, not deep inside him, just how final death was. You didn't get a second chance.

'Dad, what was this flight really about?'

Bob waved a dismissive hand, immensely relieved: either they hadn't yet got into Sharansky's files, or the guy had been sensibly cautious with his software. 'Just don't go there, David. Look, they broke into the Dubai apartment and nicked my logbook and diary. The evidence, in other words. No copies my end. They pretended to throw me off my balcony.'

'Seriously?'

'That's their style. Don't tell Mum or Sophie, OK? But these guys were satisfied — they were leaving me in peace. Basically, that type understands that a cargo pilot is not very interested in his cargo, even when he actually flies the ops. All you need to know is some technical stuff. Whether the chloroform is in a proper medical pack. Whether the aerosols or the propane or the radioactive junk are all in separate sealed crates. Whether the tiger isn't next to a ton of dry ice, which would kill it. Remember the hippo?'

David nodded. He used to be young enough to love the stories.

Bob leaned forward, dropped his voice: 'But they've got Sharansky's mobile. I'm compromised. Now, as long as your friends don't stir, and they let the trail go dead, I'm probably OK. If they carry on stirring, the nasty guys are going to get fidgety again.'

'I'm just a foot soldier: I've no say in the campaign directives. And I don't suppose they're going to let it go dead.'

David looked genuinely sorry. Or maybe alarmed. It was hard to tell behind his youthful mask, his scanty beard, his new piercings.

'Thought so. One major request, though: don't give anyone my Crowthorne address. Not ever. It's below the radar, as you know.'

The candles were blown out and mobiles flashed. At least one party girl was filming. Bob discreetly covered his face. Next thing, he'd be up on Facebook, YouTube, visible to all the world. Everything porous.

'You OK, David?'

His son was biting his lip. Unhappy about something. But then he'd been like that since puberty: thinnish, round-shouldered, did no exercise beyond the occasional kick-around. The glum waitress came and cleared away their plates. David took a gulp from his glass, his face tiny behind it.

'Look,' said Bob, 'if you have actually gone and given your friends my address, please tell me. It's OK, I'm not going to disown you. I don't bear grudges.'

His son snorted, for some reason.

Bob frowned. 'Do you think I bear grudges?'

'Nope.'

'But you snorted.'

'I was thinking about something else,' David said, turning his dessert spoon into a discreet drumstick, tapping his other hand, looking away at nothing. 'Like, the kids dismembered by the

218

landmines you flew from Serbia? Whether they bear grudges?'

'Remind me which flight.'

'Pod-something. To Berbera, Somaliland. With famous Al the McAl. The landmines were carried by truck into the main conflict zone in Somalia.'

Bob nodded, thinking a little before responding. 'Sharansky told you? Yup, well, he had a thing about it. Podgorica in sunny Montenegro. The kit would have been done up in bubble wrap and crated, then winched into a huge container. All we'd have known was that the mixed cargo, tons of it, contained dangerous goods. Explosives for a mining operation, maybe. I probably flew similar stuff for the Brits, because back then landmines were legit cargo. Still are legit, if they're for training. Somaliland was building its own state and security structures — heroically, I'd say. Maybe it needed landmines. The hold also contained lots of tents and medical gear.'

'For the victims,' David said, frowning at him. 'In Somalia. Arms traffickers' heaven. Matt acquired copies of the delivery papers in Mogadishu: not the safest job. He traced it from A to Z.'

Bob took a sip of his wine: violets, harsh back taste. 'The Swiss make weapons. And the Swiss make medicines and they make raclette and they run the Red Cross. Life is a bundle of different wires.'

That Berbera flight had paid for a term at the twins' school, but Bob didn't tell him that. The girls were leaving; one stumbled against his chair and blew him a kiss.

'Cocaine,' David said, watching them prance off in a storm of laughter.

'Really?'

'The password was e-x-p-l-o-d-e-d, by the way. Brilliant, for a peacenik. Matt's boyfriend finally remembered — there'd been some kind of joke about it. We received the files early this morning, by email. Lots of stuff about landmines, I'm afraid.'

'He and I had a deal,' Bob murmured.

'Yeah. You said. But they want to put it up on the campaign's online broadsheet, as a memorial. While the news is still hot. It's what he'd planned, anyway. But it's not exactly a scoop.'

Bob had to wave the waitress away — bad timing on her part. His heart was now being beaten by his own lead pipe. 'Am I named, David? He said I wouldn't be if I helped. And I was a major help.'

David looked away again, the spoon tapping faster. 'I asked them not to. But there we go. I'm a tiny student cog in the overall machine. No one'll read it, anyway. It's kind of really exclusive? For anti-arms nerds only.'

'But every time someone googles me, it'll come up.'

'It might. But that's the Internet for you.' He threw the spoon on the table, sat back and put his hands behind his head, clearly feeling awkward.

'Hatches, matches and dispatches,' said Bob.

'Isn't that what they call the births, deaths and marriages page?'

David shrugged. 'No one'll read it,' he repeated, as the waitress began to clear the wreckage left by the birthday treat. 'Seriously, Dad. Forget about it.'

'I'll try to. There's never any nuance in these things. No time for nuance, not these days.'

They ordered coconut cake for both of them: Olivia's speciality, once. Hers was so much better, of course. They agreed on that, and Bob did feel good, being nice about Olivia, the person who had thrown him out of his own home.

An idea occurred to him, in the same vein.

'Hey, David. Let's do a similar deal with your pals.'

'What?'

'I'll help them. Consultancy work. This way I'm a bit more in control. You can send me what they write up, each time, and I'll do a preflight checklist on it. Add info, if they want. I've a good power of recall.'

'Isn't that dangerous?'

'It's me making the decisions. I choose what to add. And I don't like inaccuracies. This way we're part of the same crew. They won't kick me, then. You don't kick a member of your own crew. You can give them my email, but not my address or number. All they have to do is to remove my name from that report on the landmine flight to Berbera. Or add a line about me being ignorant of the contents. Which is true. Otherwise, no deal.'

'Ah. Well, I'll see.'

'Tomorrow, David, if poss. Before I pass on from my temporary Gandhi phase into the Saddam period. Before the germ proliferates.'

'Like weapons do.'

'Meanwhile,' Bob soldiered on, 'you've got to promise me to have nothing to do with the Turkmenbashi business. *Nyet*. Zero. Or you may well be attending my funeral pretty soon. That's not a joke, by the way.'

David nodded, the bead in his nose flashing in the halogen spot that had revealed too much about the food. 'You're having me on, Dad.'

''Fraid not. Hear it from the source. The world out there is full of people who just want to pour acid into the spring water of life.'

★ ★ ★

The moment he got home, he cleared the laptop of anything potentially toxic: mostly emails referring to ops that smelt of illicit procurement or clandestine activities. Alerted by the Sharansky affair, HM Revenue and Customs might trawl through the machine, as was their right, and read 'hunting-rifle sights' as sniper scopes, 'NGBs' as naughty green boxes full of AK-47S, 'DGs not quite as per CM' as dangerous goods not quite as per enclosed cargo manifest, 'SAS' as second amendment science aka guns, 'lambies' as landmines, and so on and so forth. It was a freight dog's ongoing correspondence, a mutual warning system, virtual close-protection work. He didn't want to cop two years for export control violations, especially over that little rash of flights from Bratislava to Tehran in 2005, carrying 25,000 kilos of rotary drilling-rig spare parts and, he suspected, some sanctions-busting weaponry. Never probe, was his motto.

An email winged in as he was finishing: Timothy Sightly, AAW, Action Against Weapons, Manchester branch. Polite. 'David mentioned . . . discretion . . . dodgy people . . . it's a deal.'

Each such email from AAW would look good, Bob thought, if it ever came to it. It was a message from the big dice-thrower on high: turn over a new leaf, land somewhere new. No choice: you've only got one engine.

He saved all the toxic stuff on his memory stick and kept it on him. He did feel better after the hose-out. But he was worried about David. The young were so reckless.

And then, because the screen was lit and he was bored, he called up houses for sale on Scourlay, the Outer Hebrides, with 'a real rarity' in double quotes. It hit the target straight-away. Sherbet again tingled in Bob's chest as he scrolled through the description, the photos. Ex-smuggler's croft, he noted with a smile.

A life change. Divorcees in their fifties had a right to be reckless. He went out for an evening jog through misty streets whose orange sodium lamps made him feel exposed, as though in a stadium. All he could think about was Leila's breasts. He failed to understand why he hadn't just sat it out in Dubai. Her solid, silky rump. Squeezing his juice, as she called it. Her laughter.

He texted her on his return, suggestively, and

223

the response came within minutes: 'Wot's all thick and swollen? Your head? Then take an aspirin. L.'

★ ★ ★

The call came at seven in the morning. He'd not slept well, just managing to drop off again after a couple of hours of trying — at the very moment his unconsciousness unscotched itself with a sort of tearing noise that turned out to be his mobile.

It was Al. He sounded as if he'd been jogging, but he never jogged, scarcely took proper exercise, used a buggy for golf, yet passed his meds with flying colours. Bob assumed Al was in a different time zone because it was seven o'clock.

'Bob? We need to talk, urgent.'

'What's up?' He was groggy, taking a few too many seconds to recall where he was, heart sinking when he did. Crowthorne. Al could not say what the matter was, not over the phone. He wanted to meet up.

Bob croaked, 'Tea and birthday cake your place, around four?'

'It's not my birthday.'

'It's mine.'

'Christ. What timing.'

'I had no say in the matter.'

'How about I buy you a birthday meal in the D and D at CK, one o'clock? Just say yes or no.'

This was unofficial code: it took Bob a few seconds to work it out. 'Boats, boats,' Al added impatiently. The Dog and Duck at Cookham was

Al's favourite pub: they'd sloped off there through many a summer, admiring the passing craft from its pleasant Thameside lawn, but never in November.

'Confirmed.'

'Roger,' Al said. 'Don't be late.'

'My second name's Ryanair,' Bob joked. 'Hope you're checking they've put cones around the wings.'

Al had already gone. Bob was worried. The man didn't usually do scared.

* * *

He was five minutes early, but Al had already downed his pint, sitting slumped and plump-looking in a corner of what, on a weekday late-autumn afternoon, was a mere shadow of its rumbustious summer self full of jolly boating types. The log fire was non-operational, the low-beamed place slightly chilly and smelling sourly of the previous night's carousing. An artificial Christmas tree winked in the corner. It made Bob feel morose.

Al's window looked out on the river sliding directly below, glumly tugging at a bare weeping willow on the opposite bank. The music was bog-standard country and western turned down low enough so any conversation could be heard by the shy little barmaid of uncertain nationality. There was no one else present to hear.

Bob ordered a couple of Murphy's and a hotpot apiece, and brought the beers over. Al looked deathly pale under his frown. He got down to brass tacks directly.

'Hans. Hans Schmitt. Bad news. He's dead.'

'How?'

'Fell out of a seventy six.'

'Pushed off the steps?'

'It was airborne. To be precise, it was at 35,000 feet.'

'They wouldn't have opened the cargo doors at 35,000 feet.'

'He fell out of the escape hatch.'

Bob pondered on this as the hotpots arrived, clearly thawed in a microwave, ornamented with garnishes of irrelevant onion rings and parsley.

He pointed out that the escape hatch in an Ilyushin 76 is up in the flight deck's roof. 'You need a ladder to open it.'

'Exactly.'

'Where did this unfortunate accident occur?'

They were speaking in low tones, but he still felt the barmaid was noting it all down. She was certainly talking into her mobile in some foreign lingo.

'Over the Arabian peninsula. Last week. The crew were briefly arrested in Ras al Khaima but released, no charge.'

'Who were they?'

'An assortment. One or two Russians. A Bulgarian. To be honest, I didnae fancy looking into this in any depth.'

'Who told you?'

'Max Freewest. Remember him? We'd call him Face West, because he went the wrong way on the apron at Frankfurt. Confirmed face east to Apron Control then passed on to the headset operator to push back the bird face west, saw a bloody great jumbo bearing down on him, started swearing and shouting. And it was all his fault.'

'Oh, him.'

Al leaned forward over his pint. 'I was making enquiries, you know, after our knees-up. Got a bit worried when Hans wouldn't answer the phone. Max worked with him a bit out in South America. Poor old Hans. I quite liked him. Though the last thing I said to him was, 'You're a double-crossing arsehole.' It's always the same when folk die without warning. Usually you've just been rude to them or talked behind their back. So you'd better be nice to me, Bob.'

'You're not about to die, Al.'

'Wanna bet on it? Maidenhead's suddenly full o' types with ski shades in smart black Audis, kerb-crawling just behind me. I feel better talking about it. Jane has no idea.'

'This isn't like you. Hans was in with the ski-shades guys from Naples. Counterfeit chain-saws made in China. Cocaine, even. The dodgier stuff, anyway.'

Al glared at him. 'How do you know?'

'The price of three lagers and a chicken and chips in the Streep. No head for the booze, despite his Swiss banker's look.'

'You know more about him than I thought.'

Bob chuckled. 'Oh, c'mon, Al. We all knew it. He double-crossed everything in sight. His crooked friends have caught up with him, that's all.'

'You always looked so dreamy,' Al remarked

dreamily. 'Another? Christ, happy birthday.'

'Thank you. No, we're both driving.'

'Here's a present, skipper. No time to wrap it, I'm afraid.'

A pair of large sky-blue cufflinks with tiny white streaks like clouds. Bob hardly ever wore cufflinks, especially not this size.

'Topaz,' said Al. 'Your birth stone, according to Jane.'

'That was very clever of you. Will I see a rainbow when it's wet?'

'Maidenhead has its good points,' Al sighed, slumped back in his seat. He was wearing a suede coat with a furry collar, very 60s, that clashed with his sandy hair. He caught Bob's appraising glance.

'Anniversary present from Jane.'

'Very nice,' Bob fibbed.

He'd always dreaded his birthdays, but they were soon over.

He had also fibbed about poor old ex-Swissair, their one-time cockpit colleague and actually a reliable team member, if prone to lining his own pocket at the expense of others through his ability to speak French, Italian and German fluently. In fact, Bob was as convinced as Al that Schmitt was another green bottle, nudged off the wall by whoever had hired his own balcony operatives. Twenty-five floors up, 35,000 feet up: same difference, even if you landed on your feet. But he needed time to think; he needed to give Al a respite from his own panic.

'Come back to my place,' Bob said. 'Borrow the sofa. We need a private confab before headless-chicken syndrome sets in.'

He stopped. The music had been turned off and the barmaid's phone call was over. Their voices seemed very loud and clear in the silence.

'Great place to meet, Al. They say safety's in numbers, usually. Costa at Luton Airport, for example.'

'Ach, I thought you were an art lover,' Al said drily. 'Stanley Spencer. Great investment, these days. Art.' He waved a hand towards some framed watercolours of yachts.

Bob leaned forward, arms crossed on the table, and continued in a near-murmur: 'There's something that doesn't add up, Al. A few toys for the Taliban to play with, whoever the supplier, even an Israeli businessman, even the bloody Pope, whoever, they're not worth the nudging of a whole crew off the shelf, let alone a journalist. There's something else. We know what it is.'

Thankfully, the waitress was out the back, doing something loud with bottles.

'It's the drugs, Al. The snow that blew into the hold. You know my latest theory? Bensoussan can't have known about it. So now maybe he's cross. Off the gauge. You know what makes a control freak very cross? Being lied to. Hidden stuff. Business going on behind his back. I mean, let's face it, you yourself were cross about it, the subterfuge. Being used. Probably by Posh Boy Lennart. He looked like a junkie.'

Al pushed his plate away; he wasn't listening. 'There's always the croft house,' he said softly.

'The croft house?'

'The Hebridean bolt-hole. On Scourlay. I

229

showed it you. You seemed interested. But it's not ideal for Jane, not in her current condition. Otherwise I'd be tempted, I can tell you.'

Bob settled back in his seat, drained his glass, wiped his mouth, sighed. 'Six months max. Rental. Olivia has a new man. I have need of a quiet corner to sulk in.'

Al nodded. 'It'll certainly be quiet. Make a decent offer for the rent, and I legally can't refuse you, as executor. It'll have to be the Virgin Islands for us, heads right down. Dearie me. But Jane will be happier with the warmth. No offence, but I'm not sure she'd want to stare out at all those howling gales with you wandering about the house, whingeing.'

'I never whinge.'

'You will do up there,' said Al, strangely happy about it.

Bob glanced out at the river soaking up the rain, wondered if bumming on a palm-fringed beach might not be a better solution. No, that would be sad. The Outer Hebrides would be bracing. Bracing is good. Right out on the edge. It would beat Shropshire hollow.

'Anyway,' Al went on, 'she's a bad sailor, and the only way to and from the island is a leaky boat full of sacks and lambs rowed by an old whisky-rotted feller in a bobble hat.'

'No beach airport?'

'You're thinking of the bigger islands, like Barra. Barra is big compared to Scourlay. So you won't likely have a car. The island is full of unlicensed wrecks with no tax discs, some of them moving.'

'Sounds good. Get a new livery, grow a beard, dip down out of sight till it all blows over.'

'Wrong expression. Up there, Bob, it never stops blowing. And make sure you take your wellies. Anyway, you've no idea how hard it is to hide these days, once you've knocked over the hive. Even getting a damn PO box. I've looked into it. You can't just vanish. And the swarm has nae respect for fucking fences.'

'We can at least make it harder for the swarm, Al. Not worth their bother. Lie low for a bit. Pretend to be a rock.'

'Christ, what a pain. I don't want to lie low. And Jane's got her book club, her tenpin bowling. She never stops.'

Bob leaned closer again. 'The thing is,' he said, 'my money's on Pedro Diez. The Mexican connection. It can't just have been Lennart, or Bensoussan would've stopped at him. Maybe it was just Diez, grabbing an opportunity. A nice big empty bird, all paid for.'

Al looked straight at him, sandy eyebrows awry above the bleached lashes, his pale blue gaze on a scheduled flight straight into Bob's brain.

'Bob,' he said, 'for Chrissake *let it go*. Diez was a nobody. It was clearly that little Swiss sub-mafioso bastard.'

'May he rest in peace.'

'Let it go. What's come over you, skipper? You've been let off the hook. I haven't. This is the first day of the fucking Somme and you're out there with your clipboard and pencil, taking fucking notes. I'm crouched below the parapet

231

and I'm still wetting myself.'

Bob nodded, raising a mock fist in agreement. Al was always right. Commonsensical.

The music was now slow and sleepy pap: nursing-home dance music. Perhaps the bargirl thought it suited them. She came over and cleared their plates, giving Bob a nice crooked-teeth smile as he agreed to coffee.

'Let me guess,' he added, scanning her fair tumble of hair. 'Poland.'

'No. Ukraine.'

His heart gave a little jump. 'Ah, don't know it.'

'Is very special,' she sighed.

Once she'd left, following an attractive rundown of Ukraine's good points, Al leaned forward and said, 'You bloody liar. And she had eyes only for you. As ever.'

'I'm a cautious feller, remember?'

'That's what I miss, doing freight. Lissom beauties bringing your tea to the front office, all that banter. All that pleated skirt. I get lonely in my hotel rooms, these days, Bob. Not that I even fly much, now,' he added melancholically.

The little veins over his nose, his sagging cheeks, his thinning hair: Bob looked at Al and reckoned the lack of stewardesses wasn't the problem. When he first knew McAllister, they'd cluster round his copper-haired lankiness like bees.

'C'mon, they weren't all lissom. And the tea was watered-down diesel.'

'Certainly lissom no longer. Pencil-thin when I started. Take Jane, for instance. Now they're more like Russian shot-putters in drag. Hey, you're not really leaving our one big aviation family, are you?'

'Possibly, even probably. Kicking the habit. It's bad for me, being a mercenary pilot.'

'Being a *what* pilot?'

'That's what someone called me, once,' Bob said vaguely.

The waitress brought the coffee. She smelt faintly of lily of the valley and seemed to rustle as she leaned by his shoulder. 'Anything else?'

'A boat trip on the Thames?'

She laughed and said, with an ironic lilt, 'How really nice,' and left them.

Al drew his big red hand over his face and popped out again half the size. 'Ach, we just get on with it,' he said. 'Keep our heads down and get on with it. Or take the consequences, in certain situations. Do you think that's what's happening now, that we're taking the consequences — with a two-year delay for coffee and snacks?'

'Possibly. I was fitted with four engines. Marriage, home, job, kids. I've lost three. I'm gliding on one, now.'

Al nodded. 'I would've had kids,' he murmured. There was a silence: long-time cockpit brethren, they'd had this out already. Incompatibility between Jane and himself, Jane not wanting to adopt, afraid that some dark gene would resurface at puberty. Then he said, 'Hey, listen, there's something you ought to know.'

Bob was convinced his old friend was about to reveal some intimate, unappetising fact — that

233

he'd had his balls dropped at eighteen or whatever, that Jane was a lesbian, that she'd not after all been Miss Gatwick 1979, but only Miss Mildenhall.

Al pondered; Bob waited. In normal circumstances they'd have covered a fair number of nautical miles. Then Al shifted in his chair, as if he'd changed his mind, and said, 'Listen, I had this God-awful dream last night. I was in the cockpit, checking over the notification, when I saw 'HUM', circled in red. So I said to the ramp guy, who was an old mate of mine from Fife, died years ago — you know how it is in dreams — I says to him, like we always do, for a laugh, 'Fergus, I see we've got some human remains. What d'you think this is, a hearse?' And he looks at me and he says, 'It's your own corpse back there, McAllister, so handle it carefully.' And it was, it was. I went back into the rear and saw it, staring up white as a sheet, all on its own in this dim and chilly hold, lashed to a PMC pallet by five tie-down points, it was that bloody detailed. Imagine, Bob, I was carrying my own damn body!'

Bob nodded. 'Dreams go by opposites, my stepmother would always tell me.'

Al stirred his coffee. 'I know this guy who does close protection work. Ex-marine. Security consultant. Lives on a farm in Devon. If you're interested.'

'Are you?'

'You bet.'

'I can't afford stuff like that, Al.'

'You've got your nice big shoulders, I suppose.

No choice, in my case.' He looked out of the window at the river. 'There's Jane to think about.'

Bob shrugged; his shoulders would be of minimal use against a spray of bullets. He didn't mention the Makarov. Cut-price close protection.

'Randomise, randomise, randomise,' muttered Al. 'That's this guy's advice.'

10

Al didn't beat about the bush: he and Jane moved out to a secret location in deepest west Berkshire — a farmhouse B & B with blazing log fire, friendly Labrador, views of the downs — accompanied by 'Andrew', their protective membrane. Why not further afield? Because among Al's many accessories was a thorough-bred racehorse called Safety Fuse; he could discreetly watch his investment race along the gallops above Lambourn, Andrew eyeing the empty horizons through a stiff breeze at £600 a day.

Meanwhile, his client was negotiating the purchase of a second property on the British Virgin Islands under a false name: Felix Newton. Al knew a Polish couple in a large flat off the King's Road who processed false passports, driving licences and ancillary documents made in Thailand; Al and Jane had theirs already, which surprised Bob. He was persuaded to part with a small fortune to do likewise, a name decided over the phone on a crackly line. It was as hard as choosing a password.

Christopher 'Kit' Webb.

Christopher being his middle name, Webb being a lack of imagination.

'Please, Mr Webb, to spell this. Like Internet?'

A week passed. The solicitors exchanged crisp letters concerning the Worcestershire house.

Several people came to look at the Crowthorne flat. Al informed the Scottish estate agents in Inverness that he had a potential tenant for the croft cottage.

Otherwise, it was all eerily quiet. Bob went out once a day to the gym, at apparently random times, and shopped likewise, changing his route and always accompanied by the pistol in its holster. He practised whipping it out and firing with an empty chamber at the flat's mirror, and improved his reaction time by several seconds. If he hadn't texted Sharansky, he wouldn't be bothering with paranoia. But he'd betrayed Gold Teeth's order to keep mum: his only hope was that Sharansky had been eliminated by another set of scary bods with a taste for mobiles.

*   *   *

This hope was summarily dealt with by a call from Al one Monday morning. Bob was walking down Crowthorne's main street, on his way back from the dry-cleaner's with his pilot's uniform. The gold twist on the cuffs had, as usual, cost him extra: after all, it was silk. Sand had fallen out of the pockets, they said. The only other customer was a BA first officer, who tried to talk shop.

'Bob. It's Al. Bad news. What the hell's that in the background?'

'We've declared war on Germany. Phone back after the all clear. Five minutes.'

The wail of the sirens contracted and dilated in its usual manner. He ducked into a shoe shop

237

to escape the noise, which still tended to trigger a vivid horror montage on a loop: hairy hands around a little girl's neck, big teeth chomping on a finger, all blurring into a flash of personal memory that he would rather not be reminded of. Overreaction or therapeutic recycling?

The shop was empty and too quiet. He phoned back from the street.

'It's over, Al. Peace in our time. The weekly Broadmoor test.'

'Talking of which. Pedro Diez, the skipper with the eyebags.'

'So?'

'Details scanty. Location was Riga, a sixth-floor balcony was involved, and drink. Day before yesterday. RIP.'

Shoppers, harmlessness, gum-spattered pavements. A bus wheezing. Normal life.

'That is definitely bad news, Al. More details, please.'

Al scampered through them. The Latvian authorities had ruled out foul play, despite bruises: several grams of alcohol were found in his blood, there was a bottle of vodka in the room, and his reputation had followed him down. Bob's visitors had not forced vodka down his own throat. Al wasn't reassured by this. 'You know what I'm doing? Painting my old Toby lures. Gloss black and gold. To hook up the big, fat salmon. That's us, skipper.'

Back home, Bob tapped in 'Pedro Diez' and 'pilot'. There were several reports of Diez's death in various languages, and a freight dogs' blog forum from six months earlier in which Al had said what a gas it was flying with 'Pedro Diez, Bob Winrush and Hans Schmitt' and regaled the following story:

Pedro, fresh from Click Air, never went anywhere without this vintage porn mag from the good old days when they showed the boobs on the cover. One time he waved it at the ramp agent during push-back. The RA waving the gear pin and 'Manuel' (as we called him) waving the porn mag, the agent in fits. 'I'm gonna read this during my flight!' Crazy. Pedro told me he did the same when he was with Click. Presumably they gave him the push. Anyone heard from him recently?

Strange, Bob thought: Al had seemed not to recall him when asked. Maybe he was losing his memory under the strain.

It wasn't until the next morning that the latest from Tim Sightly appeared, to the same search words and in pole position. It was in the AAW's main newsletter, and described the untimely departure of Diez, 'a colourful dog of war from Mexico' and the 'ruthless carnage in Africa' facilitated by the arms trade. Bob read the rest with a wincing attention. Citing the web address of Al's blog entry, Sightly confirmed that

Diez's regular crew included Hugh 'Al' McAllister and First Officer Hans Schmitt; the latter recently died in suspicious circumstances during a freight flight (see November's post). Might there be a link between the 'accidental' deaths, over a period of six months, of Schmitt, arms broker

Lennart Burström, Captain Pedro Diez and Israeli investigative journalist Matt Sharansky? If so, what is it?

One possible link is a single return flight from Istanbul and Turkmenbashi, suspected of delivering arms to the Taliban via a final overland leg across Turkmenistan to Afghanistan. Burström arranged this flight, and the crew included Schmitt and Diez. Significantly, it was this flight that Sharansky was investigating when he was killed in Radom (Poland) by a hit-and-run driver.

Before we rush into speculation based on the ownership of the aircraft, we have to establish the identities of the lessee and the charterer, and these are hidden behind a complex web of holding companies. The list of usual suspects drawn up by Sharansky is long, and in certain cases surprising, even unlikely. However, a simple arms-smuggling exercise could not explain why any of these would wish to eliminate an entire freight crew and thus add homicide to their crimes, as well as unwelcome attention.

It has been alleged (email confidential source) that a large quantity of heroin was carried on the return flight — a flight still technically under the same charterer, though flying back to base empty. Arms dealers and drugs traffickers do not generally mix, the latter being wholly illicit; they might, however, use the same transport infrastructure. Could it be that, in this instance, there was no structural or logistical connection between the two deals, and that the heroin shipment was opportunistic and not officially cleared by the original (arms-only) dealer? This would not go down well with the latter.

Watch this space.

Bob sent the piece on to Al, ran himself a deep bath and reflected in the steam. Tim Sightly had kept his promise: no mention was made of Robert Winrush. He turned the hot tap with his toes and felt a warm sense of relief.

When he dressed in the bedroom, he saw his uniform in its dry-cleaner's plastic and wondered if he would ever wear it again. The idea of twiddling his thumbs in a cold, wet and far-off place became less attractive suddenly. Was flight necessary any longer? These guys were energy saving: they only did what they had to do. Eliminating Captain Winrush was an optional extra. They didn't usually bother with optional extras.

The phone made him jump. It was Al. He was not happy about the article.

'Why weren't you mentioned, Bob?'

'I never flew with Diez.'

'He wouldn't know that, not from my blog. He just left you out.'

'Come on, Al,' said Bob, trying to keep it light. 'I didn't fly the Turkmenbashi leg.'

'I suppose so. You haven't been talking to this saintly Slightly guy, then? Some kind of deal?'

'Sightly. I don't know him from Adam. Most of his info must have come from the late Sharansky.'

'Isn't David part of their outfit? The Arms Agin Weapons gang?'

'Al, don't go there. Do you really think I'd

want David to be involved?'

'It's a bitch. You were lucky, not being mentioned. I've never felt more bottle-shaped. Made of fucking glass, I am.'

Bob told him that the Outer Hebrides was no longer a draw.

'Why?'

'You know why. I think they've lost interest in me.'

'Happy you. Then where are you planning on going?'

'Back into freight.'

'I thought you wanted a life change, skipper.'

'I made the mistake of taking my uniform to the dry-cleaners.'

'And I've gone to all that trouble. The house was yours. Great views, fantastic fishing, empty beaches. Whale spotting.'

*   *   *

He was jogging in the woods near Crowthorne, feeling reasonably good in the circumstances. A vibration against his thigh. It was Olivia, calling him a fucking bastard. He asked her, breathless from the fierce pace he'd set himself, if this was the result of something specific or was she just giving herself a rush. She asked him in turn why he was panting. He explained.

She said, 'Thank God I don't have to put up with all that macho stuff any more. Aviation jargon, machines. Thank God I don't have to hear any of that again. Those fucking oicks you hired to ransack the house not only broke the

242

lock and one of my porcelain jars but left mud all over the white carpet. Or did you do it yourself, knowing we were house-hunting in Shropshire?'

'A break-in? When?'

'Oh, you sound so surprised.'

'Olivia, I swear on my life that I didn't hire anyone to do anything. Nor have I put a foot in our — I repeat, *our* — home since you bawled me out. Why the hell do you presume I had anything to do with a break-in?'

'Because most of the mess was in your study. Very clever. Undoing all Ben's sorting. And nothing was nicked. I've told him he should just chuck it all, willy-nilly. We've got the message. Now you can get ours. Leave us alone.'

The woods stretched wintrily all around. He scanned them. For the first time since the balcony incident, he felt a trace of fear.

'I can see why you think I had something to do with it, Olivia. But I didn't. I'll come over at a time that suits you. I'll put the stuff in store. And don't chuck it, not a single paper clip. That's against the law.'

'So is breaking and entering. We'll be out all day tomorrow. You've got a key. Don't touch anything that's not yours.'

That didn't leave much — except perhaps Zip Man's photographic equipment and organic aftershave — because the estate was not yet divided, but he didn't think it wise to point this out. Instead, he got on with being a meek (rather than fucking) bastard, hired a white van and drove over to Worcestershire in awful traffic that made him feel sympathy for all earthbound creatures who hadn't ever driven the sky.

The study was awash. Stuff was spilling out into the corridor. They'd entered neatly by the French windows: no doubt professionals looking for copies of the logbook and diary or anything else relevant to the Turkmenbashi flight and its potential embarrassment to the present government of Israel (eerily, he heard all this in Sharansky's voice). He repacked and threw it all into the back of the van, running up and down the stairs furiously with black plastic sacks until sweat dripped off his nose. He hoped Olivia and her art nerd would come back in time to see him, because he wouldn't have stopped: he was a muscular machine, pure manic male. But he did it all alone, with imaginary cross hairs in the middle of his brow. And nothing happened. Nothing could happen in this village, bar mindless yobbery and fierce mutterings between neighbours.

He took a turn around the leafless orchard, stroked an exposed beam and the lowest edge of the thatch as a kind of farewell handshake and drove out to a self-storage warehouse on the edgelands of Reading, wheeling his junk on a trolley down the aisle to a grey cell with a steel grille for a ceiling. He was given the key by a large wheezing storeman called, according to his plastic name-tag, TAG.

'Thanks, Tag,' Bob joked, nodding at his chest.

But Tag didn't see the joke: that was his name.

⋆   ⋆   ⋆

He told Al all about it. There was a big sigh.

'At least you're still standing,' Al said.

Bob reckoned aloud that just because they'd done some further research didn't mean the heavies were out to get him personally. All Al said was, 'Let it go, Bob, let it go. Head down, mouth shut. Make your surface area as small as possible.'

'See no evil, hear no evil, speak no evil.'

'You said it, friend.'

Bob reassured himself that they couldn't know about the Crowthorne address. They showed no signs of doing so. Neither did Bensoussan and his testicular knees show any signs of life on the Internet, the last article about him written in 2008. *You will be dead by Monday* was already past its sell-by date — by over two years. Bob had experienced having his room turned over once before, back in 2004, in Somaliland, in a hotel run by a retired vice consul from Cheadle who'd taken him scuba-diving. Perhaps it was something to do with the gangly pirates hanging around in the harbour, or with the naughty green boxes he was delivering onto the massive strategic runways in the middle of the bush. He took a couple of days' sick leave — the intruders had bashed him about a bit, grunting in the darkness — and was fine.

The long and the short of it was that he was concerned, but not yet headless-chicken.

⋆ ⋆ ⋆

Al phoned back the next day. He wanted a final confab, in person. Bob couldn't see the point,

245

but Al insisted. Phone calls could be hacked, tapped, whatever.

'And I can be followed,' Bob said.

'You're not a target, you said so yourself.'

'Not a primary target.'

'Anyway, you'll know it soon enough on those winding wee lanes. Hit metal. Vulva, twelve thirty tomorrow. I said *vulva*. Remember? I'll buy you one. We'll wish each other luck. Would you be interested in seeing the horse?'

Ulverton was in the vicinity of Al's farmhouse retreat. Bob briefly debated with himself whether to stay overnight again at the Old Rectory and check out the Estonian receptionist, but his sensible side won.

The day dawned grey and sleety, with a blustery wind; the last thing he desired was to battle out to the country, but loyalty was a precious thing. The slip road remained empty in his rear-view mirror as he left the M4 early to cut up through Bradfield and Yattendon into his and Olivia's old courting ground of chalky downland. He stopped the car on a long stretch of country lane and waited: no one. Woods. Leafless branches. He wanted to cry; he blasted himself with some Eagles instead.

Who is gonna make it?

We'll find out in the long run, in the long run.

He parked the Healey on the gravel behind the pub, and had fifteen minutes to spare. The wind was even worse here, so he visited the church: Olivia had liked the atmosphere, and he remembered her long fingers stroking the smooth stone of the ancient font and how much he had craved her then and there. A sob rose in his chest, which had never happened before. Gather up the threads and cut them.

Apart from a couple of flat-screens, the pub was much the same, all old farm tools and sepia shepherds. It was surprisingly crowded: smart braying types in shooting jackets vied with morose elderly couples picking at the day's special sprawled on rectangular plates. He'd come in bang on schedule, but there was no sign of Al.

A table in the nook near the toilets was free, and he sat without ordering. Twelve thirty-five. Al was never late. Twelve forty. Never. He didn't think he should call or text: one never knew with satellites, tracking systems, mobile pinging. A thick-necked man in his thirties shared the cushioned bench at the next table, drinking what looked like lime soda and studying his iPhone. He was faintly worrying: something military about him, an efficiency in the way he drank, scanned the room, spread his knees and made the bench rock.

Bob caught his eye and tried a friendly nod. The man leaned towards him and said, not looking at him, 'Captain Winrush?'

'Not in the slightest.'

'I'm Andrew,' said the man, in a nasal voice that didn't go with the rest of him; maybe because he was talking out of the side of his mouth. 'He's in the toilet. I saved you the table.'

'You're the bodyguard.'

'Close protection officer, more low-profile. More covert than overt, but that might change.

Pleased to meet you.'

A hand was proffered, hidden by the tables from the normal life beyond. Bob shook it, gingerly. A firm grip, but damp and smooth. It felt like a gay assignation.

'He's been in there at least ten minutes,' Bob pointed out.

'Nine,' said Andrew, checking his Rolex. 'Retention. Nerves. Psychological.'

'He's filled you in, has he?'

'Indeed. A complex one.'

'That means bloody nasty.'

'Oh, I'm recently back from CP work in Iraq.'

'Miss it, do you?' joked Bob.

Andrew fixed him with the full five-yard stare, but from five inches away. 'I've no intention of ever going near the place again.'

Al emerged from the toilets, looking flushed, in a whiff of close air and soap. His proffered hand was limp and dry.

'Fucking Ducks and Drakes. What a nonsense. I thought duck was male, drake female, found myself inside the skirts' cubicle. I gather you two've met,' he said, slumping into the chair. 'Christ, I stood there, desperate, and nothing came out. Maybe it's the prostate.'

He seemed to be breathless. It was worrying, Bob thought.

'Psychological,' said Andrew. 'Now pretend I'm not here. The Unknown Soldier. That's my nickname.'

Bob found the lunch peculiar: Al was not himself, huffing and wheezing, mumbling into his pint, leaving half the gristly steak.

'Death by horseradish sauce,' joked Bob.

'I've got nae appetite. Hardly surprising.'

But he did confirm that the croft-house paperwork was done. 'It's safely yours to rent from whenever you fancy it. If you change your mind.'

'Thanks, Al, but I doubt I will. I'm going back to work. Work keeps you from moping.'

'I hope your confidence is not misplaced, skipper. Just because you weren't mentioned by Tim Unsightly, a fact which still bothers me.'

'Why should it?'

'I'm a jealous man. These bad guys make Andrew here look like Snow White. Och, he's told me stories. The man's worked in circles where tearing someone off a strip is meant literally. Guys with all-body tattoos. Georgians, Chechens. Can't recall their name.'

'Vory V Zakone,' said Andrew unexpectedly, out of the side of his mouth. 'Worse than whom there is none, except for the Baltic guys, the Israeli mobsters, the Italians, of course, and maybe the Bulgarians.'

Bob nodded. Andrew's jugular lay on his thick neck like a rope.

'A lot to choose from,' he said.

'Plus the Jamaicans, the Indians, the Chinese, the Corsicans, and the Nigerians,' said Andrew. 'Along with the Albanians.'

'You've omitted the Mexicans.'

Andrew nodded. 'And many others of like ilk.'

Bob turned to Al, who was staring at his drink. 'You forget I've already met the bad guys, Al. Full frontal.'

His former crewman smiled. 'Well, things can boomerang,' he said. Bob felt something being put in his jacket pocket. 'The number to use when phoning me, and no other. It's safe from big ears.'

'How is it safe?'

'You've forgotten I'm an engineer, with a degree in electronics. You're just a spanner-and-grease man.'

'Actually, I hadn't forgotten.'

'Learn it and swallow it. Or whatever. Think of it as your credit card number.'

Bob felt the slip of paper in his pocket. 'I never had a boomerang. As a kid.'

'I'll put one in your Christmas stocking, then, along with y' tangerine. Do you want to see the horse?'

They stood up on the gallops above Lambourn in the chilly gusts, drinking brandy out of a silver flask with HM engraved on it in fancy lettering. Andrew kept some way off, in his trench coat, gloved hands folded in front of him: he looked exactly like a heavy in some TV crime thriller. The horse was beautiful, shiny as a conker and with a flash of white on its brow.

'Isn't he just fantastic?' shouted Al.

His investment tore up and down, throwing out divots from thundering hooves, the young jockey unsmiling on top. The downs spread all around under scudding clouds that were grey and creamy-white and, at one point, purple. Al was lord of all. A frigging flight engineer. The brandy burned in Bob's throat.

'I'm planning on building a biplane from

250

scratch,' he shouted over the gusts, apropos of nothing.

'Now listen to me,' shouted Al in return. 'Andrew reckons these guys are serious. Next time it won't be your study, it'll be your intestines. Do what I say for once, skipper.'

'Which is?'

'Get the fuck up to the isles. Bonnie Scotland.'

'Sounds like an order,' laughed Bob.

'Advice is all it is,' Al yelled into his ear, as the hooves drummed over the green and English turf.

★ ★ ★

Bob drove back over the limit, which was not Winrush at all. If the police stop me, he thought, I'll never fly again, unless I go into really shady outfits with aircraft kept together by parcel tape, flying everywhere by night. The sort that keep the cargo crash statistics decently high, make it look riskier than it is.

What this meant, though, was that he drove back slowly and carefully. The two crew-mates had slapped each other's upper arms, punched each other's chests and separated before it got embarrassing: Al was wet-eyed, but that may have been the east wind. He'd gripped Bob's shoulders and said, 'Skipper, take care. Use that number, whenever.'

'There's just one thing I have to say, Al.'

'Say on.'

'You're the best bloody flight engineer I ever had.'

'Get off of you. Why d'you have to say that now?'

'What's wrong with now?'

'Because you've had years and years to say it in.'

'That's how it always is, you silly bugger.'

He drove, however, as though he had a full pint on the back seat. He was rage-honked a few times by BMW types too busy on their mobiles to bother to look at the road. As he entered Crowthorne's outskirts down a leafy short cut of bungalows, there was a stench of burning plastic. At first he thought it was a wheelie bin on fire — a favourite sport of the locally produced louts. Then he realised the smudges on the windscreen were smoke, rising in serious wisps from his own bonnet.

He pulled in to inspect. He was fond of the Healey's little satisfied smile, but now its radiator was all gritting teeth. The black smoke that hid the bonnet (in a matter of seconds) flickered yellow. Not wanting to perish in a fireball, he made no effort to approach, but searched about for a bucket of water. Of course, this not being an airport apron, there was neither bucket nor fire truck. The underside was dropping flames that began to rivulet, like brandy on a Christmas pudding. Then there was a quiet *whump* and the flames leapt through the windows, curling over the soft top. It was a newsreel, taken in somewhere like Iraq. Except that on telly you didn't have the fumes scalding your throat.

The car's nose was now entirely engulfed in flames more than twenty feet tall. He backed off in case the petrol tank went up: he'd let it run low, which meant vapour. There were further smaller *whumps*, more like a brick being dropped from a height into water: the more inflammable parts. Paint bubbled, the tyres sent up blacker smoke along with a rubbery stink, and the tan soft top collapsed in a shower of sparks. The empty street of bungalows had filled up with about twenty onlookers.

'Must have been the battery,' Bob said, as they waited for the fire engine. 'I hadn't used her much.'

'You've got bits of glass in your eyelashes, look.'

★   ★   ★

His first instinct was not to think how lucky he had been, let alone that it might have been destroyed by something like a rocket launcher. This was not Afghanistan, but even so: he did not take cover. He simply assumed that the small bomb planted under the car had been faulty. The onlookers — mostly elderly with shopping trolleys — all shook their heads in the same way and said cars weren't what they used to be.

'Mine certainly isn't,' he joked.

He dismissed the idea of running away — it wouldn't help. He wished he had some mints.

The firefighters were told the same story, when they arrived fifteen minutes later, along with the police and a lot of dramatic siren effects: smoke had suddenly begun pouring from the bonnet, he'd got out smartly, it had exploded.

'You sure you've not got enemies?' the large policewoman joked.

'Only grumpy passengers in business class,' he joked back, keeping his head turned, wondering why he wasn't being breathalysed. Perhaps it was because his non-fake driving licence showed his rank as well as his occupation. Or they felt sorry for his loss: the other copper, barely out of nappies, had a thing about Healeys.

'It's all yours,' Bob said.

'Sitting in the garage doing nothing, was it?'

'How did you guess?'

'Experience, sir. Half the vehicle fires we deal with are elderly folk who haven't driven their old car for months. Poor maintenance.'

'It was a replica. And I'm not elderly. And I could take it apart and put it back together again in the middle of Africa, if I wanted to, with only one screwdriver.'

'Go ahead, sir. It's all yours.'

The firemen used up a lot of foam, the blue lights flashed on a blackened and steaming shell, the police took notes, a big trailer eventually came and towed it away for a fortune, leaving a black star shape glistening with unburnt oil, smaller than he had expected, and a coil of plastic that might have been the device. Or the CD player. Onlookers drifted away, this month's entertainment over. He was on his own.

He searched the tarmac and spotted the gleam of something silver by the scorched kerb: a possible bubble of mercury. It would have been a standard tilt-switch job, quite small, and presumably less sensitive than intended, since he'd gone over quite a few speed bumps on the trip back. He guessed it had fallen from its magnetised grip for some reason (there were a number of minor potholes in the road) and only then completed the circuit. Either that, or it was on a timer. There was also something looking like flour, if you crouched close enough. Fertiliser, maybe. All fairly amateur, but then it doesn't take a PhD in chemistry to make a minor car-bomb. Or maybe it was the battery. Or a loose fuel line. Or the head gasket.

If a bomb, he reckoned he had a few hours' grace: the time it would take for someone to know Bob Winrush was still up and about. So he walked in the wrong direction: right for his safety, that is. Thankfully, his wallet had been on him when he'd left the car. A close shave. He got to the High Street and headed for the charity shop, where he suddenly had to sit down.

'Are you all right sir?'

'Sorry. Someone's just blown up my car.'

'Really?'

The young assistant, with bright pink hair and freckles, laughed nervously. Another dafty. Get them all the time. Lonely men. As long as he isn't a loony from the hospital (though the real dread in Crowthorne isn't that someone'll make it over the razor wire and eat your brains with a spoon, but that it'll close down). He staggered to the tiny lavatory and was sick, contemplating a poster of a skeletal Asian mite, mostly eyes, holding the usual plastic bowl, with a muddy gutter as background. He seemed fairly poor himself, in the mirror, but with all five of his senses turned right up.

Back among the knocking coat hangers, *Twin Peaks*-era dresses and dry-cleaning solvent smells, he bought a homburg with a black-leather strap above the rim, a rawhide greatcoat with a hairy collar, a slippery mauve shirt and a walking stick. They said nothing except the right things when he went to the counter.

'It's for a play,' he said.

'Oh, a local one, is it?'

'Not really.'

'About terrorism?' The pink-haired girl smiled. She was more piercings than face.

'*Annie Get Your Gun*,' he said, which the twins had done at school a few years back.

'Oh, I like that. What are you?'

'Costume feller. Helluva job. You're a marvel, thanks.'

It was adrenalin that saw him through. Pilots are good in emergencies: the usual cockpit emergency lasts less time, though. He slipped back to his flat in a whiff of mothballs looking like someone dressed up as an old man, but there was no one else in sight. It was five thirty, already dark, and he groped about in the rooms to pack, using the orange light spill courtesy of the municipal council. He then slept (or pretended to) till dawn, and slunk out to the whine of a milk van, humping his two suitcases and a rucksack, quite a feat for a man in a terrible hat and coat. His breath's smoke hid the rest, or so he imagined.

He joined the early commuters for London and sat back in the train to the patter of keyboards. They all had places and people to go back to, he thought. Gardens to mow. Holidays to think about. Christmas trees to decorate. The two young jowly chaps opposite never stopped talking numbers and acronyms the whole way, with the kind of zeal he thought only priests and mullahs could summon up.

He received strange looks. He felt strange — growing into his costume, as he would instantly grow into his uniform, which he'd left on the bed. He detected a slight smell of urine from his quilted inside lining: probably the heat.

He checked into a reasonable hotel in Kensington, ditched the Oxfam chic and kitted himself out for the far and distant north in an overheated branch of Cotswold Outdoor; it was full of white-fleshed and bobble-hatted dummies, some of whom were not real. A Christmas tree sparkled in the corner. He'd sent the twins a cheque and had planned on keeping out of the festive season sight line by volunteering for a soup-kitchen run, the homeless reimbursing him with a sense of his own blessings; but that now fell into the category of good intentions. Olivia would spend it with the twins and, of course, her new skipper. He wasn't sure he could see friends.

'What should I assume about the weather?'

'The absolute worst, mate. Four seasons in a day, summer included. Certainly off the beaten track. Fab hills. But you look the experienced type.'

'Definitely. This tan's Annapurna.'

'What tan?'

He bought rather a lot of gear: retail therapy, he reckoned. Why folk love Dubai, more shopping mall than city: no need for psychotherapists, just browse under angel fish and sharks.

Why did he tell the shop assistant where he was going? It was so hard to vanish.

It was only back in his small room that he began to wonder how and when the bomb had been stuck under his car. Not in Ulverton, surely: he wasn't followed. Perhaps it had been hanging there for days, inches from his feet, the other side of the floor. Weeks, even. It might even have been a non-persistent bomb, like a non-persistent landmine that blows itself up after a while. That's progress.

Or it might have been poor maintenance. Mice nibbling at rubber.

Or not. At any rate, he was fairly confident the types out to get rid of Winrush would think the job was done — unless they checked into the *Bracknell News* website just a single click away:

Car destroyed in blaze

A crew from Bracknell fire station was called to the incident at 4.30 p.m. in Hedgers Lane, Crowthorne.

The Austin Healey Sebring had begun to smoke on entering the street and the driver escaped before the blaze took hold.

The car was almost burnt out by the time the firefighters arrived.

The police are not investigating as the vehicle had not been driven regularly for some time.

Not exactly breaking news, but still. At least they hadn't called him elderly.

He phoned the B & B via a phone box several blocks away from the hotel. Al sounded surprised.

'Oh, Bob.'

'Oh, Al.'

'Drowned in fucking suitcases. Jane's doing her nut.'

'Can't find her rocks?'

'Sorry, skipper?'

'The Healey's gone.'

'How?'

'Small car bomb. No casualties.'

'Shit shit shit. Are you OK? Nothing, Jane. Aye, it's fine. Bob had a prang. Too much ale. He's fine.'

'Not even singed,' he called out, as if to Jane. 'Someone's keeping an eye on me in the heavenly control tower.'

'Where are you now?'

'Somewhere with a lot of other people.'

'London?'

'But heading north, right to the edge. I give in, friend.'

'This is a bit last-minute. You'll have to wait a couple of weeks for the paperwork. And there's Christmas in between. Jane, please will ya stop talking for one second!'

'Al, I just need the fresh air.'

'Oh, you'll get that there. In heaps, and

moving past very fast. You sure it was what you just said it was?'

'Almost home, and she started smoking. An inferno within two minutes. I loved that car.'

'Bob,' Al said in a stage whisper, 'it may have been a normal auto fire.'

'Since when has an auto fire been normal?'

'Police?'

'They came and went. I think one of them who looked about seventeen thought I was an elderly snowhead who wouldn't piss if his pants caught fire.'

'Elderly? You? Jesus wept. Your hair's not even grey in the offing.'

'Thank you, neither is yours.'

'That's because I've hardly got any, skipper.'

★   ★   ★

Bob headed for the edge in his new vehicle, a boring Volkswagen Polo, going cheap because it was an exhibition model and white (the insurance was being difficult about the Healey). He made a stopover in Newcastle. He wanted to see Sophie before he went to ground: a natural impulse. He'd spent two weeks in Kensington battling his solemn promise not to see friends, and let his stubble carry on. He'd jogged round Hyde Park at different hours, reacquainted himself with the dinosaurs and electrons, seen films, then fallen on his sword and visited the V & A, Olivia's favourite. Feeling in jeopardy all the time gave everything a slight fizz, even museums. Life carbonated by danger. Perhaps that's what he'd missed in Dubai. Oh, Leila. He sat on various bar stools and eventually accompanied an Irish woman called Caitlin back to her Chelsea basement flat. She was forty-one and busty and drunk. When he managed an erection she said, 'And on the third day he rose again.' 'That's Easter,' Bob said, 'and today's Christmas.'

Sophie generally took her mother's side. Bob wasn't sure why she reckoned her mother to be beyond reproach, but it's not something he could have changed.

At fifteen she'd fallen heavily for horses in Worcestershire, was given her own, socialised with blue-blooded types living in houses with grounds you'd notice from cruising height, then got stepped on by Emulsion. Bob had carried a few top thoroughbreds by then and knew a horse's tonnage. She was off school for three months, had several operations on her foot and she could still stick magnets to her instep. She certainly upstaged her father's accident, despite its open fractures. So they both had this slight lameness; with her it was more a minimal roll to her gait, an awkwardness cancelled out by a life of fun, friends and laughter.

What it did was bind her closer to her mother. It also made her appreciative of not being in pain. Sophie reckoned the first time she went back to Elts in Worcester (to choose an ordinary pair of shoes) was 'the best day of her life'.

She had a slight but charming lisp and a tumble of blonde hair that was a throwback to Bob's mother, judging by a Super-8 film of the latter: a woman in a cherry-red macintosh grinning and waving by a cliff, the wind tousling her hair through the dust spots. The other films featuring his mother were 'lost', not surviving two successive stepmothers.

He stayed a night in Sophie's shared accommodation, a Victorian house with five doubles in Jesmond. He told her he was heading north to think about things on his own for a few months.

'Why?'

'Burnout. Doctor's orders. Relocating.'

'Where?'

'Scotland,' he said vaguely. 'I'll let you know.' He wasn't sure this would be wise, in fact, but he was too tired to work it out right now. 'It'll only be for nine months max. They have serious gales in September.'

'Where's the Austin Healey?'

'Phew. So many questions. Swapped it and kept the change for my travels.'

'That's really bad news, Dad. Now I can't look forward to you popping your clogs.'

'You'll get the life insurance.'

'Nah, it was the Healey I was after.'

He gave her a hug. She patted his back as he did so.

He had one of the high-ceilinged doubles to himself, as the resident was away for the weekend. He imagined that, if he had gone to university, his room would have looked much the same: a vinyl player — no, two of them — took up a corner, the desk was awash with books on psychology, and the posters were mostly retro souvenirs of 70s rock: Led Zep, Pink Floyd, Alice Cooper . . . with the exception of a huge image of a fantasy machine, like a spiky cockpit, flying between mountains; all Sophie could tell him was that Gavin was a geek and that this 'plane' was called Siegfried and had devastating guns. It responded to the pilot's nervous system. 'You'd love that, wouldn't you, Dad?'

'I can visualise all sorts of drawbacks. Supposing you're in the middle of a divorce and having a nervous breakdown?'

What she meant, he supposed, was that he'd appreciate the weaponry. Nothing could have been further from the truth.

She laughed. 'I don't think so.'

'You don't think what?'

'That you're having one. Anyway, it's just too boring for David and me if you're both having one.'

'Mum's not having one.'

'Oh come on, she's been having this sort of really diluted one for years. Poor thing.'

'She still signs off with an LOL, texting me.'

'Dad, that means Laugh Out Loud.'

'Does it? Oh. Well, not in her case. I hope.'

They were both continuing to gaze at Siegfried, for some reason. It reminded Bob of a deadly virus under an electron microscope. He asked her if she had met Ben.

'Yeah. He seems OK,' she said, followed by a shrug. 'A bit art-teachery. The multi-zip jeans are *such* a bad idea. I kept wanting to say, Ben, multi-zip jeans: why?'

She takes Olivia's part, but she's so unlike her, he thought.

They walked round Newcastle's grandiose centre ignoring the usual blitzkrieg of 60s concrete, browsed in a labyrinthine record shop and ate at a 'fab' Indian where every plate was the same yellow mush (more or less). 'I think the food'd be better in the mother country,' he said, examining a bloated tandoori chicken. 'This red's a spray job.'

He sat there and wondered why he hadn't in fact decided on India, maybe an ashram, instead of sitting out the time somewhere wet, grey and windy.

After the meal, they wove their way through a winter carnival of drunkenness to a concrete cellar in which Sophie played guest bass on a couple of songs with what looked like members of the heroin rehab unit. Bob was virtually the only person over twenty-five, yet it was so like the rock cellars he'd gone to thirty-odd years back that he lost internal decades. The music was louder than a Rolls-Royce Spey engine at three feet and he had to block his ears, which was impossible to do discreetly. Sophie, sporting 1960s sunglasses, laughed and danced and hugged her friends while her father stayed away from the press of bodies in a corner near the fire exit, keeping a smile stuck on and buoyed up by the occasional attentions of sozzled girls encouraging him to join in, mostly through sign language or by placing their lips against his better ear while gripping his upper arm.

They must have assumed he was a grizzled talent scout.

One of them, plump and pale with violet hair, said he looked like Harrison Ford — hopefully as he was a few years back. Another asked him what he did and he transfixed her by saying he was a photojournalist. 'That's just totally what *I* want to be!' she yelled during a slow track. She asked him where he lived; he said he was off touring the world. There followed a tricky few minutes when he became uncharacteristically aloof as the girl tried to ask him further questions, mainly technical. He knew nothing about cameras. She still gave him a tender wave as she merged into the general seethe. Her name was Amy, she was pretty, with dimples and a sweet nose that creased up, her lips set off by three silver studs. He wondered what it was like kissing a girl with three lip studs. She had a coily tattoo well below her collarbone, with words only partly covered by her sleeveless top.

Then Sophie grabbed his hand and got him jigging about. Endorphins started kicking in and his body took over, helped by several beers and a cocktail called Whippersnapper. The youngsters — so much nicer, he reckoned, than his own generation — didn't even chuckle as he bobbed about, getting creative, sweat trickling down his back. Dubai clubbing tended to include the older age range. Here he was on his own, stranded by the years but having a whale of a time.

Amy suddenly reappeared as Sophie went back up on stage. He found a pair of hands on his shoulders and Amy's weight against his, her sweet breath on his neck. This went on for several numbers, the friction increasing, the others not giving them much choice but to be squeezed close. He crouched somewhat to be cheek to cheek and hers was silken. In his inebriated state he told her — shouted into her ear — how fascinated he was by her lip studs, that he'd never kissed anyone with a lip stud. She stuck out her tongue and showed him the silver bead in the middle of its glistening length. They laughed. Her hair smelt of meringues, her breath of lemons. Her dimples were bottomless, as his Arab friends in Dubai would have said. His heart was alternately thumping and turning gooey, or both at once. He imagined her piercings — especially the tongue one — as cool, polished moments in a general outlook of warmth and softness ... his reverie was interrupted by the untimely arrival of her BlackBerry, suddenly in her hand and being concentrated on, the screen making her beads look like warning lights.

She came off it with a shrug and grinned at him, throwing her head back. 'I want to lock a photojournalist in my room all night!' she shouted several times into his ear before he could pick it up.

'Amy, you're too lovely for me!'

'No, I'm not!'

'What does your tattoo say?'

She started to pull her top away from her chest

to show him, and he peered in, decoding the curly words in the poor light as they snaked either side onto the steep slopes of her breasts that didn't seem to descend to the top of a bra but to yet more silken skin. He read, with some difficulty: *This chest contains red carnations.*

'That's beautiful!' he shouted.

A pincer on his upper arm, a pulling away. It was Sophie. She wasn't pleased. Amy hung on, laughing.

'She's completely smashed out of her head!' cried Sophie. 'Let her go, Dad!'

'I'm a free man! She's lovely!'

'She's on Smirnoff Ice and acid! You'll be done for date rape!'

They hit the cold damp air with Amy lost somewhere behind in the teeming sauna of the club. It was three in the morning; they returned to base with the aid of a taxi. Sophie was silent. Bob's ears were singing and his head spinning, while the pavement as they got out of the taxi was strangely sinuous. She said nothing until they got to her room; he angled into a beanbag with a grunt.

'You're not normally like that, Dad.'

'What? It was good fun.'

'That's not the point. She's not even twenty. She's a teenager.'

'Over eighteen, I presume. I was just dancing with her.'

'You were not just dancing. You were clinging. Grinding, it's known as. Hand on bum. Looking at her tits, practically diving in — '

'I was deciphering her amazing tattoo. *Red carnations* — '

'Yeah yeah. You've got a smudge of red there.' She pointed to the corner of her mouth. 'Yuk. Yuk and yuk and yuk.'

He pouted like a teenager, his head a polyphony of swaying sounds. 'Nice girl.'

'She'd dropped some acid. She wasn't in control.'

'You mean it wasn't my charms?'

'So embarrassing. Just so incredibly embarrassing,' she added, but vaguely: she'd started to check Facebook. He closed his eyes. This was his last night in England, he thought. A decent send-off. He was falling from a great height into sleep when he heard a voice saying, 'The thing is, I'm in my final year. I've got the mother of all dissertations and I'll be worrying about you. You could've waited. Mum agrees. So does David, underneath his totally this-is-trivia look.'

'It was all decided for me by others.'

'Others?'

'Doctors. Hey, I'll email. Phone now and again. It might only be a few months.'

'Uh-oh,' said Sophie. 'Amy's tagged me in a post.'

'Eh?'

'It's a new thing, it comes straight onto my own Facebook page. Look.'

Bob read:

Sophie Winrush go back to nursury school. Your Dads proper fit.

Sophie clicked on Amy's name and Bob found himself looking at the girl's sultry face, half in shadow. There was the same sentence, followed by 'Charlie's Cellar' and the time about half an hour ago. Charlie's Cellar was highlighted in blue — leading, Sophie explained, to *its* Facebook page.

'What a gas,' Bob said.

Then he saw, below Amy's compliment, a photo of a dancing couple that he realised with a shudder was Amy and himself, both looking surprisingly ill under the flash. Sophie ran the cursor over her father's image and up popped 'Sophie Winrush's dad.'

'Shit,' said Bob, this time.

Sophie pulled a face. 'Serves you right.'

'I was just having some innocent fun, Sophie.'

'I read this article about men going wild when they hit their fifties, acting like teenagers? Now I'll be even more worried about you. You weren't exactly 24/7 when we were kids, then you do a runner when you don't really need to.'

His heart gave a lurch: it had survived a three-hour bop, now it wanted to rest. 'I was present one hundred per cent when I was off duty. I always remember you stroking that moss on the balustrade.'

'Er, what?'

'Your imaginary kitten. Snowball.' She looked puzzled. 'I was home ten days every month. You had lots of activities — maybe you didn't notice. I didn't even want you to board.'

'You weren't there when I was in hospital, after my accident.'

This was Olivia's technique as well: chipping away with serial accusations.

'True. I was committed to a rotation thousands of nautical miles away. But I came back a week early.' Half a week early, but we lie on average five times a day.

'What was this commitment?'

He thought about it. He honestly had to: he remembered Olivia's panicked call coming through somewhere concrete with tiny windows looking out on grey-green bush. Around that time he'd done a few flights for Michael Harradine's Jet Line International out of Brize Norton for the MoD, mainly humanitarian stuff for Kosovo, and then he'd got more Jet Line stuff into the Congo at $10,000 a month minimum later that year, and they were too short of pilots for him to abandon ship just like that. So he reckoned it must have been that rotation: mainly military, which one doesn't talk about.

'You can't even remember, can you?'

'I'd just started a tour,' he said, 'and they were short of pilots. Mainly humanitarian work. Africa.'

Sophie laughed. 'Oh Dad, I so believe you.'

'I should have come back straightaway,' he admitted, nodding his head slowly. His tinnitus was taking off. 'I don't know how, but I should have. I did repaint your room.'

'I suppose I could've had a real geek of a dad like Lisa Hanson's,' she said, lighting a last cigarette. He joined her with a cigarillo, hoping it would remind her of his story about lighting up in the cockpit in Frankfurt and shocking the ramp agent. But it didn't.

∗   ∗   ∗

The next morning, late, Sophie called him to the laptop: Amy's remark had attracted a string of comments.

'Are you A FREAK OR WOT fancying older men.'

'Yeuch, Amy. We's gonna to sleep now and we're the same age.'

'How old, like over 40?????'

'Old men are 2 creepy and they smell yo.'

'I wanna check the dude out!!'

No replies from Amy. Sophie reassured him they were all students in higher education. One was studying English literature.

He shrugged. 'Like the telexes in the old days. Chattering away. No one took any notice. If they're stupid enough to want to read this, how do they do it?'

'Ask to be my friend. Or Amy's.'

'Would you accept them?'

'No. Only if I knew them already.'

He did a little test at the computer while Sophie spent hours in the bathroom washing her hair. Among the usual references to English setters, Florida apartments and the Gloucestershire river (it was an extremely rare name), the entry 'Winrush' yielded Sophie's Facebook profile but not Amy's kind words. It also yielded the membership list for something called Health 'n' Well-Being: incredibly, it was the private gym in Crowthorne, his name and the date of his joining. How long had that been up there? When had he ever given permission?

He could hear Gold Teeth's sing-song voice in his head: 'So, he is in Crowthorne. Here is the address. Give him my regards and say, 'One swallow, it does not make a summer.' If he is not at home, he has a daughter. On Facebook. Find out the names of her friends . . . '

Photojournalism had been a tactical error. He looked out of the window at rainy Jesmond and briefly considered posing as a writer: novels, something that required no special skills. Everyone seemed to be having a go, especially retirees. But there's the snag, he thought: it sounds like a cover. It doesn't explain the past. Besides, he had zilch imagination, and had come near bottom in English.

He searched about for something unglamorous and solitary, the very opposite of an airline pilot; and it had to be connected with the Scottish islands. What did you find on rugged, isolated coastlines, apart from climbers with a death wish? Cliffs. Molluscs. Birds.

It was a toss between a geologist, whatever you call someone who studies molluscs, or a bird-spotter.

An avian expert rather than an aviation expert.

Birders were not glamorous. He could be researching something straightforward like gulls. Their mating habits. No, their feeding habits, because they ate all the year round.

By the time Sophie re-emerged in a fug of

shampoo smells, her computer had delivered enough info about gulls in the Hebrides to get him by in an emergency. He had a laptop in the car, but he couldn't be sure they'd have Internet or Wi-Fi that far north. He knew so little.

'What's all that you've been scribbling?'

'Birdlife,' he said, packing away the scribbles in his holdall. 'I'm going to be a bird expert. There'll be nothing else to do up there.'

'You'll be found out in ten minutes. The birders here are incredibly expert, like you are about boring planes.'

'OK, I'll just evince an interest.'

He was hugging her goodbye within the hour. It began to rain.

'Remember, Sophie, you don't have a clue where I'm heading. Seriously.'

'Do you, Dad?'

'And sorry about the car.'

'This one's cool.'

'You mean cheap. White cars are naff.'

'Hey, they're not. White's cool.' She showed him her iPod and laughed. 'You're so out of date, Dad.'

She went back in. Despite the wet, he bent down to inspect the underside of the Polo, not realising she was watching from the porch.

'What are you doing?' she called out. 'Checking for a bomb?'

'I thought I heard Amy under there, OK?'

'Yeah yeah, Dad. You're not in some kind of horrible danger, are you?'

'Hanging by a thread, sweetheart.'

'If you want to really disappear, OK, you

remove the SIM card and battery and chuck your mobile into water, use prepaid phones with one time use, and put a stone in your shoe to walk different. And in your case, pursue that beard.'

'How do you know?'

Sophie laughed, resting a hand on the porch pillar. 'It's everyone's dream, right?'

Part Two

1

The croft-house was as cold as a sauna is hot. Its draughts were audible.

Al had omitted to mention that the place had last been rewired in the 1960s. Despite a droopy cable on a line of thin poles staggering off into the mist, there was no power. Bob phoned him about this and other things from Scourlay's only call box, having memorised the unhackable number; because the call was international, the preparatory pile of two-pound coins dropped like mercury. Jane and Al were basking in the sun of the British Virgin Islands. He said there had been power when he last visited.

'When was that, Al?'

'Let me see now. There's no salmon there. Nineteen eighty-one?'

'That's why you didn't know about the causeway.'

'What causeway?'

'Precisely.'

Al's picturesque rowing boat full of sacks and lambs had been superseded in the 1990s by a stone causeway that had cleared out the licence-free rust buckets, moving or otherwise, and permitted some flashy four-wheel drives to jar with the landscape.

The skeletal young estate agent claimed he'd had no idea about the lack of power until the pulling of the mains switch in Bob's presence;

his was the first customer enquiry, at least in person.

After a crossing of the Minches that had swept the glasses off the bar and set everyone (bar real sailors and the few who had taken the right pills) into what Al would call, back in his passenger days, the lobster thermidor crouch, Bob recovered overnight in a chocolate-coloured hotel room in Stornaway. He'd followed the agent's car the next morning: island-hopping, they'd taken a couple of calmer ferries, the man's hatchback nipping along the winding roads so fast it was all Bob could do to keep up. The first ferry was late, and they sat in a glassed-in shed with a couple of depressed locals and, despite it being January in the Outer Hebrides, some cheery German bicyclists in bright yellow cagoules. They thought Bob, with his scraggly new beard and shapeless fisherman's woollen hat, was a picturesque local and began taking photos: he made himself even more authentic by objecting. Within hours the snaps could be in global view on the Internet.

The agent had chuckled. 'Maybe you're a famous actor going to ground, Mr Webb. We've had one or two o' them.'

'Rats, I've been rumbled,' Bob joked, secretly dismayed. He would have to act casual.

After another ferry and some more catch-me-if-you-can motoring by the youth, they'd crossed onto Scourlay and pulled up at a broken gate with no house in sight, just pools and rocks and rough humpy pasture. The agent, called Ken, pulled on his gumboots and Bob did the same. It was raining . . . in the way, he suspected, the sun shines in the desert. Umbrella handling was made trickier by the gusts. The raised track avoided most of the wet parts, wiggling about like a worm in the hand until it rounded a small hill and the house hove into sight. No view: the cloud sliced off everything above about knee height. There was the beginning of either the loch or the sea disappearing into the mist. It was even colder than he'd expected, and the rain seemed to have sharp points.

Despite his age, Ken could remember when all this was a croft, with common rights to grazing: an undefined part, some three (not five) acres, was now 'decrofted' and 'all yours, to do with whatever you've a mind to, Mr Webb. You've certainly got the isolation,' he added, as if his latest client was cooking up some crazed sci-fi experiment to end the world. 'The summer sees one or two hikers and second-homers. They call this blackland,' he said, consulting his agency clipboard and then waving it at the peninsula's shortened horizon. 'You want to watch the ditches and drains.'

The house looked smaller than in the photos. There was not a single tree in sight; the building crouched in long, shaggy grass behind a couple of thorn bushes. Plastic tubs, milk crates and other bric-a-brac lay about, along with a fallen chicken-wire fence and a reassuring washing line with a single yellow clothes peg. The mist gave hints of a sea view, but there might equally well have been a nuclear power station out there.

The place was clearly a cement-coloured

liability. The shape was peculiar because a single-storey croft house had been stretched to one side by an extension featuring a picture window. The older part had a gleaming slate roof with a skylight each side; mossed sheets of corrugated iron covered the newer section — about a third of the whole — so that it looked as if it could be pushed back in like a telescope.

The front door was on one side of a breeze-block porch, and had to be yanked open, scraping on the sill. Bob expressed concern.

'It's fairly wet in these parts,' Ken pointed out.

'Wet's good,' Bob replied; 'you get more engine power.'

Ken covered his puzzlement with a joke. 'You'd have been better off in the Maldives.'

Bob had expected the interior to be flagged floors and stony walls, with a rocking chair before a great peat-brick fireplace and a huge wooden bed in the corner, straw palliasse and all. This was how he remembered a croft interior on Mull when he'd bicycled up as a youth to escape family life; peat smells, hubby puffing on a pipe before the blaze, dim light from a paraffin lamp. Here it was all wood. The floors were natural pine boarding, but the walls showed a 1970s taste for dark-stained plywood sheeting. The bedrooms had cream wallpaper patterned with orange asterisks, crinkled in places from damp. The kitchen was all white paint or tiles, to go with the white Raeburn stove, whose doors the agent opened and then slammed shut, presumably checking for leftovers or flight logs. Two metal-and-foam chairs sat at a rocky table as if waiting for supper. The remaining furniture looked either home-made (plywood again) or from some indeterminate date before the war.

The lad annoyed Bob by saying 'Take care' as they climbed the boarded-in ladder to the attic bedroom, which was pine-clad. It felt ship-like. Bob could only stand up in the middle, slightly crouched, and was watched in sardonic silence from the stairs. I'll sleep up here, Bob decided: he liked the ship feel, the marginally drier air.

It was gloomy: naturally, because there was no artificial light.

Ken had tried the mains switch a few times, looking at the instructions in his folder, ignoring comments from Bob. The general mouldiness reminded him of central Africa, the rainy season, with cold thrown in.

'There goes my nice hot shower,' he said.

'You'll be lucky to find anywhere else like this,' Ken retorted, 'if your mind's set on the isles.'

'I don't plan to. Your lot can call an electrician.'

'It's beyond that,' the agent sighed. 'It needs rewiring. We'll sort it, but you'll have to sign new papers in the interim.'

That would be a pain. Al had dealt with all the papers, acting on behalf of his incapacitated cousin: Bob was effectively subletting. Now Al was out of the loop.

They were in the sitting room, whose picture window that day was like a TV without the aerial. The black sofas were fake leather. The cold had increased to something viscous in which they were trapped like flies.

'Maybe I'm OK with no electrics,' Bob said. 'More romantic. The good life.'

Ken, thinking Bob was being sardonic, claimed innocence by saying he'd come out from the mainland and had only been working there a year, and the house had been on the market for three. 'It's all a mess,' he sighed, staring at his hands, already world-weary. Fifty years ago, Bob reflected, he'd have been out in all weathers, carting seaweed or hauling blocks of peat, bringing the flock home. The light was fading already.

'How far are the shops?'

'Now there's a man up with the times. There was a shop, but the causeway made it redundant. You have to go back over the causeway to Bargrennan, on the previous island. Twenty minutes.'

'Tell them I'll take it as is. Seriously. I don't want to be bothering with more papers. The rent's not high anyway.'

'They'll not be rewiring it tomorrow.'

'I don't want it rewired. I've worked out in Africa. Birds,' he added, hastily. 'Conservation.'

The youth gave a supercilious laugh. 'When folk see the postcards of this island, they say it's like the Caribbean without the tourists. White sand beaches, turquoise waters, all that jazz. But there's one big difference. Guess what that is, Mr Webb.'

'No drugs?'

'You've got to be joking.'

They walked back to the car in the gathering gloom. 'Best of British,' said the agent, like an insult. 'If you get lonely, you've got a good choice of bars in Ardcorry. But they're aye in the Tinker's Arms, with the same piped music. One tape. You can walk there and back, though.'

Bob shook a limp, chilly hand and off its owner went, headlights already on at three o'clock. Now all Bob could hear was the gusts singing in the wires and a dim *shushing* noise which he assumed was the sea. Then he noticed a tussock near his feet, its long whitish stems agitated by the wind. Here he was. Here the tussock was. Both alive in this same moment. He must, he thought, remember to buy a torch, the type you strap onto your head like a miner's lamp.

* * *

The shop in Bargrennan may have been a concrete shed with a roof of corrugated iron, but it reminded him of a cargo bay stocked with everything bar the shouting. The houses round about looked sullen, as if what they really wanted to do was get back to the mainland estate from which they'd been plucked. A few along the street towards the harbour were in stone and quite attractive, while others gained points from being painted a Kansas-style dark red.

He bought candles and matches and firelighters; the stores' complete stock of kerosene lamps with a coil of wick; a bag of slow-burning coal bricks; some pots and pans for the stove, including one big enough to stand in as a bathtub; and food — tins and pulses, mainly, as the vegetable rack's contents looked as if they'd circled the world a few times. He ordered bags of lump coal.

He also bought, in a moment of inspiration, a butane camping stove and several cylinders to back up the Raeburn; he was wise to the latter's demands from earlier years in Worcestershire. In all this wild spree, he nearly forgot the torch — a halogen headlamp type for infant potholers, supplemented by a heavy-duty hand-held. And a heap of batteries. This miraculous place (like an old-time African general stores without the hawkers) even had a battery charger that ran off a car's cigarette lighter. He went back again for paper and pens. And rope, and string. Oh, sorry, and a hot-water bottle.

'Aye, you'll be needing that,' said the woman behind the counter: round and friendly, perpetually between thirty-five and fifty-five, with large glasses and a winning smile. Her accent was soft, almost dreamy. His coming and going amused her. When he told her the croft had no electricity, she fished out some solar-powered garden lights, the type you stick in the earth.

'You'll maybe find these useful.'

'Is there enough sun?'

'Well, I doubt that in the winter,' she laughed. 'But as my father used to say, *Ye can live in sun, but ye cannae live on it.*'

He was already attracting attention to himself, just by being here. What had he said to Al in Cookham? There's safety in crowds. He had rushed into this, he realised. He might have been better off in Kuala Lumpur.

On the picturesque curve down to the harbour, in one of the older stone houses, there was a cosy-looking café called the Seaward Side. He popped in, thirsting for tea. It was empty, but a moon-faced woman in her thirties emerged from the gloom at the back, sweeping up to him in a zigzaggy yellow skirt, her leather waist-belt dangling a long tassel.

She brought him his tea in a mug that told him, in big red letters, to *SKIRL AND WHIRL*.

'Are you staying in Bargrennan, then?'

'Not exactly. I'm over the causeway. The land beyond. Scourlay.'

'It's *Scoorlay*,' she smiled, 'as in *moorland*.' She was ample but sexy, as Olivia would put it. He'd already noticed the two computers on tables at the rear, before the unlit picture gallery. A Wi-Fi sign in the window.

'I haven't got electricity,' he said, 'so you might see more of me. With laptop.'

'Reception's mostly guaranteed,' she said with a drowsy smile. 'I'm Marcie, by the way. This is Astra,' she added, as a little boy around three years old sauntered in through the door marked PRIVATE. He was dressed as Batman.

'Hello, Astra. I'm Kit.'

Marcie sighed. 'That's a nice name.'

''Tisn't,' said Astra. 'Yuk.' And gave him a kick.

★　★　★

He drove back over the causeway feeling warmer inside, thanks to a few smiles from Marcie. It didn't take much. She hadn't sounded Scottish, but a drawly northern English: a fellow stranger.

He did feel, though, that he was coming back to 'his' island. He had been here about three hours. *Scoorlay.*

He unloaded the car boot by the gate in what was effectively darkness, the wind slapping at him playfully and apparently swinging an invisible watering can towards his face every few seconds. He failed to keep to the path. His head torch wavered feebly over an undifferentiated mass of grass, rock and shadow. He had forgotten what real night looked like under cloud, terrestrially: he could barely see the hill, let alone the house. Maybe I'll hit a bottomless bog and vanish, he thought, never to be found again. Seconds later his left foot sank with a gurgle and he pulled it free, minus gumboot. This was not a good start.

He laid down his bags carefully and groped about for the boot, his wet toes starting to go numb. The water felt unnaturally cold: this was annoying. He began to regret Dubai. He was an idiot: he'd been lured into the wilderness, and without electricity, and it was freezing. Then his fingers closed on rubber and he rejoiced.

He tried walking on the dried heather bells, but these proved treacherous, as they sat on wet sponge. Using rocks as stepping stones was no good either, as slipping was worse than sinking. Apart from anything else, a burn white-watered its way down the hill and sprawled carelessly across the path. The stepping stones weren't big enough for a goat.

He squelched to the door, splashed to the forehead. He had only freighted a portion of his purchases, leaving the rest for tomorrow. The house seemed colder than the vigorous outdoors, cold in thick slabs. How nice it would have been to switch on the light, radiators, an electric kettle, to stand under a steaming power-shower. Instead, he had just the jittery little halogen that threw evil shadows from corners as the wind whistled outside.

He tried to light a candle, but the matches were wet. Somewhere he'd packed his vintage Canadian Pacific cigarette lighter that he'd kept for the occasional cigarillo and as a good-luck charm. By the time he found it in one of his suitcases, he was jabbering aloud.

In the kitchen, in the light of two candles, he peeled off his clothes, shivering like bad actors do in films and cursing McAllister and Bensoussan in that order, and rubbed himself down, staining the towel with black mud. Within a couple of hours he had the kitchen dancing to the coal bricks — the Raeburn required dusting out, but was fully operative — sufficient to fry some eggs and heat some beans, and generally thaw him out. His socks steamed on the stove's metal rail. The digital AA-powered trannie kept him company with Radio 4, albeit hissed at by the gusts.

He reckoned he was winning.

This is an adventure, he said to himself. Only

Al knew precisely where he was. Any non-junk snail mail would get redirected to David, who would scan it and send it to him by email. 'What a pain,' was all his son had said, when called from the phone box, adding, 'You can't keep hiding for ever, Dad.'

'Things change. These types fall out, get arrested, die, retire to a life of luxury. Only diamonds are for ever. I'm staying here nine months, until the September gales.'

'Tim reckons you're a rough one. Diamond, I mean.'

Bob laughed. 'Tell him I have many facets.'

Supposing they put pressure on his nearest and dearest to reveal his whereabouts? This was not the modus operandi of any of the known dodgy operators, apart from the Mexican drugs cartels — who were Broadmoor-certifiable. Which was why he didn't like the fact that Diez was Mexican.

The Raeburn roared behind its little window and the heat beat against his face; he felt pretty good as the food slipped down. Things are most definitely looking up, he thought, as he filled the hot-water bottle with water that his own vigorous efforts had boiled, taking it up to bed along with his pistol and the candle. Various noises kept him awake and he stared into the darkness, suddenly missing people. Live people of a non-murderous disposition, anyway.

The picture window had better reception the next morning — bleached grass in the foreground and a black plastic water barrel — but it might still have been the overshoot at

Gatwick: the mist had thickened. To boil water meant a further lot of palaver with wood and coal and some extra waiting, but the tea in his own *Fly Me* mug (Sophie's present) was better for it, despite its tang of peat.

His gumboots had dried by the Raeburn in a smell of rubber; he stepped outside with warm toes. The air reminded him of the stuff coming through at 35,000 feet, and he could smell the sea on it, and sea wrack, and iodine, and his own chimney. He had enough cash — even after the divorce came through, even without the flat sold — to keep him going for the planned nine months. In that time he would plot the next instalment. Every man needs a pause. But he already felt lonely. At night it was almost scary. What he needed was a guitar, although he'd only mastered four chords some thirty years back.

He found some large flat stones for the awkward burn-flow zone, then clomped to and fro with the remaining clobber.

* * *

The house was on a peninsula. This was not saying much: cartographically, the island looked like a plate smashed on a hard floor, its bits kicked together. The coastline was jagged and parts came and went with the tide: skerries, reefs, washed-over boulders, clefts with sand that looked like pleasant coves until they vanished in spume.

Cliffs were more reliable. He'd approach a grassy edge, think of the 6,000 miles of water meeting their match far below, remember the balcony incident, and tread gingerly back. The breakers rolled on slowly and hypnotically towards their fate, even in a gale.

The first gale started on his third day. He was told it was a south-easterly. After a few hours of this, he hitched on his yellow sou'wester to investigate the sou'easter: once he'd left the lee of the house, the long grass flattened all around, he felt a rearrangement of priorities: weather first, tiny human last. It was all he could do to breathe. He staggered round to the back, tugging his hood to keep it on: he was instantly wet through, transformed into nothing but a pair of salty lips. The loch had white streaks all over its gloomy surface and was chopping against the rocks so hard he could see spray.

The front skylight began to leak directly above his pillow in the loft bedroom, so he moved the bed to the corner. The sound effects of wind and rain against the slates was a bother, but the downstairs bedrooms were small and smelt faintly of pyjamas: he'd started to use these rooms as storage spaces, gathering useful stuff like planks, crates, elastic straps, polystyrene buoys, a single undamaged oar. The loo was the size of a seven-oh's, stained green and with a broken plastic seat. The tiny wash-basin was clogged with cigarette butts, rotted to a mush.

He expected the gale to blow itself out after a day or so, but a week later it was still going without a single toilet break. It was several south-easterlies, apparently, stacked and landing on the island with seamless precision.

The peninsula and its little loch were swept by every wind going. He'd hold up a wet finger and give up. But he felt safe, more or less. He had taken Sophie's advice and ditched the mobile, replacing it with a one-use prepaid type; the car was parked a couple of hundred yards down the road, tucked well off the asphalt on dry grass that curved behind a hummock; he'd check the vehicle over on departure and arrival, feeling around the hubs and tyres and the rim where the jack goes, taking a visual on everything else with a torch.

He wondered whether, when the season began, there'd be a lot more people to worry about. The shopkeeper, whose name was Kathleen, said they didn't get many tourists outside the music festival in August. The weather. It could bucket down in the summer, or clear to a cloudless sky for a week. 'There's no knowing, you see.'

'There never is,' he agreed, paying for a week's potatoes in straightforward, anonymous cash.

He bought a paper and read that every UK banknote was tainted with cocaine. There was no getting away from anything, these days.

2

His nearest neighbours were Carol and Angus
MacLean of the neat white house on the way to
Ardcorry. The peninsula's top portion was their
grazing; their nephew looked after the sheep and
doubled as the local DJ — with a taste for
'industrial rock', they added, laughing. The neat
house sat next to what looked like a scrapyard
but was in fact Angus MacLean's workshop.

Bob had met Carol MacLean in the lane on
the third day, and, eerily, she'd seemed to know
who he was. She invited him over for tea, mainly
to let him know that if he didn't fence his land,
their flock would be all over it. That was all right
by me, he told them.

He walked up the lane and arrived with water
streaming off his hood. They had two pigs, many
hens, several cows, cats and a muddy terrier. He
asked some trainee-islander questions, starting of
course with the weather.

'Layers,' said Mrs MacLean mysteriously.
'Well, you canna have too many.'

'Five seasons in a day,' added Mr MacLean,
with a grunt of amusement. He had the
creased-up eyes of a fisherman.

They hardly ever had straight northerly gales
here, they went on: the rascal who built the
house knew what he was doing — the blank back
of it faced the south-easterlies. He may have
been a smuggler and an alcoholic, but he was an

islesman, having the local intelligence. According to Mrs MacLean's long-dead grandmother, he had a long scraggly beard, bendy legs and a knotty cane.

'Oh,' Bob said, 'I've got a bit of a way to go yet.'

Carol MacLean cleaned for local second-homers and for the pub, which had three plain rooms. Angus was a scallop diver, bony and tough, joggled daily by the ocean: since he'd started with his own boat twenty-five years ago, two of his fellow divers had drowned. They talked the Gaelic between themselves. Their two teenage children were busy being educated on the mainland. Bob told them he'd been to boarding school, too. Five of them.

'Were you now?' said Mrs MacLean gently, like a hypnotist. 'They can be very fine.'

He said nothing. He shouldn't even have told them about his schools. He ought to be giving his CV an entire makeover: new registration, new decals. Christopher Webb, amateur birder. Ex-teacher. Nature studies. Various tricky schools. No, a discreet prep school in the country. The depths of Suffolk. You wouldn't have heard of it. It's not even got a website.

They gave him some hand-plucked scallops, the biggest Bob had ever seen, destined for top-class tables in ungrateful places like Dubai. He admitted water wasn't his favourite element. His socks were wet again.

'Having said that,' he went on, 'neither are heights. Surprisingly.'

He stopped himself, mumbled something

about going up ladders. They were surprised he was living where he was, given the state of it, the problems of access. Angus MacLean noted Bob's 'rugby shoulders'.

'They'll come in handy for carrying,' Mrs MacLean pointed out.

'That's it,' chuckled Angus. His skin was as brown as the earthenware teapot, but his eyes, like hers, were an arctic blue.

★ ★ ★

The evenings dragged; Bob realised his personal space was mostly confined to two minimal spots, either in front of the Raeburn or in front of the fireplace. He'd open the front door and step out into a windy dark: the paraffin lamp hung in the hall would swing wildly, making shadows leap from odd places. He'd made a colossal mistake. He missed Leila, the pools, the clubs, his friends. The sun. He dreamed of Dubai's heat, even in its worst seasonal manifestation. He missed the cockpit, its luminous spread of instruments like a night city far below: Madrid, for instance, edging a blackness that was not the sea or a lake but its huge park; New York, even its approaching glitter more stylish than anywhere else. He missed the twins, although he'd phoned them from the call box several times. He even missed Olivia: she'd laugh to see him now.

Marcie's café was closed for a fortnight — a winter break. Bored to gloominess, he ventured down to the Tinker's Arms in Ardcorry. There were only three customers — two old boys and a younger man up at the bar, all weather-singed and with fiercely blue eyes, like the MacLeans. The one tape was clearly Johnny Cash.

Bob nodded politely, waited. The younger man eventually went round behind the bar and served him his pint and chaser ('Murray's oot the back'). Bob sat at the furthest table possible and pretended to read the *Scotsman*. With his scraggy beard and woollen cap, he hardly looked the typical tourist: he fancied the news had already spread from Bargrennan that some English idiot had taken the old croft-house near Ardcorry, the one without electricity out on Carnan Tuath that gets all the winds, and this was he. Or maybe their stares were simply born from winter tedium.

The older of the two veterans caught his eye and asked how was the fishing. Bob said he wasn't fishing, or not yet. The man seemed surprised, told him that there were some fine fat trout in that wee loch (he gave it a Gaelic name).

'Are you renting, now?'

'That's right. Just a few months.'

'No electrics for years.'

'I know. They didn't tell me that.'

'They wouldn't,' said the other old boy.

The younger man said, looking at the others with a straight face, 'The summer can be quite pleasant, I hear.'

'They do say that, aye,' said the first man, into his beer.

'So the rumour goes,' sighed his friend, winking a watery eye.

They all three glanced at Bob, expectant and

suspicious at the same time.

'I don't mind the weather,' he said. 'As long as I can see the birds. Research,' he added, conveying its apparent dullness.

'Oh,' said the first man, 'you're a twitcher. I'm partial to birds myself,' he added, rubbing his thigh as the others chortled. 'So what's your speciality? Sea eagles? We have a few of them, these days. Reinserted.'

'Reintroduced,' corrected the younger man.

'The black-headed gull,' Bob said, ignoring Sophie's advice. 'Feeding habits. With particular reference to its cliff habitat.'

There was a brief silence. They glanced at one another. The younger man said, 'So you'll not be very occupied now.'

'What?'

'At this time o' the year.'

Bob looked at him, somewhat puzzled. 'Oh, they're out and about.'

'Are they now?'

'Well, I'm used to rough weather, and they're pretty easy to spot with their dark hoods,' he said. 'I saw three only yesterday.'

'Three, was it? Are you sure you hadn't been at the hooch?'

Thankfully, the barman emerged with an item of local gossip in the newspaper. During this distraction, Bob slipped out. Something was awry.

In Stornoway he had bought a stack of literature dealing with local natural history, including a bird dictionary the width of a flight-crew training manual: it was better to know a little in depth than a lot shallowly. As Doug used to tell him, 'You're a pilot once you don't expect the instruments to do what you expect them to do.' He sounded Zen sometimes, would Doug Rydale. 'Never trust your instinct: you're dealing with a machine.'

Bob turned again to the black-headed gull in the illustrated book on Hebridean birdlife. *Larus ridibundus*. The commonest of gulls. 'Its huge colonies abandon their island nests and go south to farmland or city, returning to the Hebrides only in March.' It was now the last week of January. The news got worse: the spoilsports lost the hooded look in winter, replacing it with white plumage and a chocolate smudge behind the eyes, which gradually grew in stripes and patches as the breeding season approached. This began around May.

Bob's diet revolved around oats. He missed trees. Locals stood in the middle of the road, looming dangerously out of the horizontal rain, as did sheep. The damp made his joints ache, irritated his scar tissue. He was sick of tinned artichoke hearts and the lack of a hot shower and not lifting winged metal into the tropopause. He would leave at the end of the following month and join an ashram. Somewhere hot and hidden. This decision cheered him. The end of February was a destination. He hiked, he muddied the polo's livery up and down the island chain. He phoned Al on the special number.

'Bob! How's the weather?'

'Hear that banging? It's trying to get in.'

'Oh for fuck's sake, you're making me come

297

over all nostalgic. Seriously, are you surviving, skipper?'

Bob was about to tell him that he was throwing in the towel, but something in Al's tone — a cockiness, perhaps — prevented him. 'Al, it's fine. Nice beaches, beautiful girls, no midgies.'

A chuckle over the wire hum. 'But that's another story, eh?'

'And no typhoons and no millionaires.'

'People are very nice here, too. I like millionaires.'

'Are you one, Al?'

Wire hum again, but no chuckle.

'I feel like it. I'm swinging in a hammock between two palm trees, and the sun is setting into the Caribbean and the beach is deserted, and there are some incredible yachts out there, and I'm drinking a Painkiller.'

'I assume that's not liquid valium.'

'The effect's the same. Pusser's rum, pineapple juice, cream of coconut and squeezed orange, splashed onto the ice, not poured, fresh ground nutmeg on top. We never got that in our council estate in fucking Fife.'

'Yo ho ho. You sound just like Blackbeard.'

'So I should. This was his old stamping ground. Pirates, Bob, pirates.'

'How's your peeling nose?'

'I protect it these days. How's yours, skipper?'

'Al, there are fewer people on this island than would fill business class in a 727, but they're all spies and informers. I'd have been better off in a metropolis.'

Another chuckle, with partying sounds behind: bass notes and high-pitched laughter. The yacht scene, no doubt. Al was irritatingly on top. Or just full of rum cocktails. He asked Bob if his neighbours were still the MacDuffys.

'The nearest house is the MacLeans.'

'Ah, what a pity. Carol MacDuffy was a dish. Gorgeous at seventeen. The belle of the isle. And very bright. Quite a one, too. Not that there was much competition.'

'Maybe that's Carol MacLean. Married to Angus MacLean, scallop diver. They speak the Gaelic.'

'That'll be her. The parents must have passed on. Nice folk. Is she still gorgeous?'

Bob suddenly saw her in a new light: no longer quite so homely behind her flowery kitchen apron.

'She's coming up to fifty, Al. Filled out a bit, I imagine. But holding her own. I go there for the odd hot shower and cup of tea. She lets me use her twin-tub.'

'Does she now? Diving for her scallops, eh?'

'I don't reckon she's quite a one, these days.'

* * *

Bob didn't think he'd call Al again unless there was some emergency, and he was careful now to visit the MacLeans only when Angus was present.

One time, nevertheless, the man was out. Bob emerged from the bathroom, feeling much better in clean clothes, to find Carol wielding a pair of

299

long-pronged scissors in the kitchen.

'How about it, Samson?'

'How about what?'

'A wee trim. I'm Scourlay's unofficial men's hairdresser. I think you're maybe a bit superannuated for the hippy look.'

Her breasts settled comfortably against his shoulder as she snipped, her breathing warm on his ear. Today she was wearing jeans that were too small for her in all the right places, as Olivia would put it, and a fetching furry top. Bob tried to think of rest homes, his father in his last weeks, but this neurological cold bath failed to work. He rested his hands casually over his crotch, wisps of his hair falling on them like autumn leaves. They were chatting about the export of scallops, how the middlemen got the largest cut, how Angus risked his life for peanuts. Bob said he wasn't a great sailor, but he'd quite like to go out in a boat and see porpoises. The front door opened and Bob's heart appeared to stop. Angus, with a .22 rifle in his hand. The muddy terrier panted at his feet. The scissors went on ticking.

Bob raised his hand to wave at him. 'Hello, Angus. Your wife said I looked like a hippy.'

'I never did,' Carol laughed.

'I had the long hair one time,' said Angus, dumping a dead rabbit on the table, blood congealed in its nose. 'I was quite a mover in my youth.'

* * *

300

The gales stopped after three weeks, leaving a ringing silence and a lovely mountainous landscape of bright reflectors under a blue sky that made Bob feel vaguely stoned. It was a fitful sun by the afternoon, but the day was dry and he walked the peninsula's blacklands, stumbling into ditches and drains like the lad had warned, and reached a bay to the north.

He strode the shore, elated. The sea turned turquoise whenever the sun appeared, breaking on a broad white-sand beach populated only by gulls. He didn't think he had ever seen any nicer beach anywhere: the only sunbathers were seals, spread on rocks in glossy mounds. Long streaks of cirrus down to the sea's horizon. Take that, Al my friend. You and your buried treasure.

He walked for the rest of the day without seeing a soul. In among the skerries, where it was calm, he watched a sea otter play for an entire hour. A huge bird of prey circled a sea-stack. The blue sky looked permanent.

The next day it poured — horizontally. It was amazing that the ground was wet at all, but it was.

The café reopened the following morning and he took his laptop and picked up David's emails with the scanned post. There wasn't much. Bills were all on direct debit, he could do most things online if needs be. A chilly, belligerent letter from Olivia's solicitor, quite unnecessary, concerning the Swiss account. Maybe he didn't miss Olivia. A steamy postcard from Leila, along with a photo of herself in a micro-bikini by a pool: David commented that it was now pinned up on his wall. Bob wrote back asking him not to tell Mum. Sophie had sent a chatty, loving email, and he replied in due measure. He hoped nobody sinister was hacking in.

Which pool was it? Arab tiles, palms, lots of fancy bushes. Maybe the oasis hotel they'd driven out to last year, all adobe walls and camels. Leila's collarbones were prominent above the packed contents of her bikini top. Heat, dryness and let's-get-into-the-shade. The sun had barely showed itself again, here: a one-day wonder. When Marcie suddenly appeared with his coffee, he pressed Exit. The screen returned to the twins, aged sixteen, grinning in front of a big oak near the house.

Huge dangly blue earrings, a woolly bee-striped top and a crimson skirt.

'Your kids?'

'Yup. A few years back. Twins.'

'Lovely, they look. I guess one day Astra will look like that.'

Bob doubted it, but made the right noises.

'Feels a long way away, doesn't it, Kit? The mainland? Assuming your base is there.'

'It is. Kind of. Where's yours?'

'Oh, wherever Astra is,' she said, needlessly fetching him sugar. 'The isles for now. There's nowhere like them.'

'Certainly isn't.'

The gallery took up the back area of the café beyond a bead curtain: out of season she didn't bother to light it. It was full of mostly bird photos and slapped-on paintings of cliffs, and Astra's sit-on plastic lorry parked in the corner,

302

its bonnet partly melted and the back end chewed. The café was cosy enough, with quality striped curtains, Mexican tiles and framed posters of wise sayings.

The adventure that the hero is ready for is the one that he gets.

'I like that one,' he said, as Marcie passed.

'What date's your birthday?'

'December the twelfth.'

'I knew it. You're a fire sign. Sagittarius. Likes adventures.'

'Fire. Not air?'

'Air and earth are your seasonal qualities. Not water, though. Water's out.'

'That figures.'

The ocean rushing up, mid-Pacific. An uncontrollable dive. Flat descent and at night, so no shrieks from behind. The impact of the belly in a fantastic crest of foam. Only in his thoughts and dreams, thankfully.

The twins smiled at him from an English summer afternoon. The only other customers were a group of harbour workers in hi-vis jackets over oilskins (playing cards), and a white-faced couple fresh off the morning ferry, which was hours late due to a rolling swell.

He searched on the Web for ashrams. Inner engineering, early-morning Vedic chanting, active 'jumping and screaming' meditations: these were not really his thing; besides, ashrams were not only expensive but internationally busy. Folk questing for life's meaning would ask questions, probe, want him to join in. Hit men probably used them to increase their inner calm.

Canadian therapeutic masseurs, too. Life had moved on from the 1970s. He could hear a vague and prolonged screaming through the PRIVATE door: Astra was already into the active meditations, it seemed.

He glanced out of the window: the harbour street was seriously empty, the heaving sea audible, the sleek tarmac lashed again by what they called a shower. The return mainland ferry had been cancelled. No planes, either. Certified personal safety, at no cost. The paraffin stove hummed.

He ordered another coffee, with cake, shut his laptop and had a look at Marcie's books. She was a minor rival of the book-cum-gift shop near the harbour, which sold tweed scarves, teacloths, plastic haggises from China. Marcie's dusty stock filled a small recess and had a New Age angle, but there were quite a few of Bob's sort of title, generally second hand. He pulled out a scruffy copy of *The Guns of Navarone*. He hadn't read that since he was a teenager; he wasn't even sure that he had ever finished it.

'At least you'll have the headwind behind you, going back,' Marcie joked. 'They say it'll clear tonight. I like your hair, by the way. Who cut it?'

★ ★ ★

They were right: clearance was total. He jogged to the headland's 300-foot cliffs which dominated the end of his favourite beach. Past the machair, at the peak's base, the white sand dazzled and the water was back to turquoise in long streaks, with far-off peaks stuck flat and pale onto the horizon. The cliffs were covered in birds stuck like tiny barnacles or swooping about the rock-face amazingly fast. He didn't know how birders coped.

Seals were sunning themselves again on a flat reef fifty yards out and not minding when a bigger surge swept them off in a slither of dark blubber. Big glistening eyes, mournful expressions. Running the length of the beach were dunes, with glutinous hollows he had learnt were called slacks, backed by machair. Rabbits swarmed over the grassier parts: they vanished into their burrows as he passed. Sensible creatures.

He sat in the dry section of the dunes in his fleece-lined waterproof, between harsh salt-grass and prickly creeping plants like miniature thistles. It was cold and blustery, the gusts sporadically cuffing his hood and blowing sand off the beach into his eyes in gritty clouds. Sophie would have called this place awesome. Although restful enough immediately in front, with its huge sheen of backwash, the sea, having made great play with the stacks standing offshore like bits of cathedrals, rolled against the sheer side of the headland, streaming down it in temporary waterfalls, emerging in spontaneous geysers. He missed his kids.

Awesome the place may be, he thought, but it wasn't for him. It teased you with jaw-agape glimpses, then left you to mope. He needed people. Ordinary people, not these island types who sussed you within minutes. Even the

MacLeans had sussed him. They were all too deep and brooding. He wondered if they were any relation to Alistair MacLean, author of *The Guns of Navarone*. He'd brought it along as his beach read, got through a few pages, searched about for a bookmark (he never turned down the corners: the residual impact of a charismatic English teacher long ago). The marram blades were too tough and springy to break, but he found something in his back pocket: his Emirates Airlines boarding pass, paled and crinkly from the wash.

Winrush/Robert C.
From DXB
To LHR

The remnant of another life. He slipped it in, closed the book and read his own thoughts.

Not one of Al's most brilliant ideas, re-routing him up here. Listen to that ocean: precisely like a jet aircraft's roar, not hush-kitted, and going on and on. Destination unknown. Estimated landing time, a few billion years from now. Meanwhile, his life was dissolving in wind and rain, the days left to him trickling away while some art-teacher particle rutted with Olivia, and Al swung in his sun-drenched hammock.

And there he had thought that Al was just being his usual sardonic self: *You forget what the colour blue looks like in its natural state.* How to be an optimist, unless you avoided looking up the weather?

He would go to Marcie's tomorrow and check

flights to Honolulu.

The vane of a large white feather lay by his elbow: he was shaking the sand off it when something caught his eye, off to the right. It was moving in front of the first boulders of the headland.

A figure — tiny from here. Someone running over the sand, heading for the sea. Long and loose dark hair, but the body was too close in colour to the sand for him to be certain it was a woman. He shaded his eyes, squinting as it splashed across the backwash. No sign of a swimsuit.

This was the first person he had seen so far on the beach, and it was a shock. Not a pleasant one, though. Maybe there'd be a whole crowd of them: hearty German cycling types. Or contract killers toughening themselves up for the job.

He had forgotten to bring his binos. The person hit the sea in little splashes and sparkles, hands raised high — and vanished into a black spot of head for a minute or so, to re-emerge and run back up the sand into the dunes. A dark dot between the legs: possibly a thong, possibly pubic hair.

That was it. No one else. Normal service resumed: sea, birds, seals, rustling dune-grass, gusts flapping his jacket. It reminded him of the time he was convinced he saw Olivia skiing in Dubai. Or of those UFOs floating oval and silvery at 30,000 feet, mid-Pacific, in 2001.

He waited a bit and then took a stroll along the beach towards the headland, casually glancing around him. The foot-prints were small and perfectly arched. Unlike the birds' random chaos of arrows, there was purpose in them.

Presuming her not to be a honeytrap, he followed the prints up into the dunes, where they gave out in the dense machair; but he guessed their route and found himself on a track skirting the peak's foothills beyond. The track cut up through rabbit-burrowed turf, cleared a hump of bare rock and curved down onto a road tufted by grass along the middle, and with shaggy, unmarked verges: a very minor road in an island where all roads seemed minor.

This one was visible for a few hundred yards either way before scuttling behind the usual treeless slopes. No doubt, if she was real and not some sort of sea-nymph, she had changed in the dunes and walked to her bike, or perhaps her car, its sound drowned by the wind. A spot of oil on the grass was perhaps a clue. Rabbits, seeing him motionless, bounced back to their nibbling.

★ ★ ★

He'd been invited round to the MacLeans for a hot shower and a cup of tea, but he didn't mention the skinny-dipper. Walking back in the starlit dark at around six thirty with a jam sponge in aluminium foil, he hardly needed the torch. He'd bought a litre of Talisker in Bargrennan. It kept him company as he stared into the fire, the radio's mumble behind. He flicked through the pictures he'd taken before she appeared: turquoise waters and green surf ending in white; a blurry bird. Nothing else.

Tahiti without the palms. He put the big feather into a glass and placed it on the chimney piece.

Honolulu was a bad idea: apart from anything else, he wanted to prove Al wrong.

Dawn was oddly white through the skylight: a thick sea-fog. He was grounded. He paced about finding things to do — sawing up driftwood into billets, cleaning windows, properly scrubbing areas he had skated over with a broom on arrival. He thought about Maria cleaning in Dubai; he'd not appreciated her properly. He decided to risk the pub again.

It was early evening and the place was empty. A smell of cleaning fluid, Johnny Cash replaced by a football match on the telly, the sound turned right up. He was about to leave when a stab was made at scoring and Murray the barman popped out.

He drew a pint of Hebridean beer from the painfully slow tap, wheezing behind a brindled beard: stout, somewhere in his forties. *Delicious local fare* was on offer in the season: haddock, steak, mussels. All they had now was a bowl of Quality Street on the bar and prawn-flavoured crisps. The gales had meant no fresh fish, so Bob was feeling peckish, bored of his home cooking. He took a Quality Street and tried to talk above the telly about the game, involving two Scottish league teams he knew nothing about. Murray grunted his responses, then eyed Bob suspiciously as he unwrapped the sweet and popped it into his mouth. It was a hard toffee and seemed to take up a lot of space.

'Birds?'

'That's right, yes.'

'You won't be minding the lack of power, then?'

'I quite like it.'

'Not the weather for bird-spotting today.'

'No,' Bob smiled, 'not since I arrived, to be honest. Except for yesterday. My Scottish granny from Campbeltown, she used to say, 'Carry a brolly and it won't rain.' Doesn't seem to work here.'

Murray said nothing, began to wipe the bar's immaculate wood. Bob caught his own reflection in the mirror beyond his head and thought for a second it was a grizzly local's chewing on tobacco. He selected an age-curled postcard from a stand on the bar: white beach, azure sea. Not quite the same one.

'Don't be too hopeful,' Murray said. 'That blue sky dates from 1980. I do recall it. Dimly.'

Bob chuckled politely. 'Yesterday was nice. I was up on the beach. I don't think it's this one, though. Lying back in the dune with my binos.' Murray wasn't listening. 'Do you know the beach I mean?'

'Where was that, then?'

'You follow the promontory from my house, long sandy beach, ending in cliffs. I don't know the name.'

'Aye.' He said a name in Gaelic, stopped wiping and looked Bob in the eye.

'That's probably it.'

The cloth got going again, over and over. Murray was clearly lonely, like Bob. The pub had only a couple of houses and a church near it, the rest of Ardcorry so scattered it was invisible. Bob asked him if people generally went swimming without a wetsuit, or any suit at all, at this time of year.

Murray chortled. 'I wouldn't give it a go, sir. Not even if you were a lot younger than you are.'

'I wasn't intending to,' smiled Bob, over an imaginary Kalashnikov. 'It's just that I saw someone doing just that. A woman — I believe young — running naked into the surf.'

The cloth stopped. Murray tossed it into the low sink behind, folded his arms and leaned on the bar. 'Did she then come out, after?'

'Oh yes, about a minute later. I was some distance away, so I didn't have time to follow it up, as you might say.'

'Just as well. You've seen a selkie.'

'Sorry?'

'Round here they say a selkie's what you turn into if you drown.'

'Really?'

'You take on the appearance of a bonny lass, to lure folk in. But you're ugly as sin, in truth. Smell o' fish. Hair aye dripping. Y' face all full o' lirks. Deadly.'

'Lirks?'

'Full o' wrinkles,' he said, leaving a bubble of saliva low down on his beard.

Bob chuckled, but Murray raised a tangle of eyebrow in surprise. 'Don't say I didnae warn you, Mr Webb.' He took out a pamphlet from a little metal stand and dropped it on the bar by Bob's glass. 'It's all in here. The sweets are for the quiz night, by the way. A couple of quid for the pamphlet. And the postcard's a pound.'

★ ★ ★

Bob returned to the croft vowing once again not to set foot in the Tinker's Arms. His torch probed the night fog with minimal impact. He'd never been a great fan of fog. That whole business of hurtling down through a thick whiteness, approaching minimums, waiting for visual contact, was something he found tricky to accept at first; supposing the ground wasn't where you were being told it was? He had the ground here all right, but no instruments.

He tripped over one of the two blue plastic milk crates in front of the house that had once served as flower beds and were now rooted so thoroughly he couldn't shift them. I'm only here for a little while, he thought, picking himself up from the shaggy bison hair they called grass. Until things blow over. Change as little as possible.

Back inside, crouched by the lamp's glow, he read the pamphlet: it was a local illustrated guide to Scottish legends, the selkie's pneumatic breasts hidden by long black locks. His own selkie had seemed small-breasted, although she was a fair way off. Too far to see the eyes, though. 'Some witnesses report selkies as having cold, filmed-over eyes — like drowned folk. Others say their eyes are bright but full of sadness, like a seal's. They don't stipulate the colour!'

The fog lasted a week. All he could make out was the wet plumes on the tall cotton grass growing in front; each plume was full of black spots he identified as last year's midges, now dead. Then another south-easterly, with dark-grey cloud but no rain.

He ventured out in the rainless gale to the shoreline, his face blasted by blown sand from as early as the edge of the machair. He could hardly stand upright, leaning forward sustained by wind power only, shielding his eyes. The air was passing too fast to bother with his lungs, and it was full of salt and spindrift. He'd expected to see massive waves but it was unnervingly calm, with dishwasher froth on the tideline and the water a stressed dark grey, big rollers toppling far out in streaks of white. The wind's howl was louder than a Dubai disco: he couldn't even hear himself yelling. This place was good. No hired heavies in ski shades would ever dream of venturing up here, shaking their big watches: this was not just another continent, but another planet. He pictured them floundering in the hidden bogs and ditches on the blacklands, lashed by force-nine rain. *Top Gun* guys on the wrong channel. Al, you're a genius.

There was a lull one morning and he climbed the headland's peak by a thin path, pushing down on his thighs for the last misty lap. He blew like a horse. He'd work out two hours each day, an hour in the morning and an hour in the evening, until sweat poured off him. Forty press-ups. Thirty pull-ups. Up and down the stairs, grunting like a marine. All the rest. But he had to work harder for the same result, these days. All he could see from the top was the summit itself: wind-flattened grass and a cairn. It seemed possible, suddenly: to be dead.

He tested the Makarov pistol the same day, firing across the loch water's flat calm. He was worried the damp might have seized it. The trigger was a touch stiff, requiring a good squeeze, but the shot echoed nicely off the rocky slopes. The little loch spread longitudinally: a natural shooting gallery. The grinning skeleton of a sheep lay on its shore, ribs fluttering shreds of fleece. The water was chocolate dark.

He liked the Makarov, despite its weight: it had accompanied him through thick and thin during his days as a freight dog. He'd started out with a Walther PP, but its slide was mounted too low and kept nipping his shooting hand. I'll buy a rod and tackle, he thought to himself, and some fancy lures. He heard his father's bark: *Robert, they've got to hit the water like real flies, not like ruddy bricks!*

★　★　★

The bright red call box stood in a patch of dead bracken beside the road to the causeway. The few houses visible along the way were mostly bungalows; the one opposite the call box had burned down to a heap of charred rafters. Maybe it had all got too much, looking out on rocks and tarns and grazing. *TERRIBLE ANGELS*

WANNA FUCK ME had been written in capitals on an address label and stuck on the door. He took it as a warning, trying not to look at it during his calls to his children or his confabs with the solicitor — who thought he was in Costa Rica. He didn't call anyone else, apart from Al: like the solicitor, his friends believed he was on a world tour. Midlife crisis. Time of Riley. About time young Bob moved on. Wine, women and song.

He reckoned Sophie and David were almost as happy to hear his voice as he was to hear theirs through the crackles and hiss of the phone wires swaying in the wind. He assumed the calls were safe. They kept them neutral, content-wise: no dangerous goods, no inflammables. Any news from campaign HQ was sent to Bob's anonymous Hotmail address.

'You really think that's watertight, Dad?'

'Airtight, David. Why shouldn't it be?'

'Everything leaks. There are biddable guys everywhere. The world's porous, as Tim puts it.'

'Hey, don't let suspicion rule your life.'

'You certainly haven't, Dad.'

'What, you mean my text message to Sharansky?'

'I was referring to your late career.'

'Oh, let's stick to trivia.'

At least David called him Dad, and not Bob. They called their mum Olivia. There must be meaning in that. The receiver smelt of waste substances.

He'd decided in the end to phone Al once a week, just to check on the latest position. While

Bob got whipped in the face by his anorak draw-cords, Al wiggled his toes in the sun. Here, Bob told his friend, just popping out for milk in the morning entailed a head torch and checking the double storm flaps on your pockets. Now Al was on a yacht. The yacht was his: a thirty-footer! They were moored off an uninhabited gem near Jost Van Dyke. No news, otherwise. Oh, Jane's back from California and feeling fit as a fiddle. Keep your head down, Bob: no romantic entanglements, OK?

On the way back, he looked up into a spread of welcome cumulonimbus and open patches. He wished he was out in the blue above the clouds, free of entanglements. He skirted the cottage and stood by the loch, thinking. A rent in the clouds let the sun through and a patch of bright light crept slowly over the grazing and hit the water in a magnesium dazzle. A living old-master painting that threw his shadow for a long way behind him.

He was crouched before a roaring fire in the sitting-room when the prince's soft voice in the sauna popped up. The man owned the Dubai flat, he had the Worcestershire address via the UAE work visa; but he knew nothing about Crowthorne. They'd discussed classic cars during one flight: His Eminence had a fleet of metalwork including a one-seater Maserati from the 50s and a 1921 Bugatti type 35. Get jealous. Was the humble Healey ever mentioned?

His Royal Dishrag had cousins who were top Saudis. The Saudis funded the Taliban. Evron Bensoussan, close chum of some top Israelis, was selling the Taliboys weapons paid for in Saudi cash. Shine a light under a rotten log and it all wriggles a lot more.

Bob threw on a peat brick for the smell and took another slug of whisky. The heroin did not fit in. Evron hated narcotics. Someone was sharing the transport infrastructure *without Evron's knowledge*: Lennart? Pedro Diez? Yes, this would make a mafioso type like Evron very cross. But multiple elimination usually draws a lot of attention, at least in Europe. It's an idiot's gambit. He listened, suddenly, tensing up: here was nothing like the African bush, where the night noises were loud and rhythmic and full of life, frogs and monkeys and crickets, jackals on the veldt like angry babies crying. Here it was a moaning off the cold black wave-tops, suspicious whispers, the creak of a door.

'Go away,' he shouted, tolerably pissed.

The wind ignored him.

One thing he did know: the men in their ski shades and concealed holsters would only have to enquire in Bargrennan or the Tinker's Arms after out-of-season English visitors, and Bob Winrush would be dead meat.

'Och aye,' he muttered, 'you'll be talking about Mr Webb with the straight back and broad shoulders, stuck in that hoose wi'oot the electrics near Ardcorry. Here for the birds. Feathered variety.'

Why was it so difficult to vanish, these days?

One thing he did know about the Saudis was that they were patient. They moved slowly and deliberately, like overweight gulls. He pictured a

317

royal plumpness in his dishdasha twirling a beringed finger from his bed in a five-star suite in a Kensington hotel (which he owned), and shoulder-padded minions scurrying away to the Robin Regent hangered somewhere in Essex, making a fuel stop-over in the wife-stuffed Highland castle owned by their boss, before a 40-knot gust factor over the Minches tears the frame apart — light aircraft may be viceless these days, but these guys were going too fast.

Wishful thinking. He emptied his glass.

If all this was a private vendetta by little, quick-moving Bensoussan, then he had the means to hire the top guns. The deadliest hit guys. The ones with sniper sights that could pick you off a mile away. Hollow-point bullets. Eyes of sea eagles. No trace.

All character-building, of course. He poured himself another and swirled its amber glow, lit by miniature flames. Living was in the details, like flying.

★　★　★

Marcie wanted him to comment on the bird photos taken by Kier, Astra's late da.

'Yeah, he skidded on his motorbike a couple of years back. Anyway. Can't be helped. Look at this one. What do you think of this?'

'Pretty rare.'

'It was taken on St Kilda,' she said. 'St Kilda has no roads. It's just incredible.' She consulted her catalogue. 'Bar-tailed godwit. Are they rare?'

'Depends. On the weather.'

'Oh. And isn't this one's reflection amazing? I remember Kier taking it on Harris. Knot in winter plumage.'

'No.'

'What?'

'That's summer plumage.'

'It says it's winter, here.'

She showed him. A knot was evidently a bird.

'Dead right. I'm no good with knots.'

She laughed. She found his jokes funny: Olivia hadn't done so for years.

'I'd best be off, Marcie,' he said.

He nearly fell over Astra, circling on his tricycle outside. Astra blew him a raspberry filled with genuine dislike. The local primary stood opposite, with brightly coloured railings and a giraffe mural, the apparent clone of the twins' first school in Worcestershire. He passed a plump lad of about thirteen, who held up a liquorice whirl to a friend's mouth full of dental appliance and shouted, 'These are no like your pubes, cos you've fucking got none!' And they both howled with laughter, in case the passing beard hadn't understood. Olivia had finally left crewing after being similarly insulted by a drunken male passenger, who then threw up on touchdown so violently it caught in her eyebrows.

'I've had it up to here,' she'd said to her soon-to-be-husband, down the phone from the airport. 'He didn't even use a sick bag.'

She was also pregnant, it turned out. And then Pan Am folded. Just like that. The world's most got-at airline.

Where his bedroom's sloping pinewood ceiling

went vertical, leaving a space behind, he removed three planks from their nails and cobbled together a tight frame for the wood to sit in. From the outside, nothing had changed, except for a subtle finger hold either end that allowed him to remove it in seconds. A man could vanish in his own home. He left the copy of his logbook and diary in there, plus the wad of cash. He threw in a couple of cushions and a bottle of water as an afterthought. Protect and Survive.

He hush-kitted the wooden ladder with felt and bought some thick lined curtains on Lewis; he also came back with country-style kitchen chairs, a corduroy beanbag, a couple of rugs, a wooden loo seat and a Harris tweed jacket. Olivia would have pulled a face. That night he stood in the agitated grass outside with the curtains closed and the lamps lit: there was hardly any seepage.

It was the best he could do. There was no power for an alarm system. If they wanted to train a gun on him, they just had to wait for him to emerge. No place better: cover nil, remote. He stood by the thorn bush and panned his eye over the lumpy, treeless peninsula. Villains in frogmen outfits crouched behind every silhouetted out-crop. He would not even hear the shot.

★　★　★

It was shower-and-tea day at the MacLeans. He hadn't yet mentioned the selkie.

He noticed, among the bric-a-brac on their window's deep sill, a framed photo of Carol

MacLean with her parents in front of the house. He picked it up. She was dressed in a calf-length brown coat and her dark red hair was swept back and voluminous. Her smile was a beauty queen's, she was all youth next to her dowdy-looking parents.

'What date was this?'

'Oh, I'd just been to see Blondie in Glasgow. Around 1980, I suppose. Feels like last week.'

'A festival?'

She grinned. 'It was at the Apollo. I did a lot of screaming. Good times. Single girl.'

'She hadnae met the punk rocker,' Angus grunted, pointing at himself.

Bob raised his eyebrows in unfeigned surprise. He'd imagined them somehow frozen as themselves, or emerging from crofter shawls. This was how Al had seen her, but he couldn't ask if she remembered young Hugh McAllister.

'What about you?' asked Carol.

He blinked his shampoo-reddened eyes. What would Kit Webb have been like? 'Oh, going around without socks,' he said, 'dreaming of the revolution.'

'I can imagine that,' said Carol, gazing at him. 'Even now I've cut the hair.'

'Oh dear. The ex-hippy. I'll be seeing selkies soon.'

They looked puzzled. 'What do you mean?' said Carol.

'Y' know,' he floundered, 'having visions, seeing things, tripping.'

Carol shook her head.

'All that selkie business is a load of balls for

321

the tourists,' Angus said.

'Exactly,' said Bob.

'The real selkies only surface at night,' Angus went on, 'and they look like they've been eaten by crabs and they stink o' rottenness. I've had one as close as *that*. From the boat.' His hand slapped the table a foot from his distorted face. Distorted by the memory of some indescribable terror.

'That's right,' said Carol. 'And if you turn y' head from their beautiful eyes, they howl.'

'Ululate,' Angus corrected her. 'To be scientifically accurate.'

3

He had chalked up one birdstrike in his career — out of JFK. A single Canadian goose, about the heaviest; a flock would have brought them down into Jamaica Bay. He told the maintenance bods who were cleaning out the intake area to save him some for Christmas.

Each time the weather improved, he headed for the beach with binos and bird book. He began to learn a lot more about birds: they never stopped moving, the background — sea, grass, sand, clouds — kept changing as they flew, they vanished into wheeling flocks or flickered out like flames into sky. The stiff well-behaved birds in his book were not a great help.

He didn't want to know more about selkies, not the real ones; his tourist version suited him fine.

One day he was crossing dried kelp and foam scum when he heard a mewing sound and looked up: a high-altitude bird of prey with a jumbo wingspan.

He lifted the binos: the usual teasing silhouette, but it had a white translucent fan on its tail. Sea eagle, fairly rare, recently reintroduced; a couple of pairs on Scourlay. It turned its head, catching the sun on its top wing-surface, then swayed off out of sight beyond the nearest hill. He wondered what went on in its front office. No chit-chat. No jokes. It could dive at some terrifying speed and come out of it with a vole in its claws. His reading had also told him that it was an antique bird: one of the oldest. Hardly a molecule modified for millions of years. A slight livery change, no doubt, but otherwise the veteran raptor of natural aviation.

Today the strip was as deserted as ever. He stared out to sea. He'd been feeling like an obsolescent aircraft left out in all weathers, loneliness getting into some expensive areas. But what if he was still flying? What if all this was simply a fresh leg to some destination not yet up on the board? After half a year max, he'd be back seeing the kids, find a woman to fill the heart-shaped hole, work the training schools or trouble-shoot for ad hoc charters as much as suited, or do something quite different. Open a model aircraft shop. Try his sleepy pub idea, spinning yarns behind the bar.

The ocean couldn't care less, whatever. Next parish, New York. After 6,000 miles of swell it simply swept up to him and hissed back again and repeated the exercise over and over. It turned his bare feet crimson in seconds. *The selkie must be hardy*, he thought.

A few days before he'd got very excited: the same prints near the high-water mark. This was why he hadn't given up hope. He'd come earlier today, positioning himself in the dunes danger-ously near. The showery clouds blew away and the sun began to burn. The harsh grass stems rustled around him, turning silvery further off, stirring like newly washed hair all the way to the headland. He spied on seals, waders, ran the

324

binos over the cliffs and stacks and tried to catch those endless sparks of impact as the gannets plummeted beyond the breakers. Then he saw them: gulls with smudgy heads and crimson beaks and legs. His black-headed gulls, surely, if a touch early.

He moved onto his stomach and took the binos' weight on his elbows. Some of his gulls began to fuss around a couple of tidal pools, stamping their feet in the water. He was well trained to keep awake for ages without much going on, and here quite a bit was going on. Sweeping over huge numbers of guillemots making a racket on the cliff face, then following the sleeked head of a seal beyond the surf, he caught a puzzling flash from the water, pinkish. There again. And again. In the seal's sparkly jet-trail there was a white rump, clearing the water like a sandbar.

His binos trembled. He lost her. Marram stems flickered across, blurring his aim. He picked her up again as she was turning to swim back. Her emergence point was on a vector dangerously close to his. She squeezed out her hair in front of her as she trotted through the surf. Young and slender, maybe in her twenties. He kept flat on his belly in the warm dune-sand, sighted her again and tightened the focus as she picked up her towel. She shook her hair so that it fell back behind, and revealed her face.

It was cold-pinched. It was turned in his direction with large all-seeing eyes and a frown: as if taking bearings.

Is that a glint in the dunes? A movement in the marram?

Keeping his head down, crab-scuttling to the other side of the dunes where the machair frayed into bare sand, soaking his knees in a slack, he made it home without once looking back. His heartbeat took ages to settle: *one crocodile two crocodile three crocodile* . . . Her eyes were not filmed over.

His knees dried in front of the Raeburn and he brushed the sand off, made himself a double-egg-and-bacon fry-up. He was an idiot. He would look up flights to Honolulu and spot sharks instead.

★ ★ ★

The decent weather held the next day; he jogged to Bargrennan for supplies. The several sheep standing about in the narrow road — copying the locals, it seemed — barely noticed his presence. His lungs were fiery, but the ground hit his feet in that rubbery way that gives lift; there was nothing around him but grass, hills, strips of water and sky. He hoped it would stay that way, having decided not to carry the Makarov today: it was uncomfortable jogging with the gun against the waist.

He called in for sundries at the shop. At the till Kathleen said, in her light sing-song way, 'How are the birds?'

'As fascinating as ever.'

Did Kathleen give him a look?

The door swung open. A bulky youngish man

326

in a neat grey suit and wraparound sunglasses.

The man approached them, not raising his shades. Bob watched the hands like a hawk: one plucked a cigarette lighter from the stand, the other hovered at the waist, holding coins. He seemed in a hurry.

'Is that all you're wanting, sir?' asked Kathleen.

'I believe it is, yeah.'

Accent: estuary English or lightly foreign, hard to tell. Bob gestured at him to go ahead and pay, stepping back, tensed to lunge because he was now close enough. Good in an emergency, better in a cockpit. The man nodded his thanks and paid and said, 'Decompress time,' waving the lighter. And left.

'Are you all right, Kit?'

'I'm fine. Strange man.'

'Carol MacLean mentioned she'd got a couple of suits staying at the Tinker's Arms,' she said. 'That must be one of them. Six pound fifty-three, please. I get a load stranger than that, I can tell you,' she added, eyeing Bob just a moment too long.

His hands were trembling, so of course he spilt the coins, which rolled into awkward and sticky places.

A couple of suits. Not good. Two angles of attack.

Outside the stores stood an old Land Rover splattered with bog water. It had a green-and-blue sticker on the rear window, showing the earth held by a pair of hands. Ominous, but not dangerous. A faded, peat-spattered logo on the

327

side, circled by words: THE GAIR CENTRE FOR ENVIRONMENTAL RESEARCH. No sign of the smoking suit.

A sniper with a telescopic sight would have an easy job of it on the lonely road to Scourlay: but hit men like to do it close, to verify the result. The guy hadn't given him a second glance. After all, only Al and the twins knew his assumed name, and only Al could identify his precise location (for the twins, he was simply 'somewhere in Scotland'). He was far from being the sole Englishman on the isles.

Nevertheless, he would make enquiries of Carol MacLean, just in case.

He was well on the road, supplies jiggling in his little back-pack, slightly unnerved by the occasional sun-flash off the strips of visible water, when he heard a vehicle behind him and shifted onto the right-hand verge, sprinkled with yellow springtime flowers.

The Land Rover.

As it stopped alongside, so did he, tensed to duck. A woman leaned out, holding a one-pound coin. She looked familiar: black-haired, somewhere in her thirties, a dark-eyed glance running over his face.

'Mr Webb, I presume?'

'Er, yes.'

'Every wee bit tots up,' she said, holding out the coin.

'Oh, thank you.'

'My pleasure.'

She drove off as if faintly annoyed: the vehicle had a resident clatter which he reckoned was a loose gasket. He pounded round a bend and found the Land Rover stopped again some way ahead, a large flock wobbling towards it from the other direction. He reluctantly slowed down. The young shepherd — thick neck, cropped head — stopped by the four-wheel drive to chat. By the time Bob came up alongside, he was just leaving.

'Fuck's sake,' he murmured: the last ewe was finding Bob scary. The shepherd let out a painful whistle. Bob ushered the straggler past him like a comic traffic policeman. 'Watch the rozzer,' joked the shepherd. The woman was staring at these antics through the driver's window.

'Didn't think I was that scary,' Bob panted.

'What a prick,' she said.

'Sorry?'

She glanced back at the dwindling flock. 'Oh, island politics. B for boring.'

Bob pulled a sweaty face. Her sharp chin creased in a way that he liked. Her eyes settled on him, clearly suspicious.

'You've got the croft before Ardcorry, out on the peninsula?'

'Yes, how did you know?'

'Kathleen at the shop. The local megaphone. From the age before wireless.'

A lone car was coming from the Scourlay direction.

'I'm renting it for a few months.'

'Birds, isn't it?'

'Well, more enthusiasm than expertise.'

'So I've heard,' she said, with a smile that seemed to stretch right across and then vanish.

'Have you? Right.'

The car had pulled into the passing place a few yards ahead. It tooted. The Land Rover moved off without another word from its driver.

He raised a farewell hand, taking off again with a bit more zip, playing the fit young athlete instead of the middle-aged guy keeping decrepitude at bay — although nobody, least of all the lovely contents of that vehicle, would be fooled for a minute.

Then it struck him — with a shock that made his heart miss a beat.

He leaned on his thighs and coughed, spat over the barbed wire onto the grazing. She was annoyed. Because she recognised him? Perish the thought. Surely not given the distance, that covert of marram, and with her own eyes full of salt!

But her suspicious look bothered him. Her long-nosed, sharp-chinned face was not classically beautiful like Olivia's, but when she had smiled, even though the smile was unkind (mischievous, at the very least), it was transformed.

Recognition. Simple recognition. He had known it on the beach, even. From that first and far-off glimpse of her. He had spent fifty-one years waiting for a face.

He jogged on at a gentler pace, heading towards the causeway. When things started to go sour a few years back, Olivia would accuse him — *accuse* him — of being a romantic. These days she said the opposite: that he had no heart. He had heart, all right. Someone had just pierced it.

And then there was the Land Rover again, like a mirage.

It was waiting for a massive earth mover which was inching over the causeway in their direction. He didn't fancy squeezing past the machine, an extra-wide vehicle with nasty teeth and dodgy steering, so he stopped by the concreted rocks denoting the water's edge, hands on hips and catching his breath. The water made slurping noises below: the half-mile strait must have been a lark to cross, given its currents.

She was now out of the four-wheel drive, chatting on her mobile. When she was finished, Bob ambled towards her. She was leaning against the vehicle with folded arms. Her waxed jacket was old and scuffed, her boots muddied.

'So,' she said, without preamble, 'you've no problems with Colin then, on your croft?'

'Colin?'

'The shepherd.'

'Is he the one who's the local DJ?'

'And drug dealer,' she said. Her wide mouth retracted to a pout, the dimples deepened. 'But keep that to yourself.' Bob expressed amazement, wondering if the MacLeans — Colin's aunt and uncle — knew.

'Of course. Everyone knows. He has plenty of customers on the isles. Why are you here, Mr Webb?'

A direct gaze. Eyes dark as damsons. Scottish accent, but she wasn't fair of hair or skin.

'I'm renting. The house and a few acres. The rest is still croft.'

'Without electricity.'

What did she *not* know?

'I manage surprisingly well. Large Raeburn, occasional showers at the neighbours, wood fire. Hot-water bottles. But it's dead cold in the morning.'

She smiled again; the space above her upper lip creased and almost disappeared. What was it about that smile? Her eyes caught the light, broken into glitter like small waves. 'Fairly ironic, don't you think?'

'Oh?'

'We've always managed, up to very recently. The human race. But now we're dependent. Electricity junkies. Hooked on fridges and immersion heaters and power showers.'

'Yup, gives me a rush just thinking about them. You work here, then?' He nodded towards the vehicle's discreet livery. Tiny lines under her eyes. Mid-thirties, yes.

'As you know.'

He frowned. 'Do I?'

'Mr Webb, the game's up.'

His hand went instinctively to where the Makarov would have been: heart pounding, with a dim memory of a film in which the professional assassin was a lovely woman, he had no idea what to do short of throwing himself at her.

Then she said, 'More enthusiasm than expertise, heh?'

She stared at him, not a friendly stare. He blushed, the penny suddenly dropping, and turned away to watch the earth mover, struggling like something half-witted along the causeway. Her sparkler eyes must have seen him behind the marram. He was wearing the same shapeless hat, his sturdy build and scraggy beard easily recognisable from afar.

'I'm a bird-spotter,' he mumbled. 'I like things that fly.'

'Not planes, I hope.'

'God, no!'

Her mouth stretched again, lavish and wide, disobeying her frown. 'Don't be so shy, Mr Webb. Come and see what we do. After all, we're part RSPB-funded, though our remit's general flora and fauna. I'm taking hydrological readings in the machair, which seems to be getting wetter. The locals have noticed it, so I'm establishing whether it's true. Rising sea levels. You can't just go by rumour, can you?'

'Of course not.'

She produced a card from the bag on the passenger seat and handed it to him, giving him directions he wasn't listening to: it was the second time in half an hour that he had felt her fingers touch his palm. Dr Judith Byrne, followed by a string of letters. Any time next week. Call us.

The earth mover was now close enough to make normal conversation impossible. She climbed back in.

'We'll be expecting you!' she shouted. 'Don't be shy, Mr Webb!'

He raised his hand and felt like a schoolboy. Her mouth stretched and there wasn't a frown.

He made straight for the MacLeans' house. No time to lose: instinct might take over and that was fatal. He felt the grey suits were bad news.

Carol was in, Angus was under the glittering waves. She was surprised to see him. He had a question, he said. Flushed and pleased, she made for the kettle, but he declined. She adjusted her apron and then her hair. The slim but busty girl who had screamed at Blondie had filled out, but still lay somewhere under the workaday clothes of blouse and jeans and pinny. They sat at the kitchen table; she was peeling home-grown potatoes. The radio, turned down to a murmur, was playing reggae.

'Ask away, then. You sure you'll nae try some of my shortbread?'

'There's a guest at the Tinker's Arms.'

'We've two.'

'What do they look like?'

'Quite natty,' she said. 'Grey suits, ties, folders. Business types, you know. Always on their phones. One had a wee ring in his ear. Shaven heads, but all the men have that, these days. It's to hide the baldness.'

'English?'

'I think so. Not Scots, at any rate. They didnae say much when I was there. Just talked about the wind. As everyone does.'

'Do you know how long they're staying?'

'I think three days. I've to do a thorough clean on Tuesday, anyway.'

He nodded, peeling a potato with his trusty pocket-knife from Sierra Leone. She didn't object. 'Why do you think they're here?'

'Questions, questions! Some project or other. Golf course, wind farm, weather station, flashy hotel — you name it. They never seem to see the light o' day, thank goodness. Is there something the matter?'

He looked up. 'Have they ever asked after me?'

'No. But then I'm just the skivvy,' she added, laughing.

'You're a lot more than that,' he said, without really meaning to.

Her eyes widened. 'The same could be said of your guid self. Why all these queries?'

'I'm going through a messy divorce,' he said, improvising. 'I think my wife might be snooping on me. Private detectives, all that.'

'I'm sorry to hear that. I did wonder. A man on his own.'

'Whatever, I'll be keeping a low profile. Don't let on you know me.' A simple precaution: they sounded harmless.

'Well, I don't know you, do I?' She was looking at him with seventeen-year-old eyes out of a wind-burned face in its late forties.

He took up another potato to peel, and their hands touched over the bowl. He suddenly found himself taking hers, squeezing them. They stayed like that for a moment.

'What's going on?' she said, not looking at him but at the peelings.

He closed his eyes, his breath as quick and sharp as when he was running. Her hands were warm and slightly wet. He raised them to his lips. The knuckles smelt of Pears' soap. The soap his mother would use, long ago. He hadn't smelt it in years. When he'd got back from boarding school, aged seven, after the term during which she'd suddenly died, there was still half an amber cake of it in her bathroom, streamlined by use, as aerodynamic as *Bluebird*. He'd kept it for ages.

'Angus is back at six,' Carol MacLean said, matter of fact. 'At some point I'll need to prepare his food.'

Bob opened his eyes and released her hands, feeling embarrassed. She stood and took the apron off, hanging it up on the hook by the door, then came back to the table and looked at him. Her white blouse had little yellow buttons.

'It's only three thirty,' she said. 'I'll need to lock up, in case.'

'In case?'

'In case your detectives call round. If we're going to smooch, we'd best lock up and retire.'

'Somebody might have seen me,' he said feebly. He'd not really meant this.

She locked the front door and went to the stairs, turned round to look at him. Her yellow buttons were like the flowers on the guelder rose he had allowed to flourish at the end of the orchard, to hide the new estate of crammed, executive homes.

'Don't leave your stuff there,' she said.

He retrieved his little, bulging rucksack and followed Carol MacLean up the squeaky stairs into the master bedroom. Its satiny, striped wallpaper was unrelieved by any pictures; the bed had an extravagant cushioned end of pale violet. There was a smell of talc and aftershave. She closed the curtains and turned to him. He dropped the rucksack on the carpet and *The Guns of Navarone* fell out of a side pocket. He fumbled to retrieve it, hands trembling like a teenager's, and crammed it back in.

'When you're finished with your reading, you can undo these,' she smiled, indicating her blouse buttons.

He undid them one by one with thick fingers, opening the front to reveal a flimsy nylon bra packed tight with pressed-up breasts that rose and fell, stretching and contracting their pores, their peppery scatter of moles. She was touching him below through the tracksuit's cotton looseness. She peeled the blouse off and dropped it on the carpet and pressed herself to him.

'I love smooching,' she whispered.

'Carol MacLean.'

'I'm fine. Are we going the whole hog, by the way?'

He said nothing. Her warmth and solidity were so comforting. His loneliness dissolved into her warmth.

'I'm an orphan now,' she hissed into his chest. 'I can do what I like.'

She seemed untroubled, almost unexcited, as she removed her remaining clothes. Her left breast was smaller, had a sickle-shaped scar. He kissed her throat and then her salty mouth. He thought of Angus groping for scallops in his diving suit, in peril under the cold and gloomy sea. But he couldn't stop: his desire was streamlined by abstinence. The wind whistled around the house. She listened, shifting in his arms.

'Sometimes the sea gets up and he comes hame early.'

He listened in turn, feeling her heartbeat, her

breathing; he hardly noticed wind noise, these days. 'It sounds pretty gusty.'

'Let's not be dawdling, then,' she said, pulling back the covers. Her knickers, satiny like the wallpaper, were polka-dotted, a fold of flesh hiding their elastic. He stood behind her and touched them in front: like something wrapped up, moss or paper covered in satin. Pass the parcel. She leaned back on him, her buttocks pressing his hardness, her hair against his mouth.

'You're so lovely, so lovely,' he murmured. 'Do you do this often?'

'We're not yet on the scrap heap, are we?' She moved onto the bed and waited on her side, hand tucked under her head, the duvet drawn only to her hips. 'It's an ancient custom of the isle,' she whispered. 'You didnae know that?'

A sudden gust knocked the window so hard its glass rattled.

'You look like a rabbit caught in headlights,' she said, grinning. She extended an arm. He suppressed an impulse to let its smoothness enclose him.

'Carol, I'm not sure.'

'Not sure of what, Samson?'

'I like Angus.'

'We all like Angus,' she said, with an edge of irritation.

'Someone did this to me once. I came home early and caught them.'

'Oh. What did you do?'

'I nearly shot the guy. Because of that, my wife wouldn't have me back.'

'You had a gun, did you?'

'I guess I did,' he said. 'That was the trouble.'

She snorted softly, turning onto her back. 'Then you're not what I thought you were.'

'What did you think I was?'

'Different from the others,' she said, closing her eyes. 'Different from other men.'

★ ★ ★

The next day was Sunday. Everything shut down, including the pubs. The hilltop kirk in Bargrennan would receive its line of worshippers dressed as if for a funeral. He almost felt like joining them today: he needed a stern ticking-off. He didn't think much about God, whether God was real or not, but Bob would always send up a little prayer as the aircraft began its roll-out.

He'd been on the brink. Instead of jumping, he had walked away. 'Trust your feelings,' Doug Rydale would be fond of saying, 'and you'll be chasing your goddamn tail all day.' But when Bob was returning home to the croft-house, feeling confused, Angus's van had passed him, heading for home early and at the islanders' usual boy-racer speed: a friendly wave from behind the smeared windscreen. He'd waved back too hastily, his heartbeat pounding in his ears over the wind that had mistaken them for conch shells.

That was yesterday. Today, in honour of the two harmless grey suits up the road, he was keeping his head low in the croft-house, his hidey-hole prepared and his pistol always to hand. He'd lost his bookmark and read the same

339

few pages of *The Guns of Navarone*. When dusk fell he walked to the phone box and called his children. Sophie's mobile was on message; David was in the library — for real.

'That's a very quiet pub,' Bob joked.

Once David was outside, he broke the news immediately. Sharansky had been deliberately killed. There were tyre-marks on his chest, where the vehicle had backed over him just in case. The police reckoned he had been facing the vehicle, which was stationary, when it had suddenly accelerated towards him, leaving burn-marks. The general theory was that he'd made an early-morning appointment — with the killer.

'Yup, you never know who's on your side in this game,' Bob said. 'David, please take care. Don't do anything silly.'

'You've done silly things all your life, Dad.'

'And look where it's got me.'

* * *

He woke up Monday morning having slept badly. He felt rough. He missed flying. He fished out Judith Byrne's card and considered paying a visit. As a mouse might visit a trap.

He wondered if he should take a jaunt to the mainland instead: drive down to Edinburgh, stay somewhere like the Balmoral for a few days, stuff himself with world cuisine, keep warm even in the corridors; but this would be a mistake. They'd spot something awry with his fake passport, or get on the phone to certain suite-booking clients — hotels, like airports, being shady toytowns. He should stay put, for once in his life. Let the flies settle. Six months max. Avoid porridge for twenty-four hours. Read books. Listen to the radio. Write his memoirs. The thought of the latter appalled him.

He'd had a dream that a flotilla of inflatables filled with black-clad frogmen toting automatics had invaded the island, running silently up to the croft. He'd gone downstairs in a sweat and opened the front door; the night was starry, air sweeping off the sea and rattling his windows. He put on his boots and coat and made for the loch. The water was shiny, like glazed tiles: it was the light falling from thousands of stars — the Milky Way was a visible smear. In the north-west there was something larky going on, a party, disco lights throwing up a pale reflection, but with no bass beats audible over the wind. After a moment he realised it was the aurora borealis. His bare calves were frozen.

After breakfast he checked the weather: the grass was agitated, as were the clouds, but nothing else moved. There *was* nothing else. Dr Byrne's broad smile was out of optical range.

He headed off for a run. A van was parked the other side of the gate. It was Angus's, and he was inside, shrouded in the smoke of a roll-up. The driver's door opened as Bob approached with a carefree grin.

'Fancy meeting you here,' Angus said, without getting out.

'Angus, good to see you. Not out at sea?'

'My mate's down with the flu. The captain cannae dive on his own.' He gave Bob a sharp, meaningful look. 'D'you fancy a wee boat trip, Mr Webb? Spot a few porpoises? Seals? Sharks?'

'That's kind. Can I let you know?'

Angus looked at him stonily. He had flyaway eyebrows that made his clear blue eyes look fiercer, and a muscle spasm in his right cheek. 'The water's calm. Tomorrow she won't be. Maybe rough for weeks. My wife says you mentioned a boat trip, one time.'

'Did she? Oh, that's right. So I did.'

*　*　*

Bob had never been a great fan of boats. He waited for Angus by the lonely concrete slipway in Ardcorry, beyond the Tinker's Arms, scanning the landward side for strange men. It had turned grey, with small low black clouds like flocks of sheep, and he didn't think the sea was quite calm enough, chopping and slobbering against the rocks and timber piles.

The boat was a peeling dinghy with an outboard motor, not the solid scallop-fishing vessel. They chugged out between grass-tufted islets and fearsome-looking rocks (Bob thought Angus steered too close to them), and he suddenly felt the ocean swell beneath the hull, like an adult taking charge. But this was not a responsible adult. It had no compassion, for a start, and it was (according to Bob's fingers) incredibly cold.

Angus was silent, seated in the stern with a hand on the tiller, the motor leaving a trail of dark smoke. In fact, the outboard was loud enough to make ordinary chat difficult. Bob had to twist in his seat to look out front. For some reason, he preferred facing aft, keeping an eye on the pilot. Seals slithered off rocks or stared at them with remarkably human expressions — disdain, mostly. Suddenly, Angus pointed ahead. Three sleek stone-grey backs breaking water over and over.

'Porpoise?' yelled Bob.

Angus nodded. He seemed dejected. The swell was smooth and low, lifting and dropping the boat as they hit the truly open sea in a way that surprised Bob — it seemed exaggerated. The prow pushed a V of ripples out onto the sleek flanks of water, foam-flecked from some souvenir of the crashing, catastrophic breakers glimmering much further out. The vessel had shrunk, the sea had grown, peppered as far as the horizon with the explosions of gannets. It was strange, not being able to see below the grey surface. It might have been a shifting roof of slate.

Bob looked back the way they'd come, surveying the island and its attendant islets, its peaks and troughs. He reckoned the high bulk beyond Angus's shoulder was the headland, the pale thread all that remained of his broad beach. The wind was now remarkably boisterous, the salty air devoid of anything to do with land — but it wasn't clear and empty, like the air of the stratosphere; it made Bob think of death, or at least of non-life. It was punching at his raised hood as if to remind him, and made his eyes water. This was not his element.

Angus knew what he was doing, of course.

Bob began to relax. He was losing his embarrassment in front of the man. He was glad he had walked away from the deal, this time. He felt almost good about it, and smiled at his pilot. The pilot did not smile back.

Then the engine cut out.

They bobbed about, turning as the swells took them. Bob looked at Angus, faintly alarmed. Were there oars in the boat? What the hell did you do if the motor died, or you ran out of fuel?

Angus was holding out a bit of paper. A small card.

'Have a squint at this,' he said. His Ss whistled, almost shrieked, through his gap tooth.

Bob looked, without taking it. It was his bookmark, the stub of his Emirates Airlines boarding card. He returned Angus's stare with a quizzical glance, the voltage in his heart taking on a surge. The water chopped against the hull: the sea was bottomless, to all intents and purposes. A few thin planks between, bilge slapping at his boots.

'Found it,' said Angus, 'in my wife's bedroom.'

Bob's face was a beacon, a distress flare: he raised his eyebrows free of the glow. 'Oh?'

'Man to man, Mr Webb. When I return to the hoose on Saturday, earlier than usual, I find Mrs MacLean in the shower. She never takes showers in the afternoon. She was in a queer mood.'

Bob wondered if he could swim it. He held the boat's sides — strakes, he seemed to think they were called — and mentally calculated the distance. He couldn't. It might have been a few hundred metres, or a thousand, or two miles. The land was a faint blue heap, very far away over the grey wastes of water. He didn't have the right instruments.

'Are you listening, Mr Webb?'

'Go on, Angus. Do call me Kit, by the way,' he added, conscious of sounding like his father: clipped, ex-military, fighter-pilot moustache kept till long after its sell-by date. 'Aren't we drifting a bit?'

'We're fine. I didnae breathe a word of my thoughts. She was even chattier than usual. Thank God it's the Gaelic, which is easier on the ears than the English tongue. Am I not correct?'

'Totally agree. It's a lovely tongue.'

Angus frowned. 'You look scared, Mr Webb.' He patted the outboard. 'We cannae hear ourselves think when this is working. I go upstairs to the master bedroom, and I look about, having my suspicions. And what do I find?'

'That boarding card?'

'Look at it close, Mr Webb.' Bob took it. 'What does it say?'

'Well, the passenger was a certain Robert C. Winrush. He was flying from somewhere beginning with D to London Heathrow. Date not clear. It's been in the wash.'

'Dubai, Mr Webb.' Angus leaned forward. Wiry, but his strength would be considerable. He prised scallops off the deep seabed. 'It scares me, flying. I once went in a helicopter, winched oot the sea in the storm of 92. Leave it to the birds, I say.'

'I haven't flown for years. Not good for the climate.'

'You're an intelligent man. Teaching bairns, studying birds. Do you see what I'm getting at? And don't bother saying you've not got a clue.'

How did he spot the scallops down there, in the gloom? Did he have a torch? He had placed a flat, battered tin on his knee and began to roll a cigarette.

'Don't you think we're drifting a bit far, Angus?' The boat, side-on to the swell, was now rocking so much that the bilge kept splashing onto their chins. The world was careless, ultimately. You had to meet it with precision. This would get them nowhere. But Angus didn't seem to notice. He probably had exceptionally large lungs, to go with his hands. He drew deeply on his roll-up. The air was tinged with smoke, instantly. whipped away.

'Mr Webb, I passed you on the road not a hundred metres from our hoose. The same afternoon.'

Bob frowned, as if remembering with difficulty. 'Oh, right. I was visiting Ardcorry church.'

'Not the Tinker's Arms?'

'Oh no. The church. Its churchyard, anyway. Atmospheric.'

'There are eleven MacLeans buried there,' said Angus. 'All drowned.'

Bob yelped, because a more excitable wave had pitched them to one side so far that he thought he would topple in. Angus smiled, raising his hand. Some gulls passed near them, squawking over the open water. Bob found them faintly reassuring. The grey sky was very dark to the west: stormy, even.

He pulled a face. 'A bit of dropped litter and a power-shower. I don't see it, Angus. What does the accused say?'

Angus snorted. 'What, frighten off the rabbit? I've not told her a thing. Not yet. You don't know her. She was aye liberated from the start. I cannae lay a finger on her.'

Bob was feeling a touch nauseous. He couldn't find his sea-legs, not even sitting.

'She tells me,' Angus went on, 'you're interested by the grey suits staying at the Tinker's Arms, where she cleans.'

'Not that interested. Intrigued?'

'And Murray told me they were talking about the Middle East.'

'Ah,' said Bob, relief mingling with fear. 'Maybe your wife dropped something after cleaning one of the rooms.'

'There's no Robert C. Winrush staying in the hotel. I've looked the name up on the computer. Only one Robert Winrush came up: a mercenary pilot.'

Bob almost jumped. 'We're in a jam, then,' he said.

A large moving body of water lifted them like a cork, spun them slightly, lowered them with a curious wobble. Angus's glance flickered to the west, towards the mid-ocean wastes they were approaching. There was a sudden increased coolness in the air. 'Do you think,' said the passenger, in a pinched voice, 'the weather report is not completely reliable?'

347

The skipper pulled at the motor; it started on the second attempt, springing into life like something blessed. How I love civilisation, technology, human expertise, thought Bob. They were heading for land, Angus with a bad-tempered frown of dissatisfaction. The passenger had no idea what to say, partly because he felt sick. Feeling sick, although unpleasant, was a good substitute for dying. Land was better than water. He was not good at the liquid element thing, unless it was framed by tiles.

As they were tying up at Ardcorry, he said, 'I didn't see a soul on the road that afternoon, Angus. If that's any help.'

'Just as I thought, or you'd have said straight oot.'

'I lost my wife,' Bob went on. 'She's not dead; she left me. I neglected her. She cheated on me. I didn't love her enough. I got grumpy and she just got fed up. She's with someone else now. A failed artist. Learn from my mistakes,' he added.

He dropped the boarding-card stub in the water. It floated, annoyingly, but was soon taken out by the currents like a petal and disappeared.

Angus watched it. 'You're an intelligent man,' he said. 'I knew I did right, asking your opinion.'

He shook Bob's hand: a terrifying grip.

Bob called Carol's mobile from Ardcorry churchyard, using his pre-paid phone. He didn't mention the name on the stub. She thanked him for the warning.

'I'm clear,' he said. 'He thinks I'm the bee's knees.'

'Aye,' she sighed, 'he's always been a hopeless judge of character.'

No more hot showers, Bob thought. He counted ten MacLean graves, their subjects all lost at sea. He gave up on the eleventh, but there were quite a few stones mossed over, or fallen.

★ ★ ★

He got back to company.

For three months he had not seen a single person on this peninsula. Now there were two figures on the blacklands, near the loch: backs turned. He produced the Makarov, did an SAS-style running crouch to the house, found his binos and brought the intruders closer through the tweaked-open skylight. Close-cropped heads, pale and burly, in cagoules. They were either taking photographs or checking their weapons. His hand-shake made them look worse, like a TV docudrama. He was not that surprised: they were staking out the territory for some later and more sophisticated operation called Get Winrush. There was a high mewing note and they looked up, one of them pointing.

It was the sea eagle, circling high overhead on its jumbo wings. *They look yummy*, Bob hissed telepathically. *Dive in*. It glided away. He'd hoped their shaven pates might have resembled fat mice from that height.

They began walking back, stumbling now and again. They were now close enough to spot a shadow in the skylight, if they looked up. The attic was roughly at the height of a seven-oh's cockpit, and they reminded him of two ramp agents sauntering up for the ground handling.

He waited at the top of the boarded-in ladder staircase, Makarov trained on the closed door at the bottom. He considered using the hidey-hole. He had never actually shot at anyone in his life. When the knocking resounded through the house, he all but buckled at the knees. Where were his James Bond credentials? Where had his pilot phlegm gone? At least they were knocking, rather than breaking the door down.

The floor creaked at the slightest pressure. The gunsight pinned the door below at what he guessed was chest height. The safety lever was down. His trigger finger ached from sustaining its slight pressure and the door kept trembling, drifting. No more knocking. What he expected was the punch and shatter of broken glass. Instead, dim voices. They were circling the house. By now he had realised that if you take up a firing position for more than a few minutes, you need to rest your arms on something. The pistol had tripled in weight.

He peeped out through the front skylight: they were both on their phones, by the fallen chicken wire fence, talking in nasal voices. They ducked suddenly and there was a shot, like a cut-off clap of thunder, carried late to Bob's ears by the gusts. It wasn't his shot.

They put their hands out to the sides, as in a cowboy film. Angus hove into view, cradling his .22. He was shouting at them, telling them to go home. He was, as far as Bob could catch, calling them English this-and-thats — perverts? — and how no true islander would ever surrender his property or his wife. But he couldn't be certain: the words were slurred and snatched at by the wind. Part of them might even have been Gaelic. Maybe Carol was lying in her kitchen in a pool of blood. He'd been an idiot, even going as far as he did.

And then, in a lull, a complete sentence powering upwards: '*Which one of you's Robert Windrush?*'

Their protests, high-voiced and whiny, achieved nothing. Angus was again pointing the barrel at them. If they were pros, they would take him out, rifle or no rifle. Bob tweaked the skylight open a few more inches: he aimed the Makarov at the nearest man's head. The wrap-around shades glinted. Sheep and goats, Bob thought.

The head shifted: the men were moving off with hands high and Angus was following them, still yelling.

Soon there was nothing but the wind's sigh rushing around the house — as though it was the house itself that was hurtling on without a break, destination still unknown. If Angus had, as most people did, misremembered his name, he might yet be safe.

Only boats, farms and rivers were called Windrush.

4

No schedules, no estimated arrival and departure times, no fear of being late into the front office. No one to get back to on time. No crackling voices over the radio, no telexes wondering why the precious cargo was delayed, no thinking hundreds of nautical miles ahead at every moment — just in case. There was no just-in-case, now. Except for the minor problem of someone aiming to erase him: but then everyone had that problem, sooner or later.

He was spreadeagled in the sweet, harsh marram towards the headland's cliffs. He was over halfway through *The Guns of Navarone*. The grey suits had gone; they had taken a Twin Otter from Bargrennan airport, which consisted of a shed and a windsock and 700 metres of smooth sand. He had watched them depart (alerted by Carol) from the viewing terrace of the dunes. They were never hit men; they were businessmen. Land development consultants, he'd discovered — after feeding in their names (provided by Carol) to the Internet's infinite maw. Bob was relieved, but everyone else was worried.

The policeman from Stornoway sent to have a word with Angus was a distant cousin. They had laughed a lot of the time, apparently. The men's identities had been established as genuine: neither was Robert Winrush. Mercenary pilot

Robert Winrush appeared on a website run by Israeli peaceniks: they were honouring Sharansky by displaying his recent unpublished articles. He had to close it quickly when Marcie appeared, bearing his cake.

He phoned David again from the piss-smelling call box in the harbour, the gulls deafening. The Podgorica article did not derive from anybody involved with the UK campaign. Sharansky's computer was still in Tel Aviv, obviously.

'Free speech, free access, Dad.'

'Don't let him near your daughters.'

'Is the deal with Tim off, then?'

'I'm not that mercenary,' said Bob.

David laughed. 'Are those gulls, or just sound effects to put us off the scent?'

'Oh no, look, the ceiling fan's just blown away my sweat-stained papers. Hey, are we any closer to knowing who killed Sharansky?'

'As Tim put it, we're not in synchromesh with the Polish police. They've this theory that he was an Israeli spy.'

'Don't mention the war,' Bob said.

He bumped into Carol as he emerged from the phone. She gave him only a shy smile, because folk were milling about, waiting for the ferry.

'Mobile broken?'

'I don't really own one.'

She looked at the gulls and said, 'Are you Robert Windrush?'

'No,' he replied, not inaccurately. 'I bought the book second-hand. The stub was already in it. Did Angus get at you? I think the consensus is that we had a very close shave.'

'He didn't shoot me,' she said. 'It's happened before. He knows the score but sometimes he asserts his maleness. He doesn't need to, he's the bravest man I know. A lot braver than you, for all your muscle.'

He nodded, admiring her gall. 'I'm only scared of one thing, Mrs MacLean: deep water.'

★ ★ ★

The sand was warm. The air was springlike. He kept dozing off in his coat: catching up on three decades of jet-tormented sleep.

'You haven't called.'

He looked up, startled. She was dressed in a baggy knitted sweater and was holding a towel. He looked at her as if surprised.

'You can't be thinking of swimming, Dr Byrne.'

'Usually there's no one here, but I bring my costume just in case. What are you up to? Spying on birds?' She didn't seem to imply anything else in her tone.

'Don't worry about me. I'll keep my eyes shut.'

'*Should* I worry about you?'

He pulled a face. 'You don't know me, I suppose.'

'They say you can never tell, but you don't look like a psychopath.'

'They look much like anyone, I'm afraid.'

'That's OK then, because you don't look much like anyone, Mr Webb.'

354

'Thank you.'

A contemptuous snort ended in that feisty smile. 'I hear Angus MacLean chased off some Sassenachs. On your croft-land.'

'*His* land, actually, in terms of tenancy. But next to the house, yes. Luckily, they saw his point of view.'

'Did you not know them?'

'No.'

'But he found them on the croft.'

'So? It's just bumpy grass and rocks to me.'

Her eyes narrowed above a screwed-up face as if her sight was faulty. She had what Olivia would call (with a hint of contempt) *a face with character*.

'Ewan's keen to have a chat with you, about this and other stuff such as birds. Are you free for a tea? Like, how about now, after my plunge?'

This was thrown out much more like a challenge than an invitation. Her seal-dark eyes were firmly on him as the gulls shrieked and the sea rumbled and roared from its gauze of background din. Bob consented.

She trotted down to the surf, changed under her towel, and swam in an elastic black costume cut so low at the back it was only a couple of vertebrae short of the buttocks: sinuous was the operative word, thought Bob. As far as he could see with a squinting eye, she emerged with the same face, hair in black clumps over her broad shoulders. He had not read a word since she'd appeared.

★　★　★

355

They drove to the centre in the Land Rover, following a little winding road he'd only ever taken as far as the head of a loch shaped on the map like a fist with a wagging finger: a wooden sign said PRIVATE ROAD ONLY. THE GAIR CENTRE. The shallow, shadowy glen stretched away like a location for a dinosaur film, its rocky slopes all bleached grass and scree; the loch was black with peat. The metalled track ran beside the loch shore, then cleared the feeder burn on a pitted hump of concrete, giving out in gravel in front of the house — a large severe manse of soot-coloured stone, its six long windows and crooked portico facing the loch. They stepped out of the four-wheel drive. The glen had silenced the wind and distant surf; it was all local tricklings over the hush. The banging of the car doors sent echoes flying over the water.

'Impressive,' said Bob.

They'd talked about island politics during the ten-minute drive, half of which had him lost in acronyms, the names of this and that council. Her face was mobile, her gestures energetic: she was more like an actress than a zoologist.

The manse was surprisingly bare inside, apart from shelves of books, heavy fire doors, gatherings of shabby and unmatching easy chairs, one long room with sweeping girders of brand-new pine presenting an environmental exhibition with huge backlit photos and interactive screens. It bored him instantly, but he made the right noises. Judith explained that Alexander Gair was an island man who'd recorded its wildlife and flowers and so forth way back before the war: one dim dust-spotted image of a man with cavernous cheeks, in a flat cap and cardie.

'The Richard Jefferies of the Western Isles,' she added.

'Absolutely,' said Bob, who had never heard of Richard Jefferies.

'Gair had an incredible sense of jizz,' said Judith.

'Jizz?'

'You must know what jizz is.'

'Only in its obscene version.'

She laughed. 'Wow, you've a long way to go. It's the way a bird looks, the overall impression you get. It's a complement to the field marks. Fairly subjective, but useful. The gestalt approach. You've just blown your cover, by the way.'

'Cover for what?'

'You tell me.'

'Well, let me know when you've found it,' he said, feeling he'd walked into the trap.

Gair's modern counterpart, standing in the big utility kitchen, was surprisingly short: compact, vaguely bearded, with an earring and suspicious eyes, sporting jeans and a woolly sweater that hung off his elbows. Ewan was a mountain climber.

'Hello there,' he said, not shaking hands, barely looking up. 'Judith mentioned you. Our bird enthusiast. Let's have tea.'

The dining room, with two long pine tables, had a flashy wood stove merrily aglow. Ewan fed it some more logs and they sat down to a

357

health-food version of fruitcake.

Ewan hailed from Fife. Bob stopped himself mentioning McAllister; he was playing terse. Sophie would have called it cool. Ewan was genuinely cool: never smiled, narrowed his eyes as if smoke was in them. He climbed cliffs and had prehensile fingers. He'd studied for his DPhil in Aberdeen.

Inevitably, they began to probe.

'How long are you over for, Kit?' asked Judith.

'As long as it takes for the gulls not to do what I expect them to do.'

'There's a good scientist,' said Judith, meaning it.

'Completely amateur. But keen.'

'Tired of teaching?' said Ewan.

Bob shrugged. 'Not always.' He remembered what Olivia had said about the shop, adapted it. 'I think it got tired of me.'

Ewan asked him if he kept a photographic record.

'Of the birds? Oh yes.'

'Could be useful.'

Bob found bird photos about as gripping as aircraft photos, whether an osprey or a Vulcan XH558. He was only here because of Judith's smile. He caught his reflection in the glass and took his woolly cap off, smoothing his hair.

'Who cut it?' asked Judith.

'Oh, the female barber of Ardcorry. Carol MacLean.'

'Talking of the MacLeans,' said Ewan, 'I hear Angus frightened off your compatriots.'

'That's all we had in common.'

'Is that so? They were found on your croft,' he said, as if reading from the same script Judith had used.

She explained to Ewan what Bob had explained to her.

'So you've no idea what they're up to?'

'No. Do you?'

'Not quite. Not yet,' Ewan said, examining him fiercely from under his fair eyebrows, which met in the middle. 'But I stand on the beach and look at the bird tracks and remind myself that what looks chaotic and random is always purposeful.'

'Maybe where birds and animals are concerned,' said Judith. 'I'm not so sure about humans.'

Bob told himself that there were lots of beaches Ewan could be standing on. 'What's your speciality, Ewan, nature-wise?'

'Rabbits.'

'Rabbits?'

'Have you heard of risk theory?'

''Fraid not.'

'Foraging,' said Ewan, suddenly more animated, 'involves a trade-off, right?'

'Does it?'

'It does. It's basic. A trade-off between finding the best food and getting killed by your enemies. Starvation versus predation. I'm studying the behaviour of rabbits in the presence of sea eagles.'

'That must take some doing,' Bob said.

Ewan nodded. 'Like, for how long do they come out of their burrows and expose

359

themselves? How close do they keep in a group? Because the group has more eyes and is more vigilant and there's less chance of you, as an individual rabbit, being eliminated.'

'The dilution effect,' Judith clarified.

'Safety in numbers?' suggested Bob, feeling he was spoiling things.

A mobile went off. It was Ewan's: he left the room without an apology, talking into it. Judith sat on the broad windowsill with her hands girlishly tucked under her thighs.

'Ewan is not stupid,' she said.

Bob stood looking out of the window at the loch glinting in the brief grip of sunlight. 'Clearly not.'

'Anti-predator response is a bit old-fashioned, these days, but he's doing things with it that are new. It's kind of all maths, in the end.'

'Not to the rabbits, I guess.'

Judith briefly stretched her smile even further than before, then told him that instinct was a kind of maths. 'They're hardwired to react, not make links between things, work out a causal relationship. Like, why should a stone crack a nut? Because of the hardness. The squirrel just cracks the nut; she never thinks about the hardness. It's instinct, honed by evolution.'

'Probably,' said Bob, lost in the movement of her lips. 'But instinct can also lead you astray.'

She stared back at him. 'Instinct is instinct.'

'Not in a machine environment.'

She frowned. 'Like what?'

'A nuclear power station. A cockpit.'

'Fascinating,' she said. 'I never knew rabbits flew planes.'

Ewan walked past the front of the house balancing a three-bladed propeller on his head, as if playing at helicopters.

'There's our wind turbine. He thinks the best spot is on the north side. Near the sand filter. I'm not so sure.'

Bob thought Ewan had been a bit rude, not coming back to tea. But he was glad he hadn't. 'He'll take off if he's not careful.'

'I don't suppose you approve, as a bird enthusiast.'

'Oh?'

'It's not very good for birds.'

'Flying?'

'Wind turbine.' She put on a terrified face. 'I'm swooping into one. Slap slap slap slap.'

'True,' he smiled. 'Birds don't like propellers. And vice versa.'

'This is hardly going to be very grand,' said Judith, looking at him carefully. 'Hardly of industrial size and capacity.'

'You could tie silver ribbons on the blades,' Bob suggested.

'Really?'

Ewan had disappeared. Bob could easily imagine him taking off vertically, his compact body whisked over the sea until gone for ever.

'Ewan's not so great, as a mechanic,' she said.

'What type is it?'

'Search me. Normal, I guess. Why, are you an expert, Mr Webb?' she added, leaning forward conspiratorially.

'I installed one for my school,' Bob fibbed. 'I can have a peep.'

Veteran of stopgap maintenance regimes on prop-driven planes deep in the bush, he worked it out quickly. The wind turbine was an off-the-shelf model designed for normal English winds: the package included a shut-down system, but the blades were glorified planks. The kit was propped against a wall in a roomy outhouse facing the garden in which a huge vegetable patch bore labels in kids' writing over its bare earth: more hope than vigour. The tower's pole stretched the length of the outhouse. Ewan was back to his constitutional grumpiness.

'You need blades with variable pitch,' Bob said, who missed oil on his hands, the turn of the bolt. 'They adjust themselves to the wind speed. And maybe you need the type that bend back and twist, just to be safe. And I'd recommend a furling system rather than relying on a shutdown. You don't want your tower to collapse. And talking of the tower, that pole looks a bit short, given some of it's buried.'

'It was gonna go up on the roof,' said Ewan.

'Not a good idea.'

'Why?' asked Judith.

'A house creates a heck of a lot of turbulence. Planting it well away somewhere in the grounds where you've a view of the sea, that would solve the problem. Hills are bad news, but cliffs are good.'

Ewan's sour look went sourer: his pug nose curled up like an oyster hit by a squirt of lemon.

362

'Cliffs? What's good about cliffs?'

'The air hits with a wallop, lots of bumps, but then just flows over it fairly easily, if there are no hills or trees.'

'Sheep?' joked Judith.

They walked round to the outside of the high garden wall. You could see the glitter of the sea between a broad cleft in the hills, beyond a spread of machair.

'Carry out your data checks just here,' Bob said. 'The wind speed, and where it generally blows from. I'd say you'd get enough air — the prevailing wind's off the sea — but I'm worried about those south-easterlies.'

Ewan's nose almost disappeared. 'South-easterlies?

'Those gales that go on and on. They turn north-westerly in the end, all that hail and sleet we had last month, but you still want to check. You could get a certain amount of figures off the Met Office, I suppose. But you want to get the ground info, too. Air's weird, it can do crazy things. A hill with a certain shape can make it deviate in a completely unexpected way. You can't generalise. That's why airports are all different.'

Ewan did not look happy. The sun caught on a wave far out. He said, 'How come you know so much about wind?'

A bird of prey was circling overhead, silhouetted against the bright sky. They all looked up at its peeping. 'Well,' Bob said, 'birds use wind all the time. Along with thermals.'

'What is it?' asked Ewan, pointing up.

'Buzzard, looking for a juicy mouse.'

'I'd have said it was a hen harrier,' Ewan said. 'By the way, I'd always thought black-headed gulls don't hang about here in the winter.'

'They don't.'

'Oh, but they do. Complete with their black heads. Their summer plumage. According to the expert.'

'The expert?'

'You,' said Ewan, thin lips doing their best to smile.

Judith tried to shut him up, but he carried on regardless, in an accent that seemed to thicken for Bob's benefit. 'Someone in the Tinker's Arms, whose name I canna remember, told me. 'You've not got a clue,' I said. And he said, 'Witever. I was informed so by the bird expert from England. And that's all about it, son.''

'The music was a bit loud at the time, the stroboscope flashing.'

Judith giggled.

'Aye, maybe that was it,' said Ewan, his dryness wrinkling the air itself.

His mobile buzzed and he went off, talking into it. Like a grown-up, thought Bob.

'Never mind Ewan,' Judith said. 'He doesn't like mystery.'

'Do you?'

'It's what got me into science. Asking the right questions. But never expecting the right answers.'

'I'll see you around, Judith. We've got some extremely soggy machair on the peninsula.' He was hoping she would offer him a lift, gaining more time together.

'Are you OK walking?' she said. 'It's only about half an hour. I'm on office duty now, more's the pity.'

* * *

It took forty-five minutes, but he didn't mind. He was on the croft's path, just rounding the hill, when the shot sounded.

It was so close it made his ears buzz, and the boggy ground at his feet seemed to splatter. He ducked down pretty quick among the heather and tussocks, wishing they were a bit taller, and reckoned this was it. He had no idea where the shot had come from, so his own gun ranged around rather helplessly.

He lay for half an hour in a state of cold, muddy expectation. Every sound was heightened, as if his tinnitus had temporarily taken a break, although the blood kept thudding in his ears: he could even hear the dry heather bells shifting and ticking and the chirrups of distant seabirds. This is all too interesting to lose, he thought. A small winged creature settled on his coat, and it was then he noticed the hole in his pocket.

He had a vague memory of feeling the pistol's jerk on his thigh: he gingerly checked its clip. It was missing two rounds, only one of which he'd intentionally squeezed off, over the loch that time. The gun was old, 1965 Bulgarian military issue.

Back home, he stripped it on the kitchen table

and found sand around the firing pin, which meant that it was no longer free-floating — gunked up enough to fire when the slide cycled. He also studied the trigger parts and the safety catch looked a bit worn, but the sear notch wasn't at all rounded, so it couldn't have let the sear bar slip.

Whatever, he was lucky it hadn't gone off at any time before, hitting himself or someone else: Astra, Judith, Marcie, a stranger. The sand inside was white, not Dubai's. He should never have taken it to the beach: he'd lost a camera in Hawaii like that, decades back. One day, perhaps, experience would teach him something.

Accidental discharge, anyway. Which is what his father used to say about his son's procreation when the bastard had been at the gin and felt joky, settling into the settee.

Bob stripped and lubricated the beast, cycled it without a round and inserted a full clip. The gun was old, but he was sentimental about it. He dropped it a few times on the table, muzzle first, but nothing happened. He was ninety-nine per cent reassured that he wouldn't have a testicle blown off. Only eventual personal extinction could rate one hundred per cent.

★ ★ ★

'How did it go up at the Centre?' asked Marcie, with the usual mug of coffee and a ginger biscuit. Her skirt was turquoise, her face soft and round.

'Do I need to ask how you knew?'

'Nah,' she said.

'The tea and cake's not as good as here,' he smiled.

'They're a brainy couple though, aren't they? There's not much they don't know about wildlife.'

'Are they a couple?'

'They go on holiday together in this converted van,' she said, wistfully.

'Brains aren't everything,' he went on, covering his disappointment. 'Quite a few of the guys in Broadmoor have very high IQs.'

'Broadmoor? Jesus. What's Broadmoor got to do with anything?'

He was looking at his scanned post when Astra came in. The post included the decree nisi to sign, all tight-lipped legalese. His marriage was to be *dissolved UNLESS* anyone objected. This was it, then. Finito. In a few weeks the decree absolute would come through and the dissolving would be complete. There'd be no *UNLESS*.

He pre-empted Astra's target practice by bundling him into his arms and dangling him upside down by the ankles. The delighted squeals brought his mother hastening out of the gallery area.

'That's probably against at least two laws, you know.'

'There are nae laws on this island,' Bob growled, 'except obedience to the Saaabbath. Which means — ' Astra's miniature legs had powerful pistons inside — 'all wee bairns should be seen and not hearrrd, or go strrrraight to hell!'

'Not in this case,' said Marcie.

His words made Astra squeal louder, swinging himself towards Bob's groin with flailing arms. Bob felt the child needed to see someone professional, but chuckled along. Astra's long hair brushed the pinewood floor. The child suddenly relaxed, his eyes closed, and for a split second Bob thought he had fainted.

Then a tiny voice emerged: 'Swing me,' it said.

Bob swung him gently like a pendulum, as he'd swing the twins, years ago, one after the other. Twenty-five years of marriage ending on a lawyer's dry snigger. A final signature required. How would he disguise the postmark? He could send it to Al, and Al could post it from there.

'That's what Kier used to do,' Marcie murmured, her lower lip crumpling in a way that Bob had to make a huge effort not to imitate in turn.

'I'll need to use your printer,' he said.

★ ★ ★

He posted the decree nisi, duly signed, to Al's PO box on the Virgin Islands. From one island to another. A favour from an old friend. He'd slipped some white sand into the sealed envelope, to nestle among the papers; Olivia and her arty particle would appreciate that. Best wishes from the land of buccaneers.

He sat by the loch and got pished. On his own with the Talisker. Just this once. Quality time. Total class. On the other hand, he was now a free bird. The sheep's grinning skeleton was unsettling. He talked to it. That helped. He shouted shite for ten minutes, over the dark-chocolate waters. Nobody to hear but the waders he could not even identify. Oh fuck it, let's say oystercatchers. Who cares? He waded into the marshy bit through the reeds and rolled up his sleeves and tried to tickle trout. It was hilarious. His father was watching from the opposite bank, fishing in a light drizzle. Bob's bared arms were black with peatiness. He shook his fists and shouted and threw stones at his father, who shook his head.

'I don't care! I'll land them like fucking bricks! I'll do what I fucking like!'

You always have done, whispered Olivia, standing next to his father. Voices carried far in this glen, it was so quiet. He pulled out the Makarov and used up an entire clip, getting rid of them across the water, but he was so pished and cold he missed them entirely.

5

That night he dreamt of Joseph H. Kenley. Not for the first time. Kenley did what he liked too.

He showed up in multi-pocketed bush gear, waving a Bible. *Holy machete lore*, he'd call it. His willowy form, his long limbs and fingers, his Bambi eyes, the tribal scars nicked over his sharp cheekbones: just the same.

'Your wife has sent me because she loves you,' Kenley said in the same earnest tone he'd use about his divine mission, brown eyes bloodshot from too much cola nut, too little sleep, and whatever else he was on: cocaine, rum, LSD. Bob hadn't seen it at the time. He looked out of the kitchen window and saw the red earth of a compound, a lad in a camouflage jacket smoking right by the glass with automatic rifle shouldered, the forest trees bunching up beyond the barbed wire, and other men laughing, playing cards. But on the windowsill there was still the tea caddy and his keys and an opened packet of digestives, clear as day. No sign of the 707 he'd thumped in right by the loch.

'You've occupied my peninsula,' Bob said. 'You've brought your men where they shouldn't be. This isn't right. That's not part of the deal. You gave me your word you wouldn't come back.'

'Then fly them out, Captain Winrush. Fly them out.'

The rest was a blur. He woke up in the attic bedroom, shivery but too hot under the blankets. A breath of the usual malaria, a whiff of the old life. The systems breaking down. A mixed bag.

He was bad for twenty-four hours.

Olivia was calling his name from the Worcestershire garden, which had a huge meadow behind it full of white horses cantering about instead of the estate. Why was she calling him Kit? He staggered to the front skylight, opened it to a near-windless day full of sparks. The hill's slope on the left descended from the giddying ridge to a lone figure at the bottom, standing with her eyes shielded by her hand.

'Mr Webb, I presume?'

He let Judith in after stumbling on the attic bedroom's steps, turning his two new Yale locks with difficulty. She wondered why he needed to lock up at all: no one did on the island, apart from the odd second-homer.

'Automatic,' he mumbled.

'You've been on a bender, Kit,' she said.

He nodded sheepishly. He didn't want to get into the malaria thing, invent travellers' tales.

'I was on my way to your machair,' she said. 'The curtains were all closed. It's two o'clock in the afternoon. My father died of a stroke when I was fifteen; he'd lain on the floor for a day and a night, they reckoned.'

'Alone too, was he?'

'A drunkard. Separated from my mother when I was five. I stopped seeing him. He was only the other side of town. Edinburgh's not so big, after all. That was bad, but I was a judgemental

371

teenager. So you see I was acting on precedent.'

'Thank you,' Bob murmured. He felt terrible, but he was over the worst. She made the coffee nevertheless.

'You don't look like a boozer,' she said.

He nearly replied that, as a pilot, he couldn't be. Instead he shook his head and said, 'We all have our days. I think it was the whisky.'

She said, in a mock-American voice, 'The news was received with amazement.'

She relit the Raeburn, got the hearth fire going, refilled the paraffin heaters, forgot there was no electricity and opened the fridge door to packets of rice and spaghetti. She made him a hot-water bottle and generally fussed. It was rather nice, and he said so.

'My pleasure. It's a sweet wee cottage,' she said, tracing a cross on the kitchen window's condensation. 'Can I look around?'

'I wouldn't call it sweet, but it's certainly wee. Go ahead. Could you pass me the sugar?'

She did so. 'Do you want a spoon?'

'Top drawer.'

She opened the wrong top drawer, rummaged under papers as if the cutlery was eccentrically underneath. 'Och, d'you know your passport's in here?'

It was sitting in her hand: the old one. Captain Robert C. Winrush, pilot. Thick with visa stamps. The new false one was upstairs.

'That's fine. Leave it in there,' Bob said, a little too sharply.

She closed the drawer without opening the passport, saying how awful everyone looked in their photos, not being allowed to smile. He stirred his coffee. What else was there lying around that might be embarrassing? He was still too malarial to think straight. The moment of stress had pitched him backwards. He put his head in his hands. It would have fallen off, otherwise.

She saw him up to bed with an aspirin. He took his dressing gown off; he was in pyjama shorts. She eyed his scarred leg.

'You've been in a scrape.'

'Car crash. Icy road.'

She tucked him in, like a nurse. All that was missing was the goodnight kiss.

'I'll look in on you, later. On my way back from the machair.'

'You're an angel. I mean that.'

Her smile made her upper lip vanish again, all but touched her earlobes. 'You've not got a clue,' she said.

★ ★ ★

The intervening hours were a fog. He woke up to find her where he'd left her, on the edge of the bed, frowning and in miniature. An enormous hand felt his forehead. He was a young knight with folded ankles.

'You're awful hot. Have you got a thermometer?'

'I'll be fine. I feel better already.'

'I thought you might be in a coma.' She held up an empty bottle of Talisker. 'I found this floating in the loch, with a message inside it. I think you've caught a chill.'

'Message?'

She unfolded a piece of paper. 'It's a right scrawl,' she said. 'But here goes. *You're my little bird. How much does a little bird weigh?* She turned the paper the other way up, peered closer, her mobile face flashing perplexity. '*It depends on the fucking bird. As far as I can fucking tell. UNLESS*. Unless what?'

He smiled, his dry lips cracking. 'My handwriting's terrible. How was the machair?'

'Ever so wet. I think the world's going to end tomorrow. Or maybe next week. If we're lucky. My boots and socks are drying downstairs, if that's OK.'

She showed him her bare feet, raising them in turn. They were slender, deeply arched, with no sign of webbing; Olivia's feet were flattish, the bit of her she would disown and that went with nothing else: not her slim waist, long neck, svelte legs. Oh, wife.

'Thank you,' he said, not really concentrating, closing his eyes because they ached with the light. He had seen the rest of her, firm and smooth as a seal, but she didn't know that. 'As soon as I'm better, I'll invite you round,' he said. 'You're a remarkable person.'

He looked around; there was no one. The attic bedroom stretched out as long and narrow as a dormitory. It was the dorm. There was a letter from home on his bed, not a good one. He felt incredibly alone and tears came into his eyes.

'Here we go,' she piped, coming up the stairs.

A bowl of porridge oats in hot milk, sprinkled with cinnamon.

She looked down at him, hands on her hips. 'Have you been crying?'

'Just glad to see you, as they say.'

★ ★ ★

The first hints of spring had brought a change. Fresh mould had appeared in corners, despite the Raeburn, the paraffin heaters and the fire kept roaring in the sitting room, and he began to think about it all as if he cared. He inspected the outside walls for damp patches, studied the drains, made rough measurements, found the boggier bits, watched how the rain escaped, ran his finger along sills, and actually bought a ladder and cleared the guttering. As if he cared.

Colin was exercising his grazing rights, and Marcie had customers. She offered him her power shower. Bob said no; then she'd insisted and he'd said yes, feeling traitorous. He'd emerged glowing and dressed, but with the towel over his shoulder, through the door marked PRIVATE. The customers that day were a middle-aged English couple, already bowed like old folk. 'We're from Cheshire,' they said. 'You two've got a lovely little establishment here.'

'I'm just checking my emails,' Bob replied, which they thought was a terrific joke.

One from Al, acknowledging receipt of the divorce papers and attaching photos of his property in 'Ruislip': white colonial-style mansion dazzling in the sun; flowery bushes and lawn around a curvaceous azure pool; and the 'private beach' — a tropical version of Bob's, curved into a palm-fringed bay, hammock in the foreground. Marcie caught the last image on the screen as she fiddled with plates in the little galley.

'Ooh, that looks nice. Could *almost* be here.'

'Ruislip.'

'Thought I recognised it. Your next stop, for the birds?'

'Nope. No black-headed gulls.'

'You chose the wrong species,' she sighed, heading back to the couple with some sponge cake. It was eleven o'clock.

'That does look scrumptious,' said the English lady as her sponge cake was lowered.

'Like its cook,' snorted the man — short, fat and bald.

'Can't take him anywhere!' his wife wheezed.

'Putting teeth in his mouth spoiled a good arse,' the returning Marcie murmured in Bob's ear. 'As my da used to say. A friend's place, is it?'

Al was there on the beach, bare-chested, tanned and waving a straw hat. His private beach. He can't have done *that* many brown envelopes. This was serious wealth.

'A distant cousin,' Bob said. 'Likes to show off.'

'To the poor relation, who doesn't even have hot water.'

Thankfully she pulled away to the galley's sink. He opened the other messages: nothing from Sophie amongst the spam, but the one from David was bothersome.

Tim Sightly had written a report for an

anti-arms journal about various dodgy flights, including one from Gostomel to Tehran: it was based on original research by the late Sharansky. The packing lists consisted of the usual — mineral exploration machine parts, rotary drilling-rig spares — and Tim wanted Bob to check it over, any further info welcome. 'So glad the deal's still on.'

The guy's terrier doggedness was quite something. David had signed off his message with 'love' and a cross. That was something, too.

Bob turned the screen slightly and opened the document, diminishing the font size. Marcie passed him, seeing only a sea of dull-looking text, heavy with acronyms and real names and footnotes, with only the word 'flight' repeated.

'Birds, birds, birds,' he grimaced.

He decided to print it off: the printer was on the next table with a fax alongside, the latter even dustier. Perhaps it came into its own in the season, perhaps not. He connected the flex and clicked the button and the printer coughed and whirred as he stood up.

'State of the art,' he remarked.

'Like me, hun.'

It was a report of just four pages, the last being a grid of packing lists and three different flight plans — from proposed to final. Familiar enough. The last page was emerging when Marcie came alongside with a bill in her hand for the Cheshire couple. He shielded the printer as if unconsciously.

'No problems? It sticks sometimes.'

She moved to his left, her eyes glancing down.

The paper was hard to read because it came out upside down. 'That looks like a lot of fun. Don't pull on it before it's out. As it were.'

He liked Marcie's familiar earthiness, but not just now. He tapped a brief note to Sightly, saying he would get back in the next few days. He signed off the message to David with 'loadsa love' and five crosses.

The English couple were open-mouthed: they'd seen him pay.

★   ★   ★

Sightly's report was spread before him on the kitchen table. Just reading it had hooked him again: the aviation drug. Being airborne, rotating to take-off, feeling the thrust and the lift, getting all that metal bulk to ease upwards and coast, apparently weightless. He tipped back just as he'd do as a kid in the old wicker chair in the hall, his father holding it by the corners and making engine noises, jerking it when they hit turbulence, spotting an Me109 and giving it such a long burst that his son's teeth rattled, then shrieking into a spiral dive to avoid its Hun friends ('rather fed-up, those chaps'), pulling out after they'd cleared the cloud base and could see each stook in the fields, then stalking a Heinkel over the sea and blazing away but to no great effect, landing with a damaged wing and glycol smoke pouring from the peppered nose.

'Not a bad show,' was all his father would say, lighting his pipe. 'Now the tea and paperwork.'

The report, entitled 'A Proliferation of Lies'

and acknowledging Sharansky's posthumous contribution, tracked a recent cargo flight from Gostomel to Tehran, with a complex final flight plan of about 15,000 nautical miles involving some ten legs during which a lot of interesting cargo could have been soaked up. There was even a stopover at Pyongyang. This wasn't the North Korean shindig that Al and he had been roped into a few years back, but a lot more recent.

The Ukraine-Iran link itself was virtually standard, but the thrust of the report was that this flight was a sting intended to frame a big-time arms trafficker called Igor Karnosov (the name new to Bob). The crate, an Ilyushin seventy six, had been impounded and searched at Colombo, with some thirty tonnes of arms and ammo on board — officially listed as, among other things, drilling-rig spare parts.

He let his eye drift down a long paragraph detailing the plane's leasing, wet-leasing and chartering history — the usual sequence of Chinese boxes, designed to blind. It certainly would have blinded him, too, except that his eyes were suddenly opened, and rather wide, by the location of the main shareholder of one of the companies incorporating the outfit that had chartered the aircraft for the last five legs. This shareholder, Swallowtail Trading Ltd, was where the trail of shell companies petered out. It was registered in Panama, although the director was based in the British Virgin Islands. His name (almost certainly fake) was Keith Price. No address in either case, of course: Bob knew that

379

tax-haven companies were all brassplates, their directors virtually untraceable. But something at the back of his neck tingled.

One swallow does not make a summer, Captain.

A swallowtail being a butterfly, but Gold Teeth did not have a perfect command of English vocabulary. Bob saw in his mind's eye that display case at Al's, full of bright wings: the smell of camphor, the thoraxes pinned to the foam.

He felt better, he felt worse, depending on the way his thoughts blew.

Swallowtail appeared to have links, according to the report, with various drug cartels, mainly Afghan and Mexican — goods from the former coming via China, the latter near enough to do it by yacht or speedboat.

His father's motto in the Spit: *Take your time, punch hard.*

Bob grimaced. He should have stuck to white rhinos, arctic foxes, live crickets out of Brisbane, a Hercules maindeck full of Cadbury's Creme Eggs. Or self-loading passengers.

He wandered over to the loch and stood by the neck portion of its goose shape. A fish surfaced, the ripple going on and on, suddenly glittering as the sun came out from behind a sliding cloud. Marcie would have said it was a sign. If Al had anything to do with that heroin deal on the return Turkmenbashi leg, let another fish rise.

An instant later, the corner of his eye caught someone heading for the cottage: at this distance, from the far side of the loch, he couldn't identify who until, through the binoculars, he could just make out Judith's waxed jacket.

He sprinted back as best he could without falling. He'd left the front door unlocked; Judith was nearly there; Sightly's report was spread page by page on the table. His yelling of her name went unheard. By the time he leapt over one of the blue milk crates, the peat had hit his eyebrows.

Judith was in the porch. Her hand was on his arm; he was too breathless to make sense. She looked shocked rather than pleased.

'I wouldn't ever have dreamed of going in,' she said. 'I'm on the way to check out my readings.'

'Cup of tea? Something stronger? Al fresco, even?'

He gathered up the papers on the kitchen table before she was halfway in, stood there beaming.

'You sure you're better, by the way, Kit?'

He'd set up a driftwood bench on the blank south side of the house, facing the peninsula. They took their tea out to his home improvement; Judith made great play of the fact that the bench wobbled. 'It's my suntrap,' he said. 'But it hasn't caught anything yet.' Bands of sunlight were obediently travelling at single-engine speed over the slopes, the loch, the rocks, the distant machair, and striking occasional sparks off where the sea lurked. To Bob's surprise, she offered him a cigarette, which he declined.

'Don't tell Ewan. I have one a day, max.'

The smoke blew across him, but she didn't notice.

'Basically,' she began, folding her bony hands, 'Ewan reckons he knows who you are.'

He barely concealed the lurch inside him.

'Good for Ewan,' he said. 'What's the prize? A *Crackerjack* pencil?'

'Before my time. Put it this way: he knows who you're not. The rest is intelligent guess-work.'

'Impress me.'

'You're not an ex-teacher of nature studies; no one's called it that for decades. It's called science studies and you don't do birds, not these days. The only bird most kids know is a robin.'

'We called it that at the exclusive little prep school in deepest Suffolk where I taught. Weird uniform. Squirrel-red.'

'Then you should know a buzzard from a hen harrier. We had a clear view of its silhouette. They're completely different.' Her dark eyes were on him again.

'Maybe I need glasses.'

She shook her head in mock-despair. 'And you didn't know what jizz was.'

The plank felt like emery board. 'I'm very specialised, Judith.'

'Yes,' she said, 'in wind farms.'

'Eh?'

'We were a little gobsmacked by your handyman's lecture on turbines up at the manse.'

'Air and wind. It's where birds operate.'

She sighed, looking out on the panorama.

'Ewan reckons you're working undercover. He wants to put this fact on his blog.'

'His *blog*?'

'The centre director's blog, yes. I said that was unfair.'

'It is. Defence counsel requests more information.'

Judith explained that there were worrying rumours involving a new energy company called Scottish Torches. They wanted to plant twenty wind turbines on the peninsula: she swept an arm and they seemed to rise like phantoms, turning their vast white blades. This is a bad day, thought Bob: trouble always comes in twos and threes.

She told him that the croft's landlord had a multi-megawatt allowance to export electricity to the national grid; the local and national powers-that-be were to be approached, and were expected to approve. A lot of money was involved. Bribes, dodgy politics. Ewan had looked into the possibility of buying the croft, but of course had got nowhere.

'The RSPB will make a fuss and they'll be fobbed off with your silver ribbons or whatever,' she went on. 'According to a mole in contact with Ewan, the cabling will not go underground, but be carried across the island on massive pylons.'

Bob squeezed his eyes shut and opened them to the same prospect: life as a strip mine, free of pretty illusions. The landlord was Al McAllister. Al McAllister was God, at the centre of everything. The true skipper all along.

'I can see why they chose here,' he said. 'It never stops blowing.'

'As you're confirming to the grey suits? From your on-site readings?'

She was looking at him with raised eyebrows, like a clown face. The cigarette in her fingers.

'If you don't fib,' he said, 'you end up somewhere better, my mother used to tell me. Before she died. This is the first I've heard of it.'

'You look genuinely upset,' Judith noticed.

He nodded and said, 'Who chased off the grey suits?'

'Not you. I hate guns.'

'Well, I wasn't unhappy about it.'

'So you say.'

'Aren't you all for it, given it's green and the Centre's got its own propeller?'

She explained how their turbine was tiny, on a human scale. 'Apart from the pylon question, a full-size turbine is set in concrete that goes down as deep as it does high — some fifty metres high. Tons of CO^2 given off in its manufacture. It's made of metal, which has to be mined, smelted, assembled, transported. It wrecks the landscape, makes this terrible hum, kills birds.'

Sounds like aviation, Bob thought to himself. 'Yours might still have a birdstrike,' he said.

'Offshore's better,' she went on regardless. 'Onshore wind power's what I call shiteology. You need more heat, so you cut down a forest instead of pulling on a sweater. You know what Americans do? They spin-dry their washing in the sunshine states. That's shiteology.'

'Like skiing in Dubai,' Bob suggested.

'Oh, Dubai!' She waved her cigarette about. 'Shiteology's headquarters!'

The glass towers flashing, the lemons ripening around the pool, the tiles cooking the soles of your feet. Here, a grim bank of cloud was moving in from the west: normal service resumed.

'So if you're never a wind-farm agent or a private investigator or an agent provocateur from some English security firm, what are you?'

'I've said.'

'Military? Your hairy barrel chest, your obsession with fitness, those scars on your leg.'

'Oh, skiing accident. Open fractures.'

Her eyes were almost as dark as the pupils, until she moved her face slightly to catch a last warm band of sun and they turned into two reservoirs of burnt oil, flecked with greenish dots. He felt short of breath as he gazed into them.

'I've said,' he repeated.

His hand resting on his thigh found itself covered by hers. The long slender fingers were surprisingly chilly, but then it wasn't warm when the sun was in. She had peat in her finger seams; at least, they were darkened, stained from all that digging about.

'Why don't I believe a word you say, bird man?'

'Scars to prove it.'

'You said those were a car crash. Ice.'

'I did,' he said, vaguely remembering. 'I was delirious.'

'Why should I believe you twice?'

His instinct was to plant his lips on her broad mouth, but instinct has to be fought: getting entangled with a selkie would cause all sorts of leaks in the hull, already carefully holed by Sightly's report.

'There you are,' she said, squeezing his knuckles. 'You've made the whole thing up.'

He said, staring at the hand duet, 'As my father would tell my second stepmother, 'My son talks a lot, Samantha, and some of what he says is quite interesting.''

'You had two stepmothers? Poor you.'

'Nah, I did make that one up,' he said hastily. 'Sorry.'

She took her hand away. They sat in silence.

'Couldn't Ewan have come himself?'

'He never sent me,' she scoffed. 'I'm a grown-up. I'm thirty-four.'

'That's almost grown-up.'

'I've been picking up the wrong message. And that's all about it. See you around.'

She stood and strode off towards the machair in her stout boots, without once looking back. She was sure-footed and sinuous. He could see why the energy outfit was interested — in the peninsula, not in Judith: her long black hair was horizontal in the gusts. KEEP OFF THE BEACH WHEN THE WIND-SOCK IS FLYING.

Maybe she expected him to run after her. He sat on the bench and waited until she was a dot, then went round to the front. It had started raining, hard. There was a moaning noise towards the road: Colin was in the grazing, surrounded by drenched beasts with prominent cheek-bones. He raised a hand from inside a vast hooded sou'wester.

She didn't call in on the way back. She would have been very wet. He'd built up a blazing fire for her.

Being a mystery was a pain.

6

Scottish Torches had a website, all happy faces, charming windmills and green hills, but no mention of Scourlay. They seemed to be into coal, too.

What if he refused to leave? Could he be an obstruction? The selkie's hero? Or would he just end up with far too much electricity in his back yard, driven crazy by the hum?

The croft's executor, of course, would have been fully abreast all along. He felt a need to phone his old friend: the man who had twice saved his life, once in distressing circumstances. It did no one any good to think the worst of people. It was perfectly possible that Al had seriously nasty neighbours and was himself in danger.

'Why didn't you tell me, Al?'

'My fool of a cousin agreed to the idea four years ago. Twenty-odd giant propellers that don't go anywhere. The fight agin climate change, whatever. Honestly, I'd forgotten all about it. Then they made this offer.'

'How much?'

'Three times the fucking ask price. I tussled, they demurred; I turned about-face, they caved in. It was all done through the solicitor. It'll take a few months to go through. What's it to you? You'll be gone by the time the diggers come. Actually, skipper, I thought you'd be screaming to get out after a fortnight, keen to know what dry weather and people look like.'

'I've made some very good friends.'

'Male or female?'

An instant's hesitation on Bob's part, and Al was chortling.

'By the way,' he said, 'you could always use a pay-as-you-go mobile. Chuck it every so often.'

'Oh, like arms dealers. Drug gangs.'

It was Al's turn to hesitate. 'There are so many snooping gadgets these days. Just thinking of you, as ever, skipper.'

'By the way, how long is High Ridge Drive?'

'Eh?'

The charred rafters across the tussocks seemed to move, an effect of the storm-gathering light.

'I'd like to send you a postcard to remind you how pretty this unspoiled part of the world is. I don't want it to fall into the wrong hands. Are there lots of houses on High Ridge Drive?'

'What an odd question. We're one of twelve, though we don't see them. Properties tend to use up a lot of room in the Virgin Islands. My childhood council flat would fit into our bathroom, with room to spare for the jacuzzi.'

Bob knew a lot about Al's childhood in Fife: the damp walls, the alcoholic mother, the sickening father who died when Al was eleven.

'I'm well impressed, Al. What's your number?'

'You don't need to bother with a number, skipper. Just don't be an idiot and put Al McAllister. The name's Newton. Felix Newton.'

Bob rang off. Just twelve houses on High Ridge Drive.

And he knew Al well. They'd shared too many long hours together. That hesitation of his yawned to a chasm into which Bob stared and saw disagreeable things. The way he'd said, *Just thinking of you, as ever, skipper*. It was not right. It was strained. Even with the thousands of miles between them, and the tin-can quality of the voice, he could tell. When Bob had mentioned his relief over the grey suits, Al had laughed. It wasn't a laugh you'd take home with you; it was anxious, a cover. A cover for what? *Terrible angels wanna fuck me.*

Plenty stuff you don't talk about in Cargo World.

Back home, he closed his eyes and consulted his internal world map, not having brought his heap of tatty aeronautical charts — rescued from Holier Than Thou and now residing in the self-storage hangar, like so much else.

What he'd forgotten was the proximity of the Virgin Islands to Central America; and he saw how, if bits fell off a jet between Mexico City and some steamy port city in west Africa, they might well fall into Al's pool.

Al had been shifty: he'd hidden the wind farm instead of coming clean. Embarrassed, perhaps. Top-secret deals. But drugs?

There'd been drugs on the return flight from Turkmenbashi; drugs always meant serious money. Al was the possessor of serious money. Maybe he did organise that home substance run — in cahoots with the Taliban. Opportunistically

. . . with Evron Bensoussan not counted in. That would, as Bob had already calculated, have given the latter's flowery shirt a large dark sweat patch of fury.

He made himself a mug of strong tea and took notes with a trembling hand. There were lots of arrows sweeping over the page.

If Al McAllister had truly risen in the fallen world, would that put Al himself out of danger? Possibly. And his former skipper? Probably. And what would happen if the former skipper threatened to expose things? Would he be in danger from Al? No doubt.

Or, as Bob put it in his diary: *NO DOUBT!!*

★   ★   ★

A rapping on the door, at dusk. It sounded fierce. He picked up the Makarov. It was Judith.

'On my way back from the machair.'

'I didn't see you go out. Or have you been basking for three days?'

She laughed. She was cold, even shivering. He cleared up his notes and made some more tea and they sat by the hot Raeburn. She'd taken hydrological readings, consulted old charts, taken samples of soil. The machair did seem to be wetter; there were signs of old potato patches where it was now boggy or pooled.

Bob nodded and said, 'You're a remarkable woman.'

'As long as you don't call me *feisty*,' she said feistily.

He accompanied her to the gate with a torch.

The night was clear, bright with stars. At one point they stopped and stared up.

'Excessive twinkling,' he commented. 'Stormy weather imminent.'

'Who says?'

'Old lags.'

'Grey seals steer by the stars,' she said, her eyes faintly agleam.

'Do they?'

'They pop their heads up in the middle of the ocean and take bearings. Only recently proven.'

'Is that what you do? When you're swimming out there at night?'

'What?'

They had cleared the bluff and the only sound was the dim roar of the shoreline: hush-kitted, travelling nowhere.

'It's so quiet,' said Bob.

She was in silhouette against the deep blue flush at the horizon, beneath which was the land's absolute black.

'For the present,' she was saying. 'There's a protest meeting in Stornoway next week. Will you say a little word, as the peninsula's only inhabitant? It'll be in the papers, maybe make the *Scotsman* or the *Guardian*. They love that sort of thing. Photos, even. You could look all moody by the loch in your funny cap. You'll get fan letters from teenage girls.'

'I'd rather not. Sorry.'

'Why?'

'I need to keep my head down. High predation risk.'

'You become more fascinating by the minute. I

hope you're not on the run from a murder. None of the Christopher Webbs on the Web are you.'

'I'm not a criminal. I think I told you. My ex-wife. American. Her brother's a lawyer, works for Goldman Sachs.'

'Oh,' said Judith, as a jet's lights winked across, too high to hear, 'why didn't you *say?*'

He could have put his arm around her, gazing up at the stars. Instead he thrust his free hand into his pocket; his knuckles knocked the grip of the Makarov. The night sea went on sounding, not caring either way. His neck ached.

The jet's lights vanished, taking his heart with it. He craved to be up there, suddenly, knowing where he was coming from and where he was going.

★　★　★

Bob wasn't happy doing it, but he eventually emailed Sightly, asking him to provide a full address and details — including the name of the director, main shareholder, the nature of the links with the Mexican drugs cartels, whatever, of Swallowtail Trading Ltd. And to avoid involving David.

The Land Rover was outside the shop. He hadn't seen her for days. He hovered, pretending to watch gulls over the harbour, and Judith appeared.

'Kit Webb, have you been swimming yet?'

Patchy cloud, no headwind, temperature nudging a freak twelve degrees. Spring was flowering on the machair; a bush by the cottage threatened to be a hydrangea (banned by Olivia), but the water still felt icy. 'I do a lot of hiking, Dr Byrne.'

'Hop in.'

'I've no towel or togs.'

'The wind will dry you. You can jump up and down.'

Judith changed behind a dune, but not into nakedness. He was glad: naturism had never been his thing — he recalled a beach during a stopover in Brazil in the 1980s full of weighty German hausfraus who'd shaved their tender parts and kept smearing them with sun cream. As Judith walked towards the surf in her black costume, hands out on bent wrists, hair falling down her long olive-coloured back, he thought of the first time he had seen her. Her costume vanished. She hardly paused before disappearing into a minor wave.

The sunlight and the sea's turquoise were an illusion of heat. He kept his boxer shorts on, stopped dead once the icy water had clamped them to the top of his thighs. His legs already burned pleasantly, but the rest was goose-pimpled from the breeze. He remembered being given cold baths at school: it was a punishment. This was also a punishment. Once immersed, he'd be fine. It was like his first ever solo flight: once the wheels leave the ground, you'll be fine, Bob.

The sea seemed to inflate, rolling up almost to his navel, nudging him backwards. Judith waved from some thirty yards out, shouting 'Softie' as he splashed the nape of his neck. At first he thought she was shouting his daughter's name: he almost turned round to check. A second swell arrived, the lie of the ocean surface painfully delineated across his midriff. He blanked out intelligence and dived forward. A flash of torment as the body adjusted — rotating temperature gauges taking thermometric readings, pulling and resetting circuit breakers until the new levels were reached and he was seriously uncold.

They braved it for about five minutes; she was a strong swimmer. Her body brushed his at one point, and it felt sleek. They had a crawl race which he let her win. Then she came up behind him and put her arms around his neck and said, 'Carry me out, stranger.' So he did so, on his back, pacing softly over the giddying backwash, hopping across the tangle of wrack in which a faded plastic Tesco bag rather spoilt the effect. He put her down and she laughed, hugging herself, shivering. Their skin had lost its glaze in goose pimples. They ran up and down a dune, drying in minutes. They were startled by a sudden flurry off to their right: a black-headed gull, attacking something out of sight, beating its wings.

Bob pointed. 'Risk theory! Trade off! High predation area!'

The gull flapped up, squawking, then swooped so low that he had to duck.

'Irritated fowl syndrome,' he said.

She laughed. 'You know, amateur birders aren't usually beefcakes with a gift for one-liners.

395

Look at that body. I'm well impressed.'

'I'm working on it,' he said, pulling in his tummy, slapping it.

'Maybe you're SAS, on a secret mission.'

She lay down on her back in the dune's sunny hollow, stretched out in her flimsy one-piece, her wet hair sprawled in a black star-shape behind her, and closed her eyes.

'This is paradise,' she murmured, 'apart from the hordes under their parasols.'

He nodded. 'And the smell of the fast-food joints.'

'And the motorway's a wee bit close, and it's on stilts.'

He scanned the emptiness. 'As for the high-rise hotels . . . '

She opened her eyes. 'What's happened to your scars?'

The cold had brought them out: they snaked over the flushed, goose-pimpled skin like a pattern on one of Olivia's shop dresses, ivory pale.

'Looks pretty bad, Kit. Car or skis?'

'Scars you see, scars you don't.'

'Tell me a scar I don't see.'

He pulled his shirt on and sat down near her. The sand was detectably warm. He let his thoughts drift to the usual black rock.

'One day, when I was at boarding school, aged eleven, the headmaster called me to his study.'

'A boarding-school story,' she said softly.

'They're the best. So Mr Dodson-Watts shook my hand and asked me to sit down. He handed me a framed studio photo of a young woman, saying that I had to put it on my bedside table. It was in colour, and she had bright red lips and was fairly beautiful: like a film star. It had been sent to him by my father. That's very kind of Daddy, I thought: a present. It must be to do with growing up. I seriously thought that. 'This is your father's new wife,' said Dodson-Watts. 'You must give me the old photograph on your creaser, as this one is to replace it. Those are your father's express instructions, Winrush.' The old photograph was of Joan. Joan had been my stepmother since I was seven. Quiet person. She felt like my mother to me, obviously. The new one was called Samantha.'

He stopped. What was he up to? He was saying much too much. He'd been lured into saying far too much.

'Joan had died?'

'Not at all. Divorce.'

'What's a creaser?'

'Oh. The little bedside table. In the dorm.'

'And did you?'

'What?'

'Replace it?'

'I went to five schools,' Bob said. 'I got chucked out of four. You see? I'm not that much of a mystery.'

She stretched a bare arm out and touched the scars, following them with her fingertips. His heart began to rock his entire body. There was a mewing sound: he glanced up. It was spying on them from on high, in silhouette, wing tips adjusting to the laminar flow, white fan-tail

397

glowing; even from this far down he could see its head cocking from side to side, judging angles, gauging distance, taking accurate readings on two dots in the marram. Judith's fingertips had paused on his thigh. They burned away there, forgotten about, her eyes turned to the sky, shimmering like silver discs.

'Sea eagle,' he said.

'I know that,' she scoffed, her fingers leaving his skin.

It banked away towards the machair, the sun catching its head, part of a wing, and vanished for a moment into its own knife's-edge thinness — spotting another dot too big for a mouse, with a longish shadow on two thin legs, heading away from the beach towards the road: but Bob didn't know that then.

What he did know was that the spell was broken. He was cross with himself: he'd been lured out of cover, exposed, in return for getting something out of his system that would be still there tomorrow, and for ever.

He went behind a dune to change and almost stepped on what the gull had been fussing over: a small rabbit, eyeless and gutted. Dropped by the sea eagle, perhaps, as not being worth the fuss. Pulling off his damp boxers, he decided to say nothing about the rabbit.

Judith had dressed, was tugging at her salt-stuck locks with a comb.

'Why did the headmaster call you Winrush, by the way?'

'What? Oh. Just my nickname. Wind Rush. I rushed like the wind.'

'I like it. Can I call you that?'

'No, basically. Ugly memories.'

She looked at him through a hanging screen of hair, and grinned. 'I will in my head.'

7

Although a weekly power shower at Marcie's was now routine, he'd pop into the MacLeans now and then for tea or a dram — if Angus's white van was outside. The conversation was forced, but he needed the company and not to visit would have puzzled Angus.

Carol said, one time, when Angus was on the phone in the sitting room, 'How is your consolation in the café?'

He'd shaken his head. 'You've got the wrong idea, Carol.'

'Och, then so has the whole island.'

'Then all five of you are wrong.'

He'd return home most times swinging a bag of fresh scallops — *for your sins*, Angus would joke. They were always peculiarly large: plump and fleshy. Not like the wee ones scraped up by the industrial clear-cutters, Angus told him — 'along with aye else in the way'. From this we grew, he'd think, breathing their smell of the seabed. And they were scrumptious.

There was white clover along the path, but the springtime weather had turned Calvinist. It was cold again. After ten minutes jogging on the road's verge, he could have filled a glass from each shoe. An elderly woman sped past him way above the speed limit, sending an arc of water over his entire body. That was unsupportive, he thought.

He was in no-man's-land. Old rope. He hiked until it hurt.

Nothing from Tim Sightly. He avoided phoning Al, but he did send him a postcard, chosen at the Tinker's Arms, to allay any suspicion of suspicion.

'I've got one of your hooded gulls, here,' Murray had said.

'The beach one is fine.'

'Or a selkie, here.' A cartoon drawing, red-lipped, breasts like balloons. 'Have you seen her again?'

The bar trio were watching: their night's entertainment. A youngish customer in a leather jacket, bony-faced and dark-eyed and silent in the corner, made no attempt to hide his interest.

'I've barely scratched the surface,' Bob said, which went down very well, although the stranger looked bemused.

Bob drank up quickly and left, looking over his shoulder along the road, feeling about as safe as a clay pigeon. He'd filled two notebooks with bird observations, he didn't have a girlfriend, he was beginning to sense the jizz thing, he was totally harmless. This was how he now spent his days, the lack of electricity somehow slowing them down, softening their edges, making him wince at the glare of places still wired to the real world. He didn't spell trouble for anyone. Not even Olivia.

Right on cue a police car, minus flashing light but careering around the bend in the Ardcorry direction, had him jumping onto the verge near the MacLeans. Carol was out front, scattering ash from a bucket onto her roses. In the dim light, she might have been eighteen.

He waved and she came up to the barbed-wire fence.

Bob said, 'Did you see that police car appreciating the view? Something exciting?'

'Visiting the old ladies. Aleck is a lovely man. He likes his tea and a wee chat.'

'Why does everyone round here drive like a maniac?'

She smiled, a crooked incisor catching the dusk under her full upper lip. 'It's the tarmac, Mr Webb. We've nae got over the novelty.'

'And wind farms? They're pretty novel.'

Her face tightened. 'Don't disappoint me.'

'In what way?'

'I'm the only one who doesnae believe you're working for them.'

'I'm not. Thank you for that. But I'm afraid the landlord is all for it.'

She nodded. 'That bruiser.'

'You know him?'

'Hughie McAllister? He'd come our way a few times to fish, with his no-good cousin, Robbie. Who'd use the place to store cannabis.'

'Really?' He checked himself, lowering his level of interest. 'Yet more smugglers, then.'

'Oh, you know what youth is. A lot worse now. But that McAllister was a bit of a brute, a loud-mouth. Keen on the drink. Laid into Angus one time. A bridge too far.'

'Rivals?'

She avoided his eye, studying the point where the road curved out of sight. 'McAllister never

402

came back, so we never knew whether his broken jaw mended right. No doubt he's now saying how backward we islanders are. They all say that, these business types, each time we say no to some new horror.'

Bob touched his own jaw through its thin beard, thinking of Angus on the tiller, the open sea, those big hands. Scallops prised free in a billow of sand as the oxygen roared. Not many had ever taken on McAl and won: they generally finished under a litter of chairs and glasses and beer mats, like something washed up.

'Perhaps you're all way ahead,' he said, unconvincingly.

* * *

A long parcel arrived at Marcie's, as planned.

'I hope it's not actually a gun, Kit.'

'Marcie, would I ever order a *gun*?' It was deep in bubble wrap, a tripod nestling beside it. 'See? A spotter's telescope.'

'Oh yes. Ewan up at the Centre's got a few of those.'

The times he saw Ewan, passing in the Land Rover, there was no wave, no smile. One morning he was sitting in the café. Bob greeted him; Ewan nodded, avoiding his eye.

'How's the fan, Ewan?'

'The which?'

'The wind turbine.'

Ewan now looked at him as a falcon does a field mouse before diving and taking off its head.

'You smell of smoke, Mr Webb. No smoke without flame.'

With that, he paid up and left. He was perfectly friendly to Marcie, who had heard the exchange.

'He's Taurus,' she said. 'Incompatible. But he has climbed Annapurna.'

'Do I smell of smoke?'

She wrinkled her small nose. 'The shower's always there if you need it.'

What's the definition of a freight dog? A man who only changes his shirt once a week.

Once, when he was screen-gazing, Marcie put her hand on his back and leaned forward, her blue butterfly earrings fluttering, her armpits winning over the natural deodorant.

'You know, the first time I saw you, you looked really familiar? Did you ever hear about Angus MacLean's diving partner?'

'He drowned.'

'I'd seen him the previous evening. Standing at the door, looking in, all wet and pale. Except that it wasn't raining, and he never came into Bargrennan that day.'

'Oo-er.'

'It was a *taish*. Gaelic for someone's spirit appearing just before they actually die. Second sight.'

Bob pulled a face. 'So you're in two places at once. Hey, you must think I'm about to die a lot, Marcie.'

'Oh no, you always look really, I dunno . . . '

'Packed to the doors with life.'

He slumped, playing dead, and she laughed,

ruffled up his hair. 'You're dead honest, y' know?'

He pointed to one of her framed posters: a picture of a loch and *Water is modest and humble because it always takes the lowest ground. Lao Tzu.* 'That's humble me,' said Bob. 'I'm water.'

'That's the one thing you're not, Kit. Fire, plus air and earth as seasonal qualities.'

Banter, like cockpit banter. Nothing in it.

In return for the shower and endless free coffee and so on, he'd give Astra an hour or two of his undivided attention in the living room. They'd build farms out of bricks, for the plastic animals. Despite Bob's protests, Astra would dive-bomb them with various sci-fi hardware, reducing them to rubble that he'd inspect for victims with squeaky relish, bouncing on his knees. Bob's efforts to introduce other games got nowhere.

Then he was dive-bombed himself by the most surprising news since Olivia had filed for divorce.

He was writing a quick note to David when there was a *ping* and the pop-up announced another email. Tim Sightly. At last! Astra also popped up — for real. Marcie was busy with a group of French OAPs in wasp-like cycling gear near the door. The little lad leaned on Bob's thigh and attacked it with what looked like an F/A-18 Super Hornet showing characteristically carefree flying qualities and unlimited angle of attack, just as the thigh's owner received confirmation that Keith Price, the director of

Swallowtail Trading Ltd, did not exist under that name, although his address appeared to be High Ridge Drive, Tortola, BVI.

Al's luxury house was also on High Ridge Drive.

For all Bob knew, High Ridge Drive trundled along for several miles, with its villas and its pools and its sea-view. Or maybe this was just a brass plate, an empty garage, a shed with nothing inside. A tax dodge with a roof.

Or it was Hugh McAllister's address.

He felt bad, he felt worse, depending on the way his thoughts blew.

There was also an office in Liverpool. The number two director was 'a certain Alfredo Rivera Morales living in Madrid, who also does not exist, according to the Spanish authorities'. A certain 'equally untraceable' Jane Tutt — presumably Jane's maiden name — was allotted ninety-nine per cent of its shares last year, when it incorporated a company called Universal Executive Ltd, registered in Hong Kong. Tutt also owned significant shares in various other companies, 'list still being compiled'.

Astra's bombing of his thigh was growing more intense, as bombing tends to when the results are disappointing. Universal Executive Ltd dealt with recruitment, quality control and wet-leasing contracts for a string of further companies, some linked with Evron Bensoussan, others to hair-raising guys known to have connections with drugs cartels like Juarez, which 'operates transportation routes out of Chihua-hua'.

The kind of routes, Bob thought, that the late Mexican skipper with the eyebags, Pedro Diez, had flown.

'Is any of this of interest?' asked Tim.

'Nah,' Bob muttered, chewing on his thumping heart.

Astra paused. 'Whassat you says?'

'Astra, go to your mum.'

'Cos you didnae want it.'

Pedro Diez, the legendary character with the adult reading material. Not good company. Maybe that's why Al had suffered a convenient case of memory loss on being asked about him.

Tim reckoned that UE Ltd effectively owned a trio of other outfits — Dorsay Ltd, Takao Ltd and Fairhope Ltd — suspected of 'laundering Mexican drug money as well as arms dollars, via accounts with Wachovia and Bank of America'. Tim added that these three names were varieties of roses. He was certainly thorough.

Al and Jane were rose breeders. They were also top-end crooks.

Nowhere in Tim Sightly's email was there any indication that he knew the true identity of either Keith Price or Alfredo Rivera Morales — or for that matter Ms Tutt. In fact, he ended by saying:

Hope this is of help. It looks to me like a grey-market outfit shading to black where it touches drugs. It would take a large budget and a team of experts months, maybe years, to unravel it all and make a case. Obviously if any of this rings louder bells, do let me know. Take care. Tim.

The Super Hornet had shifted its target to Bob's face; fortunately, its climbing capacity was severely limited — until its pilot bailed out and it flew through the air without a controlling hand. It struck just above his eye. Bob yelled an adults-only swear word and ordered Astra to 'Get!' so effectively that he took fright and ran straight into his mother's arms.

It was as much the email as the pain. Blood welled and snaked into his eyebrow, which helped his case. The OAPs buzzed away conspiratorially in French as Marcie led him into the kitchen, with Astra clinging like a ship-wrecked sailor to her knee and sobbing uncontrollably. Bob guessed it would be on all their travel blogs by the next morning.

As Marcie dabbed, wondering whether it needed stitches, her musky scent wreathing his face, Bob was regretting contacting Tim Sightly, who knew nothing of the link between the heap of stinking garbage he'd summarised and Flight Engineer Hugh McAllister.

It was disappointing. Bob didn't do drugs. He didn't like them. Or rather, he didn't like the people who peddled them, from the billionaires flitting about on their luxury yachts to the little guys on the street, from the coke-fuelled crazies running the world's economy to the souped-up kid who runs his car into a wall, killing his friends.

David had once pointed out to him that

alcohol was a drug.

'Alcohol's legal,' Bob had replied, 'and drugs are illicit.'

'Exactly, Dad. And weapons that kill millions? Blow children's limbs off? Send shrapnel into a woman's unborn baby? Cluster bombs with their little bomblets hanging around like really interesting toys?'

Of course, you could legalise drugs tomorrow and the entire crooked caboodle would collapse in a cloud of dollars. He was already aware that above-board outfits like investment banks allowed clients to launder drugs money, but that in itself was no great recommendation. The fact was, Al was making big-time cash in a totally illicit business. That bothered Bob a lot. All roses have thorns. *A bit of a brute, a loud-mouth.*

'I don't think you'll need stitches,' Marcie murmured, her breath on his cheek. 'Astra's not usually a violent kid.'

'All roses have thorns,' Bob said.

★ ★ ★

The bar trio plus stranger had been replaced by several wet campers, which suited Bob. He sat thinking about things in the pub's corner where the smaller electric fire looked lonely.

He was struggling to picture Al as Mr Sort-It, aiding and abetting, trustworthy, discreet, getting the heroin or whatever safely off the hill, dissolving it into lucre.

Sharing the transport infrastructure: just the

odd packet at first. Maybe when the Taliban had come on board in their flared suits, they'd made him an offer. Just a small parcel, tuck it under your seat. Turkmenbashi's stink of crude wafting up the fuselage: anything's possible. This wasn't Maidenhead.

Or perhaps Al was in on it before: he'd been pretty keen to carry on in Istanbul. Maybe Lennart, Schmitt and Al had simply used their captain as a cover. *The man hates drugs, won't touch them for fame or money.* But they'd not anticipated him pulling out of the extra arms run. He remembered Lennart sweating with fear in the airport shed. Never walk away from a deal. Never cross Evron Bensoussan.

If the man with testicular knees had ever got a whiff of the heroin deal, he'd have flipped. Arms to the Taliban was already stretching the business envelope; buying their heroin was tearing it.

And Evron would have heard the noise, once Sharansky started walking his dog in the cattery. All participants to be eliminated. Except for McAllister? Al hadn't really taken flight: he'd gone to his own burrow. The man you can't do without. Scary friends. A burst of laughter from the campers made him jump.

And the croft-house? Al must have felt it was the safest bet: keeping an eye on his errant captain. Had Bob pushed him into it? He couldn't quite remember. Al had blown hot and cold about Scourlay. Maybe he'd just given Bob the illusion that it was his decision. Like the illusion that you're flying a plane, when it's the avionics.

Bob could see it beginning to get a bit cross-wired for Al. Twitch a thread in Israel, Russia, Afghanistan, and it pulls something in Mexico, Spain, Addis Ababa. Wherever. Easy-Drugs. Heroin Air. Nîmes to Liverpool. Accra to Minsk. Dnepropetrovsk to Bangkok. You name it, the spider spins it.

And somewhere in all this, the squeak of a wheelchair: Evron Bensoussan's paralysed daughter, and her raging father in his flowery shirt. Bob pictured Al growing anxious by the pool: checking the amber lights, the green lights, the critical alerts, and not quite managing. *And now there's bloody Bob, bothering me from the old country, moaning from the fog about the propellers. I'm no joking, Jane. The fucking giant propellers.*

Bob felt the weight of the pistol in its holster. It reassured him. He mustn't drink too much, but on contemplating his half-full, half-empty pint glass, he wondered about having another chaser. Its pure flush.

Never mix arms and drugs, they say; but Al was being commissioned to do just that. So why did he ever accept? Easy money, in hallucinogenic quantities. He had all the contacts, the expertise. He may simply have slipped deeper and deeper into the bog to a point where, if he tried to extract himself, he'd leave his wellies. Like the entire human race, Bob thought.

We should all have stuck to roses.

* * *

411

Back in the cottage, he poked at the fire: sparks raced up the chimney. Al McAllister had always struck him as the most honest guy he knew. He'd have assumed Einstein was not that bright, probably.

I get people wrong, that's all.

Around 2005, Bob freighted some 300 army personnel — rebels or regular, he was too confused by the changing alliances to work it out — from Kigali to a bush airstrip just inside the Central African Republic. They smoked in the hold, they were drunk or stoned, they laughed and sang and yelled, and he was happy to get shot of them.

A few days later he chewed on a cola nut and agreed to deliver another batch from a different group. They were politer, calmer, quieter, led by a willowy youth with Bambi eyes who told him through the seven-oh's cockpit door all about his plans to change the world. How refreshing, Bob thought: this guy talked peace and love, he read English poets like Wordsworth, he had a soft voice and long, elegant fingers. Bob had apparently freighted quite a tonnage of equipment for Bambi's group, and Bambi was grateful: freight dogs are never thanked, usually. The weather was rough and knocked them about a bit and Bob asked after the lads in the back.

'They're healthy,' the doe-eyed youth joked.

Then all the dials on the number two engine wound anti-clockwise and they felt a shuddering. As the plane was heavily loaded, fifteen tonnes over the maximums, he'd used additional thrust on take-off. Up to then, he had kept to reduced thrust for this particular beast, lessening wear on engines that he knew were near their sell-by date and getting far from tip-top maintenance. Now they had a problem.

Bambi noticed nothing, he was too busy telling Bob about poetry and the Bible until the co-pilot — not McAl, but a scar-faced Belgian called Jean-Luc — bawled the man out in French. Anyway, the two of them concentrated and despite melted turbine blades in the starboard engine, lashings of rain, a ten-knot tailwind and mist swirling in the treetops, they landed with no more than a bit of a bump.

Bambi shook Bob's hand, none the wiser, and he and his hundreds of lads melted likewise into the trees. Bob even gave them a wave, before gauging the chances of an engine replacement by next year.

'Bless you,' Bambi had said.

A week after that, in another overworked and ageing plane, he and McAl landed some mixed cargo in the same spot in Central African Republic, burst a couple of tyres when they pressed the worn brakes a touch hard, blowing the thermal plugs, and were forced to stay put a couple of days. A colonel — paunchy, jolly, vaguely reminiscent of Idi Amin — drove them out in a jeep down a track redder than Worcestershire to visit the nearest big village deeper into the country. A nasty smell blew towards them as they alighted, much worse than copper-mine sludge, and there was a deeper buzzing on the bush soundtrack. The smell seemed to use up all the air. It seemed solid.

'You see what Joseph H. Kenley's men have been up to, Captain. Why we must continue the fight.'

Men, women, children. Some just looked as if they were pretending, in funny positions, all elbows, but of course they weren't. One woman sat upright in a hut, worms teeming in the sockets of her eyes, her feet and hands missing, stomach bloated by gas. She'd taken a day to die, they said.

The guys that had done it were not the first, rowdy lot he'd carried here, as Bob had assumed, but the second: the quiet bunch led by Bible-loving, poetry-quoting Joseph H. Kenley. Machete lore. Bob didn't believe the colonel at first (the sides kept changing), but survivors trickled in from the forest and confirmed it. Several hundred victims. Guns and panga blades and terrible spells that would pass on through the generations.

'They are the worst,' the colonel said, 'to these ignorant peasants.' His son was at Marlborough.

Bob threw up in the charred remnants of a hut and got a blinding headache. He had all sorts of silly notions in his fever — that he was a carrier of plague, and so on — and took several days to pull out of it, lying on a pallet in an airstrip shack that stank of the nearby latrines, with a Pepsi-Cola bottle on the sill (a candle holder) that loomed large in his delirium. His right arm suffered from what a doctor back in Worcestershire was to call rigor, as in rigor mortis: a temporary rigidity, a kind of paralysis.

Al nursed him, making sure the water was

boiled, erecting a mosquito net, counting out the malaria pills, stamping on the huge cockroaches (they'd still lumber off). Bob went home on sick leave, not quite himself.

Olivia always thought it was straightforward bush fever. Well, in a way it was. He told her it may have been a spider bite, one of those giant bird-eaters that make their nests under the houses' eaves. She asked him to show her the bite, but he had so many red bumps that it was pointless: now and again they'd produce little worm heads, like tiny white moles taking a peep. He walked about with central Africa in him — in more ways than one. The twins had always loved it, in a sort of ghoulish way; now they were hidden behind screens, headphones, and hardly noticed. Al was tougher: he had the capacity to shrug. That's why Bob had found his recent intolerance of the local Berkshire yobs a bit out of kilter.

'Why are you reading poetry?' asked Olivia, amazed.

They were in bed, Sunday morning in May, wood pigeons cooing through the open window. One of his father's old anthologies, won as a prize at school, the pages smelling of 1930s damp and coal smoke.

'Wordsworth,' Bob said. 'We did him in English with nice Mr Bentall, before I got expelled after the chapel incident.'

'And?' She looked worried; she'd reckoned her husband was getting better. But he was, he was.

'Don't really clock it,' he said. 'But thought I'd best check.'

The northern, sea-surrounded days were long, and getting longer: he'd go to sleep in light and wake up early, thinking it was late.

He kept looking at his *NO DOUBT!!* alarm in the diary, and wondering about the best approach. This problem's handling procedures were not encoded; they kept altering.

He knew Al better than most, but folk have many sides, and the business side was unfamiliar. He was always thrifty, though. In the pre-hush glory days of Ostend's Hotel Ter Streep, where anyone up at the bar would be expected to stump up a collective round for the other crews, he'd be absent at the crucial moment. 'I'm a Lowlander,' he'd joke when Bob complained. 'Money is flat that it may lie still.'

It's also round that it may roll: he was rolling it, all right. And now what? Bob regretted his long-distance calls: he'd sounded tetchy, peevish. All that grey suits nonsense. Wanting to buy the place.

It wasn't so much Al who was scary, but the world he moved in: about as much compassion as the infrared payload on an unmanned drone. And you never knew who was in on it, once the loaded mule had started trekking down the Afghan hillside or wherever. All he did know was that lower rungs do not and must not see whose boots are on the higher rungs: it seems that rule had been broken in this case. And those rungs stretched right up into the stratosphere, into the playground of the gods: politicians, the military, corporate heads, top bankers. What's that written on the wing? DO NOT WALK OUTSIDE THIS AREA.

He felt their cross hairs warm on his neck.

And why had Al suggested a pay-as-you-go throwaway mobile? Bob paced up and down the attic bedroom and then out and around the house, tripping on tussocks, wishing he had never left passenger for freight. He hadn't even bought a dinghy for the loch, for those long afternoons on the water, fishing. A cloud of midges suddenly appeared, like a black thought bubble above his head. Here we are, mate. Another year. Only doing our job. They descended onto his eyes and nose and lips, then a gust came and they were gone. Or maybe they didn't like the smell.

It was late afternoon. Fresh green bracken had grown up around the phone box. By the time he was standing inside it, he was shaking. Not typical of the skipper. What he had planned to say to Al was, 'Pull the plug on the wind-farm project, and I'll keep mum about Swallowtail Trading Ltd, about which there ain't much I don't know.' But it occurred to Bob that, even if Al himself didn't phone Contract Killer Inc. and book a job for a few thousand dollars (rates being cheap in these days of high unemployment), Winrush would be lucky not to end up with his excised face stitched to a football. The Mexicans were in Liverpool and probably Glasgow. Near neighbours. He pictured sombreros emerging onto Bargrennan's beach airstrip and being snatched away into the surf. If Mossad was the problem, he had a different picture: wigs flying off.

He lifted the receiver. What was he supposed to do? There was a movement in the burnt-out bungalow: a stripe of sunlight, manoeuvring through a slit in the low-slung cloud, crept away over its charred guts, to continue on across the blackland beyond.

That was it. That's as much as you're getting.

It shimmered on what must have been the sea, seemingly far off. Then the grey lid shut tight again. That's what a lifetime is. It doesn't wax then wane, it flits. You don't have time to see what's lit up, not properly.

'Al? How goes it?'

'As good as ever. I'm sitting on a chair in the warm ocean, Painkiller in hand. Are you keeping your head down, skipper?'

'Right out of the wind. How's your jaw?'

'My jaw's fine. Why?'

'I hear it got broken, last time you visited.'

There was a silence. Bob realised his mistake.

'Did you tell your informant you knew me, or are you still sane?'

'Of course I didn't. You're just my absent landlord. You're not popular, either. The wind farm.'

'You seem to be getting involved in the local community. Is that wise, skipper?'

'Give me a break, Al.'

'You sound nervous.'

'It's the line. Eaten into by salt. Never felt better.'

Walking back, he realised he'd have to tell Tim Sightly not to bother with Swallowtail any more: further enquiries, however unlikely, might give Al and his mob the wrong idea. Bob was the skipper, and as the skipper he strongly disapproved of his subordinate's actions. But he'd have to keep his mouth shut, now.

Marcie's place was still open. He was sending the don't-bother message when Judith came in. She didn't spot him. He hadn't seen her since the swim, nearly two weeks back.

He ambled across once Marcie had served her, heart bumping in quick time. She looked up and smiled without her eyes and said hello. He asked how things were.

'Fine. And yourself?'

'Busy. How's Ewan?'

'Unhappy.'

The café was empty bar a young male hiker with a stubbly chin and smart trekking jacket, studying his mobile by the front window. Fortunately, the Cuban stuff playing over the speakers made their talk less audible.

'You seem cross.'

'We had a row,' she said. 'Ewan was there.'

'Where?'

'On the beach, when we went swimming. He's now totally convinced you're some sort of undercover agent luring me onto your side.'

'Do I look it?'

'Very much so. Undercover means just that. A police helmet would give the game away.'

He thought of the grey suits and felt obtuse. Of course. A contract killer would not come to a remote Scottish island looking like a contract killer.

'I'd love to know who I'm supposed to be working for.'

'The wind-farm project's gathering pace. Scottish Torches deny specifics but are working like crazy behind the scenes, oiling the wheels before it's rolled out into the sunlight.'

'I give you my solemn word, I'm not working for Scottish Torches, the FBI, or any other outfit,' Bob said. 'And I'm equally sad about the wind farm, because I like birds. Especially sea eagles.'

She sighed. 'Ewan's under a load of pressure. Drastic funding cuts. He doesn't want me to have anything to do with you. And he's the boss.'

'We're just friends, aren't we?'

'He didn't believe me on that one, either.'

'I'm flattered. I guess that's it, then. And if I prove that I'm just a birder in midlife crisis, waiting for his final divorce papers?'

Astra ran in from nursery school and began to swipe Bob's legs with a Mickey Mouse bag.

'Nuts!' he shouted. 'Nutty nuts, Uncle Kit! I'm gonna fly into your eye!'

The young hiker in the window tore his own eyes away from his mobile and watched. Marcie came to lull Astra with the help of a chocolate biscuit and telly.

'It's release after being force-fed at school,' she said, instead of telling him off.

8

It had begun to rain, so Judith gave him a lift back from Bargrennan. It was gloomy outside; he invited her in for a farewell splash of Talisker.

'Are you luring me again?'

'Just to admire my spotter's telescope.'

'A spotting scope, as real birders call it.'

'When required.'

'And your massive gun collection. And your split mind.'

'No, that's private.'

'It's pretty wet out there.'

'I keep the Raeburn going all day, these days.'

Ensconced in front of the blazing fire on the blanket-covered sofa, her hair tied up to leave two long curls dancing over the ears, she told him about the previous resident of the manse, an eccentric recluse murdered by persons unknown in the 1970s.

'Ask Carol MacLean. She's fey, of course, being an islander. Clairvoyant. Och, that new mainland ferry, it's going to sink, they said — thirty years ago. Anyway, she saw his *taish*.'

'Remind me.'

'Gaelic for someone's ghost, except it appears before death and not after. She was about twelve. She saw him walking up the road, near your gate, heading for Ardcorry.'

'Perhaps he was.'

'No way. He was smothered in his bed about

the same time. Anyway, he was bedridden.'

'In two different places at once,' Bob said.

'Except one's the spirit. It confused the Feds for a bit.'

'Marcie saw a *taish*. Angus MacLean's diving partner, funnily enough — '

There was a sudden fierce rapping on the front door, exactly like Judith's. Bob's nerves were trained to react steadily to surprises, but today he jumped.

'That can't be you, can it, Judith? Your *taish*?'

'I'm all here,' she said, turned pale. 'It could be Ewan.'

'He's not scary.'

'Anyone's scary, potentially.'

'Too true. Stay put. Check your seat belt. No need for concern.'

He ran up to the attic bedroom. Perhaps Carol had confessed to Angus. He opened the front skylight carefully and popped his head out, but the closed porch hid its secrets. He grabbed the Makarov from the hidey-hole, checked the clip out of habit, released the safety catch, donned his Harris tweed jacket and cradled the weapon in the outside pocket. Meanwhile there was another rapping. It would be clear, from the reddish glow in the windows, that the house was occupied; the world outside was in cargo-hold gloom.

He went downstairs and stood to one side of the door, opened it carefully with his gun in firing position in his pocket — and faced, not Gold Teeth and cronies, nor an angry Ewan, nor Angus with his rifle, but a drowned rat of a hiker, trembling with cold, his white cheeks alternately glistening and blackening under the swaying glow of the hall paraffin lamp as the air swirled in. A head torch flashed into Bob's eyes. The man had rain still dribbling off his smart green waterproof jacket and stubbly chin.

'Rather wet,' he said in what might have been a German accent. He held up a GPS aid, like a large yellow mobile. 'I think the water fell in, total fucked the battery.'

He explained, while his outer clothing steamed before the Raeburn and filled the kitchen with the smell of feet, that he'd tried to take a short cut to Ardcorry, but kept hitting either marsh, bog, or rock. He hadn't wished to disturb, but had no choice. He was staying in the Tinker's Arms.

'The day started with much sun and quite warm,' he said mournfully.

'Three seasons in one day up here.' Bob sighed, feeling indigenous. He remained standing. 'You were in the café in Bargrennan, weren't you? An hour or two ago? In the window seat? Or was that your *taish*?'

'Pardon me?'

'Anyway,' said Judith, 'what's wrong with a paper map?'

'I know, bloody stupid. Not so much progress after all.'

'The evolution of intelligence isn't a straight curve,' she smiled.

His small eyes focused on her with puzzlement. Bob told him to drink up. He took a slug of Talisker and almost choked. 'I think I am the

423

beer drinker.' He grinned. Bob got him a bottle of stout.

'No electrics, no fridge, I'm afraid.'

'This is OK. I like it like piss today.' His features seemed to clear: squarish face, small nose, puckered chin you could almost plonk your glass on.

'I'll bet you're German or Dutch,' said Judith.

'German. And you?'

Judith laughed. 'Edinburgh.'

He was trekking around Scotland, he said. 'John o'Groats. Lots of hills.'

'The Highlands?'

'Yes. So beautiful. And you?'

Bob hesitated. The youth's grey eyes were fixed on his face.

'He's our bird man,' Judith announced, smiling. 'Everything you want to know about black-headed gulls.'

He nodded slightly. 'That's good. They said to me this in the pub. The famous Mr Vebb?'

The youth's hands were both visible, one of them round the stout bottle; Bob's hand was clamped to the Makarov. 'Mr Webb is my research partner,' he said. 'He's out. Up on Lewis for the week. My name's Geoff. Geoff Smith.'

Judith was looking at him with a puzzled frown. Everything had slowed down, leaving him plenty of time to think and act. The hiker looked momentarily puzzled above his dark polo-necked sweatshirt. Beyond the smell of feet, of wet wool steaming, there was something else: cheap aftershave, bland hotel rooms.

'Mr Webb's keen on cliff nests,' Bob went on, with a hint of contempt. 'I don't like cliffs. They give me vertigo. Mudflats, me.'

The hiker nodded. 'I think maybe I saw him on a cliff. Real near from the edge. Does he have a beard?'

'We birders all have beards, more or less. Self-neglect.'

The man turned, as Bob guessed he would, to Judith, who was still looking bewildered. A tiny muscle twitched under his eye. Once, twice. 'I like all animals,' he said, over-pronouncing the s. 'Not so much sheeps.' He smiled without altering anything but his mouth.

'No,' said Judith, not quite keeping up. 'They get in the way, somehow. I'm Judith, by the way.'

'I am Ulrich. Where is your toilet? I'm exploding.'

'Take this lamp,' Bob said.

As soon they were alone, he turned to Judith and hissed, 'Look, for health and safety reasons I'm not Kit Webb, I'm Geoff Smith. OK?'

'Who's Geoff Smith?'

'Me. Kit Webb is on the cliffs the other end of the islands. Kit Webb is not me. In case.'

'In case what?'

'In case he's checking the chamber on his semi-automatic.'

'You're scaring the shite out of me. He seems harmless enough.'

'Before he goes, I'll be caught short. OK? In case he's put something in the loo.'

'Like what?'

'An incendiary bomb, for instance.'

'Christ, I'll call the police. They've got a helicopter, somewhere.'

'No.'

A rattle and squeak in the pipes: the chain being pulled. He raised a hand for silence. 'I told Kit,' he began, in a loud voice, 'that we had established the aggression as being directly linked to gull density on specified food patches. His figures are not relevant to exposed mud-water margins. You see what I'm saying?'

'Yes,' said Judith, feebly.

Ulrich came in, clean-faced and with shiny hands. Bob ignored him. 'I'm not letting Kit reconfigure my figures,' he went on testily. 'When he gets back from his bloody cliffs I'll have to tell him. His log-linear model of capture rate was crap.'

'Kit's always been a mystery to me,' said Judith, in a stronger voice.

'Sometimes I don't think he's very professional, as a birder. He didn't even know about trade-off.' Bob turned to the hiker, who was hovering by the Raeburn. His hands were clear of any pocket. 'Sorry, we're being rude about our colleague.'

'The famous Mr Vebb?'

'Oh, not so famous.'

The young man's expression shifted into a simper: there was a plastic quality to his skin, now it was clean. 'For sure famous in the pub. They told me this Mr Vebb was seeing black-head gulls during the winter. It seemed to be something very difficult about it.'

Maybe he wasn't so young, Bob thought. Late

twenties. 'They were laughing?'

'Sometimes the natives of backwards places think of things in pretty funny ways,' Ulrich said, donning his trekker's jacket. Bob's hand tightened around the Makarov's wooden grip, slippery despite its notches. 'There of course always are special qualities to natives, that they know much about local experience, and you even can say they are having so much reflections who are wise.'

'You are so right,' breathed Judith, almost flirtatiously. 'Kit was saying just that, before he went off to the cliffs at the other end of the Hebrides.'

Ulrich glanced at her. There was a rasp of Velcro as he undid the double storm flaps on his jacket pocket, and his hand disappeared. 'The path of return, is it simple? It is growing more darker.'

Bob's body had gone into a kind of seizure or cramp, which meant the Makarov felt glued to his skin, which in turn was stitched to the pocket lining. This had never happened to him in the cockpit, or even in some of his more hapless moments on the ground. The prospect of shooting someone was quite different from charming your way out of trouble. He kept his gaze fixed on the man's hidden hand, and then it slid out with his yellow GPS unit. Bob detectably jerked into relief mode.

'Now it is working,' Ulrich said. 'It was playing a trick on me.'

'No use here,' Bob muttered. 'I'll show you the way to the road.'

'So will I,' said Judith.

'I was having no expectations of such treatment!'

Bob told Judith pointedly that she didn't need to come. He had no immediate strategy, bar buying time.

'OK, *Geoff*,' she emphasised. 'Take care on your travels.'

He excused himself and popped into the loo on the way out: nothing stuck on anywhere. Limpet projectile bombs were one of Mossad's favourite devices, normally carried by motorbike and clamped onto the driver's window in stalled traffic. He pulled the chain for the sound and went out to find Ulrich joking with Judith in the porch. They left her on the threshold; she waved, looking as if they were setting off for Canada in a storm.

Bob made sure he stayed just behind: the path, anyway, was single file. The man had stepped aside at the beginning to let Bob go ahead, but he'd said, rather unconvincingly, 'After you. It's a Hebridean tradition.' Some of the solar garden lights had gone, doubtless trampled by sheep. Moving helped the cramp. They tramped in silence through the furious gloom. Bob could hear his breath inside the hood, like an astronaut, as he blinked away the rain, which was throwing itself at them in spasms. It was as grey as a winter dusk, although it was not yet seven o'clock in the far north in early May, and he could see the wavering spot of his head torch touch the tussocks and heather and rocks.

As they rounded the hill and approached the gate, Ulrich slowed down, but Bob kept a pace behind, verbally guiding him now and again so that he only squelched a couple of times. The man's hood was up, but his hands were either on the straps of his little rucksack or swinging loose. Bob guessed German hit men would be from the east, driven to it by unemployment, abuse, misery. Or straightforward greed. Prices ranged from a few hundred euros to well over ten thousand — plus expenses, he assumed. He wondered what Al would be coughing up, with maybe help from the yacht-loving billionaires or some grant from a security service. He was half-enjoying these thoughts, because of course he knew deep down that young Ulrich was just a helpless hiker.

About thirty yards from the gate the helpless hiker stopped and pointed: the black clouds had a rip in them to the northwest, creating a marvel of gold cut into fanned pieces. Bob had transferred the gun to his waterproof, standing close in such a way that he could fire without moving, both hands in his voluminous pockets.

'It must be completely romantic here,' Ulrich commented. 'You can't complain too much of this.'

'It's a job. Kit moans all the time.'

'Kit?'

Bob's heart felt as if it was trying to ram its way through his ribcage; a mould of the Makarov's notched grip could have been taken off his palm. All he wanted was for this guy to hike out of his life. 'The famous one.' Bob found himself grinning, water dripping off the end of his nose.

Ulrich turned and looked at Bob, as if reflecting. 'Oh, OK,' he said, with a rather sweet smile. As the golden shafts were put out by a thick soot-black coil he started walking again and then, some fifteen yards from the gate, he froze so that Bob almost bumped into him and he said, 'Skipper!'

'Yup?'

Bob registered his mistake as the elbow came plunging at his solar plexus in a crackle of impermeable plastic. Sprawled in the sodden grass, his breath somewhere in New Zealand, all he saw was the stub muzzle of a gun pointing at his face in a sudden bloom of light he half-thought was his death but turned out to be a sweep of headlights.

Ulrich crouched down, his shadow rather large on the slope behind as the vehicle rounded the curve and sped by. Bob lunged forward and took him in a dirty rugby tackle that slammed him onto his back, although slamming onto sponge does not hurt, let alone wind. The man showed great strength and determination as Bob, unable to find his pocket, let alone his weapon, attempted to swipe the jutting jaw. His own chin had been hit by a knee and his tongue self-nipped, so the taste of blood warned him of what was to come. He half-noticed a gleam through the rain as they struggled, Ulrich's face a pair of white eyes and white lower teeth in a mask of streaked peat mud. There were tennis-player grunts as they flailed; Bob had the advantage in strength, the other had youth.

The gleam was a wavering torch with Judith

behind it now calling out, 'Kit! Kit!' Bob yelled at her to keep back, but his throat was not functional and he choked instead. They rolled over and over, and something, perhaps the man's elbow, hit Bob's cheek. He was scrabbling for the gun and slugging the man at the same time, mostly missing, when a chunk of metal slid between them: Ulrich's gun, not Bob's, pressing against one of his ribs. When the shot went off he felt the kick as heat travelling down to his toes, leaving his ears to vibrate like loose gaskets. Everything went from tyre-rubber-tight to limp.

The shot had entered under Ulrich's jaw: his strong chin and lower teeth were yesterday's news; his eyes were still open, filling up with rain they weren't blinking away. The top of his hood had a hole in it.

Judith came up, her torch beam catching the dead man's savaged face.

'It was his gun,' Bob panted, on all fours. 'I didn't pull the trigger. He was trying to kill me.'

She said nothing. The close-up wind-tossed tussocks went this way and that as he looked at them.

★ ★ ★

By the time they'd dragged the late Ulrich back into the croft, hands under each arm, his boots bouncing along the track (Bob was too shaky to act the lone fireman), his death stare covered by his own sweater, a strip of horizon sky had begun to clear and a searchlight sun was playing over the exposed stretch, before the hill hid them

431

from the road. A couple of cars and a king-size camper van rolled past: they would have seen, if they'd bothered to peer hard, three figures stretched flat out in the grassland through the sparkling drifts of rain.

Judith went on saying nothing the whole way. Finally inside, soaked through, their faces black from peat mud and bogwater, Ulrich in the spare downstairs room among boxes and bottles, she said, 'I need a fucking cigarette.'

She smoked three in the kitchen, trembling by the Raeburn in her underwear and Bob's dressing gown, hair dripping onto her shoulders; he heated some water, washed and changed and nursed his bruises, of which there were many, with an especially stormy one on his cheekbone. His tongue was a nuisance: swollen and crusted where the bite had penetrated. But compared to Ulrich, damage was minor.

'I saw my father dead.' She shivered. 'That's the only time.'

She'd asked who Ulrich was. He'd told her that Ulrich was a contract killer.

'Hired by whom?'

'I'm not sure.'

She nodded. 'I knew you weren't ever just a sheepskin rug but this is still a very scary thing. Because I am scared. I am scared of you, as a matter of fact. One minute that young guy was standing there, just there, and then . . . there's a crime happening. Murder.'

'Attempted murder, yes. I've never shot anyone in my life, OK?'

He stroked her hair, but she flinched. The

432

Raeburn was a happy inferno through the tiny glass window. He poured each of them a large Talisker; Ulrich's beer was still on the table, virtually untouched. He'd not wanted to blur his aim. The whisky stung Bob's tongue, but calmed his nerves.

If his hands and knees were still wobbly, it was not just because of the slice of action: he'd gone through the smart hiking jacket and found a passport, scribbled names and numbers, a handkerchief, a small bottle of Dettol and a throw-away mobile; the latter happily glowed when he pressed. The passport had the killer's name as Franjo, not Ulrich, and his birthplace as Petrovaradin in Serbia, but he'd spent the last few years in eastern Germany and Poland, judging from the visa stamp and various stapled tags.

Bob requested a few moments' quiet from Judith, and scrolled through the messages. He found several with a BVI code. It was a number he didn't recognise. Al doubtless had an array of SIM cards: the crew would play a lot of poker and he now saw them fanned out tinily in that freckled hand.

He read the messages sent and received.

Arrivd Oban. Ops confirmed for Sunday after arival Wensday. U.

Repeat: confirm target by name KIT WEBB. Tall, beard, not as in photo supplied.

In my room Ardcorry. Fucking grate weather. Target spotd in cafe of Bargrenan?

Deal with target in his house only.
Target spotd joging, beard and uggly hat, maybe 50 above.
Confirm name KIT before action.
In targets toilet. He and girl say his Jeff Smyth.
Lie? Use SKIPPER. Discard mobile after!!
I tell you x 100 till it go in yr brain, Im top brand product.
Confirm hit successful after, top shit. Then our side will go to work.

Once his hand was steadied again by another squirt of Talisker, Bob sent a message of his own:

Confirm of target disposd with. No problems. Last words was, 'Tell that shit McAllister his a hypodermic.' No understand, I say. Then one bullet his brains go out and I have to use mopp. Once recieve yrs, will dispose of phone. Over and out.

An unnerving few minutes later, the reply came winging back over the oceans' corrugated glaze:

OK. Windrush toast. Second half in yr account tomorrow. I don't know a McAllister from my ass. I'll check it.

Bob frowned, wondered for a moment at Al's cheek, then began to be alarmed. He opened the previous received text, read the final sentence.

Then our side will go to work.

434

He stood, grabbed the torch, told Judith he'd be back in half an hour, then sat down again. If he phoned Al from the call box, he'd know his former skipper was still alive. If it wasn't Al on the other end of the phone, then that final message began to look ugly. McAllister was the last of the crew.

Only one way of finding out. He asked Judith not to disturb him for five minutes, went into the living room, stared into the fire, did thirty press-ups and thirty sit-ups, dialled the number from Ulrich's mobile, blowing hard.

'Yeah?'

The quality was poor, but it wasn't Al's voice. And he would never say 'Yeah?' He'd say 'Hello.'

'Ulrich here,' Bob panted. 'No problems.'

'Why're you phoning?'

'Confirming target disposal. You gonna get Felix now?'

'How you knowing his fucking name?'

'Papers.'

'Burn fucking papers. Get the fuck out the Scottie island, OK? You read me? Dispose of this fucking cell phone and go.'

'I'm no idiot. Over and out.'

The voice was a mash of accents: all the world was in it.

He had a few minutes left on the throwaway, and dialled Al's home number. It was a calculated risk: he had no guarantee that his former shipmate hadn't contracted the job of elimination to some pro in the Virgin Islands, keeping himself at a distance.

A few rings, then the cough of the

answerphone. 'Felix and Georgina Newton here. If you have a message . . .'

Georgina? That was classy. He let a few seconds pass, cleared his throat, then said in a husky sub-foreign accent, 'Warning. Your life may be in danger. Take a break abroad. Immediately. Depart in the next five minutes, max. A friend.'

It sounded silly, he thought afterwards.

He returned to the kitchen and sat at the table next to Judith. He held her hand, which was cold. He was reasonably certain Ulrich hadn't got backup; he was a lone wolf. Twice the cost, otherwise. Judith was peculiarly calm. He said maybe it was best she left; he'd accompany her to the gate.

'And shoot me dead?'

'I didn't shoot anyone.'

'I don't believe you. I don't believe a word you say. I still can't even *scream*. What's the use of screaming? Oh, thinks the sea eagle, that sounds interesting.'

He fetched the Makarov and Ulrich's stubby pistol and placed them on the table. He turned up the paraffin lamp to full.

'Watch,' he said. 'Now this Glock is a subcompact, the smallest, for what's called concealed carry. Handbag stuff in places like Moscow or LA. It's got a capacity of ten rounds. That means ten bullets. So if one went off, that leaves?'

'Nine.'

'Assuming it was full, which I'm sure it would have been. Ten chances to kill me. And you.'

He opened the clip and counted out the cartridges. There were nine, including the fresh bullet in the chamber.

'Now for my pistol. It's called a Makarov, made in Bulgaria in the 1960s. Soviet issue. Pretty reliable, if scruffy-looking. One bullet in the chamber, unfired.' He unclipped the magazine. 'Full to the brim. Eight rounds. Not a single bullet fired.' He put the clip back, empty.

Judith picked up the gun. 'It's heavy.'

'Russian. Nice and simple.'

Judith smiled. 'So what are you doing with them?'

'The Glock I'm chucking. It's unreliable. I'll keep the Makarov in a safe place. That's a bit more reliable.'

'Why keep it?'

'Self-defence. I'm not sure the enemy are going to swallow this one for long. Maybe, maybe not. They might come back.'

'What about Ulrich?'

'I'll deal with it.'

She stayed seated and lit another cigarette. He went through two cigarillos, worrying someone would call round now the rain had stopped. But very few people had called round in the months he'd been here: he should have held a party.

'All I could see was a wrestling match,' she added.

'Yup. I never thought being a prop forward at school would one day save my life.'

'So the gun went off by accident.' She

sounded unconvinced.

'No, it didn't,' Bob said. 'Glocks don't go off by accident; it has safety features. You have to fire it intentionally. I think he thought it was pointing at my chest. But for a few millimetres' difference, it would have been. If you want to go to the police, I can't stop you.'

She nodded, her black eyes gleaming in the dim light.

'If you keep that horrible pistol,' she said softly, 'I probably will. You're an armed man. If you chuck it along with the Glock, I won't.'

'You're serious?'

'Very.'

'I'll think about it.'

'There's nothing to think on, Kit.'

'The Makarov's an old friend.'

'Please yourself. I trust you enough to think you won't shoot me, but then I'm probably very naive. It's just that there's something about you.'

He smiled. Feeling faint, he went outside without a gun, saying he was checking for further visitors. It was after midnight and almost dark; the wind had got up again and was blowing from the north-north-east, the long cottage heading straight into it. He could hear the crash and churn of the sea against the northward cliffs: distant sighs and moans, the air full of sand and salt and dark distances. He took some deep breaths.

He came back and held her hand again. It was quivering.

'I'll chuck both of them,' he said. 'They'll get

me anyway, if they want to.'

'You'll still be a dangerous feller to hang around with.'

'Yup. I'll feel naked, but there we go.'

'More like an animal,' she said.

'You bet, selkie.'

He held her warm hand and tried not to think of the body in the hold as the wind streamed past the windows and on into the night, although the two of them weren't moving an inch.

9

She asked for another Talisker. He poured it, and a splash for himself. He needed to keep steady.

'Are you a bad man, Kit?'

He shrugged. 'There's a lot worse. But I'm not a really good and beautiful person, like you.'

She smiled, her hand twitching under his.

He said, 'I feel I can trust you.'

'Do you?'

'I do. With the truth. I've not got much to lose, anyway. They know my name, my hideaway, even my beard. I thought they knew this through a friend. But now I'm not so sure. It's a mystery, how they know everything. Gadgets, probably. My friend may well be next.'

'Why?'

'I was a freight dog. In ordinary English, a cargo pilot.'

'I've always been wary of pilots,' she said, shaking her damp black hair.

'I walked away from a deal. Arms for the Taliban. Illegal, of course. And very embarrassing for some seriously important people if it ever got out. It involved drugs, too. I didn't know that then, I walked out because the Taliban deal was sprung on me, without warning. One by one the crew have been dealt with, and a journalist investigating the whole thing. My friend was the flight engineer. I flew with him a lot. I think he may well have been up to some shady business, even very shady, but I had no idea until a few days ago.'

'Have they got him as well?'

'Probably, in a kind of joint operation. We each made a mistake. Actually, he made two. His first was to cross into the drugs world, which is a place of unadulterated fear. Much scarier than the arms world.'

'How is it scarier?'

'Being murdered by an arms dealer is very rare. In the drugs world, killings are two-a-penny and you're lucky if they just shoot you.'

'His second mistake?'

Bob sighed. 'Protecting me, staying loyal. At least that's what I reckon. And my mistake was helping the journalist. I'd already been menaced, beaten about a bit. I left a message on his mobile; the phone was taken by his killers.'

'Who were the killers, exactly?'

'It's complicated. That's all I can say. They have a habit of reading your thoughts.'

It felt good, telling her. He'd been susceptible to loneliness up to now. She didn't bat an eyelid: that surprised him. She just frowned and cocked her head, puzzled. He felt coshed — the room swayed and bumped — but he struggled on.

'I know there's no reason to believe me, I've told you too many tall tales. I am, however, just divorced. My ex-wife is not vindictive. Not that vindictive, anyway.'

'Kit, I believe you.'

She covered her face with her hands and began crying, so gently he almost didn't realise. He put an arm on her back but she shook it off.

Then she blew her nose and gathered her damp clothes from around the Raeburn, dressed, and within ten minutes had left, taking her torch but saying he mustn't accompany her. She didn't seem angry or scared. It was another mystery. All she said was that she'd check on him tomorrow afternoon, when she had to take her readings on the machair.

He was the scared one: not scared of another visit, but of Ulrich next door. Had Carol Maclean seen his *taish* on the road? Worse, was she seeing him now?

* * *

The throwaway vibrated at two o'clock in the morning, moving steadily over the stool that served as his bedside table. He watched it for a moment — he hadn't yet managed to sleep, leaving the paraffin lamp glowing softly — then picked it up, readying his Ulrich voice. The caller was pure rasp, a kind of bottled psychotic.

'Why have you no disposed of this fucking phone?'

'No confirmation of the other job.'

'It's done, fuckface. Now you no dispose of this, you'll never be hire by us again, right?'

'I'm gonna go to university now.'

'Eh? Whassat?'

'The university of life. Better than death. A lot better.'

He ended the call, breathing against a tight straitjacket of pure anxiety. The alpha-male type who runs the world. Who knows exactly why the stone breaks the nut. Who understands all the causal relationships.

He dialled Al again: this time there was nothing. No answer-phone, nothing. They must have pulled the phones out, he thought, before doing what they were there for. He saw Al drifting all day in a reddened pool, or his lifeless hands dangling either side of the hammock. Bob felt in his bones that he was the last green bottle, and wondered if they'd left Jane alone.

★ ★ ★

He'd set the alarm for some two hours before sunrise: it wasn't completely dark. He had prepared the stretcher the night before. A couple of poles, sheets, a blanket to cover the body, good sailor's knots, straps to haul it, as Native Americans used to freight their stuff. He'd rolled the body onto the stretcher and felt ill. He was sick into the tussocks, with the final glow of yesterday fading to the west.

He'd made good progress by the time the next day's glimmer showed the way more clearly than his head torch. The straps were over his shoulders and around his belly, but the end of the stretcher would snag on heather roots and cotton grass and hidden stones, then slide easily for a while. The wind had dropped to a fitful gustiness, and the dark grey loch was dead calm. Everything was the colour of lead. The smells were stronger and fresher and sweeter from the grassland. By the time he hit the beach, the sky was light grey, the sea moving like mercury.

The sand was easy just up from the tidemark; he came to the rocks and lumbered on in grunts over their slippery black facets, their hollows full of sky-reflecting water like see-through holes. His shoulders were sore from the taut straps, the cargo heavier and heavier, but he made it to the skerry-like edge at the base of the cliff. Here he overlooked the deep cleft where, even on calm days, the surf would thrash about and send up flashes of spume fifteen feet high, then be sucked out to expose kelp before crashing back again. The sea roar and the screeching of the gulls meant that he couldn't hear anyone coming. There were human voices wailing in the din, but that was projection.

He unstrapped Ulrich, held the blanket, then rolled him over the edge. He caught a glimpse of his mutilated face, like a silent scream, before he bounced and disappeared into the general turmoil. He fell very fast, arms waving. He seemed to surface briefly — a flash of pink and a shinier green in the green surge — as the wave crammed itself boiling into the narrow gulch. Then there was nothing. It was as easy as that. It had taken an hour and a half from take-off to landing.

The poles and sheets were soon flotsam, too.

That day they'd swum together, Judith had told him about the prevailing currents: the body would be swept around the cliffs and away, not onto the beach. He'd never been here this early. Perhaps someone walked their dog every day at this time, along the grey sands by the mercury sea. Which goes on crashing all night, exactly the same.

Daybreak suddenly blazed.

Was Al really gone? He could google the Virgin Islands' local news. Everything could be found out . . . except what was essential: why people did the things they did. Why, when you looked at a human skull, you sometimes felt frightened not of death but of the species that skull represented, as if you yourself were drawn from something else. Why the sea kept rolling and lashing itself in and out without a single break.

He dropped the Glock down a deep, lightless slit in the rocks, where the sea could be heard rather than seen. Then he fished out the Makarov. He'd put all the rounds back. Pointing the gun's muzzle upward, he squeezed. It sounded no louder than a cough over the sea's surge, and seemed to bounce a few times off the rocks. The gulls wheeled, untouched. Then he threw his old friend down into the darkness, retrieved the spent cartridge and dropped that down as well.

He considered building a small cairn. Unfortunately, it would be visible from the beach — through binos, at least. And his hands were trembling, as if they'd lain flat on ice for ages.

★ ★ ★

He went to bed with what felt like a stomach ulcer. He heard Judith calling from outside. He let her in and staggered back to bed. She brought up tea for both of them. She placed the

445

tray on the floor and then held up his passport, one hand jokily on her hip. The air felt chill.

'I was just looking for a spoon, Captain Winrush. Wind Rush was a lot prettier.'

He felt relief, not dismay. 'Yeah, prettier and also safer. Don't tell anyone else. I've got two kids — they're students.'

'You're a dangerous man to know.'

'Exactly. I'll have to become a birder on Tristan da Cunha. Two weeks by boat, no proper harbour, treacherous currents, lots of potatoes, zero crime. I don't think they'd bother to put themselves out that much.'

'In and out of Dubai, I see.'

'So?'

'Not quite bonny Scourlay. Not quite centre of the green-hued conscience.'

He shrugged. 'A job. Get it where you can. I flew a converted crate for a sheikh. Sauna and jacuzzi in the tail end.'

She was quiet for a few moments, then said, 'You were really a gunrunner, weren't you?'

'A flying warehouse,' he said. 'A mixture of things in the hold. Like life. Good thoughts, junk thoughts, bad thoughts. We keep the world moving. Without us, it'd seize up.'

Her eyes travelled over his face until they settled on his hands, folded on his chest. 'You're very like a dead knight on his tombstone.'

'No, that's my father. Knight of the skies. He was a Spitfire pilot; lost his leg in the war when he was nineteen. Thank God I'm not him, and never was.'

She pulled up the covers, went over to the

skylight and looked out. 'Where do you think he'll be washed up?'

'Hopefully a long way away. Murray down at the pub'll report him missing; they'll check out a few bogs and cliffs. He'll just be another hiking casualty. Let's not mention him again.'

'What's the worst thing you ever carried?'

He struggled to think about it. 'I carried some badly crated lizards that got out and under the pedals. But in terms of smell, the — '

'You know what I mean.'

'People. Some army chaps, rebels.'

'I mean when you were a cargo pilot.'

'That was when I was a cargo pilot.'

'OK, you might well have carried a serial killer when you were flying passengers. I'm talking about goods, things. That you knew about.'

He thought hard: no one had ever asked him this question before.

Minsk, 2003. His plane grounded for three days with spongy controls. Another crew, all Russian, slipping and laughing on the ice, their pilot still not recovered from his birthday vodka bout. Asking Bob, OK, to step in? A few dozen bombs under canvas, a badly lit hold. The bombs were taller than a man and, as one of the crew laughed, twice as heavy. Bound for Khartoum. He was bored in Minsk. He swapped tales on the way there: for instance, about his recent trips in and out of El Geneina, West Darfur, carrying UN inspectors in a Beechcraft 1900, waiting five hours while the gravel strip dried out after a squall — a 'haboob', everyone called it. El Geneina: dust and donkeys and AK-47S.

Yawning aid workers who hadn't slept after a night of shooting, not really up for the participatory food-security-assessment workshop in the big tent. Halfway to Khartoum the crew told him what they were carrying: ZAB 250/200s, incendiary bombs full of petrol jellied by polystyrene and benzene so it sticks.

Napalm, Judith.

A big brown envelope and lots of jokes and an infected skeeter bite on his neck. He knew fuck nothing.

That beat the landmines out of Podgorica, because he was fully aware that the stuff was dropped on ordinary people and burned for hours.

'Tiger parts for China,' he said aloud. 'A crate of striped heads with robust fangs. Tiger livers in ice. Cures for impotence, toothache, myopia. It'll eat the world empty, will China.'

'That's bad, Kit.'

'I probably shouldn't have done it. I've made a bit of a mess of things, all round. I've chucked both the guns, at least.'

He lay back, all wear and tear, on the pillows. Judith turned and crossed her arms and said, 'How're you going to clear up the mess, then?'

'Interference,' he murmured.

★ ★ ★

Marcie reckoned he looked like death warmed up. The British Virgin Islands' news website had a brief report among a crowd of investment adverts:

A fatal shooting incident has been reported in High Ridge Drive, Tortola.

According to reports reaching BVI news, a blaze in the luxury villa belonging to residents Felix and Georgina Newton have revealed two bodies suffering from bullet wounds. These are believed to be the latter parties. A gun was found on one of the bodies.

The fire took hold at about 5.30 p.m. on Friday, although no gunshots were heard.

Reports indicate that the house was not badly damaged. It is thought Mr Newton had financial worries, and a verdict of suicide is likely. Police are investigating the matter.

He felt like squealing, but not in a way that would attract predators.

So he would have to proceed cautiously, alongside Tim Sightly. Maybe they could start with the prince: softly does it, we wouldn't want to wake the cheetahs.

Astra ran up yelling and was about to launch a ground-to-air missile attack with a plastic rocket when he stopped and stared.

'Uncle Kit, why're you crying?'

'Am I? Oh yes. Birds don't cry, do they, Vauxhall?'

'Course they well do,' he said, clutching Bob's thigh and resting his plump cheek on it. 'My name's not Woksore, anyway.'

Bob stroked his silky hair. Al and Jane had never had kids. He'd better go to the funeral in shades, he thought, if he went at all. You never know who might be watching.

'I cry a lot,' came a little, muffled voice. 'Cos I like chips.'

Marcie came up and asked Bob if he'd heard about the missing German hiker.

'No. Blown off a cliff, was he?'

'They don't know. He was staying at Murray's, in Ardcorry. Murray's in trouble because he didn't bother to take the guy's details; just trusted him and scribbled his name or something. That's against the law.'

'Poor Murray.'

'Anyway, Carol MacLean can't clean the room until he's found. She said he was a nice quiet chap. Called Ulrich. She saw him near your gate late yesterday afternoon, but the police don't take her seriously any more. You know, what I told you about the *taish*?'

'Vaguely,' he said, blowing his nose.

'I think he might have come in here, but the photo's really bad. Makes him look like a psycho.'

'They all do,' he said, pretending not to listen properly.

'What's a slyco?' asked Astra.

'Whoops,' said Marcie.

★ ★ ★

Tim Sightly was burrowing into Swallowtail Trading Ltd; a link had been established between the outfit and Scottish Torches. The paper trail consisted of a lot of charred areas, after the fire, but it seemed that the mythical Alfredo Rivera Morales (aka Hugh McAllister) had a substantial holding in the energy company. Al had discovered a new career skill late in life: how to launder money. Or rather, his own soiled washing. Scottish Torches' website had frozen. A brief piece tucked away in the *FT* announced its demise. One more bright green hope that ran too fast.

The Centre's Land Rover flashed him as it crossed the causeway into Scourlay. He stopped.

'Ewan.'

'Have you read about Scottish Torches?'

'Of course. An unlucky speculation.'

'The Centre committee's thinking of buying the croft. Preventive measures. We'll need to fund-raise massively at a bad time, so it won't go through until the winter, earliest. But I thought I'd warn you.'

'Ewan, you're a gentleman.'

★   ★   ★

Bob's offer was snapped up, since it was over the asking price. He started work on the house straightaway, given it was summer. He solved the transport problem by buying a mule: Antonov coped with sacks of lime, bales of straw, slates and other natural products with no more than the odd *haw*. Astra loved riding on his broad back — the only time the boy kept perfectly calm.

Bob decided not to have electricity, however provided; a touch hypocritical, otherwise. This decision was made the day Ewan found a dead gull at the foot of the Gair Centre's turbine,

451

blood massed over its black hood.

'Only a gull,' he muttered when the subject came up.

'Never mind,' Bob said. 'It'll be a sea eagle next time, I'm sure.'

The decree absolute arrived that afternoon, sent on by David. Bob stood by the loch and opened the envelope. A fish rose and made ripples. The sheep's skeleton grinned. He'd never look at the papers again, so he read them carefully.

'Only a gull!' he shouted. Because the thick white cloud was at fifteen feet, there was no echo.

★　★　★

He would have liked to have known who had sent Ulrich. No one except Al had been aware he was here. But he refused to believe it of Al. Maybe they had threatened Jane. Given Al the Chinese burn. Started the electric drill whirring.

On a hunch, at Marcie's, Bob googled 'Kit Webb' and 'Winrush'. Nothing but a long list of Kit Webbs. Then he remembered Ulrich's final text messages and Angus's happy mistake. He changed 'Winrush' to 'Windrush,' a confusion he'd had to put up with all his life. He immediately fell on the Centre's blog. The entry was dated a week before Ulrich's visit; the day after Judith and he went swimming.

You read it here first, folks. We have a new mystery neighbour on the island, by the name of

Christopher **Webb**. This is likely to be about as genuine as a nine-bob note. He is English, tall, broad-shouldered, has a stubbly beard and sports a dockworker's shapeless woolly cap. He may be a certain Mr **Windrush**, in disguise. Well, he says he's a birder, but heavy doubts remain. There are several possibilities to my mind: either researcher or private-security spy for Scottish Torches, drugs broker or simple arsehole. Or all four. The Centre would be grateful for any help on this matter, and that's official. Eh man I dunno, I can hear you say, but in these days of undercover agents scrounging free beers out the green movement at great expense to the state, we cannot be too careful. Better oot than in.

He didn't blame Judith: better oot than in. To her, initially, it had only been a nickname. Then he remembered that Ewan had spied on them that day on the beach. The man was sharp, beady-eyed, suspicious: you couldn't get much past that sort of mind. Now all he'd have to do was mention it to Angus, or Angus might call up the blog on his computer, and another boat trip would be in the offing.

Marcie came up as he quit, hands shaking.

'Are you OK, hunk?'

'I'm great. Just great.'

'Here's your coffee. You're all pale.'

'Marcie, you're made to make others happy. A bit like Ewan.'

'Ewan?' She looked astonished. 'Thanks very much!'

'I'm sure he makes some people happy.'

'Depends which people you're talking about.'

'Those who read his blog.'

'That's Judith and maybe his mum. Apart from him. He's not exactly sociable, so no one's interested.'

Bob sipped the excellent coffee. 'You're so right, as usual. Hey, I want to buy a painting, by the way. A bit of the café in my house.'

'Really? I was wondering when, actually. You choose.'

'The one of that cliff, lots of thick white swirls at the bottom.'

She beamed. 'That's mine.'

'I didn't even know you painted.'

'I stopped when Keir died. I don't know if I'll ever have the urge again.'

They stood in front of it. The paint had been applied with a trowel. It was £250.

'What do you like about it?'

'It's probably where my gulls roost,' he said, touching a clot of white. 'I want to be reminded, even when I'm at home. Stops me brooding.'

'I feel all tingly inside,' sighed Marcie.

'Maybe that's the urge,' he said, as Astra burst in.

⋆　⋆　⋆

The project kept trying to revive itself, passed from meeting to meeting in glass towers. Other grey suits passed by, to talk their language of flexing, winning, unrolling, delivering; of goals and strategy; of initiatives and processes and framework and change. 'It's not rocket science,' they'd insist. The twenty-odd turbines would provide electricity for 21,000 households, most of it exported to the mainland. Bob listened, heard each group out, said his position was unchanged no matter how much the money on the table, and suggested they try to go frugal instead of fattening the belly. Blackouts would be one solution. Eating by candlelight. Three-day week, remember?

'We hear what you're saying,' they'd say, in turn, as Antonov hee-hawed outside. But that was a fib. They just thought the islanders were backward.

The last time, as they were leaving, one of them — his hit-man look softened by oval glasses, a mumsy fringe and projecting teeth — turned by the porch and said, 'You think we're baddies. Wrong. We're the good guys; we're the knights in shining armour; we're saving the world.'

'You're not saving the world,' Bob said; 'you're making money. Except that it's now the recession.'

'Nylon and rubber tyres were invented during a recession.'

'They saved the world too, did they?'

A cloud of midges came to Bob's rescue and the men stumbled off.

★ ★ ★

The sea eagles circled, mewing, as he walked to the beach for his dip. They kept an eye on him; the sea didn't, it just seethed blindly around his waist before the plunge. There were a few cloudless days that first summer, when the sand dazzled and the flat-calm water broke malachite-green on the empty stretches with nothing but a sigh. The Centre visitors — mostly teenagers — played cricket, with Judith as longstop, but Ewan hit the hard rubber ball so far beyond the boundary it vanished into glitter, and (like Ulrich) never came back. Otherwise, Bob kept his distance from the manse, even though a section of Ewan's blog had been discreetly removed.

He stayed loyal to the café, where Marcie's new paintings filled the walls and a tall Ghanaian photographer called Kojo had filled the place of Keir. He had been shooting a re-enactment of waulking songs for *Woman's Weekly*, fallen for Marcie's charms and the landscape in that order, and swapped Leeds for Bargrennan. Astra's pinpoint attacks were now shared. Bob pretended not to know much about Africa and the two men got on like a house on fire. Once, walking the beach on a misty day, he saw Kojo in the distance and thought for a split second that it was Joseph H. Kenley.

Now and again, a person-sized lump of jetsam would be sprawled on the sands ahead, but it was always harmless. Harmless to Bob Winrush, that is; not to the fishes or the birds, stopping themselves up with bottle tops, nylon cord, rubber crumbs, the plastic silt he'd freighted for years.

The birds never did what he ordered them to do, so his field reports felt hesitant, full of deviations and qualifications. They weren't scientific enough: when it was the laying season, he cared about the eggs too much, and the fluffy juveniles, and the whole thing.

Of course, under pressure, he caved in and told Sophie and David where he was. Before they headed respectively for Cambodia and Peru, they stayed a full fortnight over the decent weather, arriving together on the first bright day of the spell, fresh from Olivia's new Shropshire place, which leaked in several places. Apparently Olivia and Ben kept bickering, mainly because Ben being an artist was not very practical, he filled the dishwasher wrongly, that sort of thing. But his work was 'cool', said David.

'He takes details from famous old paintings, but only of reflections, the blurry upside-down bits in pools and rivers. Then he puts them the right way up and enlarges them, massively.'

'So?'

'They look awesomely modern. Impressionist or even abstract. He says it's ironic.'

'Sounds a bit like cheating to me,' Bob said.

'Sour grapes, Dad.'

Sophie was impressed by the view. 'I thought it was even wetter here and just incredibly windy all the time?'

'Nah. That's just a myth to keep folk away.'

'How's your biplane project?'

He showed them the drawings. 'First things first. I need to build a hangar.'

Angus MacLean took them out porpoise-spotting, and told them yarns that they believed. They reckoned the Bargrennan Music Jamboree beat anything in Spain, Hungary or wherever, but they couldn't see why their father bothered about the birds.

'They're only gulls,' Sophie insisted, when they went again to the beach. 'They feed and fight and lay eggs and sleep. And screech, unfortunately.'

'No one's perfect,' he told them, bent to his telescope. He was tracking an individual as it swooped over the ocean: it had no black tips on its snow-white wings — an outsider, an anomaly. It was called McAl. 'Not even you two. Though you come close.'

Judith stirred in the sun. 'And me?'

'You're the exception that proves the rule, sweetheart,' he said, still squinting through the scope's eyepiece, turning up the magnification. 'But do selkies really count?'

She stubbed out her day's one cigarette in the sand, flicked it into their picnic basket and leapt up.

'You bet, pilot.'

And plunged back into the surf as he lost the bird and plunged in turn into the sky.

Acknowledgements

I was brought up with aviation as the natural backdrop to my life: my father Barney Thorpe worked for Pan Am for thirty-five years, taking early retirement just before Lockerbie; my brother Jimmy joined the RAF at the age of 16, while my grandfather was briefly in the Royal Flying Corps after serving as an infantry officer during the First World War; lastly, this book has gained immeasurably from the detailed advice of my nephew Daniel, who has been working as a landing agent at Frankfurt airport for eight years. My own three months working in Pan Am wash-up provided insights that would need another book to extrapolate.

★   ★   ★

Many others have been an aid and inspiration to this novel; I owe a particular debt to two UN arms experts, Mike Lewis and Brian Johnson-Thomas, who know as much about arms smuggling as anyone and have been extremely generous with their time. I thank Val Rice, my father's former secretary, for tirelessly checking details, and Barbara O'Grady and Maureen Blaydon, former Pan Am stewardesses, for their insider knowledge. Likewise, I am grateful to ex-PC David Buckley for his insight into police procedure.

459

Thank you also (as ever) to Zoe Swenson-Wright, my agent Lucy Luck and to Sharon Black for their careful reading and invaluable suggestions; to Tessa Thiery and Andrew Rissik for providing regional particulars; to my editor Robin Robertson and all the crew at Cape for guiding in the beast safely; to my children Josh, Sacha and Anastasia for promptly answering erratic queries, and to my wife Jo Wistreich for her insights, support and on-board patience.

We do hope that you have enjoyed reading this large print book.

Did you know that all of our titles are available for purchase?

We publish a wide range of high quality large print books including:
Romances, Mysteries, Classics
General Fiction
Non Fiction and Westerns

Special interest titles available in large print are:
The Little Oxford Dictionary
Music Book
Song Book
Hymn Book
Service Book

Also available from us courtesy of Oxford University Press:
Young Readers' Dictionary
(large print edition)
Young Readers' Thesaurus
(large print edition)

For further information or a free brochure, please contact us at:
Ulverscroft Large Print Books Ltd.,
The Green, Bradgate Road, Anstey,
Leicester, LE7 7FU, England.
Tel: (00 44) **0116 236 4325**
Fax: (00 44) **0116 234 0205**

Other titles published by
The House of Ulverscroft:

THE STANDING POOL

Adam Thorpe

Two Cambridge academics, historians Nick and Sarah Mallinson, take a sabbatical with their three lively girls in a remote Languedoc farmhouse. But the farmhouse has a history of its own, and the illusion of Eden begins to retreat. The couple feel the vulnerability of being among strangers, and being strangers themselves — even in their own place, and even to their own children. Sarah frets about the danger of the swimming pool and the presence of wild boar, while the local hunters' guns concern Nick. And what should they make of the gardener, Jean-Luc, who lives with his invalid mother in the village and whose private world involves collecting arcane rubbish, spying on Sarah's naked dips in the pool and hammering nails into a doll . . .

THE BURNING SOUL

John Connolly

Randall Haight has a secret: when he was a teenager he and his friend killed a fourteen-year-old girl. Randall did his time and built a new life in the small Maine town of Pastor's Bay, but somebody has discovered the truth about Randall. He is being tormented by anonymous messages, haunting reminders of his past crime, and he wants private detective Charlie Parker to make it stop. But another fourteen-year-old girl has gone missing, this time from Pastor's Bay, and her family has its own secrets to protect. Now Parker must unravel a web of deceit involving the police, the FBI, a doomed mobster named Tommy Morris, and Randall Haight himself . . . because Randall Haight is telling lies . . .

THE 500

Matthew Quirk

Mike Ford was following his father into a life of crime, but chose, instead, to go straight and work his way through Harvard Law School. Now he's landed the ultimate job with the Davies Group, a powerful political consulting firm run by the charismatic Henry Davies. With money and privilege, he rubs shoulders with Washington's heavyweights. Mike believes that everything has finally come right. However, he's about to discover that power comes at a cost. Henry Davies is looking for a protege for a crucial deal that must go right — at any price. Mike soon learns that being on the side of the lawmakers doesn't mean your work is legal. And there's no place for a moral code when you're on the devil's payroll.